MONSTROUS AFFECTIONS

*Fifteen
Beastly
Tales*

MONSTROUS AFFECTIONS

FIFTEEN BEASTLY TALES

edited by

Kelly Link
&
Gavin J. Grant

WALKER
BOOKS

For Bill and Linda Link

First published 2014 by Walker Books Ltd
87 Vauxhall Walk, London SE11 5HJ

This edition published 2019

2 4 6 8 10 9 7 5 3 1

CONTENTS

Introduction

et's be honest. We have questions about monsters. That's why we put this book together. That's why you're reading this book right now. On old maps, cartographers would draw strange beasts around the margins and write phrases such as "Here be dragons." That's where monsters exist: in the unmapped spaces, in the places where we haven't filled in all the gaps, in outer space or in the deepest parts of the ocean. At all the seams of the worlds and relationships that we build for ourselves. Sometimes we see the monster in a mirror. Sometimes we find the monster in the face of someone we love. Sometimes we fight monsters, and sometimes we love them. Sometimes it isn't bad to be a monster.

Sometimes monsters inhabit our skins. Doesn't everyone wonder, at some point in their lives, if they are monstrous? Haven't you wondered? What about the parts of yourself that you keep secret? What about the things that you want, the things that you long to say, the worst thing that you've never done, the times in your life when you wish that you could destroy the world? Are you a wolf dressed up in a girl's skin? Are you a boy held together with bolts? Do you dream of night, or do you fear the dark? Do you long to be dangerous?

In this anthology are stories about what it means to discover that monsters are real, that all families have secrets, that friendships can mutate into something strange and awful. There are also stories about learning to accept and celebrate one's own peculiar gifts and talents. There are stories about the monsters that guard the boundaries between life and death, the known and the unknown. Sometimes they grant a gift. Sometimes they exact a price for that gift.

Here's the thing about monsters: they exist in violation of the way we think things ought to be. They're a sign that something is wrong with the world. And *isn't* there something wrong with the world? Have you noticed this? Us too. So maybe it's not a bad thing that monsters exist. Maybe the world should be different. Maybe we ought to spend more time being monstrous, being strange, being different.

If monsters exist, then the world is larger and stranger than we ever hoped it could be. Like the margins of those maps, the stories in this anthology are a place where we can safely contemplate monsters — kraken, vampires, greater and lesser demons, and even stranger things — and what it means to be monstrous.

But before you begin reading, here's a pop quiz. Best to take it late at night, when you are alone in your room, when the night is dark

and everyone else is sleeping. Turn the lights down. Pick a nice sharp pencil, one that can double as a weapon in an emergency. No do-overs, though. Be honest. Why not be honest?

Ready?

Monsters: A Pop Quiz

There are no such things as monsters.

    YES   NO

You would know a monster if you saw one.

    YES   NO

Monsters are
- A) hairy.
- B) fangy.
- C) slimy.
- D) strangely attractive to me, although I don't know why.
- E) all of the above.

You would absolutely consider dating
- A) a vampire.
- B) a mutant spider creature, as long as it had a really good sense of humor.
- C) a really attractive person who turned into a wolf once a month and ran around in their fur and ate stuff I'd rather not know about. I'm a dog person, okay?
- D) anyone, really. I'm not picky right now.
- E) none of the above.

When summoned by a text message to a mysterious blood ritual in the dead of night, you
- A) go through my closet twice. It's important to look good when I'm going to be very, very bad.
- B) hatch a plan to disrupt the ritual and bring down the dark forces.
- C) hatch a plan to disrupt the ritual and rule the world from a throne of skulls.
- D) set my alarm for another ten minutes. What's the rush?

You are beginning to think that the person you like is a vampire, so you
- A) avoid garlic.
- B) accept that everyone has their quirks.
- C) look forward to arrival of the obligatory werewolf love interest. Twice the fun!
- D) consider my life choices.
- E) ask my friends on Tumblr for advice.

When do you let your significant vampire other bite you?
- A) Random vampires can bite me in any alley in town. I'm into casual necks.
- B) First date, to test the chemistry.
- C) Third date, so my vampire knows I wouldn't do it with just any unholy member of the undead.
- D) I'm not Miss/Mr. Bite Now. I'm into commitment. Eternal vampire bliss or no dice.

If you see something move down in the dark of a storm drain, you
- A) assume it's a monster, get my trusty weapon, go down into the tunnels underneath my town, and attempt to slay it.
- B) assume it's a monster, go home for a leash and some raw meat, and attempt to befriend it.
- C) assume it's a monster, reapply lipstick, and attempt to date it.
- D) assume it's not a monster and do nothing. Try to ignore the shiver starting at the back of my neck and my growing sense of dread. Assume it's not a monster until I'm alone in my room late that night, trying to get the last problem for Physics done, and it's long after midnight now, and I keep taking my earbuds out of my ears because I thought I heard something. Assume it's not a monster until something brushes against the back of my neck and says, around a really impressive mouthful of teeth, "$Vf = -25.5 \ m/s$."

Monsters can look exactly like people. Sometimes you can't tell.
- YES   NO

Sometimes monsters look exactly like people you know.
- YES   NO

INTRODUCTION

If anyone in your family is a monster, it's your

- A) mother.
- B) father.
- C) brother.
- D) sister.
- E) me.
- F) I don't have any family. I am a foundling discovered running wild on the moors under the full moon.
- G) I don't have any family. I ate them all.
- H) We're all monsters: it runs in the family. Imagine how much fun we have around the holidays.

It's kind of creepy the way vampires are always hitting on high-school kids.

TRUE   FALSE

Sometimes you dream about blood.

YES   NO

Your friends can be kind of scary sometimes.

YES   NO

No, really. Your friends are scary.

YES   NO

You are a monster.

YES   NO

What was that noise?

- A) The wind
- B) Nothing
- C) Something. I don't know.
- D) It was coming from the closet.

What's under the bed?
- A) Shoes
- B) Dust bunnies
- C) Evil shoes
- D) Evil dust bunnies
- E) Monsters
- F) All of the above
- G) There is nothing under the bed. There are definitely not any monsters under the bed. I've checked three times and there are still no monsters under the bed. The monsters are definitely somewhere else.

When you were younger, you were afraid that something was in your closet.
YES   NO

There's nothing in the closet. Really.
TRUE   FALSE

Are you sure there's nothing in the closet?
YES   NO

Maybe you should go look in the closet, just in case.
YES   NO   I DON'T WANT TO. YOU DO IT.

Check again. Just one more time. Go ahead. We'll wait right here.

Kelly Link and Gavin J. Grant

Moriabe's Children

PAOLO BACIGALUPI

Alanie had never seen a kraken, but her people spoke of them often. The kraken were out beyond the breakwaters of Serenity Bay, the hungry children of Moriabe. They writhed in the depths and sometimes rose to the surface to hunt. A kraken's tentacles could encircle a sailing ship and crack its spine. Kraken snapped masts like kindling, and swallowed sailors whole.

None but the most foolhardy and desperate hunted kraken. But sometimes, it was said, a captain might return from the open ocean with the prize of one of Moriabe's children, his ship wallowing low in the waters as he tied to the Prince's Pier, his fortune assured thanks to the bloody mountain of flesh piled in his hold.

Alanie sold oysters in Greyling Square, and she had seen hopeful ships set sail on hunts, but she had never seen one return with a kraken in its hold — and most ships never returned at all.

Alanie sold oysters and accepted whatever prices High Street cooks offered when they came down from the mansions that ringed the white cliffs of the bay. After her father died, Alanie prayed to Moriabe that she might find and sell enough oysters so that she and her mother would not be forced from their home on Middle Street, and each day she returned home with too little for her efforts.

Alanie often lingered in Greyling Square until darkness fell and then stumbled home by the light of the stars. And while she lingered, she listened to the talk of the other fishmongers as they compared their business days and their netted catch, and sometimes they would speculate on what it might be like to return to port with a hold overflowing with kraken spoils.

"I saw Greyling when he caught his prize, so long ago," old Bericha said, as she plucked out the last of her flankfish and beheaded it for Tradi Maurch's cook.

"The prince threw a fete. Maidens tossed rose petals at his feet as he went up the cliffs to the prince's manor on the point. And behind him, his sailors came, too. Urn after urn, full to the neck with reddest blood and greyest poisons and blackest inks."

The ink went to lovers' notes, a syrup-sweet filigree to the protestations of devotion that suitors spilled on vellum. The blood went to wealthy bedrooms and was mixed with wine, an aphrodisiac said to besot lovers for days. And, of course, the poison also had its place. Wrung from the kraken's tentacles, the grey viscous poison was slipped via servant entrances to the betrayed — the ones who had been foolish enough to believe the sweet calligraphy of love, and yielded to the madness of trust. Kraken poison found its way into Calagari wine and Rake Point mead and flankfish stuffing, and former lovers thrashed and collapsed, frothing blood and spittle, praying for forgiveness as they gave up their lives.

Ink and blood and poison, tender meat, powdered tentacles — all found ready markets in the High Street mansions where they ringed the bay atop white marbled cliffs and kept sharp eye over the prince's commerce.

The fishmongers gossiped and wished, and packed up their water carts and dragged them sloshing from the deepening shadows of Greyling Square, with copper bits in their pockets and visions of untold wealth in their tired dreams.

Alanie had never seen a kraken, but her mother spoke of them often. Sinolise spoke bitterly of the creatures that had taken the *Sparrow* and her crew. She spoke of Alanie's father, whom Alanie remembered as a giant of a man, black-bearded and laughing.

Alanie's mother said the kraken were always hungry, spawned from a cold trysting between Moriabe and Stormface, an object lesson that lovemaking in anger resulted in terrible things.

Sinolise said the kraken were always hungry, and it wasn't just a man's body they sought to consume, but his mind.

A man could lose his head hunting kraken, mad for the profit that might result. He forgot wife and child, love and life. Kraken muddled a man's thoughts until he dreamed of becoming another Orin Greyling, a legend who might be spoken of for generations. It happened all the time. A man lost his wits in pursuit of kraken, and when he did, it was his family who suffered. It was his family who were forced to flee to pastures far beyond the city. It was his wife who

was forced to find a new man who would accept a pauper woman and daughter into his home.

The kraken stole not only sailors' lives, but also the lives of all those people who had been foolish enough to believe in them.

Alanie had never seen a kraken, but her father had spoken of them often.

"I saw them, Alanie. With my own eyes, close as touching, just beneath our *Sparrow*'s beam."

He told her how the *Sparrow* had wallowed, half drowned, leaking between her boards as Moriabe and Wanem clashed in a lovers' battle and the *Sparrow* was trapped in the heart of the tempest.

"Half of Moriabe was down in our hold. Every time a wave crested, I was sure poor *Sparrow* would founder and we'd all be dragged down.

"For two days and two nights, we fought that storm. We bailed and bailed. We lost Tomo and Relkin to Moriabe's and Wanem's fury. We fought Moriabe's waves, and we battled Wanem's torrents, and none of us believed that we could survive. Waves taller than our masts, Alanie! Winds yanking us about like a toy on a string. It was all I could do to keep the *Sparrow*'s prow to the rise of Moriabe's next embrace. Every time we climbed a wave, I was sure it would be our last . . ."

He trailed off, and then abruptly smiled.

"When dawn came, we were so exhausted and waterlogged and broken down that at first we thought we had drowned and gone to the distant shore, but instead of the warm song of the Rising Lands, it was the sun, giving us all her warmth.

"The waves steamed mist, and the sky was bluer than the shell of a

bluestem clam, and Moriabe was as still and calm and loving as a cat nursing kittens, and our only company was a pair of dolphins bearing Tomo back to us. It was as if Moriabe herself had decided old Relkin was enough sacrifice, so she gave us back our skinny cabin boy.

"We thought we were blessed that day, Alanie. We bailed water from our hold, and every time we dumped a bucket into the sea, we thanked Moriabe for making peace with Stormface. She was so still and calm in that moment, just sunshine and wavelets, all the way to the horizon. Bitty little wavelets, gleaming like mirrors . . .

"That's when we saw them. Just below our hold. Huge, Alanie, so big . . . I've seen a black whale breach and knock a frigate aside like a toy, and a black is nothing to the kraken. A snack, perhaps. The kraken are so large, you can't fit them in your eye. You cannot see the whole of them, not when you're close. Nothing holds a candle to the size of them, except maybe bluebacks, and no one dares hunt them.

"We stood there, staring. Me and all the rest of the men, jam-jawed, every one of us. All of us looking down into the water, and not a one of us making a sound as they passed and passed and passed. It was something extraordinary, seeing Moriabe's children. Huge long tentacles trailing behind them, down there in the water. Dozens of them, and any one of them might have dragged our mortal *Sparrow* down without a second thought. They are greater than we, by far."

He paused. "Everyone talks of kraken, but no one knows the truth. That prize Orin Greyling brought home in his hold? The one they say was as big as his ship?" Her father shook his head. "It was but a babe, Alanie. Nothing but a tiny little babe."

Alanie's father had seen the kraken, and he never forgot its awe. And when he was near poverty, ruined by poor trade, and with hundreds upon hundreds of useless black-whale oil casks turning rancid

in his warehouse, he remembered how the kraken surfaced after Wanem and Moriabe fought in a tempest and then made amends, and he would hunt.

Armored with his own desperation, armed with poisoned harpoons and the lore of Greyling's triumph, Alanie's father sailed the *Sparrow* into the teeth of a building storm, his crew a band of hopeless souls who anticipated nothing but debtors' labor in the marble quarries of the white cliffs if they failed in their mission — a ragged band of gamblers, betting on a future that was already beyond their reach.

Alanie had never seen a kraken, but they spoke to her often.

In her dreams the kraken spoke to her, and when they did, they called her by name.

Alanie. Alanie.

In the darkness of her new father's chink-stone manor, wrapped in quilts before his hearth, listening to her mother and the man she had chosen for shelter as they rustled and groaned in the man's bedroom, Alanie stared into the flickering fires as the kraken called to her.

The kraken sang of ocean currents and cities beneath the waves. They sang of shipwrecks and gold and the lost wines of ancients. They sang of urns of olives and whale oil, the marbled statuary of Melna and Calib, a carpet of treasures spread across the seafloor, woven with the bones of sailors.

The kraken called to Alanie when she was asleep and stalked her when she was awake. They sang to her as she walked the pastures learning the trade of shepherd from her stepbrother, Elbe. They whispered to her when she scrambled down the cliffs to the beach

where she hid from her new family and hunted for oysters. They chuckled predatory in her mind when she straightened from scrubbing shells and caught her stepfather standing too close, his gaze lingering too long on her body.

Every night as the embers of the kitchen fire turned to ash and glow, the kraken came calling.

Alanie, Alanie.

Alanie had never seen a kraken, but she remembered the first time she heard their song.

She'd stood at the end of Prince's Pier, a tiny girl alone on the longest finger that poked into the bay, looking out across calm waters to the froth of the breaks and the channel where her father would return. Around her, sailors loaded bales of wool brought into the city from the pastureland. The great storm rains had soaked the bales, and the sailors and stevedores cursed the weight of the wool, while owners and captains argued over the merits of drying the wool or shipping it immediately.

All across the pier's oiled planks, water beaded and steamed as the sun rose and warmed the white cliffs that ringed Serenity Bay, and it was then that Alanie heard the singing. She heard the snap of timbers and felt the prick of barbed steel in her skin and tasted blood in her mouth.

Alanie stood at the tip of the pier, bathed in sunlight, trembling, listening to the delighted singing of the kraken as they fed.

That night she told her mother that Father was dead and would not be returning, and her mother beat her for the news. Her mother beat her for cursing a sailor beyond the breaks, and beat her for

telling lies, and beat her for her lack of faith; and Alanie fled her home for the streets, and all the time Alanie heard the kraken singing as they ran their tentacles through the shattered *Sparrow* and ferreted out the last drowned bodies of her father's crew.

When Alanie returned home, she found Sinolise sitting in the shadows, a single candle flickering on her mother's face, turning her bones to hard, sharp angles. The woman did not look up at Alanie's return, and Alanie saw that her mother was afraid.

Her mother — who had seemed so important and authoritative as she ran her Middle Street household and its servants — was now adrift. A bit of storm wood tossed into an ocean of uncertainty.

With a surge of fear, Alanie realized that her mother was weak. Sinolise was not a woman who supported herself as the fishmongers in Greyling Square. She was a woman who wanted others to care for her. She'd chosen a man with a ship to his name on the assumption that her marriage would bring her servants and a house farther up the white cliffs, far away from the fish guts among which she'd been raised. Sinolise had chosen a man of the sea in order to abandon it, and more foolish she to have thought that way.

Alanie went to bed, knowing that she was lost in an ocean greater than any her father had ever navigated. She wondered how she was meant to sail its currents and shallows with no knowledge or skill of her own.

A week later news came of the *Sparrow* wreckage, and Alanie found her mother down on her knees in the kitchen, burning her father's clothing in the fire. Alanie saw her mother's hatred and fear — that Alanie had known of her father's death before it could be known.

A month after that, without money to pay them, their two servants

were gone, and not long beyond, just before Summerturn, Alanie's
mother announced that they would be living in the country.

Alanie would have a new father — a stepfather — a man who was
a widower, and who had lands and sheep.

Eliam was a man who didn't mind a woman who brought with her
the child of another man, and came without means to his doorstep.

Alanie had never seen the kraken, but she remembered the first time
they spoke her name.

The man who was meant to replace her father called himself
Eliam. His wealth was known, his generosity as well. He was tall
and strong, his beard was brown, and he kept his hair in a long braid.
He was as powerful as her father, but different in the eyes in a way
Alanie couldn't name.

Eliam smiled as Alanie's mother presented her. He touched
Alanie's hand and exclaimed over her and complimented her dress
and tresses.

"Why, you're nearly a woman," he said.

"You look the age of my son, Elbe," he said.

"Such a lovely daughter," he said.

Sinolise took Eliam's attention as a compliment, but Alanie turned
rigid with fear, for she heard the kraken whispering.

*Do you know how we hunt blueback, Alanie? That whale is greatest
and most powerful, but we together are stronger. We do not hunt the
blueback — we hunt the blueback's young, for the blueback must forget
herself, then.*

*We hunt and poke at the children of old blueback, and of course she
must defend. Parents must save their little ones, and so the great ones*

forget themselves and dive deep, chasing us away, and then we seize a great mother and we hold her to us, and we twine our tentacles in seafloor corals, and we hold her fast.

All our kinfamily come, and we hold that mother to us, and we nip at her flesh, and the salt water turns misty black with the blood of her great heart, and at last she tires and sips of Moriabe, and then we have her to us.

And later, if we like, we snack on her children, too. Once we've drowned the mother, the children are no match.

That is how we hunt the blueback. We trick the mother and seize her and drag her down.

We are the children of Moriabe, and the blueback, though she swims in Moriabe's embrace, she is not one with the sea. We breathe the waters, but old blueback must needs breathe the air above, and if we hold blueback tight enough, she may thrash and twist and beg, but in time, the great one breathes of our mother, and once a creature has sipped of Moriabe, that one is ours.

See how your mother sips and drowns?

She is gone, and you are vulnerable.

Above or below the waves, it is the same.

The hunt is the same.

The kraken whispered to her, and Alanie saw it was true. Her mother fluttering to impress the man, using words to tend and flatter, while the man's eyes lingered only on Alanie. Eliam was no husband and no father, Alanie realized. He was a wolf who tended lambs.

Alanie bolted for her room and slammed her door, and plastered her body against its planks, and wished that her father was not dead in the embrace of Moriabe, and that the kraken did not speak true, and that she had not tasted her father's own blood in her own mouth as he died.

Alanie sobbed and wished for impossible things while the kraken whispered that her father was no salvation. His *Sparrow* lay beneath the waves, and they themselves nested within its hold.

Alanie's mother pounded on the door and begged to be allowed in, and Alanie heard her apologizing to the man who would devour her.

"This isn't like her," Alanie's mother said, again and again. "Alanie is a good girl. She will listen to you. I will make her listen."

Terror of abandonment made her mother's voice rise and crack as she sought to assuage her future husband, and Alanie heard her mother's words and Eliam's indulgent chuckle, and knew that her mother was lost. Sinolise would sacrifice anything for this new man. Eliam was meant to preserve Sinolise from fish guts and sea, and she would do anything to serve him.

The kraken chuckled and rolled lazily in the deeps of Moriabe.

The young blueback is the sweetest to consume. No gristle at all. They drown easy once the mother's gone. We wrap our tentacles around them and drag them down, whenever we like.

Alanie had never seen a kraken, and yet she swam among them.

She tumbled in the fast black flows of Moriabe's currents and nested in tangled writhing piles of kin beneath the ancient shells of massacred cathedral crabs. Alanie felt the grit of sand on her skin as she buried herself up to her eyes for ambush, and she tasted blood in her mouth when the kraken fed.

Sometimes the kraken songs were so loud that they drowned Alanie's ears with their feeding joy. When Sinolise instructed Alanie as to which belongings they would take to their new home, Alanie could only stare at her mother's lips and guess at the woman's words,

for kraken voices crashed and foamed inside her skull like surf off the breaks.

At other times the kraken voices were only whispers, as when they pursued narwhal pods beyond the icy northern horizons, their voices faint as fingers on Alanie's coverlet. But more and more the kraken were with her, sometimes close and sometimes far, tidal in their company, but never gone entirely.

When Alanie rode the cart to her new home, kraken rode with her, amused at the wheeled conveyance piled precarious with her and her mother's belongings, and when the kraken saw the chinkstone and thatching of Eliam's hall, with its storm-shutter windows and heavy wooden door, they murmured to themselves as to how it might be pried open for the food within.

But they were most impressed when they spied Eliam's sheep in his lush green fields — they marveled at prey that waited so contentedly to be slaughtered.

The kraken watched and listened as Alanie was taken into her new father's household, but they recoiled and flooded Alanie's sight with black-ink flight at the sight of Eliam's son.

Elbe was a boy of Alanie's age, and yet his eyes were those of a Graybane warrior's, returned from shoreline slaughter, and they seemed to laugh and mock her when he called her sister. A ghost of a boy, haunting the dark silences of his father's hall. Elbe's ancient knowing eyes clung to Alanie as he shadowed her through the echoes and stone of Eliam's manor.

Bluebacks beget bluebacks. Eels beget eels, the kraken murmured. *Beware.*

Room after room, hall after hall, Elbe stalked behind her as Alanie explored the kitchens and libraries and examined her spare clean room, where no lock barred her door. Always Elbe's knowing eyes followed her.

At last Alanie paused in Eliam's great hall and stood staring up at hunted trophies upon the walls. Byre elk with barbed ivory antlers, and snarling grey wolves, and the heads of mountain apes arranged by tribe and mounted in studied lines. Snow-lion pelts sprawled across granite flagstones, three times Alanie's length, and their white lush furs smothered her footsteps as she walked from kill to kill.

"In winter, he goes to the edge of the Scarp," Elbe murmured in Alanie's ear, standing so close that she flinched and drew away. "He hunts with bow and knife," Elbe said. "He likes the chase. The look of a heart draining in the snow. I've seen him stand and watch a stag bleed out for hours."

Alanie shrank further from the ghostly boy, but Elbe ignored her retreat and instead pointed to the dead and told their tales.

Eliam ranged forests where wind pines towered and forged through waist-deep snows where none but snow lions laired. He followed blood-spattered trails, relentless, undaunted by the worst of Wanem's ice-blind storms and careless of the Scarp's avalanches. Eliam ran his prey until at last it collapsed exhausted in the drifts, ribs heaving with its last living breaths, finally willing to give up life and flight, in favor of rest and death.

"He likes surrender in his toys," Elbe said. "He wants their welcome when his knife finally cuts them true. He likes to see them lift their throats to him. In the end, they all lift their throats and make his cutting easy. They're like your mother that way. So very desperate to please."

Alanie blanched at his words and turned to flee, but Elbe seized

her arm and yanked her close. His lips pressed to her ear. "Make no sound," he whispered. "Make not a sound. Listen to me while you still can. Listen like a rabbit, for surely you are prey. Do you not hear their trysting? Listen silent, sister, listen close. Already my father consumes your mother. If we slip to his chamber door, we'll hear her as she groans. But she is not the prey he most desires. I've seen his eyes on you, Alanie. You are the one he desires to hunt."

The boy drew away, and to Alanie's surprise, she saw pity in his eyes. Pity of what was to come. And the sight of his grieving eyes frightened Alanie more than any of his words.

"We're not so different, you and I," Elbe whispered. "We see the monsters others deny. We know what comes knocking at our chamber door. Run now, sister. Run and never look back."

"But my mother —"

"— is weak and wants to feel his teeth."

He pulled her to the manor door. "Don't make me earn a bloody back for nothing. Run, Alanie. Run for the ocean and follow the cliffs to the bay. Find a ship and sail, and remember that my father has never failed to catch his prey."

Still Alanie hesitated, but the kraken whispered in her ear.

A young blueback is easy to catch once its mother has sipped of Moriabe. So soft in our beaks. So easy to drag deep. Drown the parent first, then dine on the child. Sea or land, the hunt is the same. The hunt is always the same. First the parent, then the child.

Alanie fled.

She fled across green fields and rolling hills, sobbing with fear and running still. When she reached the sea, Alanie bore north, following the rise and fall of white marbled shores. The sun sank toward the ocean as Alanie ran. Shadows lengthened and fields reddened.

Moriabe wrapped the sun in her quilt, turning day to night, and still Alanie ran. She plunged through black pine forests and scrambled up and down ragged cliffs, and still she ran, her breath burning in her lungs and her legs turning weak. Her guts knotted, and still she ran. When she broke through the last of the forest and saw the burning lanterns of Serenity Bay and the white cliffs of the town luminous under the moon, she fell to her knees with relief.

In the end, it was for naught.

Eliam caught her on the Prince's Pier begging for work or berth or pity as the morning sun broke above the white cliffs. He seized her wrists in one strong hand and dragged her away from the docks, joking with the sailors and warehouse owners that children were always headstrong. He tossed her over the back of his horse as easily as tossing a sack of oats, and when still Alanie fought, he struck her face until her lips broke and bled.

When they arrived home, Alanie's mother stood at the manor door, wringing her hands with concern. But when Alanie fled to her, Sinolise struck her for a defiant child and returned her to Eliam's waiting hand. The boy Elbe watched with his ancient warrior's eyes as Eliam led Alanie into the manor, and said nothing at all.

Later, Elbe stripped his clothes to show Alanie what his father had wrought on his skin, and she traced the wounds of his bloody battles with her fingertips. The boy's flesh hung from his ribs in tatters and the coral knots of his spine showed through the shredded meat of his back.

But by then, Alanie hardly cared, for her own back was bloody as well.

———⊁———

Alanie had never seen a kraken, but they called out to her often. When Eliam whipped her bloody, the kraken thrashed and disappeared in clouds of blackest ink, calling for her to flee as well. When Eliam pinned Alanie in the kitchens and fumbled at her skirts, they lashed out with poisonous tentacles and snapped sharp beaks and called for her to fight.

And Alanie did flee, and she did fight. She fought until she was exhausted. She fled once and once and once again, and each time Eliam dragged her back, and finally she fled no more.

Eliam hunted too well, and his belt bit too deep.

The kraken recoiled at being hunted down. They lashed out at the monster that pinned them, and each time they shrieked that they had warned her about the beast who stalked her.

We told you, they said. *We told you how the hunt was done.*

Moriabe's children were not creatures to be preyed upon. They reviled the monster who ran them down, and they were with Alanie less and less. They went distant hunting for narwhal pods or else sank deep in Moriabe's blind trenches. The kraken nested in the wreckage of the sailing ships they'd broken and slept beneath shifting seafloor sands, and when Alanie called for them, they sang, *We are of the sea, and you are of the shore. We are Moriabe's children. No one hunts our kind.*

My father hunted you, Alanie retorted, but the kraken only laughed.

It was we who hunted him, they sang, and their voices were faint and fading.

Alanie had never seen a kraken, and she heard their voices not at all. So silent were they that Alanie began to wonder if she had been

simply mad, fooling herself into believing that Moriabe's children had spoken to her in the wake of the storm that had reshaped her life. She called to the kraken and she cursed them and she cajoled, but nothing moved them, if indeed they had ever been moved at all. Alanie was alone.

Alone she learned to bar her bedroom door with cedar chests, and alone she took the whippings for her new defiance. Alone she learned to ghost the halls, as silent and careful as a rabbit, alert for the wolf that stalked her. Alone she learned to survive as best she could. Her eyes became sunken and ancient, and she became watchful and fearful, but she survived.

And still she remembered the kraken and how they'd called to her. And no matter how much she hated herself for seeking their voices, still she tried.

Alanie, Alanie.

She remembered the first time she'd heard their song, and so she waited, implacably patient, hoping to find them once again, waiting for one of the great storms that brought the kraken to the surface. Waiting for Moriabe and Stormface to clash in a lovers' quarrel, just as they had when her father had seen the kraken in his own time.

Alanie waited and survived, and at last a night came when Wanem lashed the manor's shutters with wind and rain, and Moriabe's waves rose high. That night Alanie dreamed of kraken in the deeps, and in the morning she ran across the rain-drenched fields to the cliffs, to look out across the blue calm waters of Moriabe's quilt as it shimmered with golden sunshine.

Alanie scrambled down rocky trails to the beaches far below and picked her way across the kelp-draped stones to the water's edge. She waded out amongst crystal tide pools, stepping barefoot past

anemones and bluestem clams. She hiked her skirt as Moriabe's waters rushed and foamed about her knees, and she closed her eyes and listened, straining for the taste of blood in her mouth and the rising strain of kraken song.

She listened for her name.

Alanie. Alanie.

If she listened close, she imagined she could hear them still, their voices tumbling in the surf. If she listened close, she could imagine great vast creatures swimming in the depths of Moriabe. She could imagine that Eliam did not squeeze her wrists until they bruised and pretend that Sinolise never turned away from a daughter pressed against a kitchen block. Alanie could imagine and pretend, and listen for the sound of kraken, and hours could pass. The sun could climb in the sky, and gulls could wheel and bank and hunt, and dolphins could cut the far blue waters, but if kraken called her name, their voices were drowned in foam and surf.

When Alanie at last opened her eyes, the rising tide had soaked her to the waist, and Elbe squatted on the shore, his knowing eyes upon her.

By reflex Alanie searched the cliffs, afraid he had been followed, but she spied no sign of Eliam.

"I thought you might keep walking," Elbe said.

Alanie waded back to shore and spread her skirts to dry. "I was listening to the ocean."

"My mother said the same. And then one day she walked out into the heart of Moriabe. She walked out into the waters, and when it became too deep to walk, she swam. And then she kept on swimming. Father was in a rage at that. Nothing escapes him on land, but she was in the sea. He called to her and shouted. I watched him waving his arms and raging, but he was too much the coward to swim after her into the deep ocean. He stood on the shore and screamed and screamed like Wanem, and she kept swimming. And then she stopped, and Moriabe took her. In the end, it was easy. She ducked her head and sipped of Moriabe, and it was done. And I was alone with him."

"Why didn't you tell me?"

"And tell you the one true escape?" Elbe laughed. "If you go swimming, sister, then there is only me. There aren't enough cedar chests to block a door that he wants open. What wouldn't you do to keep from hearing that man's knock? What wouldn't you do to keep his attentions focused elsewhere?"

"But you told me to run, when we first met."

"I hoped . . ." He shook his head. "I liked your eyes. You did not look like someone hunted, then. I knew your mother wouldn't save you, but I thought, perhaps . . ." He shrugged. "I was a fool. My father never fails to catch his prize."

They were quiet for a while. At last Alanie asked, "Why do you not go swimming, too?"

"I tried once. Soon after. I couldn't breathe the water the way she did. I'm a coward, I think. I swam back to shore. He whipped me for it. He was terrified that he would lose his heir. He keeps a boat close now, to row after me in case I try to follow her."

He was quiet awhile and then said, "I know that everyone says that the great storms are caused by Moriabe's and Stormface's love quarrels. But I think they're wrong."

"Oh?"

"I think Stormface is like my father."

"And what is Moriabe, then, if Wanem is such a creature?"

"Moriabe . . ." Elbe fell quiet for a long time. "I think that when the great storms rise, she is fighting to defend her children. Moriabe isn't like our mothers at all. She is something else. Stronger. Fearless. And when Stormface comes to her door as my father does to ours, she battles him and fights him, and she forces him to flee." He nodded out at the blue waters. "And then, when she turns calm like this, it's because her children are safe again. Moriabe defends her children — that's what I think."

Above them on the cliffs, Eliam called out, and Elbe flinched. Alanie looked up at the man who stalked her nights, and her skin crawled. She thought of Elbe's mother, swimming out in the deeps, and wondered at parents who would do anything to save a child.

Eliam called out again, and Sinolise appeared as well, demanding that they return.

Alanie reached for her brother's hand. "Come with me," she said. "We'll swim together. We don't have to be afraid." And though Elbe looked at her with terrified eyes, he followed where she led.

The waters rushed around Alanie's ankles as she strode into the ocean. It swirled about her knees and clutched at her thighs and tangled her skirts. From high on the cliffs, Eliam shouted for their return, and Alanie's mother begged for their obedience in her high frightened voice, but they were far away, and the waves were loud, drowning out demands.

A wave came crashing in, frothing up around Alanie's ribs, and she gasped at the chill of soaking clothes. She kicked free of skirts and blouse, and pulled Elbe deeper into the waters. He seemed to struggle for a moment between the pull of her hand and his father's voice, and then he, too, was tugging off his clothes, and the ocean rose

to their chests, and they pressed on, and Alanie thought she heard Elbe laughing as if suddenly free.

The next wave lifted Alanie's feet from the stones, and then she was swimming, letting Elbe's hand go so she could stroke hard through the surf. She dived through an oncoming wave and surfaced on the far side, shaking her head to clear water from her eyes. Elbe surfaced beside her, swimming hard, and then they were swimming together, matching each other stroke for stroke, swimming with all their will.

Behind them, Eliam galloped down the path to the shore. His threats and demands echoed across the waters, but the ocean spread between them, blue and wide, and he stood powerless on the shore.

Alanie swam and Elbe kept pace, and then the ocean's current caught them, and they were swept away from shore. Moriabe cupped them in her currents and carried them fast away from where Eliam dragged his boat into the surf.

Alanie turned on her back, resting and treading water and staring up at blue sky as the current carried them. Beside her, Elbe was smiling. His eyes seemed almost young. The white cliffs of shore were distant now, but when Alanie checked Eliam's progress, she found to her surprise that he gained upon them.

"He's quick," Alanie said, trying not to despair.

"He was born to hunt."

Eliam used his great strength to advantage as he leaned into his oars, and his boat fairly shot across the waves.

"I don't have the will to drown myself," Elbe said quietly.

"You won't have to," Alanie said, wanting to believe it was true. "Just swim with me. All we have to do is swim."

She tugged his shoulder and kicked off again, and Elbe cursed and followed. Stroke after stroke, they swam through blue glittering waters, rising and falling on Moriabe's waves. Panting and paddling still. Kicking, always kicking deeper into the blue, until at last their strength gave out and there was nothing left to do but float.

The two of them bobbed on Moriabe's quilt, flotsam specks on the open ocean. Alanie's limbs felt loose and sinuous in the waters, limp and used. She didn't resent the exhaustion, but wished she could have swum deeper. She wondered if she had done enough. She wondered if Moriabe truly cared for anything at all. She wondered if kraken were close or far. She wondered if she had ever heard their voices.

Eliam closed the distance, straining at his oars. On the waves, he looked small. Not the monster that Alanie had known on land, but only a tiny man in a tiny little boat, far out upon a wide, deep ocean, a man who thought he was a hunter.

Alanie narrowed her eyes as she stared at him, and then she lay back and spread her arms wide to float on Moriabe's quilt, and she called to the kraken. Alanie imagined them in the deeps, lying in tangled piles of kin. She imagined them swimming sinuous through the dark shadow waters, and she called to them.

Do you know how I hunt the blueback? I seize his child, and he forgets himself. Come and see what I've baited forth. Come and see how I have learned to hunt.

Alanie could hear Eliam's cursing as he drew nearer, and Elbe had begun to sob with fear, but Alanie cared only for the deeps.

Again and again she called out to the kraken.

The hunt is the same on sea or shore. The hunt is always the same. I have listened; I have learned. Come and see what follows me.

Again and again she called, and down in the deeps great shadow creatures stirred and shifted. Alanie felt the currents change, and she redoubled her calls, and Moriabe's children slid from beneath ocean sands and eased from night-black trenches.

The hunt is the same on sea or shore, Alanie sang. *A great blueback has forgotten himself in the chase to save his child. Come and hunt; come and see.*

The ocean currents shifted and swirled. The waters around Alanie began to froth as kraken surged upward.

Come and hunt; come and see.

She could feel the kraken rising from the depths, feel the ocean rushing past her skin, faster and faster, see the sunlight streaming down through the waters, and the specks that floated far above, so small so small.

See what I have baited forth, Alanie called. *He is soft. No gristle at all. He is soft.*

Moriabe's children surged for the surface.

Eliam was still shouting and Elbe had grabbed Alanie's arm to point at the boiling waters all around, but all their words were lost. The ocean's roar drowned them out completely. The only sounds in Alanie's ears were the voices of the kraken, rising.

Sister, the kraken called. *Sister.*

Alanie spread her arms wide, welcoming her kin.

Old Souls

CASSANDRA CLARE

A graceful and honorable old age is the childhood of immortality. —PINDAR

The entrance to the nursing home was both grand and unobtrusive, Leah thought, as if nobody wanted to be reminded that beyond the high white wall that hid the building from the road, past the elegant sign saying *Silver Pines*, behind the inoffensive clapboard front of the huge, rambling Victorian, were old people who were unlikely to ever leave the place alive.

She sighed and tried to push the depressing thought away. She was having nothing but depressing thoughts these days, and the lack of anyone to talk to about them didn't help. Once she'd been able to talk to her mother about anything, but not anymore.

"Are you nervous about your first day of work?" asked Grandma Ruth as they bumped up the gravel drive. Grandma drove the way most old people drove: all white knuckles and squinched-up eyes as if she were being tortured.

Leah scrunched down in her seat, trying to avoid her own reflection in the mirrored sunshade. The pale blue uniform everyone at Silver Pines had to wear clashed with her olive skin, and her braids ("hair must be tied back at all times") made her look like Rebecca of Sunnybrook Farm. "Nothing says I have to do this except Mom. We could just turn this car around right now and never tell her I didn't go."

"Oh, I don't think so," said Grandma lightly. She pursed her lips, painted the same shade of seashell pink as her nails. Her hair was perfectly set, too — once a week at the beauty parlor kept it looking like a shiny helmet. "It'll do you good to get out. You can't hang around the house with me forever watching my programs."

Leah wasn't so sure about that. Grandma's house smelled musty, but it was dark and peaceful, and she was starting to develop an interest in *Days of Our Lives*.

"So instead of spending time at home with one old person, I get to go out and spend time with a lot of old people?" she grumbled.

"At least you'll be moving," said Grandma, and mimed walking with her fingers. They were drawing up at the circular drive in front of the home. There were massive wide stairs leading down from the front door and two wheelchair ramps. A woman in a white suit was standing on the steps, looking ostentatiously at her watch and then at the car, as if to indicate her annoyance at Leah's late arrival. Leah felt an instant swell of resentment. It wasn't her fault Grandma's sedan didn't have GPS. "Besides, a young girl needs her walking-around money. When I was young —"

OLD SOULS

"Right." Leah had no desire to hang around and listen to the reminiscences of the old. She jerked open the car door and jumped out. "See you at five."

"Try to memorize every patient's face," said Mrs. Minchel, the head of Silver Pines, as they hurried through the first-floor corridors. "Greet them, say a friendly hello. They may not remember their name, but you can remember it for them. Don't say anything else, though. No conversations. Just 'hello' and 'good evening.'"

Say hello, remember their names. Leah hurried to keep up with her boss. They were passing into the group rooms of the home — the activities room, in which a game of bingo was going on; the exercise room, where a teacher was leading some of the younger residents in a series of slow tai chi movements. Everyone looked fairly cheerful — maybe it wouldn't be so bad, Leah thought. Maybe she could make friends with the old folks. Maybe they'd be charming and pass on some life lessons, like old people in movies.

Mrs. Minchel *click-click*ed on her high heels into the television room, where old people napped in front of the screen. A male nurse in blue scrubs was leaning over a woman so old that she appeared to be a shrunken figure with a tuft of white at the top, like a cotton ball pasted onto a doll's head.

He stood up and turned around as they came into the room. Leah was startled at how young he was. Ringlets of red-brown hair, cut in an old-fashioned style, framed a pale, youthful face. He was very slender, to the point of thinness, and looked as if a high wind could blow him over. Even his scrubs hung loosely on his body.

"Hello, Brooks," said Mrs. Minchel, her voice warming. "This is

Leah, our summer intern. She'll be dealing with the laundry, cleaning the game rooms, and doing a few other activities. Let her know if she can be of use to you in any way."

He ducked his head and muttered, "Sure, ma'am."

Leah looked at him curiously, but he avoided her gaze, ducking around her on his way out of the room. The old woman he'd been talking to looked after him as he went, her wide old eyes dark and wet, her lip trembling.

"So why can't I have conversations with the patients?" she asked. "He was."

Mrs. Minchel turned around without a word to the old woman in the chair. "Because some of them have Alzheimer's or dementia. They could become violent if you said the wrong thing. Brooks is an old soul — he knows what to say to them. You're inexperienced." *And immature*, her tone implied. "Stay away from the patients, and deal with the sheets."

Whatever fantasies Leah had been entertaining about becoming friends with the charming old people who populated the home were slowly suffocated that first week. Mrs. Minchel's edict that she not say anything to the residents besides "hello" and "good evening" stifled any attempts at conversation — not that anyone seemed all that interested in talking to the girl who pushed carts full of linens stained with puke, blood, and worse through the halls of the facility.

Besides, most of the residents were either silent or asleep when she saw them. The very oldest residents were kept on the third floor, where the rooms were big and open but always seemed to smell like dust and urine. On her third day, Leah trundled her cart into one

and, thinking it was empty, began to lift the pictures on the night-stand in order to dust under them.

A sudden shrill screaming nearly made her drop the silver-framed photo she'd been holding. What she'd taken for a huddled heap of blankets had transformed into a screeching old lady, her tufted white hair standing up like a duck's fluff, her mouth an open black hole.

Leah began to back away. "I'm sorry — sorry —"

The old woman was still screaming as Leah thumped into something behind her. Hands came up around Leah, circling her arms. Cold hands. She gave a cry of surprise and turned to see Brooks, setting her gently aside so that he could move toward the old woman in the bed. He bent down over her, making soothing noises, not English, just a rush of murmured words in a language Leah didn't know.

She stood with her arms hanging awkwardly at her sides as the old woman lapsed into faint sobs and then silence, her wrinkled cheek pillowed on her hand while she slept.

Brooks rose to his feet. "Come with me," he said, and took Leah's hand. He drew her out of the room and into the corridor where she had left her laundry cart.

"Thanks," she said. He released her, and she leaned against the wall. The old lady's screaming had shaken her up more than she realized. She suddenly wanted a cigarette.

"I'll see you later," he said. He started off down the hall.

"Brooks, wait."

He turned around. He was still pale, the weird luminous pale she'd noticed when she'd first seen him. His brown-red hair curled against his cheeks and temples. His fingers were bloodlessly bitten, ragged with scraps of skin. When he moved to tug awkwardly at his scrubs, she saw the peach-colored circle against his skin. "You smoke?" she asked, pointing at the nicotine patch.

"Trying to quit," he said.

"So you don't have any cigarettes on you."

He shook his head. His eyes were an odd fathomless dark brown, like holes dug into the earth. "No."

"You don't look old enough to be a nurse," she said. "Or to smoke."

"I'm older than I look," he said, neutrally. There was a tinge of something to his voice, not quite an accent. He sounded more like someone from an old movie, with a slightly stilted way of speaking. She wondered where he was from.

"Old enough to have trained to be a nurse?"

"It didn't take that long," he said with a shrug, the bones of his shoulders pushing up his scrubs. "I should go — I'm supposed to read to Mrs. Ellis."

Mrs. Ellis was one of the second-floor residents. She was somewhere around ninety, with a kind, lined face and a smile that made Leah think that maybe getting old wouldn't be so bad.

"You're awfully nice to the old people," she said. "You know what Mrs. Minchel said about you?"

He shook his head.

"She said you have an old soul."

"She was right about that," he said, and left.

"Are you enjoying Silver Pines?" asked Grandma Ruth. She and Leah were eating dinner the way they usually did, on TV trays positioned in front of the couch. *Wheel of Fortune* droned on in the background. Grandma had a habit of taping a whole week's worth of game shows

and then watching them all at once, as if there were actually a continuing story to them that she was paying attention to. It made Leah want to hit her head on the wall.

"No," Leah said, forking up some meat loaf. Meat loaf, chicken, matzo ball soup, *cholent, kasha varnishkes* — her grandma had a rotating menu of food she cooked, and it never varied. Today was Wednesday, so it was meat loaf. It was so completely unlike the food Leah had at home, where her mother was always cooking macrobiotic meals with kale and locally farmed fish.

Grandma frowned. "Why not? I was hoping you'd make some friends."

Leah stabbed at her plate. "With ancient people?" She saw a look of hurt flash over her grandmother's face and quickly amended her comment. "Mrs. Minchel says I'm not allowed to talk to any of the patients. So it's hard to make friends."

"Aren't there any other volunteers? Nurses or candy stripers —"

"No one calls them candy stripers anymore, Grandma. And no, I'm the only intern. There's a nurse, called Brooks. He's not that old, but he's — weird."

"Weird isn't necessarily bad." Grandma Ruth had stopped eating and was watching TV again, murmuring the revealed letters under her breath. "What about your friends from home?"

Leah thought of the hundred unanswered texts on her phone, the e-mail addresses she had blocked. "They haven't tried to get in touch."

Grandma turned her gaze on Leah, her eyes bright and sharp. "I find that hard to believe. You always had such good friends. What about Rachel?"

Leah set her fork down. She couldn't believe Grandma remembered Rachel. Though she'd looked after Leah enough times

when she was little and Rachel had come over — she remembered Grandma leaning over them while they both were finger painting, laughing when they got the paint all over their clothes and faces. She'd thought Grandma was awesome then, like a parent who let you do anything you wanted.

"We're not friends anymore," Leah said.

"Really?" Grandma stood up, picking up both her plate and Leah's. "That's odd, since she's called here for you at least twenty times."

Leah swallowed down the sudden hot bitterness in her throat. "Grandma —"

But her grandmother had already disappeared into the kitchen.

Leah looked back at the TV screen. The phrase up on the board was THERE'S NO PLACE LIKE HOME. The laughter of the crowd rattled inside her head as she remembered her mother silently handing her a packed bag while Grandma waited in the driveway.

"Leah?" Grandma was standing in the kitchen doorway, holding the cordless phone in her hand. "It's Rachel."

Leah stood up, knocking over the TV tray. "You *called* her?" she hissed.

Grandma just shrugged and held the phone out. Leah trailed across the rug and took it reluctantly, pressing the receiver to her ear. "Rachel?"

"Oh, my God, Leah!" Her friend's voice gushed down the phone line, horrible in its familiarity. Just hearing Rachel talk flooded Leah's mind with memories. The car, both of them in it, silent, stuck at a red light. The windshield wipers going. Rachel telling Leah she was lucky her mom was taking her to the clinic and paying. Telling her about a girl she knew who hadn't had the money and had kept throwing herself down the stairs, trying to end it that way.

"Rachel," she whispered. "What's going on? You called —"

"I called you, like, fifty times," Rachel said. "Look, I wanted you to hear it from me and not some other way. Ryan's going out with Sadie."

Leah felt like she were drowning in something that burned her eyes and choked her voice. Drowning in poison. "With Sadie? But she knows, she knows what he did to me —"

"I guess she doesn't care." Rachel sounded furious. "Look, just so you know, I've stopped talking to her, and so has practically everyone else. No one thinks it's okay. I hate her now, okay? I hate her."

You should hate him, Leah thought. "It doesn't matter," she said.

"What?" Rachel sounded outraged. "Of course it matters."

"It doesn't matter what Ryan does," said Leah. "I don't care."

"Leah —"

Leah clicked off, cutting off Rachel's voice. She handed the silent phone to her grandmother, who was staring at her wordlessly. "Don't call my friends again," Leah said, and headed upstairs to her room.

"Why do you hate it so much here?" Brooks asked.

Leah was sitting on the back steps of Silver Pines' kitchen. They were concrete and utilitarian. In fact, everything was utilitarian and plain out here. The nursing home looked nothing like it did from the front; it looked more like the blank back of a mall.

Leah flicked ash off her cigarette. "I didn't say I hated it."

"It's fairly evident, though, from the way you behave." Brooks was leaning against the wall behind her, his long arms pale against the darkly painted clapboard. It was one of those drippy gray June days that seemed like an affront to summer.

"It's not here, it's just . . ." She waved a hand. "Everything."

"You're unhappy," he observed.

"You're insightful." She'd been surprised when he'd joined her on her smoke break. She'd thought he probably wanted to bum a cigarette at first, but he didn't seem inclined to do that. Instead he seemed to want to stare off toward the dripping trees in the distance.

"I guess I've seen a lot of unhappy people," he said.

She snorted. "You make it sound like you're a million years old." She dropped the butt of the cigarette onto the ground and watched it splutter out.

"I'm not," he said stiffly.

"I didn't say you were. It's just —" She toyed with the frayed strap of her sandal. "Look, I don't mean to be bringing you down somehow. It's true, I don't want to be here. My mom sent me here as a sort of punishment."

"Punishment for what?"

She looked up at him. His auburn hair curled in the humid air. There was a red mark on the inside of his wrist, probably where he'd pulled a nicotine patch off. "I was pregnant," she said.

He stared at her. "You had a baby?" he asked.

"No." She stood up. "No. I didn't have a baby."

He didn't say anything else. Leah turned around and went back inside.

Leah sat in her room at her grandmother's house with the window cracked open, staring at the glowing screen of her computer. The familiar blue and white of Facebook blinked on her screen.

She'd come home to a dozen texts urging her to check her Facebook.

She'd found more messages there, telling her excitedly that Ryan had cheated on Sadie with another girl. Ryan had changed his relationship status to "It's complicated," and Sadie had abandoned her page completely. She hadn't updated in days.

Leah struggled to remember what Sadie looked like: a mousy girl, with pale brown hair, who had always looked at Ryan sideways under the fringe of her bangs.

Sadie totally walked in on Ryan kissing Amanda at Mark Davis's party.

It turns out Ryan's been cheating on Sadie for weeks, months even.

Ryan's such a dog, really, I don't know why anyone likes him.

I do!!!! (The last with a picture of Ryan, looking soulful, attached.)

Sadie's such a slut she got what she deserved.

I hope Leah knows it proves Ryan's just a scumbag.

Sadie's the slut, she's nothing.

Nothing

Leah flipped the computer off and leaned out the window into the drenched night.

Silver Pines had a wi-fi network, though hardly anyone ever used it. The password was taped up in the big laundry room, where huge washer/dryers went all day long and the whole place stank of bleach and disinfectant.

For some reason, the best reception was in the residents' rooms, especially the ones on the second floor. Leah sat on the floor of Mrs.

Ellis's closet, scrolling down Facebook on her phone. She could hear Mrs. Ellis's gentle breathing. It made a strange counterpoint to the faint beeping from her phone as her page updated.

Rachel had posted that she was glad Ryan had cheated on Sadie.

Lucy and Amanda had posted to Sadie's page telling her she was a slut. Sadie hadn't replied. There was more, too, more angry posts. It was strange to see the messages there, like watching someone hit someone else, someone helpless, in the face.

Part of her wanted to leave Sadie a message, too. Something like, *I told you so.* Or *What did you think would happen? He wouldn't even drive me to the clinic, you know that? What kind of person does that?* It felt like a bad, ugly part of her, and it ached in her stomach like the undigested pit of a fruit.

The door to the room opened, and Leah hastily slid her phone under her sweater so that the glow wouldn't give her away. She saw shoes crossing the floor, the blue hems of nurse scrubs. The creak as someone sat down in the chair next to Mrs. Ellis's bed.

"Iris," Brooks said. Leah jolted hard enough to nearly knock against the door of the closet. It hadn't occurred to her that Mrs. Ellis had a first name or that Brooks would know it. "How are you feeling?"

Mrs. Ellis murmured softly. Leah had to lean close to the crack in the door to understand the words. "My husband," she said. "He's overseas, in Anzio. They won't let me write to him. How will he know I'm thinking about him, if they won't let me write to him?"

"I know," Brooks said. His voice was low and soothing. "But your husband is a soldier. They know letters don't always get through. You know how I know that? I was a soldier too, but not in the same war as Mr. Ellis. In the one before it."

Leah's mind raced. Brooks a soldier? Maybe he had been overseas

in Iraq? But how could that have been "the one before"? Mrs. Ellis was ancient. If she'd had a husband in a war, it must have been World War II at least —

"You would have been a little girl," said Brooks. "You probably didn't know anything about it. The trenches and the Somme. The way the gas would come rolling across the fields, green and yellow. You'd have a few seconds to put your smoke helmet on, and then the place would be full of gas. It's heavier than air. It would fall like a curtain and blot out the light. It could be hours before the wind took it away and you saw how many had died. Or sometimes they'd die right in front of you, clawing at their throats and their eyes. At least your husband was spared that."

Mrs. Ellis murmured something soft. Leah thought she might be patting Brooks's hand.

"Or we could talk about the things you do remember," Brooks said. "New York. Do you remember the elevated trains? The Automat? Or when you could see a picture for a dime? I remember going to the picture palaces back when it meant something to be able to see a movie —"

The door swung open. Leah heard Mrs. Minchel, obviously standing on the threshold. "Is everything all right in here?" she asked.

"We were talking about movies," said Brooks.

"Of course you were," said Mrs. Minchel, her doubt clear in her tone. "Now, come along, Brooks, we need you downstairs in the activities room."

Leah heard the scrape as Brooks pushed his chair back and a soft noise of protest from Mrs. Ellis, drowned out by Mrs. Minchel saying something else in her strident voice. She burst out of the closet the moment the door opened, to find Mrs. Ellis looking at her with faded blue eyes, paler than the linen pillow she rested against.

"The Strand," she said, in her rusted old voice. "On Forty-Seventh. It was the loveliest place."

Leah fled.

Leah was lying on the roughest part of the shag carpeting in her grandma's house, just at the foot of the stairs. She was holding the receiver of the phone against her chest. It had been ringing on and off for the past hour, but she'd managed to mute it every time before her grandmother heard it.

She looked at the receiver screen. Six missed calls from her mother.

She could remember her mother standing on the front steps of their house as Grandma's car idled in the driveway. Leah standing with her green duffel bag at her feet. Her mom with her hand on Leah's shoulder. "It'll be good for you, being at Oma's," she said.

"You just want to get me away from Ryan," said Leah.

Her mother crossed her arms and pressed her lips together, staring off into the distance.

"You don't want us to get back together," Leah said.

"He didn't go with you," said her mother. "To the Clinic." She always said it that way, like the C was capitalized.

"He was busy," Leah said, knowing even as she said it how threadbare the excuse sounded, like a worn-out blanket.

Her mother sighed. "Talk to your Oma," she said. "She understands more than you think."

It was poker night tonight, which meant Grandma was in the

kitchen with her friends, playing cards. Leah could hear a whoop every once in a while when someone won a hand. The phone rang, and Leah muted it again. Only half her mind was on her mother. The other half was on Brooks and what she'd heard him saying to Mrs. Ellis. She'd looked it up online. The things he'd been talking about, trenches and gas attacks, they were things from World War I. From a hundred years ago.

Why was he pretending he'd been there?

Leah commenced a desultory search the next day, but Brooks wasn't in any of his usual places at the old people's home — not in the activities room or the TV room or the dining hall or on the concrete steps behind Silver Pines. She finally decided to check the second-floor rooms, starting with Mrs. Ellis's. There was no one there; Mrs. Ellis was curled on her side, peacefully sleeping. With her tuft of white hair, she looked like a Q-tip.

Leah moved to the next room. Mrs. Ambridge was ninety-eight and had aphasia, which Leah had discovered meant that she mixed up words with other words. She was always saying things like "purple chocolate dinosaur" when she meant to be asking for another helping of spaghetti.

Leah pushed the door open carelessly.

The first thing she saw was the blood. It was splashed across the white tile floor like a streak of scarlet paint.

Mrs. Ambridge was lying in her bed, her eyes shut. She looked as peaceful as a figure on a tomb. Her left arm was stretching out, because Brooks was holding her wrinkled, pale hand. His mouth was fastened to her thin wrist. Blood ran from his mouth, over her skin, splattering on the floor.

Leah gasped. She couldn't scream; she couldn't get enough air in to scream. Brooks heard her anyway, and his head jerked up. His eyes looked feral and wild. His chin was smeared with blood.

"Leah," he said, his voice choked, and blood ran out of the corners of his mouth.

Leah ran. She didn't remember running later, only that she had, out the door of Silver Pines and across the grass, plunging into the woods that ringed the property. She ran until the light was nearly blocked out, and something caught her arm and swung her around, so hard that she tripped over a root and fell to her knees on the ground.

She looked up at him, standing over her. Brooks. He wasn't even out of breath, though he must have been chasing her. There was dried blood in the corners of his mouth and some spattered on his blue scrubs. Leah remembered reading somewhere that scrubs were blue because in the days when nurses had worn white uniforms, patients had reacted badly to the sight of red blood against the white.

She didn't understand why blue was better.

"You're a vampire," she said.

He just looked at her. He was still the same Brooks, pale and tall and bony, with the same sad eyes. She tried to read those eyes, tried to read what was behind that sadness. Anger? Viciousness? She had seen what she was sure she was never supposed to see. Surely he cared.

"You could kill me," she said. "But I won't tell anyone about you. No one would believe me. Everyone already thinks I'm crazy."

"You're not crazy," he said. "But it's not like you think."

She shook her head. The birds were chirping in the trees. The sun was shining down on them. And there was a vampire standing over her.

"You were alive," she said. "In World War One. All that stuff you said to Mrs. Ellis, that was true."

He walked a little away from her and looked at the trunk of a tree. She could run, she thought, but he'd just catch her. He was clearly faster than she could ever be. "I was human then," he said. "I was alive. Signed up at sixteen, just to get out in the field. Lied about my age. I didn't know what it would be like. The shells, the guts everywhere. I wanted to be a medic. Wear a red cross. But the gas came one night while I was sleeping and tore out my lungs. I was buried and I woke up like this." He shook his head. "I don't know why. I must have been bitten while I was alive. I don't even remember it, but it must have been enough to get the virus in my bloodstream."

"You live on blood?" Leah said. It was only half a question.

"I can eat," he said. "I breathe. I go out in the sun. I smoke cigarettes. I drink coffee. But blood — blood carries memories."

"What does that mean?"

He took a shallow breath. "The beat of the human heart is the music of remembrance," he said. "When I drink blood, I see the memories of the person whose blood I'm consuming."

Leah shrank back. He turned and looked at her. And laughed, without humor. "You think I'd want your blood?" he said. "You're sixteen. What do you remember? The mall? Your friends? The boy who dumped you?" He shook his head. "You're thinking of movies. The ageless vampire and the teenage girl. But the truth is you — you're a child to me. Inside, I'm an old man. No matter what I look like." He touched his hand to his face, the smooth skin there, with an expression of distaste.

"I remember more than that," Leah said in a whisper.

His eyes narrowed. "I guess you do," he said. "You've known some pain. But — why do you think I work here?"

"Old people don't fight back?" Leah said, her words harsher than she'd intended. She shouldn't make him angry, she knew. But he didn't seem angry. His eyes were far away.

"They remember," he said. "The way they are outside, that's the way I really am. They know what I know. Some of them, they remember New York before cars. Horses pulling advertising wagons through the streets. A nickel to ride the subway. The first time anyone ever saw a plane take off. Irving Berlin, now that was real music. In the twenties I was a rum runner. You don't even know what that is, do you? You don't know a time when people sewed their own goddamn buttons on. You don't remember calls being put through by manual switchboard exchanges. You never lived without a cell phone in your hand and a computer on your lap." His hands were fists. "You don't understand my world. Telegraph and radio and Model Ts. My world is dying. When the last person who remembers my time dies —"

He broke off.

"Then what?" she said in a whisper.

"I don't know," he said. "I don't know what I am. I don't need blood to survive, but I need it to feel. If I don't have it, I'm afraid of what I might become."

"Maybe nothing would happen," she said. "Maybe you'd be all right."

"I've lived a long time, Leah," he said. "In all those years, I've never met another vampire who was *all right*." He touched the blood at

the side of his mouth. "The things that are commonplace to you, computers and satellite and the Internet, are abominations to me. I remember my father telling me about the first message sent over the telegraph," he said. "You know what it said?"

She shook her head.

He stared at her and through her. "*What hath God wrought?*"

"What hath God wrought?" Leah muttered, poking at her peas with her fork.

Oma raised her eyebrows. "What did you say?"

"Nothing," Leah muttered, and took a swig from her glass of ginger ale. "The first telegraph message."

"I know. I didn't realize you'd been studying your history trivia." Oma looked more closely at her. "You look pale. Are you all right?"

Leah said nothing. She was thinking about the phone buzzing under her hand with unanswered calls from her mom and of Brooks saying, *I need blood to feel.*

Oma sighed. "I know," she said. "I'll never understand." Leah looked around the kitchen, saw the curling old drawings she had done in kindergarten still pinned to the fridge. There were no other drawings, nothing newer. She was the *bas-yekhide*, the only child. "You know why Mom sent me here?" Leah said. "Don't you?"

Oma set her fork down. "Why don't you tell me?"

So Leah told her. About Ryan, and about the way he'd made her feel special and loved and unique until the day she came to him about the problem she thought was theirs and found out it was only hers. How her mom had taken her to the clinic. The drugs they'd given her that made her feel far away and floating. How it hadn't hurt then but it had hurt later, when she felt like she'd been kicked in the stomach, but nothing had hurt like finding out Ryan wouldn't answer her calls. That he had another girlfriend. That he looked right through her like she were invisible.

Like she were nothing.

When Leah was done, Oma reached up and patted her blue-white hair into place. "Leah, Leah," she murmured, and then opened her arms. "Come here."

Folding herself into her grandmother's lap, Leah could feel how small her Oma was, how birdlike her bones. For all that, she felt strong, as if there were a structure of hard wire under her soft, wrinkled skin. "I thought you would hate me," Leah said.

"*Shayna maidel*," said Oma. "Let me tell you something. You know I used to be a receptionist when your ma was growing up, didn't you? For a doctor. It was a long time ago. They didn't have clinics like the one you went to. Women would come in, ones who couldn't afford to have a child, whose husbands beat them and their kids, or little girls sometimes, younger than you, who'd been forced. And he had to send them away. The law said so. He would have gone to jail otherwise. So a lot of them found someone else to do it for them. They'd come back later, with knitting needles or broken glass still stuck inside them. Sometimes their stomachs would blow up like balloons from the infection. That was when we knew they were going to die. It was a terrible time, Leah. Do you think I'd want something like that for you?"

"I don't —" Leah said as her Oma stroked her hair. "I didn't know you felt like that about it."

Oma laughed softly. "Just because I'm old doesn't mean I don't understand life," she said. "I wish more people remembered what I

remember. It's one thing to hear about it, but if you remember it, it makes all the difference."

"Why didn't you say anything before?"

"I knew," said Oma. "But I thought I should let you tell me about it. You're my grandbaby and you're safe — that's the most important thing. More people understand than you think. You should talk about it, Leah. It's secrets that poison us. When you let the truth out, that's when you're free."

The sun was shining the next day, for the first time in what felt to Leah like weeks. Big bars of yellow like sticks of butter slanted in through the windows of Silver Pines, across the rugs in the activities room, in the hallways, and in Mrs. Ellis's room, which was empty.

Mrs. Ellis had died the night before. Sometime while Leah was talking to her Oma, Mrs. Ellis had gone to sleep and never woken up. Leah stood in the hallway, watching the orderlies taking away her things: the small cardboard boxes filled with photographs and books, her faded patchwork blanket folded on top.

Mrs. Minchel was standing in the hallway, shaking her head. "Leah," she said, looking up sharply. "You shouldn't be here. Go down and see if they need help in the laundry room."

"But her things —" Leah began.

"They'll go to her family," said Mrs. Minchel, not unkindly. "Now, don't worry about it, all right? She was old. She had a full life."

Leah did an about-face and half ran down the stairs, through the lower hallway, and out the back door of the Pines. Even the sunlight didn't do much to beautify the concrete stoop and dirty on-ramp that led to the delivery door.

Brooks was sitting on the ground by the back door, in his scrubs, his hands dangling over his bony knees. His shoulders were shaking.

"Brooks," she said.

He didn't look up, so she sat down next to him. As Leah watched him, he scrubbed away his tears with wet hands, streaking them across his already-blotchy face. She had thought somehow that there might be blood in his tears, but they were clear, like anyone else's.

"I'm sorry," she said. "I know you liked her. Mrs. Ellis."

"She remembered," he said.

The wind blew, rattling the leaves on the trees, blowing trash across the concrete lot.

"You know what makes someone a monster?" he asked.

She shook her head.

"Being alone," he said. "They're dying. One by one. They're dying and one day they'll all be dead and I'll be alone. The only one who remembers."

"You can make new memories," she said.

He shook his head. "I've tried. To live among the living. To be like them. Every day I wake up though, and those memories are like a dream. The only thing that seems real is my mortal life. The blood . . . The blood gives it back to me for a little while."

"That's why you don't want my blood," she said. "What do you think will happen? When they're all gone? Won't you have to — to go on somehow? You said you don't need blood to live."

"Not to live. Just to want to live," he said, and then: "I think I'll fade. When they're all gone, I think I'll be erased. I'll be nothing."

Nothing, they'd written on Sadie's page. *Nothing. You're nothing.*

"I won't have anyone," he said. "Anyone to talk to."

"You can talk to me," Leah said.

He snorted and looked away. Leah thought of the talk she'd had with her grandmother the day before, and the way she'd woken up feeling different. Lighter. Ryan had been a dream, a dream she'd had her whole life that had ended with her mom driving her to the clinic, pale, her hand on Leah's knee, saying over and over, "As long as you're sure this is what you want."

Leah had been so angry that it hadn't been Ryan that took her, that he loved her so little, that it hadn't occurred to her to think about it the other way: that she had a mother who loved her so much.

"It seems to me like maybe you get to choose," Leah said. "We all have the way we thought our life would happen. And then there's the way that it does happen. And you can cling to the way you imagined it would be, or you can accept what really happened and let it change you."

"Change is forgetting," he said.

"Forgetting's not so bad," she said, and smiled. It felt strange to smile, but good. Ryan was the past now: Ryan would be forgotten, papered over with new dreams and new loves. Just because one dream had ended badly didn't mean they all would. "As long as you remember enough to do it differently the next time."

He looked up and over at her. For the first time, she thought, she saw a spark of real life in his brown eyes. "When you forget," he said, "when people forget you, you disappear."

She put her hand on his shoulder. It was cold, hard under her touch. "Even if you change, I won't forget you," she said. "I won't let you disappear."

Leah could hear her Oma moving around downstairs, humming to herself as she set the table for dinner. The sun was going down outside, all red and gold with streaks of pearl. It was beautiful. It had been a long time since she had realized a sunset was beautiful.

She thought of the orderlies carrying out the small boxes of Mrs. Ellis's things, of the way a life could be packed up, totaled in a handful of objects, a few photos, the fragile dust of memories.

She picked up her phone and sent a text to Rachel. *Call me, okay?*

Then she dialed an unfamiliar number. It rang a few times before it was picked up.

"Hello?" Sadie said, nervously. Leah's name must have flashed up on her phone. It took courage to answer, Leah thought.

"Hi," Leah said. "Sadie, it's —"

"I know," Sadie interrupted. "If you're calling to yell at me, go ahead. Everyone else already has."

"I'm not calling to yell at you," Leah said.

"You're not?"

"I'm not," Leah said. "I saw the messages people were leaving on your Facebook. Saying that you're nothing. I just wanted to tell you, I don't think that. You're not nothing. And you and me, we should talk. We have the same — the same memories." She paused. "Everyone needs someone to talk to. So they don't forget."

Sadie gave a choked little laugh. "I wouldn't mind forgetting Ryan."

"Then we can remember to forget him together," said Leah, and leaned back against the pillows of her bed.

Ten Rules for Being An Intergalactic Smuggler

(THE SUCCESSFUL KIND)

HOLLY BLACK

1. *There are no rules.*

That's what your uncle tells you, after he finds you stowing away in his transport ship, the *Celeris*, which you used to call the *Celery* when you were growing up, back when you only dreamed of getting off the crappy planet your parents brought you to as a baby. No matter how many times you told them their dumb dream of being homesteaders and digging in the red dirt wasn't yours, no matter how many times you begged your uncle to take you with him, even though your parents swore that he was a smuggler and bad news besides, it wasn't until you climbed out of your hidey-hole with the vastness of space in the transparent alumina windows behind you that anyone really believed you'd meant any of it.

Once you're caught, he gives you a long lecture about how there are laws and there's right and wrong, but those aren't *rules*. And, he says, there are especially no rules for situations like this. Which turns out to be to your advantage, because he's pissed but not that pissed. His basic philosophy is to laugh in the face of danger and also in the face of annoyance. And since he thinks his brother is a bit of a damp rag and likes the idea of being a hero to his niece, it turns out that *no rules* means not turning around and dumping you back on Mars.

He also turns out to be a smuggler. Grudgingly, you have to admit that your parents might not be wrong about everything.

2. *Spaceports are dangerous.*

Your uncle tells you this several times as you dock in the Zvezda-9 Spaceport, but it's not like you don't know it already. Your parents have told you a million stories about how alien races like the spidery and psychopathic Charkazaks — fugitives after their world was destroyed by InterPlanetary forces — take girls like you hostage and force you to do things so bad, they won't even describe them. From all your parents' warnings about spaceports, when you step off of *Celeris*, you expect a dozen shady aliens to jump out of the shadows, offering you morality-disrupting powders, fear inhibitors, and *nucleus accumbens* stimulators.

Except it turns out that spaceports aren't that interesting. Zvezda-9 is a big stretch of cement tunnels, vast microgravity farms, hotel pods, and general stores with overpriced food that's either dehydrated or in a tube. There are also InterPlanetary offices, where

greasy-looking people from a variety of worlds wait in long lines for licenses. They all stare at your homespun clothes. You want to grab your uncle's hand, but you already feel like enough of a backworld yokel, so you curl your fingers into a fist instead.

There are aliens — it wasn't like your parents were wrong about that. Most of them look human and simultaneously inhuman, and the juxtaposition is so odd that you can't keep from staring. You spot a woman whose whole lower face is a jagged-toothed mouth. A man with gray-skinned cheeks that grow from his face like gills or possibly just really strange ears loads up a hovercart nearby, the stripes on his body smeared so you know they are paint and not pigmentation. Someone passes you in a heavy, hairy cloak, and you get the impression of thousands of eyes inside of the hood. It's creepy as hell.

You do not, however, see a single Charkazak. No one offers you any drugs.

"Stop acting stupid," your uncle growls, and you *try* to act less stupid and keep from staring. You try to act like you stroll around spaceports all the time, like you know how to use the gun you swiped from your mother and strapped to your thigh under your skirt, like the tough expression you plaster on your face actually *makes* you tough. You try to roll your hips and swagger, like you're a grown lady, but not too much of a lady.

Your uncle laughs at you, but it's a good kind of laughter, like at least you're sort of maybe pulling it off.

Later that night, he buys you some kind of vat-meat tacos, and he and some of his human "transporter" buddies get to drinking and telling stories. They tell you about run-ins with space pirates and times when the InterPlanetary Centurions stopped their ships, looking for illicit cargo. Your uncle has a million stories about narrow getaways and hidey-holes, in addition to a large cast of seedy accomplices able to forge passable paperwork, but who apparently excel at getting him into dangerous yet hilarious situations. You laugh your way into the night.

The next day your uncle buys you a pair of black pants and a shirt like his, made from a self-cleaning material that's both hydrophobic and insulating, plus a shiny chromium steel clip for your hair. You can't stop smiling. And although you don't say it out loud to him, in that moment you're sure that the two of you are going to be the greatest smuggling duo of all time.

3. When someone says they'll pay double your normal rate, they're offering to pay at least half what you'd charge them if you knew the whole story.

The *Celeris* stays docked in the spaceport for a couple of weeks while your uncle buys some used parts to repair the worst of wear and tear to her systems and looks for the right official job — and then an unofficial job to make the most of that InterPlanetary transport license.

You try to keep out of your uncle's way so he doesn't start thinking of you as some kid who's always underfoot. You don't want to get sent back home. Instead, you hang around the spaceport, trying to make yourself less ignorant. You go into the store that sells navigational charts and stare at the shifting patterns of stars. You go into the pawnshop and look at the fancy laser pistols and the odd alien gadgets, until the guy behind the counter gets tired of your face and orders you to buy something or get out.

After a while the spaceport seems less scary. Some of your uncle's friends pay you pocket money to run errands, money that you use

to buy caff bars and extra batteries for your mother's gun and holo-graphic hoop earrings that you think make you look like a pirate. Just when you start to feel a little bit cocky and comfortable, your uncle informs you that it's time to leave.

He's lined up the jobs. He's found a client.

A little man with a red face and red hair sits in their eating area on the ship, sipping archer ethanol, booze culled from the Sagittarius B2 cloud, out of a coffee can. The man tells your uncle that he supplies alien tissue to a scientist who has his laboratory on one of the outer worlds, where the rules about gene splicing and cloning are more lax. The little man has come across a particularly valuable shipment of frozen alien corpses and needs it to get where it's going fast, with few questions asked.

The assignment creeps you out, but you can tell that your uncle has been distracted by the ludicrously high offer the man is wav-ing around. It's more money than you've ever imagined being paid for anything, and even with the cost of fuel and bribing Centurions, you're pretty sure there would be enough to refit the *Celeris* in style. No more used parts, no more stopgap repairs. He could have all new everything.

"Half now," the man says. "Half when the cargo arrives *intact*. And it better get there inside a month, or I will take the extra time out of your hide. I am paying for speed — and silence."

"Oh, it'll be there," your uncle says, and pours a little archer etha-nol into a plastic cup for himself. Even the smell of it singes your nose hair. "This little ship has got hidden depths — *literally*." He grins while he's speaking, like the offer of so much money has made him drunker than all the booze in the sky. "Hidden depths. Like me."

The red-haired man doesn't seem all that impressed.

You have lots of questions about where the alien bodies came from and what exactly the scientist is going to do with them, but a quick glance from your uncle confirms that you're supposed to swallow those and keep pouring drinks. You have your guesses, though — you've heard stories about space pirates with alien parts grafted on instead of their own. New ears and eyes, new second stomachs tough enough to digest acid, second livers and new teeth and organs humans don't even have — like poison glands or hidden quills. And then there were worse stories: ones about cloned hybrids, pitiless and monstrous enough to fight the surviving Charkazaks and win.

But you're a stupid kid from a backworld planet and you know it, so you quash your curiosity. After the client leaves, you clean up some and fold your stuff so it tucks away in the netting over the bunk in your room. You go down to the cargo hold and move around boxes, so the way to the secret storage compartment is clear for when the redhead comes back with his alien parts in the morning. That night you look out through the transparent alumina windows at ships docking on Zvezda-9, and you get excited about leaving for your first mission in the morning.

But in the morning, the *Celeris* doesn't depart.

It turns out that it takes time to get ready for a run like this — it takes supplies and paperwork; it takes charting a course and new fuel and lots of batteries and a ton of water. The whole while you careen between sadness over leaving Zvezda-9 now that you've become familiar with it and wishing you were in space already. You visit your favorite spots mournfully, unsure if you'll ever see them again, and you pace the halls of the *Celeris* at night until your uncle orders you to your bunk. His temper is a short-sparking fuse. He sends you to buy supplies and then complains loudly about what

you get, even though you're the one who'll be doing the reheating and reconstituting.

The client arrives in the middle of the night. You sit in the shadows above the cargo bay and watch what he loads — a long cylindrical casket, big enough for several human-size bodies. Smoke curls off of it when it's jostled, as though it is very, very cold inside.

An hour later you're back among the stars. There, your uncle starts to relax, as though space is his real home and being on a planet for too long was what was making him tense. Over the next week, he teaches you a few simple repairs he has to do regularly for the *Celeris*, shows you a few of his favorite smuggling hidey-holes, teaches you a card game and then how to cheat at that card game, and even lets you fly the ship for an hour with him hanging over your shoulder, nagging you about everything you're doing wrong.

Considering that he turns on autopilot while he sleeps, letting you put your hands on the controls while he watches isn't that big of a vote of confidence, but sitting in the cockpit, gazing out at the spray of stars, makes you feel important and wholly yourself, as though all your time laboring in that red dirt was worth something, because it brought you to this.

Mostly the trip is uneventful, except for an evening when your uncle comes up from the cargo hold and won't look at you. He downs a whole bottle of archer ethanol and then gets noisily sick while you watch the computer navigate, and you fiddle with your earrings. He never says what set him off, but the next day he's himself again and you both try to pretend that it never happened.

Then you wake up because the whole ship is shaking. At first you think you're passing through an asteroid field, but then you realize

something bad is happening. There's the faint smell of fire and the
sound of the ship venting it. Then the gravity starts going crazy —
lurching on and off, bouncing you against the floor and the walls.

Once it stabilizes, you manage to crawl out into the corridor.
Your heart is pounding like crazy, fear making you light-headed. You
clutch your mother's gun to you like it's some kind of teddy bear.
There's shouting — more voices than there should be on board. You
think you hear your uncle calling your name and then something else.
Something loud and anguished and final.

You head automatically for the cockpit when a man runs into
the corridor, skidding to a stop at the sight of you. Based on the
mismatched array of weapons and armor, you figure he's got to be
a pirate — if he was a Centurion, he'd be in uniform. He reaches for
his weapon, like he's just shaking off the shock of seeing a kid in her
nightgown aboard a smuggling ship, but you've already swung your
mother's gun up. You blast him in the head before you allow yourself
to consider what you're doing.

When he drops, you start trembling all over. You think you're
going to throw up, but you can hear more of them coming, so you try
to concentrate on moving through the ship, on remembering all the
hidey-holes your uncle pointed out to you.

The lights go out all of a sudden, so you have to feel your way in
the dark, but soon you've found one big enough for you to fit yourself
into and you're shut up inside.

Snug as a bug in a rug, your mom would say.

You start crying, thinking about her. You know your uncle is probably dead, but you don't want to admit that to yourself yet, so you
pretend you're not thinking of him when you wipe away your tears.

4. If your ship gets raided by space pirates, don't hide in the cargo hold, because everybody wants what's in the cargo hold.

The *Celeris* is a small-enough ship that you can hear the pirates walking through it, talking to one another. You try to count different voices, but all you can figure out is that there're more than five and probably less than ten. Which doesn't mean that much, since they boarded from another ship and there could be any number of them back there.

Did you find it? You hear them say, over and over again. *We've got to find it before it finds us.*

Which doesn't mean anything to you. You wonder if they attacked the wrong ship. You wonder if your uncle got murdered for nothing, for less than nothing, since the credits he got paid are in his bank account and not anywhere aboard the ship.

You hear the acceleration of the engines and feel the odd sensation of forward momentum. Which means they're probably taking the whole ship, not just gutting it for parts and leaving it to spin endlessly in the void — which would have meant no life support for you. Maybe you'll survive this, you think. Maybe no one even knew you were aboard, maybe they thought the guy you shot was shot by your uncle. If they docked on a planet, even a terrible planet, maybe you could sneak off the ship and hide in the station.

To do that, you need to make sure you stay hydrated. You'll need food too, but not right away. A bathroom, ideally. You and your uncle usually ate in the little kitchen area — he called it the galley — off the main cockpit, where there's a small burner, lots of packages of freeze-dried food, tubes of paste, and a jar of nutrient powder. You're sure that some of the pirates have raided it by now, drinking through your uncle's supply of archer ethanol — you've heard them, rowdy and full of good cheer, like they'd done something heroic instead of something awful.

If they catch you, they'll most likely kill you. You're using up oxygen, just breathing. But you know all the other things pirates might do instead — sell you, use you, cook you, eat you. Your parents loved to tell you how bad things could get when you talked about wanting to have adventures in space.

There's food in the cargo hold, you know — those were the supplies that went on the official roster as his official shipment. Your uncle had the papers to sell that stuff to a homesteader planet. He'd been planning on sending you down to haggle with them — and had loaded you down with plenty of pieces of dubious bargaining wisdom in preparation.

Don't be afraid of silence, he'd told you. *Silence shows your strength.*

Have a bottom line, he'd told you. *Sometimes to make a deal, you've got to walk away from a deal.*

But it turned out that pirates didn't care about negotiating. Just like your uncle had told you in the beginning, there aren't any rules.

You doze impatiently waiting for your chance to slip down to the cargo hold. Your leg cramps from the position you've folded yourself into, and finally you decide that even though you can still hear voices, they're faint, and you're going to have to go for it.

You unfold yourself and step into the hallway. The floor is cold against your feet, and you feel light-headed from being in one position so long, but you begin to pad your way toward the cargo bay. There's a steel ladder to a crow's nest above the cargo bay, and as you climb down it, you know that if there's a pirate patrolling beneath you, he's going to see you before you see him, your pale nightgown

fluttering around you like a white flag of surrender. There's nothing you can do about it, though, so you just try to keep on going and stay quiet.

You're in luck. There's no one there. You climb all the way down and start to open the shipping crates. You find luxuries that settlers love — caff bars, tins of coffee, jars of spicy peppers, fermented soy, and plenty of both salt and sugar. Ripping into one of the caff bars, you realize the stuff won't keep you fed until the pirates dock, unless they dock very soon. Worse, there's nothing to drink.

Despairing, you grab another caff bar and begin to look over the few remaining crates. You find some machinery — farming stuff — and what appears to be an array of tents suitable for a desert environment.

You're freaking out, sure that you're about to be caught, when you remember the secret hold, where the alien bodies are being stored. There might not be anything particularly useful there, but it's at least a little more spacious than your last hiding place, and if you keep to the corners, you'll have a great shot at picking off any pirates who discover the compartment before they can spot you.

It takes you a few tries to get the hatch open, but you manage it and slide down into the darkness. The only lights are the dim blinking green and blue and red buttons on the side of the cylindrical casket. You crawl over to it and look at the buttons. Maybe, you think, maybe it has life support built into it. Maybe you could dump out the contents and put yourself inside if things got really bad.

You squint at the control panel. There's a large button, clearly labeled: VIEW SCREEN.

You press it.

5. If your ship gets raided by space pirates and you wind up hiding in the cargo hold, even though you know it's a bad idea, don't go poking through the secret cargo.

A square of the shiny white case turns clear and the inside glows. The whole thing hums a little, as though expecting more instructions, a thin mechanical whine. You lean down, looking at what's inside, and then it's all you can do not to scream.

There's a Charkazak, its eight terrible black legs drawn up against the shiny black carapace of its chest. Its humanoid face, with black lips and red tattoos along its cheekbones. A chest that rises and falls with breath.

That thing is alive.

You stumble back, falling against the steel, more scared than you were when you faced down the pirate in the hallway, more scared than when you felt the blast hit the side of the ship and realized the *Celeris* was being raided.

You've heard horror stories about the Charkazaks all your life, on the news, whispered about at slumber parties of kids on the farm, and even on Zvezda-9. They were a race of warriors who worshipped death, becoming bodyguards for the most corrupt merchants and glorying in being soldiers on the front lines of the most awful wars just so they'd have more opportunities for bloodshed. They were so awful that they wouldn't follow InterPlanetary laws regarding who it was okay to kill and who it wasn't, nor did they believe in things like surrender or mercy. They invaded planets, brought down ships, and generally behaved like the monsters they appeared to be. When Centurions were dispatched to discipline the Charkazaks, they fought back with such viciousness that the only way to keep them

from overrunning the galaxy was the obliteration of their planet and all the Charkazaks on it. Those that were off-planet when the Charkazaks' homeworld was destroyed became even more vicious than before. And as you look at the living one cocooned in metal, you feel like a child hearing those stories for the first time — more like a child than you've felt since you stowed away after that last stupid fight with your parents.

This — *this* must have been what the pirates meant when they worried about it finding them before they found it. You wonder how the redheaded dirtbag who hired your uncle acquired such a thing and to where you'd really been transporting it. That Charkazak is the reason your uncle is dead.

The whine gets a little louder, and one of the red buttons on the side of the case begins to blink, like a throbbing pulse. Between that and the dim light from the screen, the secret cargo area feels too bright, but you wait and wait and finally all the lights switch themselves off.

You wouldn't think you could sleep with that thing near you, but you're so relieved to be able to stretch out your limbs that you sleep after all. You dream of someone calling your name from very far away. When you wake, your body is stiff with cold and everything is still dark. You realize that you're freezing and that if you don't get warmed up fast, you might be in serious trouble.

Tents, you remember. There are tents up in the regular cargo hold. But as you feel around in the dark, you can't quite make out how to open up the hatch. Then you remember that the casket lit up — surely that would be enough for you to find the latch by — so you go over and press the green button again.

It lights up the case and you try not to look inside. You scuttle up instead and grab a couple of tents. You're dragging them back down when you hear the tramping of heavy footfalls. They speed up, like maybe they heard the thud of the material hitting the floor, and you swear under your breath. You move as quickly and quietly as you can, back under the floor, yanking the cover of the hidden compartment into place.

The light is still shining from the casket, and you're afraid that the glow will show through the seams and reveal your hiding spot. You press the green button again, hoping that will turn off the view screen, but it doesn't. The other light — the red one — starts blinking again, and you're panicking, because it's brighter and more obvious than the glow from the casket.

Push to open, the red button says. And as the footfalls come closer, as you hear the pirate feel around for the latch, a sudden strange calm comes over you. Since you're going to die — or worse — you figure, screw everything. Screw the pirates, screw yourself, screw every god-damn thing. You owe your uncle some final revenge. You're not going out like some dumb farmer kid. You're going to give those pirates exactly what they were looking for.

So you press the button. Twice. There is a horrible loud sound, like a giant exhalation of breath. The top of the casket slides open.

6. And if you do go ahead and poke through the secret cargo, then for the love of all that is holy, watch out which buttons you push.

For a moment, you almost believe that you can take back the last five minutes. It seems so impossible that you could have done what you did. You were tired and freaked out, but you'd been pretty clever right up until then, clever and quiet and careful. Not crazy. No death

wish. For a moment, you're just angry, so angry — at yourself, at the world. It feels so unfair that you're going to die because of one stupid decision, one bad moment.

"Hey," the pirate calls. "Kid, we know you're on board. We knew you'd show yourself eventually. Now come on out, and we'll go easy on you."

You snort, because it's a ridiculous thing to say. What does that mean — *go easy on you* — like surely he knows that implies nothing easy at all? Plus, it's too late. He's swaggering around, cocky, without realizing that you're both about to be dead. You're all about to be dead.

"Come out, come out, wherever you are," he calls, a laugh in his voice.

From the casket the Charkazak unfolds itself, bathed in the glow of the light from within. It rises, up and up and up. Eight legs, two sets of arms with six-jointed fingers on its shining onyx chest, and large luminous eyes. It might have human features, but you can't read its expression. It seems to shudder all over, then swings its head your way.

Fear makes you nearly pee your pants. You freeze so completely that you don't even draw in breath. It moves toward you — fast, its legs a blur — and leans down, all wide eyes and flaring nose slits.

Your mother's gun is lying beside you, but you don't grab for it. You released the Charkazak, after all. There's no point fighting it.

You whimper.

"Come on, girl," calls the pirate. "You think I've never been on a cheap old smuggling ship before? You think I can't find you? Come out or I'm going to make you sorry."

You close your eyes, but you can still hear the scratch of Charkazak feet against the floor, can smell the medicinal odor that clings to it from its containment, can hear its ragged breaths.

"I know you killed Richard," says the pirate, his voice falling into a false, honeyed tone. He's come closer to the grate that conceals the hidden cargo area. Maybe he knew where it was all along. Maybe you were a fool, thinking they didn't know where you were. He laughs. "You did me a favor there. I owed him money."

You hear the slide of metal on metal and open your eyes. The Charkazak is no longer in front of you. You let out your breath all at once, so fast that you feel dizzy.

"Hey, there, you —" the pirate says, then there's a gasp and a wet, liquid sound.

You sit in the cargo hold for a while — you don't know for how long — too scared to move. But then you force yourself numbly to your feet. You walk past the body of the pirate, with a massive bloody hole in his chest like that Charkazak thrust a clawed hand into his chest and pulled out his heart. The pirate's gurgling a little, but his eyes are shut, and you wouldn't know how to help him, even if you wanted to, which you don't.

You go straight to the galley, passing two more bodies. They are bent at odd angles, one missing the top of her head, her long red-blond hair in a cloud around her face. There is an odd spatter of red along one wall, and laser blasts have blackened the corridor.

In the galley, you wash your hands and then make yourself a cup of tea. You eat an entire sleeve of sugar cookies and then you heat up a freeze-dried package of salty, soy-drenched noodle soup and eat that too. There's no point in dying on an empty stomach.

After that, you feel super sleepy, your eyes heavy, so you go back to your tiny room, climb under the covers, and close your eyes.

7. On a spaceship, there really aren't that many places to hide.

The Charkazak isn't like the pirates. It's a monster, and you can't hide from monsters. So you don't.

But it doesn't come for you.

You go into the bathroom and take a shower. You change your clothes and check your mother's gun for ammo.

Out in the hallway, the bodies are gone. You return to the galley and drink more tea, noting how the food has been picked over. You didn't count the night before, though, so you're not sure what was eaten by pirates and what was eaten by the alien.

You make some oatmeal with reconstituted milk powder.

While you're eating, there's movement in the hallway. You duck under the table, hoping that you're not worth the Charkazak's notice. Maybe you're like a rat to it, some kind of ship vermin. Maybe you don't matter. You wrap your arms around your legs and *hope* you don't matter.

It skitters into the room, and you can't help noticing that as large as it is, there is a certain gliding elegance to its movements.

Then the Charkazak's body crouches low, bending forward, two pairs of arms reaching to the floor to take its weight. Its head tilts under the table, looking straight at you.

It blinks. Twice.

"Um, hi," you say, because you don't know what else to do.

It keeps looking at you, tilting its head the other way this time.

Don't be afraid of silence, your uncle told you, but you are afraid. You don't have the upper hand in this situation. You don't have anything to bargain with in trade for your life.

8. *You'll catch more Charkazaks with salt than with sugar.*

"I could make you something," you say, "if you don't know how to cook."

"I know how," it says after a long moment, and you're completely startled by its voice, which has a little hiss behind it and an accent you're not used to but that you understand easily enough. It's a young voice, a not-much-older-than-you voice, and you have no idea what to make of that.

Of course some part of you knew that Charkazaks could talk — or at least understand commands. They couldn't have betrayed any treaties if they didn't talk, couldn't have committed treason if they hadn't sworn fealty to the InterPlanetary government, but you're still surprised. Monsters aren't supposed to sound like everybody else.

It — *he* — leans up and begins to move things on the counter, turning on the water heater and setting out two tin cups. His many legs move, swift as a centipede's, and equally disturbing.

"I am going to make some of this red fern tea," he says, opening one of the tins of leaves. "You will drink it."

You listen to the crinkle of paper, the whine of the steam, and the sound of water splashing into the cup. Tea making is confusing, because you associate it with comfortably curling up with your holo-reader and sleeping off a minor illness. Monsters aren't supposed to be able to make tea. If monsters can make tea, then nothing's safe.

"What happened to their ship?" you ask, because he *hasn't* killed you so maybe he'll *keep on* not killing you.

You hear the metal spoon clank against the sides of the cup. "Their ship is unharmed."

Which means that everyone who'd once been inside of it was dead.

The Charkazak leans down again and passes you a cup with his delicate, multi-jointed fingers. It's warm in your hands.

"Th-thank you," you manage, and take a sip. Then you start to cough. It's *salty*, like your mother described the seas of old earth.

"Is there something wrong with it?" the Charkazak asks, folding his limbs under him, so he can look at you.

You shake your head, terrified. You force yourself to take another swig and try not to choke. You don't think you quite pull it off, though, because he looks oddly stricken, studying you with those large, pale eyes.

"Was this your parents' ship?" he asks, taking the cup from you and drinking deeply, as though he's not afraid of tasting your spit or getting your germs. As though he really, really likes salt.

"How do you know the *Celeris* isn't mine?" you ask. Then you remember that you're trying to get him to think of you as some kind of ship vermin, entirely unimportant, and wish you could take back those words.

"*Is* it yours?" he asks, not seeming unwilling to believe it, just confused.

"No," you admit. "The ship belonged to my uncle, but I'm pretty sure he's dead."

He tilts his head and narrows his eyes, studying you. "You freed me," he accuses softly. "By accident?"

You don't want to tell him that you thought of him as a bullet to the head. Your big murder-suicide plan, now staring at you with that implacable gaze. "I —" you begin, but you can't think of a lie fast enough.

He nods and picks up something from the counter. Then he

leaves, the sharpness of his many steps across the floor a reminder of just how fast and lethal the Charkazaks are.

Once he's gone, you draw up your legs, wrap your arms around them, and feel smaller and stupider than ever.

You no longer believe that he'll just kill you outright, but that makes you realize how bleak your future has become. Even if the Charkazak dumps you off at some space station, even if you drain your uncle's bank account of all his credits, the only place you have to go is home. You didn't learn enough from your uncle to fly the *Celeris* yourself. You've got no way to make any money back on Zvezda-9. You're just a farming kid with delusions of grandeur.

Of course, you're not sure that the Charkazak will let you off the ship. He's from a fugitive race, hunted by InterPlanetary Centurions — he might want to keep you around so he could shove your face in front of any call screens until he moved outside regulated space. Then you'd be in the same situation you were in with the pirates; he could sell you or eat you or . . . well, you've heard stories about Charkazaks ripping humans apart in a sexual frenzy, but you're trying not to think about that.

You decide you're going to make dinner for him. You break out more rehydratable noodles and start in on making a vat-meat goulash. There's a tube of apple-quince jelly and some cheese that you figure you can either make into a dessert or some kind of first course.

Halfway through, you think about cooking for your uncle, and tears come to your eyes. You have to sit down and sob for a little while, but it passes.

Once the food's done, you pad through the halls of the ship to find the Charkazak. A smear of blood still marks one of the walls, wiped by something but not wiped clean.

TEN RULES
FOR BEING AN
INTERGALACTIC
SMUGGLER

9. *The dead are a lot less trouble than the living.*

You look for the Charkazak in the cargo area, but you find dead bodies instead. They're lined up on the floor, the cold keeping them from decaying quickly, but they're still a mess. Eleven pirates, men and women, scarred and tough-looking, and your uncle, all with their eyes open, staring at a nothing that's even bigger than space. Your uncle's shirt is blackened from blaster fire. They must have shot him soon after boarding. You lean down and take out his identification card from his pocket, running your finger over the holo-picture of him, the one where he's not horribly pale, the one where his lips aren't blue and his eyes aren't cloudy. The one where he isn't dead.

You wanted to be just like him — you wanted to have adventures and see the universe. You didn't want to believe there were rules.

See where it got him, your mother would say. *See where it got you.*

Leaning over his body, you close his eyes. "I love you," you tell him, brushing his hair back from his face. "I love you and all your hidden depths."

On your way out, you can't help but notice how nine of those eleven pirates died, though. They were sliced open or stabbed through. One was missing a limb as though it had been pulled clean off her.

You find the Charkazak in the cockpit, pressing buttons with those long, delicate fingers, his dagger-like feet balanced easily against the floor. He turns toward you swiftly, a blur of gray skin and gleaming black carapace, his body hunched, as if braced for flight.

"I made dinner," you say lamely, heart pounding.

He doesn't immediately respond. You watch as he slowly relaxes and wonder if, for a moment, he'd thought you were stupid enough to attack him.

"It's ready, b-but I could j-just bring you a plate if you're b-busy." You're stammering.

He touches the screen again, twice, quickly, then begins to unfurl toward you. "I am honored by your hospitality," he says, and each time he speaks, you are startled anew that he sounds almost human. "We will eat together."

You go together through the hall, with you walking in front. You can hear him behind you, can hear the clattering sound of his many feet, and you steel yourself not to look, because you're afraid that if you do, despite everything, you'll run. You'll scream.

10. *Good food is universal. And it's universally true that you're not going to get any good food in space.*

In the galley, he manages to perch on the bench while you plate the goulash. He waits, watching.

Finally, he says, "I'm called Reth."

Which is odd, because of course you knew he must have a name, but you'd never have asked him for it. "I'm Tera."

"Tera," he echoes, and then begins to eat, his long fingers making him seem like a mantis.

You wait until you've pulled out the cheese and apple-quince paste to ask him the question that's been haunting you. "What are you going to do with me?"

He tilts his head, studying you. "I know you're afraid. I even know why."

You are silent, because of course you're scared. And of course he knows why.

"They caught me off the salty sea of Callisto — and I heard them

talking while they processed me. I am on my way to be harvested for experiments and organs, just like the rest of my race."

You study his strange face — those luminous eyes, the grayish color of his skin, those tattooed marks that remind you of the stripes on a tiger, his high cheekbones, and the sharp elegance of his features, which make him both almost human and very alien. You hear the anger in his voice, but he's got something to be angry about.

"I know what they say about my people. I know the rumors of savagery and horror. Not all of it is untrue, but the war — the reasons you have heard it was declared, those are *lies*. The InterPlanetary government wanted us to fight their wars, wanted our own government to sacrifice its children, and when the Charkazaks would not become a slave race, they decided to destroy us and engineer the army they desired from our flesh."

He could be lying, but he doesn't sound like he's lying.

He could be mistaken, but he doesn't sound like his knowledge is secondhand.

"I'm sorry," you say, because you can't imagine being hunted across the galaxy, whatever the reason.

Reth shakes his head. "No, don't say that. Because I have become like your legends about my people. I can kill quickly and surely now — and as for where I am taking this ship, I am completing the course that your uncle had set. I am planning on docking and destroying those scientists who would have cut me open and used my body for their experiments. I am going to destroy their laboratory, and I am going to free whatever creatures are being tormented there." He slams down two of his fists on the table and then seems startled by the action. He looks over at you with haunted, hunted eyes. He was trying to stop you from being scared, and he thinks he's scared you worse.

But he hasn't really. He's just startled you. You never heard of any Charkazaks saving anyone, and the anger in his voice is righteous fury, not the desire for bloodshed. He might not sell you to anyone, you realize. Might not rip you apart or eat you. Might not even mean you any harm at all, despite being the scariest thing you've ever seen.

You force yourself to reach across the table and touch his arm. His skin feels smooth, almost like patent leather. He tenses as your fingers brush up his arm and then goes entirely still.

"This dish you made is very good," he says suddenly, and you can hear in his voice a shy nervousness that fills you with a sudden giddy power. "I told you I knew how to work the cooking things — but all the food was unfamiliar. I ate one of the green packages and found it entirely strange. I feel sure I was supposed to do something more to it, but I wasn't sure what. . . ."

You keep your hand on his arm a moment more, fingers dragging over his skin, and his words gutter out. You wonder when the last time it was that someone touched him — or touched him without anger. You wonder how lonely it's possible to become out in the void of space.

The comm crackles at that moment, a voice booming from the speakers in the wall. "Centurion ship *Orion* hailing the *Celeris*. Are you there, Captain Lloyd?"

Reth's eyes narrow and he rises, looming above you on those long black legs.

"I know what you're thinking," he says softly. It makes you try to imagine what it would be like to grow up with all the universe against you. "But if they know I'm here, they will destroy your ship. They won't face me — they've heard the same stories you have. They'll kill us both to avoid facing me."

Don't be afraid of silence, your uncle told you. *Silence shows your strength.*

You know it's not the nicest thing you've ever done, especially because you're pretty sure Reth's correct about the Centurions' likelihood of blowing up the ship rather than fighting him, but you make yourself stay quiet as the seconds tick by. Reth needs you to go to that comm, but you need things from him too. Promises.

"Please," he says again.

"If you want my help, you have to agree to my terms," you say. "Agree that you'll teach me how to fly. That we'll split the salvage profits from the pirate ship fifty-fifty. And that we'll be partners."

"Partners," he echoes, as though he's trying out the word, as though he doesn't know what to do with it. As though you're giving him something, instead of asking for something from him.

Have a bottom line, your uncle told you. *Sometimes to make a deal, you've got to walk away from a deal.*

But there isn't going to be any walking away this time. There's nowhere to walk to, not for either one of you.

"Agreed," he says, and the relief in his voice is enormous. You probably could have asked him for a *lot* more, and he would have agreed. You're even worse at this bargaining thing than you thought.

"And you have to agree that once we finish attacking the planet of the mad scientists, we'll take some actually profitable jobs," you amend, trying your best to sound tough. "Since I don't think we're going to get paid for the last one."

The comm crackles again. "Captain Lloyd, are you there? Please respond."

"Agreed, Tera," Reth says softly, like a vow.

11. *One more for the road. There really are no rules. There are laws and there's right and wrong, but those aren't rules. You make it up the best you can as you go along.*

You grin at Reth and go over to feed your uncle's ID into the comm. "This is Captain Tera Lloyd of the *Celeris*," you say, once you get the right frequency. "Captain David Lloyd — my uncle — is dead, and I have taken control of the ship. We were in distress, but you're a little late to be of much help, *Orion*."

Reth watches you speak, smiling a fierce alien smile as you tell the Centurions to buzz off, swearing up and down that they don't need to board and you don't need a tow. Finally, you agree to a small bribe, pull out your uncle's ID card, and wire the credits over.

The whole thing reminds you of one of your uncle's stories. You hope it would have made him laugh. You hope it would have made him proud.

You know you've been wrong a lot since you left home, but as you look out at the stars and the Charkazak begins to explain how the controls work, you begin to believe that you might still have a chance to become one-half of the best smuggling duo of all time.

Quick Hill

M. T. ANDERSON

1. COURTSHIP

That fall, the songs were all about saying good-bye. The hits were all about the end. The last kiss and the final embrace. The empty room. Waiting alone. Promises you hoped you'd keep.

The boys in town disappeared one by one.

The paper ran pictures of them.

Then they ran more pictures when the bodies were found and shipped home.

Don Thwait couldn't wait for the basketball season to start, but he was worried there wouldn't be enough rubber for basketballs.

His friend Mike made jokes: "I don't know what Thwait will do if he can't dribble. That guy dribbles everywhere."

Don Thwait punched his friend Mike. His friend Mike punched him back.

Mike was always a ham.

When the kids walked down the hills into town to go to school, the mill windows along the river were dull with frost.

When the first sun hit the glass, the frost shone in long scratches like the swipe of furred claws.

In church, they prayed for the boys who had gone off to the front. After a while they started praying for girls, too. The minister begged for victory. Thwait took the prayers seriously. When the hymns came, sometimes he couldn't actually sing because his voice had caught and wouldn't move. He had to clear his throat and start again.

It hit different people in the congregation on different Sundays. During the Intercessions, when the minister said that people should say the names of those who they held in their prayers, there would be a sob in the silence, and everyone would swing their eyes across the bowed rows to pick out who'd broken. An old man folded in his pew, say, would look down at his kneeler and wouldn't stand when everyone rose.

The acolytes floated up and down the aisle with candles and white gloves.

Tammy Strickland was in Don Thwait's class. She had dark hair and freckles. Thwait always thought she was pretty, but he never took much notice of her before the others talked about her once after basketball. The other boys said:

"She lives in — it looks like a witch's house. How does she get so pretty in that house?"

"She's real ginchy."

"She's a smooth catch."

One of the team announced: "I laid her."

Everyone stared.

It was Richie Sledge. He held up his hand. "Yeah. I laid her." He made a popping noise with his lips. "Belvis laid her too. Tammy's a swell lay."

Thwait could not stand talk like that.

Richie Sledge and Thwait got along on the court but not off it.

Thwait said, "It's not true, Richie. You haven't."

Thwait didn't know whether it was true or not, but he didn't want it to be. Tammy Strickland looked too beautiful and too sad for that.

"It is very true," said Sledge. "She'll do anything if you give her a little firewater." He jiggled his hand like he was tapping drops from a flask into Tammy's tipped-up mouth.

Thwait did not want to stay around for this kind of conversation. He did not like conversation of this type at all. He walked out of the gym.

Later his friend Mike said something about it. "Do you think that Tammy really . . . with Belvis and Sledge?"

Thwait shook his head and said, "Sledge."

The trees on Quick Hill were completely nude. Most of them were silver. The leaves were tangled in sticks near the ground. Briars and dead bracken were wound like barbed wire between fallen trunks.

On the top, there was a tomblike barrow lined with stones.

No one went up Quick Hill. It was too overgrown. It stood between a neighborhood on one side and a loading dock for one of the factories on the other side.

On the side of Quick Hill near Don Thwait's house on Crab Apple Lane, a grade-school group, earlier in the fall, had strung construction-paper hands up in the branches with colored yarn. The hands looked like they were saying, *Stop*. Now most of them were curled; the colored paper was blotched.

The children did not trace their own hands to make these hands. If you were a parent or teacher, you did not want anything to be able to detect a child's particular hand and come to know that hand and seek that child out.

When the cold came out of the north, the paper hands spun slowly where they hung.

Thwait and Mike watched to see which houses got stars. It would happen like this: The house would become more withdrawn, as if it didn't have people in it at all, as if it were shutting up, and then the mother in the house would tape a star to the window. This meant that their son or daughter had died. They were given the stars by an organization in Washington, D.C.

Their boys had died in North Africa, fighting the Germans, or on messy atolls in the Pacific, fighting the Japanese. Tobruk. Attu and Kiska. The Bataan Peninsula. Of course, Pearl Harbor. The

war was going badly. The cabinet radios coughed up news all day of troops trapped in the Philippines and on Guadalcanal. Rommel's push across the deserts. There was a congressional inquiry into how the federal augurs had missed signs that a whole airborne strike force would sink half the U.S. fleet in Hawaii. Senators held up black-and-white photos of wet entrails and bellowed that the American public demanded answers.

The women whose sons had been killed while serving were called Gold Star Mothers because of the paper stars they got in the mail. They were proud to be Gold Star Mothers. Everyone in town was proud of them.

Despite the pride, no one wanted to be one.

Though the town was gray and full of fear and all the businesses now were staffed by older men standing behind counters where younger men used to stand, Thwait and Mike were still excited about the future. They were newish at living, and so food rationing and reports about armaments and air-raid bells did not seem all that strange to them or all that important.

They talked about the positions they would play on the basketball team when they were seniors. (Point guard, said Thwait, who was a good team player, but who Coach always made play forward on account of his height.) They argued about which branch of the armed services was better to join. They talked a lot about vehicles: whether they would drive a tank or a plane, whether they would pick up their girl one day in a Bugatti or a Horch, when there were cars for sale again, after the war.

"D'you rather fly a fighter or a bomber?" Mike asked.

"Bomber. It's steadier work. You just fly and then you drop the bomb."

"If you had to fly a fighter though, what would you fly?"

"I said I'd fly a bomber."

"I'd fly a Jap Zero. I'd blow you out of the sky. They dance with you like a lady."

"Grumman F4F Wildcat can beat a Zero."

Mike gave a wild laugh. "I'm in a Fritzy Focke-Wolf. FOCKE-WOLF." He riddled Thwait with ak-ak fire.

Thwait rolled his eyes. "It's pronounced Focke-Vulf," he said.

Then they talked about cars. Mike described pulling up to the curb in something fancy and a lady in a fur coat getting in and kissing his nose, murmuring, "Mon Michel."

He said, "She'll smell like roses and Paris."

Thwait blinked. For a moment, it occurred to him that driving the one machine in a year might mean they never got a chance to drive the other in five years or ten.

A busload of ladies came to town saying they had the gift of a spirit hive and they would cherish your breath if you would buy war bonds. They put up posters all around town. They were cherishing breath for the war effort.

There was a long line for the cherishing. It was held in the grange hall. You bought your war bonds at a card table by the door, and then you were facing the ladies. They were dressed normally, in blouses and skirts and sweaters and jackets, but they were all chained together in a row with delicate little gold necklace chains that led from neck to neck. You went up to a lady and breathed in her mouth,

and she caught your breath. She would close her eyes and swallow it. It was safe with her. Then your breath was kept for if you ever needed it.

A lot of the kids from the high school were sent to the cherishing by their parents. "You get down there!" It didn't work most of the time — people out on the fronts were still dying in tanks, in gullies, in infirmary beds, in pieces. But there were those stories about someone lying on a battlefield who breathed their last, the death rattle, and there was silence, and then they got a different breath back and rose coughing.

Don Thwait's lady wore horn-rimmed glasses and was on the old side. He held his face close to hers and she said, "Just blow a soft column of air toward my mouth, honey. Real easy." He released a breath. She sucked in.

He felt guilty, but he wished his breath were being guarded by more of a looker.

At night he thought about Tammy Strickland and what Sledge had done with her. He crushed his legs together. He tried to bat his own hand away.

Tammy Strickland had never thought much about Don Thwait until that summer. He was tall, but he was quiet around girls. Then one day she had been in line at the grocer's with her mother, and Thwait was in front of them. Tammy saw her mother read the name on Thwait's ration book as the boy tore out the stamps and handed them to the grocer.

When the boy had left the store, Tammy's mother said to the grocer, "That's the Thwaits' boy?"

The grocer nodded.

Tammy's mother said, "Belongs to the hill?"

The grocer nodded. "That family. His great uncle was the last one. During the influenza."

Tammy's mother leaned to the side to watch the boy across the street.

"It's about time," she said, shaking her head. "They should marry him off."

Tammy had not understood a word of this at the time. Her mother wouldn't tell her but just said, "It isn't decent."

Tammy Strickland lived on a small dying farm just outside town. The goats gave milk, but they were also her pets, and she had always loved them and gave them glamorous names: Lulu, Anastasia, Esmeralda, Princess Immaculata. You got used to the smell after a while, and from the time she was a little girl, she talked to them. Her mother had once even worried that maybe one of them had become possessed — goats were weaker that way than other animals — and was about to say that Tammy couldn't visit them anymore, but Tammy's older brother, Townall, said, "Hush, Mom. Those goats are just plain goats. They don't talk back."

He took Tammy's mother out and showed her that the goats all had their reflections in brass. Even so, she fed them little crosses and signs of warding made of straw. She made Jimmy, the billy goat, sleep on ash shavings.

Townall was always doing things for Tammy. He took her skating

with his friends and so on. He taught her to play ice hockey. He made her a dollhouse when she was little and even made her small nanny goats out of spools.

Townall died in the Dutch East Indies. There was no mark of metal on his body from the bomb. He had been bobbing in the sea when he was killed. The impact of the explosion underwater was so great that the face of his corpse turned red instantly, scarlet and beaded from the bursting of all the capillaries right beneath the skin.

Tammy didn't know what do with herself after they got the telegram. A few months later, Tammy and her father tried to figure out about where Townall must have been in the Pacific when he died. Tammy went to the library and looked for a record of the action, but the newspapers didn't report a lot of things, especially because the war was going so badly. Based on the date of Townall's last letter, the Stricklands figured he'd died in one of those naval encounters where the papers said, ". . . escaped with only light casualties."

The late Townall Strickland was not statistically significant.

After they got the telegram, Tammy spent more time taking care of the chickens, which didn't need taking care of, and the goats, which weren't interested in pampering. Tammy's mother — who spent her days clutching at her husband's sleeve and, as Tammy thought, generally making herself a nuisance — decided that she'd been right all those years before and one of the goats really did have a secret rider. After Townall's death, it was a bee in Mrs. Strickland's bonnet. Tammy's mother sent away for a U.S. Department of Agriculture pamphlet on the spirit possession of livestock and spent most of the summer of '42 sprinkling the goats with human mother's milk and walking them widdershins around Quick Hill.

She wouldn't let Tammy go near her own nanny goats, though

of course Tammy slipped out sometimes to talk to them and whap their ears around. Tammy and her mother fought all the time about the goats.

It was after one of these fights that Tammy had slammed the front door shut and stomped into town. The mist coming off of the lawns was lit by the summer lights. She could feel things growing all around her. Water was running in all the ditches.

She walked up and down Front Street. That's where she saw Richie Sledge.

"Hey," she said, walking past him.

And he said, "Say, Tammy."

It was dull and uncomfortable. It happened a few times, not always with Richie Sledge.

After she had been with one of those idiots, she'd go back to the house and slip into the barn and sit near the goats with the showgirls' names. They whickered softly and congregated, hoping for handouts. She felt guilty toward the goats, guilty toward the chickens. She felt like all the animals wanted her to still be a little girl, not grown-up.

She held Esmeralda's long face and said, "I'm sorry. I'm sorry."

The goats looked back at her with eyes that were slit horizontal and alien, as if they peered into another dimension, where they saw around her some magnificence no one else could see.

Tammy could see clearly that Thwait was watching her at school. She caught him looking at her through a window when she walked down the steps. She smiled at him.

She couldn't tell whether he was handsome. He was tall and he looked strong and friendly, but his face was very pale and strange. His clothes were very neat and tidy.

One night she asked Richie Sledge about Thwait. Sledge said, "You sweet on him?"

"I just asked."

"He's a hill fucker."

Tammy turned her head away. She didn't know what he meant.

"I'm serious," said Sledge. "His family is the hill fuckers."

Tammy sighed dramatically about Sledge's indecency. She thought maybe too dramatically.

Sledge said, "I'm not kidding you. When they want the spirit of the hill or whatever that thing is to take mercy on the town, they marry it to someone in his family. Quick Hill. With a full wedding."

"That's the stupidest thing . . ."

"It's from Indian times."

"Do they sacrifice him or something? Like in Chicago?"

"No. Remember his uncle? Did you know his uncle? Crazy Thwait? Back when we were kids? Off his nut. They married him off to the hill back in the Great War or something. To stop everyone dying. My dad says they should marry Don off to the hill now. Before more of our boys in khaki are, uh, you know."

He had clearly just remembered that her brother had been killed.

He was sometimes nice like that, thinking of her. Then when they ran into some of the other boys, he would walk away from her and leave her behind. He would say, "Me and Tammy were just having a little fun. My pal Tammy, huh?"

———◆———

Don Thwait had found out when he was very little that someday he might be betrothed to Quick Hill. He and his father had been dragging his sled back home in midwinter.

He asked his father, "Where did you meet Mom?"

"Bean supper."

They walked a little farther along the ice-scarred road. Little Thwait said, "What did they mean when I fell off my sled?"

"What did they say?"

"That I just met my girl."

"Don't listen. You don't listen to noises that animals make."

"The Johnsons are people."

"Those squirts are too short to be people."

"They're kids."

"Don't worry about it. They're basically chipmunks."

But then, when the two of them turned around the base of Quick Hill, Mr. Thwait changed his mind, and stopped, and rocked with one foot on the dirt of the street and one foot in the snow of the hill. He kept rocking. Looking up the slope, he said, "You know, there's something to be proud of. A tradition. We're important in the town."

He told him then about the family's proud heritage, going back centuries to the burning raids. He talked to him about Great-Uncle Stew, and the Great War, and the Spanish flu, and how people all over town were dying back then and wore masks to keep off the contagion, and how the wedding was held, after which Stew was married to the hill and claimed the hill talked to him and had opinions and darling things to say just like any lady paramour. "Uncle Stew saved the town."

Young Thwait began to cry. "I don't want to marry the hill," he said.

His father shuffled him away quickly. "Hey, quiet," he said. "We're right next to it."

Thwait sobbed, "I don't want to marry a hill. I want to marry Mom."

His father hissed to make him quiet down. "It's all right. It's all right. Just don't say anything. The hill gets angry easy."

From down the street came the rhythmic chock and hiss of someone shoveling a path in snow.

Thwait tried not to think about it. The hill was in front of their windows. It was in front of their front door. When he walked out in the morning, it rose up before him. When he came home in the dark, he could hear it breathing.

He wanted to settle down with a girl in a house. He planned to move far, far away to a distant city. It wasn't fair. He would have a house in St. Louis, where no one knew about the Thwaits and the town. He could already picture his wife's legs. He couldn't believe that someday he would be allowed to touch a woman's legs when he wanted to. He would be allowed to run his hand along her calf and have her laugh like a cricket rising up out of hot grasses. He wanted to love a woman and to be proud of their child.

He already pictured the angle at which they'd hold the newborn tilted, to bounce the kid to sleep.

They played a game against some kids from Pepperell. Thwait's team won, 58–50. It was close for most of the game. Afterward, they went to Lucian Belvis's house, and a few of the players from

Pepperell went with them. One of the fellows from Pepperell was Belvis's cousin.

They went to Belvis's house because he lived with his grandmother and she didn't really know what was going on. Also, Belvis lived in a neighborhood where the air-raid wardens never told anyone to shut up, because they didn't go out much in winter.

It was starting to snow when they got there.

Some of the girls were there, too, and at first everything was very quiet, because Mrs. Belvis, Belvis's grandmother, kept bringing in things to eat and drink, like hot chocolate. They thanked her. Everyone murmured and there was some laughing.

Thwait kept looking at Tammy Strickland, but he couldn't look at her for too long. He was embarrassed. His friend Mike made jokes about him staring, like saying, "Clamp up your jaw, sonny."

Thwait looked away.

Mike said, "Just kidding, Thwait. Feast your peepers. She's poetry on a davenport."

Thwait glared at him.

Then Mrs. Belvis said she was going up for the night and you all make yourself at home. Congratulations to everyone on a magnificent game of basketball. She went up the stairs.

People were only sweet for a few minutes after Mrs. Belvis shut her bedroom door. Then people began petting on the rug.

This always made Thwait uncomfortable because he thought people should do that kind of thing alone, in the comfort of their own car.

Mike muttered, "Now comes the swak parade." Mike had had a girlfriend the year before, but she had moved away. He was bitter.

Thwait crossed his arms and didn't know where to look.

M. T.
ANDERSON

Tammy was sitting rolling a mug back and forth in her hands. One of her girlfriends was talking to her, but she was obviously not listening.

Thwait saw Sledge nod across the room toward Tammy. Sledge was standing near the pocket doors, talking to one of the Pepperell kids. Thwait heard Sledge whisper, "Have a tête-à-tête with her. She'll do more than kiss. Find a place to sit her down."

"Oh, yeah?"

"Sure. Say it's for the war effort."

Sledge and the Pepperell boy went over and sat on either side of Tammy. They started talking to her and laughing. She made a face and pushed at Sledge with spidery hands. He didn't move away but started whispering in her ear. She shook her head. He reached up and held on to her skull and kept on talking at her ear, louder and louder.

She shoved at him again. He just laughed.

"Come on, Tammy," he argued. "You got two hands."

Thwait was not aware of anything but feeling a bright deep hurt for her, and he rose up and walked over and pushed Sledge.

He wanted Sledge to push back. He wanted to fight, and looking at Sledge's clever face, he wanted to hit it. Sledge stood up.

Thwait found himself moving closer to Sledge.

Thwait knew then a little bit of what it must be like being in one of those bombers near Midway or the Coral Sea, slanting sharply down toward the deck of an enemy cruiser — tumbling toward the target — the pleasure of speed, anger, inevitability, and immense detonation.

Sledge stared him in the eye. "Hey, Hill Fucker," he said.

Thwait explained to Sledge, "We can fight, but you know I'm bigger than you."

"Got to be big, to fuck a whole hill."

Thwait explained, "I try to use my strength with gentleness."

Thwait wondered why he had just said that when just a second later he punched Sledge in the face.

It felt very good, and Sledge went backwards. Everyone was talking in the papers about the effectiveness of surprise attack.

The boy from Pepperell had his hand on Tammy's knee, but she wrenched it off and stood up. She furiously flung her way across the room and hurled around coats, looking for hers.

Thwait looked down at Sledge, who was pushing himself upright on the back of the davenport, holding on to his face. Sledge was twitching. Thwait could tell Sledge was trying to decide whether he could hit him back safely.

Thwait said, "My left is slower than my right. You should try for that side."

The boy from Pepperell said, "Who is this guy?"

Thwait walked away from them. He felt good. He said to Tammy Strickland, "Mike and I will walk you home, if you want us to."

She said, "Mike could want to stay."

"No," said Mike. "Everyone will look at me funny, and it will be terrible."

Sledge said to Tammy, "Go back to the goat farm, chippy."

"Whoa, whoa, whoa," said Mike, and bundled the other two out the door.

It was beautiful and still and cold outside. The snow, which was small and bitter, still fell. It felt nice and new to be outside after the greasy air of Belvis's parlor, the thick breath of petting. Tammy and Thwait were looking at each other. They both felt like they had just put on a play.

It didn't matter that Mike was along. They knew that they would have plenty of time to talk alone in the weeks to come.

They skated on small puddles in the road. All three of them grabbed at one another for balance. Tammy was the best at skating. Thwait watched the snow land in her black hair.

An hour later, after he left Tammy at her house, he got to his own house and felt the hill watching him as he turned up his walk. It loomed in the dark.

He walked her home from school on Monday. She did not invite him in.

On Thursday afternoon, he came over and knocked on her door. She saw him through the window and ran outside, still putting an arm in her coat. He thought it was because she was excited. She was — but, more importantly, she didn't want her mother to see him. Tammy was afraid that her mother would yell at her in front of him or say something about Don marrying the hill.

The leaves were all wet and clogged on the ground and gave forth a dark leaf wine. The air smelled like vinegar.

Tammy took Don's arm first thing.

Don and Tammy had just a marvelous time that day. They talked about everything in the world. They walked out to where the town got thinner. There were more pastures there.

Don said, "Don't you want to go into town? We could get a sand-wich."

Tammy shook her head. She didn't say anything, but the truth was she didn't want to see Sledge. She knew Sledge would ruin every-thing. She said, "Look! Everything you say is all steamy."

Don blew in the air and pretended he was smoking a cigarette.

They talked about their families. Don did not mention that his family belonged to the hill. He talked about his mother and father being nice. He thought they were swell parents. Nothing about the mystical marriage in times of civic need.

He listened when Tammy said that her mother was crazy since her brother died.

"I'm sorry," said Don. He did not know what to say about someone who had died, and he didn't want to say the wrong thing. "Was he in the service?"

"Yeah. Navy."

"I'm sorry."

Tammy scuffed her heels through the mud. It was a more playful thing to do than her face looked. She said, "We miss Townall all the time. My mother has been awful since he died. She got real protec-tive of me."

"You mean she can't see me with you?"

"Probably not. She's afraid of everything. U-boats in the goat pond."

Don Thwait laughed. Tammy smiled. It didn't seem as bad as it had before.

Don did not know what to do about kissing her. It got dark around four thirty, so he had to take her home. They were almost at her house. He wanted to kiss her, and he figured he should, just so she knew he liked her. But he didn't want her to be afraid he was just like Sledge and Belvis — pretending to be nice just to get fresh.

She was hopping along next to him, avoiding puddles. It was even better that she was hopping. That made him like her even more. She was like a different person than at school.

So he took her arms and said, "Someday I want to kiss you."

Tammy didn't look at him.

He didn't know what to say. He thought that maybe saying that had made it okay, so he leaned in.

He saw her duck, as if she were ashamed of the kiss. She smiled politely at him and backed away.

She ran into the house.

He stood outside like an idiot.

But he saw her wave through the window.

On the court, Richie Sledge and Belvis acted like jerks toward him. They never passed to him. They always went in for the shot themselves, even if that meant they lost the ball. They passed to each other or to other team members. It was as if Thwait was a ghost on the court: not there at all.

Tammy and Don walked home together every day. They wrote each other notes throughout the day and slipped them to each other in classes. The full winter snow came and lay on all the mills in town around the black river. Don and Tammy were falling in love, so it looked beautiful to them.

The Carmichaels' son David was killed in Tunisia. The Saltonstall boy died of malaria somewhere in the Pacific. Louis Franco drove over a mine; there was nothing left of him to send home. Danny Loesser, who was looking forward to seeing Rome for the first time, having spent all those years learning Latin (*I love, I will love, I have loved*), had his head taken off by shrapnel in Sicily. The Gagnons' kid was seized on by a tactical ghost, something sent by a hell of a shaman, and hanged himself from a railing on his carrier.

In the Great Lakes, there were seen serpents, monstrosities, leech-like and heaving.

All up and down the East Coast, U-boats sounded near lonely beaches and slid off to torpedo the shipping.

There was constant expectation of German victory. The winter was harsh, and many thought it had in its winds the stench of Teutonic curse. Every letter from a kid at the front read like the last, quavering words of a patsy about to be beheaded in the *Niebelungenlied*.

No one thought that the war could be won anymore.

Still, the Andrews Sisters harmonized about how grand it would be when the boys got home, come apple-blossom time.

The goats pushed their foreheads against Don's hands. It was like a sporting event with them. They all jostled to play with him first.

Tammy told him their names. Don fed them potato peels out of a squashed pie tin.

Don and Tammy had sneaked out together to visit the goats.

They had to disguise their footprints inside of Mr. Strickland's big boot prints so their tracks wouldn't show up in the snow. Then they had to be careful when they went into the barn that the goats didn't run around too much. Mrs. Strickland in her mania had hung bells around all their necks. She said that if a bell helped St. Anthony Abbot warn off the devils in the deserts of Libya, it would work for goats, too.

Don and Tammy stood among the herd and handed out kitchen rubbish.

Don asked, "Did the bell work for St. Anthony Abbot? He still was tempted by all those monsters with chicken feet."

Tammy shrugged. "Saved his pig, anyway. He had a cunning little pig." She added, "I can't believe I eat ham."

The goats milled around them and drew their lips across Don's fingers.

Tammy asked him, "What do you think of them?"

"I think they're swell."

"I always want to keep goats and sheep when I'm older. And a border collie." She shifted her back against the railing. "But I don't want my husband to be a farmer. It just goes on and on."

She looked at Don, and she could tell Don wanted to say something about her husband in the future. He was trying to say something.

All he said was, "I don't want to be a farmer."

Gently, carefully, she said, "You planning on getting married?"

Don blushed. She could feel him looking at her, at the shape of her, at her arms and her neck and her mouth.

"Yeah," he said, gutturally.

Then they kissed for the first time right there in the barn. They stood with their arms around each other and really kissed, and there was nothing wrong about it.

They laughed for a long time after that, because they both felt like they had found a place away from everyone else. They whispered and kissed again and whispered until Don realized what time it was and had to get away. He slipped out of the barn and staggered along the footstep holes left by her father, while Tammy hissed after him, "Keep away from the house! Mother will think we've been tying the billy goat's beard into elflocks. While it told us poetry."

Don snorted one laugh, and then she couldn't see him anymore. His crunching was faint. He was trying to step softly.

She closed the barn door and felt like she was full up to the brim with nectar. She couldn't believe that things could be so good. She saw her flock, her family, watching her attentively. They wanted more peelings. She would have given them fresh home fries, if she could have, and carrots and beets.

She could not contain herself. She took Esmeralda by the ear and said into the goat's sloping face, "He loves me! I think he loves me!"

"Yes," said Esmeralda kindly, as Tammy reared back. "Anyone can see that."

Quick Hill was buried in snow. It stood above the town. At the top, around the empty barrow, there was a grove of beeches. Their skin was smooth and silver. Their leaves, though dead, did not fall down but clung, cupped with little ribs like chrysalids.

They chattered in the wind. They were agitated all around the empty barrow.

Don and Tammy sat on either side of Esmeralda. They asked for an explanation. She told them that she was the only possessed goat. The others were all dumb brutes, though easy, she said, to live with, except Queen Claire, who bit.

The spirit in Esmeralda had fled from the Midwest, beast to beast, because she said that things were not good in the plains. Something was eating the heartland. Livestock out there was being killed in barns, and the papers had been told not to report it. There were stories of squat metallic shapes that came from the north warping across the grassland — that before they set out, some *Wehrmacht Zaubergruppe* assigned each one a town to havoc. On farms there were rumors that metal twists lurked in culverts during the day, then bandied out at night to cut the throats of cattle. They especially searched out spirit-riders, since the riders otherwise could cry warning.

So Esmeralda's rider had jumped into animals being shipped east, one touching another, her leaping between hearts and hides and leaving behind scent and color and many mulching bellies for dim eyes or twitchy ears. She had made it to New England in a Guernsey, which was about as stupid as she could go before she lost clarity.

"I am here since September," said the goat's rider through the goat's mouth. "I looked around in a white-tailed deer, and I knew I wanted to stay with you, at your farm." Esmeralda said to Tammy, "I could tell you were someone I was safe with."

Don Thwait smiled with love at his girl. "Isn't that something?" he said. "That's how perfect you are."

"You two," said Tammy, embarrassed. "You're both too much."

The train tracks ran into town from the south. There was a switching station there near the factories, which was all confusion. The snow between the sleepers was painted black with soot.

The factories had all been turned to war work. They were making blankets and uniforms. The trains brought people from far away to work in the sewing rooms and machine shops. They got off at the station with their cardboard suitcases. They were staying four to a room in the hotels, and couples were taking in lodgers. You couldn't recognize people on the street anymore. Now there were gangs of men walking with sandwiches.

The newcomers complained about the cold and about the snow. They razzed the locals about it while they waited for change at the cash register.

North of the town, the tracks continued. They split at that point, and each headed its own direction, into the forests, the White Mountains, the Green Mountains, Quebec.

Up there, darkness fell even earlier.

The first body was found in an alley beside the tracks. His name was Lavalle, and he was new to town. He worked as a mechanic at the woolen co. His face was slit and so was his neck, as if something had taken three swipes.

Some people said it was a spy who had done it, sent to cause panic and lower morale. Some people said it was a madman who'd shipped in with all the workers. Some said it was a monstrosity.

The body was found at a time when battles were being lost everywhere.

It was about then, late in the winter, that people began to say it was time for a Thwait to marry the town hill.

Tammy and Don sat side by side on the sofa.

Don's mother tried to smile. "So you're Tammy," she said. "Who we've heard. . . . So. Much . . ."

Don's father said, "It's good to meet you, Tammy."

Don's mother and father exchanged a look. No one seemed very comfortable.

Don offered, "Tammy is a swell drawer."

They both sneaked out once to skate together by moonlight. It was harder for Tammy to slip out than Don. She was late, and he spent fifteen minutes standing under some big old white pines, shifting his shoulders up and down and clapping his hands together. He bounced on his toes. The pines fumbled over his head.

She arrived. They grabbed at each other's hands and raced toward the pond.

It wasn't frozen enough.

Instead they kissed and went home.

Walking through the town at night, they both felt a great love for the place — for all the little boxy houses and all the people they had known since birth. Something about sleep and about snow, which was like sleep, made it beautiful. Don said, "It's the best town ever." Tammy started to sing "Silent Night," even though Christmas was over.

The next morning Isobel Michaels, a girl eleven years old, was found slaughtered in her bed on Harmon Street.

One of the city councillors came to see Mr. Thwait. They sat in the living room.

Don knew what the councillor had come about. He went upstairs and crouched down quietly by the cast-iron vent in the floor. He knew it was wrong, but he had to listen.

"There was an editorial in the newspaper," said Mr. Lumley, the city councillor.

"Just because Dick Baker writes an editorial doesn't mean my son has to jump."

"This killer . . . Some people say it's a spy. Kraut who parachuted in. But you know what other people . . . They're saying it's the hill."

"It's not the hill."

"How do you know?"

"The hill isn't like that."

"Isn't it?"

"It's a hill."

"Mr. Thwait."

"Do you think it has some kind of servant?"

There was a long silence. Then Mr. Lumley said to Don's father: "I don't know. Do you?" He sounded almost menacing: "Maybe you know."

There was another long silence.

Mr. Thwait said, "It's not time yet."

Mr. Lumley said, "How many have to die before it's time?"

Don was giddy with anxiety. He wished he could see his father's face. All he could see was the cast-iron vent, which was a rosette thick with scratched white paint. Light came from below.

Mr. Lumley said, "You know his girl? Tammy Strickland? We called the principal. She's not a good girl."

"That's outrageous. I met her, and she is —"

"She has a reputation." Don heard Lumley's lighter flip open and the flint strike. He heard Lumley exhale. He smelled the smoke of Lumley's cigarette.

Lumley said, "She is not of a good moral, uh, standing. You understand what I mean, Mr. Thwait? If Donald does something . . . A girl like that could ruin our chance, see? She is not a good match for your boy at this time. Not for a Thwait."

Don Thwait spent the next day training at the Y. He thought it might make him feel less violent. He didn't like those emotions.

He lifted and punched until lunch. He ran until it was dark and sleeted.

Mike's older brother came home for a week, furloughed before he shipped out again. He had been in the Pacific, but he suspected he would be sent to the Atlantic.

The kids went to Mike's house to see him. He was different from when he was in high school. He didn't pay them much notice.

Kids who'd be enlisting the next year asked him about whether it was better to be in the navy or the marines or the army. He talked a little about it, but he didn't seem very interested in their questions. Mainly he said that on a destroyer, it was so goddamn hot that the metal walls sweat. Over a hundred degrees belowdecks, and above decks so goddamn hot that rubber-soled shoes got tacky and

stuck starting around fourteen hundred hours. The men all crammed down below, bathed in one another's water, waiting for a Jap torpedo to blast through the wall. Then, on one of the islands, the constant rain, nothing dry, you're sitting in a hole with water up to your waist, and at night all the bushes and trees are rattling on every damn side of you, and in one of them's a Nip Type 96 with your name on it.

Mike did not joke like usual. He watched his brother smoke.

Tammy and Don didn't talk at all. They were worried Mike's brother would suddenly get angry and yell at everyone. You could feel the anger just under his skin.

One of the boys — slated for the army — shook his head with sympathy and said, "You fellows give so much. You're heroes."

Mike's brother said, "Once. I was a hero one time." He held up a finger. "After a skirmish, heard some whimpering, and saw it was a Jap we'd shot, almost dead. One of the other boys — Saunders — was teasing him with a knife. Even though the Jap was almost dead anyway. Saunders was yelling all sorts of bull crap at him about torture and started to scalp the kid. But I couldn't stand hearing the screaming. So I took my pistol and stuck it in the Jap's eye and killed him." He stood up. "That's the closest I got to being a hero."

The army boy argued, "But all of you fellows are making a sacrifice."

Mike's brother crossed his arms. "Making a sacrifice doesn't mean being a hero. Making a sacrifice is about sacrificing something."

He looked at Don. "Thwait," he said, with menace. "You thought about making a sacrifice?"

A week after the editorial about Quick Hill, the newspaper ran a bunch of letters in which people said that the Thwait heir should

realize what had to be done for the town and do it immediately. They said there was no time to lose.

People did not have to sign letters in the newspaper, except with a fake name like "Concerned" or "Had Enough."

Then there was an article about how Donald Thwait's cousins were girls and so couldn't marry the hill, because the hill was female. The article ran a picture of Don from one of the basketball games. There was a quote from Don's father saying that it wasn't time yet to marry the boy off. Mr. Thwait pointed out that because Don didn't have any brothers, there would never be another Thwait — no Thwait named Thwait — if Don married the hill. Don would be the last Thwait.

Then the town's compact with the hill would be over, said Mr. Thwait. Did people really want that to happen? The article suggested that people were willing to take that chance.

Now that everyone knew Don's name and everyone — even new kids at school — knew his face and that he was betrothed to the hill, he never felt easy. People talked to him about it wherever he went. His history teacher, Mr. Allen, had a son overseas and watched to see what Thwait would do. Don did not go to the snack shop anymore. He did not know who "Concerned" was — the person who had written into the paper, talking about him as "Don," like a friend, complaining that "Don" did not take his duty to the town seriously. "Concerned" was furious that Don was dating. Don realized that anyone could be "Concerned." Don saw "Concerned" in every pair of eyes, blaming him. He did not feel safe anywhere because of "Concerned."

The closest he felt to safe was huddled on a stool in Tammy's barn with her huddled next to him. Esmeralda sat on the straw in her pen and watched them benevolently.

They tried to talk about simple things, the tokens of small talk — pets, teachers' romances, the mob under the basket on the court, how to set picks and stop the other fellow from shooting — but really all Don and Tammy wanted to do was hold on to each other. They hugged so hard they could feel the sticks in their arms and in their fingers beneath all the wool of jackets and coats.

She said to him, "We could save you."

He pulled his head back from hers so he could look at her face.

She repeated, "We could."

He said, "Go away? Off to St. Louie or something?"

She blinked. She looked miserable.

She said, "No. Not go away. We . . ."

Then he understood. They didn't know what to say to each other.

"They'll kill me," he said.

"If we don't?"

"If we do."

She thought about it. She said, "Then what if we did go away?"

He was amazed. He said, "You'd go with me?"

She considered. "Maybe," she said. "Maybe. All right. All right, I'll go."

He cackled and hugged her. She kissed him too hard and hurt his nose.

Then they started to think things through. He said, "I wish I could just join up. I always thought I'd join up when I was old enough." He sighed. "I could lie, I suppose."

"You don't want to go someplace together? Until you're old enough?"

"What'll we do?"

"It doesn't matter," said Tammy.

They both knew that this was not a good answer — so they grinned at each other, thrilled by the excitement of it all. They started to make their plans.

Mrs. Bateson was a friend of his mother's. She was pregnant, and got down on her knees in front of him.

"You don't *understand*," wept Mrs. Bateson. "I had a dream I gave birth to a wolf."

Don stood awkwardly. "Mrs. Bateson," he said, "I'm real sorry you . . . Well, I'm sorry you knelt. Can I just help you up . . . ?"

"It's for the next generation."

"Mrs. Bateson . . ."

"The wolf was tearing at my . . . when I was nursing him, he . . ." She waved her hand back and forth in the air.

"It was a dream."

"No," said Mrs. Bateson. "It happened to a woman in Ohio. Please. I've known you since you were three."

Don stood, holding out his hand to help her rise. She did not take it. His parents did not come back into the living room to lead the woman out.

His parents did take him to the Episcopal Church to talk to his minister and the Congregational minister, who would conduct the marriage service. Several of the town council were there, too. Everyone talked to him quietly about duty.

Don admired the Gothic woodwork in the church office and wondered how the cherry was milled. While they talked to him, he couldn't help but almost smile, because he knew that in a couple of days, he would be on a train, and Tammy would be asleep with her head on his arm. He would watch new places come toward him. He would go out to where it was flat and there were no hills.

When Don looked up at Christ, Christ's arms were spread wide, not in pain but in welcome. And Don could already feel them wrapped around him and Tammy, the three of them standing together.

Don and Tammy had a strategic meeting with Mike and the goat.

Don was afraid that when he bought his ticket to flee, he'd be recognized by the stationmaster. Too many people knew Don's face. All the police officers in town knew him now and glared at him when he walked with Tammy. Don asked if Mike would buy the tickets for them. Mike said sure. Don could tell Mike was trying not to show fear. Don pulled out a lot of bills from his pants pocket. He had made the money in the fall, stacking wood and helping people from the church with odd jobs. He handed it to Mike and said, "Thanks."

Mike and Don, strangely, shook hands, as if it were already years later, and they were men.

The four of them planned that Tammy and Don would not enter the station together. Tammy would get to the station about ten minutes before the train and wait on the platform. Mike would walk by the gate and give her the wave to say that everything was on schedule. Don would stay inside the station until the last minute. She and Don would ignore each other if they ran into each

other. They didn't want anyone remembering them together. Once the train had gone an hour or so toward Boston, they would find each other. From Boston, they would take a train west. Tammy had a grown-up cousin in Illinois they might be able to stay with for a couple of days, until Don got a job jerking sodas or something.

That was how they always talked about his future job: "jerking sodas or something." Don and Tammy had no idea what they would do for money. But the blankness in front of them was part of the thrill — as if they stood ready to jump from a cliff above the sea, hands gripped together tightly, and what lay before them was nothing but empty sky.

Tammy stood on an oak stump and looked around her house and her yard. She hadn't really noticed how much the house needed paint. She felt bad that she was leaving her mother and father. She would send them a card from Boston, so they'd know she was safe but wouldn't know where she was heading.

Tammy wondered what was on postcards from Boston. She guessed maybe the Bunker Hill Monument or baked beans.

In two hours she would be getting on the train. Earlier that morning she had started crying without feeling anything. She figured she must be missing the town already. Whenever she felt upset, she just thought about Richie Sledge's glances at her — all the boys now, when they thought Don wasn't looking. She would never see any of them again, until she was a grown woman and came back to visit her parents sometime. She would have her and Don's children dressed up socially.

Staring at the house, she worried that maybe her mother and father wouldn't let her come visit. And then she worried that even if they did, the boys around town would make jokes about her to her kids.

She didn't know whether she would ever see the town again, and, frankly, she didn't care.

M. T.
ANDERSON

One hour before the train, Mike knocked on Don's door as if nothing was happening and asked Mrs. Thwait if Don could come out and go goof off with the guys. Mrs. Thwait said she didn't see why not.

Don trotted down the steps and gave her a hug. It was a long hug. He tried not to cry while he said, "Okay, Mom, I'll be back late. I'll probably have dinner at the Cartwells'."

He looked at her face. He knew he would not see her again for years. He stared at her so he could remember her later, and so she could remember him when she discovered he was gone.

He went out on the stoop. Mike was waiting.

The door of Don Thwait's house where he had grown up closed behind him.

He stood confronting the hill. It was black and silent. The wind blew past, and all the trees on the hill rattled.

"Let's go," said Don. He and Mike treaded off toward Mike's house. That's where Don had hidden his bag of stuff, the things he was taking with him.

They didn't talk. They kept trading glances.

Finally, Mike said, "We should look like we're having fun. Normally."

"You're right."

Mike said in a loud gangster voice, "Whaddayou? A wise guy? Why I otta . . ." He shook his fist.

It was not a funny or good imitation.

The grove at the top of the hill could still be seen above the roofs of houses.

Tammy had not told any of her friends that she was going. She did not trust them not to gossip. She told her mother that she was staying overnight at Stacy's. She left with a paper bag of things.

It was forty-five minutes before the train.

By the time they got to Mike's house, Don's heart was beating. He looked at his watch and said, "Forty-five minutes."

Mike nodded. They went inside.

Don said, "We'll wait here for twenty-five minutes. We can make it to the station in ten."

Mike nodded. He looked sad. "Okay," he said.

"Sorry you can't come with me," Don said. "We'll send you a note to tell you where we end up. You can come out and visit."

"Sure."

They sat on Mike's bed and didn't say anything. Don had his bag on his lap.

Mike said, "Do you think that you left yourself enough time?"

Don said, "I don't want to get there too early."

He looked out the window.

Several big cars pulled up in front of the house. One of them was the police.

Don felt his hands go numb.

Out of another car stepped the Congregational minister.

"Damn," said Don, and dropped to the rug.

Mike stood up, gaping at the cars.

Don headed for the stairs. "We got to go out the back door."

He thumped down the steps.

He said, "Must be the hill. The hill told them! That — that *bitch*!"

He did not often swear.

There was a loud knock on the front door.

He loped toward the kitchen.

There were two people pounding on the front door now.

Don thrust off the sink and swiveled around the icebox. Mike was right behind him.

Don rattled the back doorknob. "Locked!" he said. The little floral curtains bobbed.

Mike reached over to a hook by the door and got a key. He gave Don the key. Don unlocked the door. He pulled it open.

There at the kitchen door were his mother and a policeman and Mr. Lumley from the town council. His mother was crying.

"Don," she said.

Tammy stood on the train platform. It was dark out and very cold.

There were a little girl and her mother both wearing green. The little girl said, "I want the train to come now. I want it to come forever."

The mother said, "That would be a very long train."

The 6:38 pulled into the station.

Don didn't know what to do. There were people at the front and back doors. They had cars.

He tried to pretend nothing was happening. "What's going on, Mom?" he asked.

She looked at him shyly.

Mr. Lumley stepped into the kitchen. "Thank you, Mike," he said.

Don looked at his friend.

Mike put his arm out and touched the cabinet for a long time. Then he turned and walked away down the hall.

Mr. Lumley said kindly, "This is what everyone wants, Don. Mike too. His brother shipped out. He's going to be in U-boat territory until who knows when. Now come along."

Don Thwait could not think right. He was supposed to be on a train. There was something wrong, and he was supposed to take her hand or put her head on his arm.

Tammy waited at the station. The train sighed. A man in an old beaver coat climbed up the steps and got on. Tammy hung on to the metal railings of the fence with both hands and looked for Mike. Cars went past with their lights on. There were people on the other side of the street wearing hats, hurrying back and forth.

Any minute, she knew. Any minute, Don and Mike would be there. She reached down and picked up her paper bag of things. The lip was curled and soft.

Don was supposed to be in the waiting room, where he wouldn't run into her. It could not hurt to see if he was, if she just peeked.

There was no one inside except the stationmaster.

She waited. A few more people got on.

Mike did not come.

Finally, it was 6:38, and the 6:38 left the station.

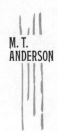
The barn was dark when Tammy got home. She sat there in the cold. The wind pressed up against the old grimy windows. Esmeralda sat on the hay, her legs folded under her. She chewed from side to side.

"Mike came by," said Esmeralda. "He told me that there was a problem. He said that you should just wait here and Don would be by in an hour."

"Wait here? What was the problem?"

Esmeralda just chewed. "Ask Mike," she said. "No one's let me out of this stall all afternoon."

"We're just going up the hill. We're just going up the hill," said Reverend Baxter as they half dragged Don Thwait through the snow. "We're just going up the hill. Just going up the hill, Don."

His mother said, "We can't make you do anything."

Mr. Lumley said, "It's a war. You'll damn well marry the hill."

It was not an easy going. Twigs scratched at them all. Old thorns clacked as they kicked at them. The wind was high now and shook all the trees. Their flashlights swept across patches of snow and flailing branches. There were strange marks in the snow as if something had made its way there earlier.

As they went up, Mr. Lumley kept shouting the names of the men who'd died overseas.

An hour passed and Tammy waited. She waited for another hour before she realized that someone was lying to her.

She said, "This is wrong. Something's wrong."

Esmeralda said, "He's probably married by now."

Tammy looked at Esmeralda. Tammy was aghast.

Esmeralda said, "We all want safety. I don't want to move again."

"What do you know?"

"He's not coming. Mike told me they found him."

Tammy shrieked and ran at Esmeralda. The goat backed into the herd, but Tammy half climbed, half toppled over the fence and scrambled toward the possessed. She grabbed Esmeralda by the head and yanked the long face around to hers. *What are you talking about?* she demanded.

The face she looked at did not show any sign of being able to speak back.

Tammy let go of Esmeralda the goat. She stepped backward and looked at all ten females.

All of them looked back at her with their alien eyes. None of them spoke.

Tammy left the barn and ran for Quick Hill.

Don Thwait did not know exactly what was happening. On top of the hill, he felt very at home. He saw the lights of his town through the trunks of the trees. It had been his family's home for three centuries.

Don's father said to him, "You want to serve, don't you? You've wanted to serve."

"In the air force," whispered Don.

"You'll be safe here," said Don's father. "And it's better for the town. It's like you took all these young men and pulled them out of the water after their ship had been bombed. You'll save their lives."

Don said, "But I'll be giving up my life."

The adults exchanged looks.

"She's just a girl," said Mr. Lumley. "Is your, ah, romance really more important than those boys out there in the ocean? Do you see how selfish? Right? How incredibly selfish your dream is?"

Tammy found the paths where the snow had been trampled. She heaved herself up toward the grove at the crown of Quick Hill.

She found some of the men of the town standing with the Thwaits near the door of a tomb. Don Thwait sat on a piece of cut stone. His elbows were on his knees and his head was hanging down.

He looked up when she came into the grove.

She stopped dead. She could tell he had made his decision.

"Don?" she said.

He did not smile to see her. He just said, "I want to be a good person."

She told him she loved him. He nodded.

Even as she said it, she was not sure it was true anymore. She wondered if she would love someone else some time.

He said, "I love you."

She went to him and put her arms around him. He put his arms around her. They already knew they were saying good-bye.

He said, "We'll talk every day. It doesn't matter that I'm married to the hill. We can still talk."

Tammy was crying. She thought she maybe actually did love him.

She put her face in his neck. Her nose ran on his collar. She thought about the hill receiving him with his collar wet from her nose.

She wanted the hill to reject him.

He let go, and then held on to her again. She was solid and real in the moment; he was solid and real, and they were together on top of Quick Hill in this time.

They knew they could not stand like that forever.

Neither one wanted to step away from the other.

The wind blew on the heights.

"All right, now," said the Congregational minister.

He put his hand on Don's shoulder.

Both Don Thwait and Tammy Strickland stepped back. Each one thought about who had let go first. Tammy thought it was Don and was surprised that she blamed him, just for the single step with his heel.

Don was already walking into the barrow.

The minister walked in behind him.

Snow began to fall softly as the rites were read underground.

2. MARRIAGE

Through the frozen apple boughs, the lights of town are ringed with woven coronas of mist and ice, and far away there is motionless smoke. All dark in the trees and he is alone. He thinks the other people have gone now, the people who were on the hill; some time they went and left him, perhaps some days ago.

And he curls closer to the dirt and winds himself in taproots, from which come warmth. Among frozen beeches he sees the girl Tammy, who watches for him. The small falls are whiskered with ice.

Let them slumber sweetly, says the hill, all my creatures.

And comes new time wakeful, all unlocking. First felt in blinking of water behind ocular ice and lidded oak leaves, then rains. He huddling in the barrow, no chill there to him. His delivered bread is no longer frozen. Through bark the tree sap rises like matins light crawling across cathedral columns, and it is full day. *I'll be seeing you in apple-blossom time*, says Don to hill, *say the Andrews Sisters*, and he laughs, because it will be that time soon, in the old orchard on her flank where he lies and watches clouds.

The deaths, the scored edge of metal that kills these people — it has to stop. And he and the hill excise it from their dream.

A rupture it is, the killer, and a girl on her bike is screaming in the woods and, slumbering, Don and hill swaddle the sharp edge away. Don can feel it kicking as it is removed, soothed, smoothed into vacancy. The girl emits a high radio whine as she stumbles toward lights, leaving the bike with wheels spinning. The sharp edge still fights, but he and hill muffle it further, and then he cannot remember it or what it was any longer, because it is past and gone. The hill quiets him.

And throughout him and his limbs spread upon the clod extends the love of this place and its people, loved with her (smilingly), the thoroughfares and busyness, its quiet moments and soiled window-panes (gaze through to brick walls or far swales; the people alone or several, in stuffed chairs that face in different ways, so they can make their noises at each other). And bless Myron Glikman of Fitzwilliam Street, who parades and trains in the Arizona heat. And bless Sarah Pratchett, who liked jigsaw puzzles with her gran, who now is set to ship out and nurse in Europe. And bless — and bless — and with each one, the hill asks him of them, and he knows them as he did not before, and knows too what scratched in their walls. He feels the hill's

vast expertise at benediction (cereals; furrows; bird eggs; expressive parasites).

Quickening.

Sleep in heavenly peace, he says, exultant, demanding rest for them all beneath the moon: the little girl tantrum-smeared and sobbing in bed; the cad now snoring next to someone else's jumpy wife; those who labor in insurance; also the women, new to town, new to these factories, bringing the breath of other places and stories about fast cars or wheat told while they bend over the machines, and bolts spin out between the rollers.

And in those years, he advocates for settled nights and bustling days, and throughout all of it, love for the people of that place. (They leave him baskets at the hill's foot and seem unenthusiastic when he visits the grocery and exchanges fistfuls of leaves for cans.) Now his knowledge of her is greater, and he knows even of her infancy (glacial moraine) and the long years of waiting, and birds come and go. Her till and sweet humus. And all that vast history, and all those born of the dirt of that town now standing around the globe, and he no longer understands how he could want only eyes, only touch. (He presses against the rock of his barrow and, with joy, embraces it motionless for a week.)

(Thanksgiving. Down to visit his folks — right in the front door! The whole family gathered at the table, even his cousins, nine and fifteen. Thanksgiving, joyful reunion.

You two, over here, says his mother, pulling gently the terrified girls. *We'll all just let him alone. He won't hurt us. Let him alone.*

He has not spoken for two years. He croaks: *I would like some pop.* The glass shakes in his hand. The things of people no longer fit him well.

He lowers his head to his father's plate, bites, eats thigh, and lopes out.

Later yellow jackets congregate on his fingers to mob the gravy.)

Blessings, blessings, and his people are winning the war. He overhears the congregations of spirits of other places, their vast stances in prairies and in chaparral, in lagoon and shipping port, their parliaments, their twittering ancient tongue.

The war is won. He cannot stop laughing with delight that night and creeps down to watch the parade from the recessed doorstep of McMurphy's Electronics. The faces of his children glaring with relief — home. Oh, the dinners that will be served.

Then he is ancient. For a long time he sleeps. The snow falls gently on his barrow, but gently and long mean heavy and deep. She and he whisper their dreams to each other.

("I saw him at the parade," says Mike.

Tammy asks, "How did he look?"

Mike shrugs. "Crazy. He smells like shit. Because he sits all day in his own shit."

Tammy gets up from the table. "He's a hero," she says.

Mike eats a sugar cube. "He's off his nut." Then, as she leaves the diner: "Tam, Tam! Tam!")

In the barrow, the hill's husband dreams of local grasses.

3. THE SOLEMNITIES

When Tammy's father died in 1973, she came back to town with the kids. The mills were shut up, and Main Street was not doing well. The power lines all hung lower than she remembered.

She was going to be there for a week. She had to move her mother

into a nursing home and then shut up the house and prepare it to sell. The kids were ticked off about having to come and spent a lot of time in the empty barn, smoking where their gramma wouldn't catch them.

Tammy dragged boxes of old documents onto the dining-room table and sorted them while her mother slept on the sofa. She made a stack to ask her mother about. Most of the papers could have been thrown away years ago: offers for aboveground pools; news articles about neighbors winning pageants; utility bills from the '50s.

She had heard from a high-school friend that the only Thwait had died. He had last been seen sometime in '67, shambling around the back streets. When no one saw him the next spring or summer, the town coroner went up to the grove on the peak of the hill and found his body. It was buried up there in a pit with the other husbands, according to custom. There were no more Thwaits left for the town.

"Good thing," said Tammy's friend over breakfast. "That guy creeped everyone out. Remember him in school? He was really quiet. Then — wow. Humping the hill. Doug used to talk about him to frighten the kids. 'If you don't eat all your . . . chicken or whatever . . . if you don't eat it, the Thwait will break in tonight looking for it. He's real hungry . . . Real, real hungry.'" Tammy's friend put up her claws, made crazy eyes, and clacked her teeth.

The realtor suggested that Tammy should have the house painted before she put it on the market. It was going to be expensive to paint, though. Tammy asked whether she couldn't hire some local teens to do it cheap, rather than pay professionals a mint. She wished she could at least scrape it herself. When the realtor left, Tammy went back to sorting papers. She and the kids dragged all the old crap no one would ever want out to the street. It sat there for a day before the dump came. In that time Tammy was surprised to see the broken things people took.

That week Tammy made the family simple meals like grilled cheese or spaghetti. She couldn't bear to think about complicated cooking. Everything in the kitchen was dirty and nothing was in its place. Her mother complained that the toasted cheese was burnt.

One day Tammy left her mother in the care of the kids and walked to Quick Hill. It was a warm day in early spring. The clouds were always brief. She discovered a rough path up the slope. Cigarette cellophane and cans of Old Milwaukee Light were tangled in the grasses. Some of the beer cans were bleached white from the sun.

She walked up through the old orchard where she had glimpsed him several times before the war ended. It was not as overgrown as she remembered it. She did not like to think about the weird expressions he had made on his face when he saw her.

She came to the grove at the top of the hill. She could hear the traffic of the highway and the main streets through the branches.

There was the stone he had sat on years ago, with his head down. She suspected it marked the burial pit. She peeked into the barrow. It was empty. There was a condom wrapper on the dirt. Using leaves as a glove, she picked it up and hurled it into the bushes. She didn't want people leaving their trash.

She stood for a long time in the grove. She said his name once, quietly — *Don* — and wondered if he could hear.

There was one time, she remembered, that some women had come to town offering to preserve people's breath. A lot of the kids from the high school had been sent by their parents to ward off sudden death. They had all been so scared back then. The whole town. Don Thwait, she recalled, had been a few people in front of her in line.

She watched him particularly, because she had just recently heard about him and the hill, and she was curious. Tammy inspected his sweater. He stood with his hands on his pockets but not in them.

A woman in glasses called out, "Next? Over here, honey," and he stepped out of the line and walked over and stood there in front of the woman, waiting for instructions. Tammy noticed how quiet he was within himself, how straight he stood.

Then he bent forward and breathed into the woman's mouth.

Tammy wished she could have been the one to cherish his breath. She would have held it in her chest.

Now, standing in the grove on the top of his hill, over the spot where he lay, she inhaled deeply; and when her lungs were full, she did not let go.

THE
Diabolist

NATHAN BALLINGRUD

For many years, we knew our monster. He was a middle-aged man, prickly of temperament and reclusive of habit, but of such colorful history and exotic disposition that we forgave him these faults and regarded him with a fond indulgence. He was our upstart boy, our black sheep. He lived in a faded old mansion by the lake and left us to gossip at his scandalous life story. It was a matter of record that he had been drummed out of a prestigious university that had employed him in the southern part of the state, his increasingly eccentric theories and practices costing him his job, his reputation, and — it was whispered, and we believed it because it was too wonderful not to — the life of his own beloved wife.

Dr. Timothy Benn, metaphysical pathologist.

Theomancer.

THE DIABOLIST

Sometimes the sky around his house would light up after dark with whatever wicked industry kept him awake, bright reds and greens and yellows igniting the bellies of the clouds like a celestial carnival show, or like an iridescent bruise. Once he seemed to have tipped the axis of gravity, so that loose objects — pebbles in the road, dropped key rings, toddlers tossed into the air by fathers — fell toward his house instead of the ground. This only lasted a few minutes, and we responded with bemused patience. It was one of the quirks of sharing a small town with a known diabolist.

And so it was that we enjoyed the company of our resident monster and the particular glamour he afforded us, until the day he died, and you found him there.

Dearest Allison.

We didn't know you like we knew him. Like him, you were sullen and withdrawn, but you lacked any of the outlandish characteristics that made him so charming to us. You did not puncture holes in time and space. You did not draw angels from the ether and bind them with whores' hair. You only lived, like any awkward girl, attending ninth grade in a cloud of resentment and distrust, hiding your eyes behind your bangs and your ungainly body beneath baggy clothes and a shield of textbooks clutched to your chest. We saw you in class, sitting in the back row with your head down; we saw you weaving like an eel through hallways choked with strangers; we saw you when you came down from the mansion on pilgrimages to the grocery store, where you were as disappointingly mundane in your selections as you were in every other aspect of your life.

After school, after shopping, we'd watch you climb into your father's car with the tinted windows, engine growling at the curb, and disappear up the hill into the mansion.

For all the attention you paid to us, you might have been moving through a world erased of people.

We loved your father, but we did not love you.

The miracle began the night of his death. We imagine the scenario: He put you to bed, kissing you lightly on your forehead. You asked him a small, domestic question: about homework — or, no, about an imminent camping trip that you were excited for. He answered you noncommittally — he did not want to disappoint you, but after all there was work to be done. He walked downstairs and retired to his study, in the room overlooking the lake. He poured himself a healthy measure of single-malt Scotch and retrieved a crime novel from his bookshelf. Reclining in his easy chair, we like to think that he enjoyed some of these small pleasures for a while. Then he closed his eyes, leaned back, and quietly died, felled by the interruption of some mysterious inner function.

You came downstairs the next morning, Allison, and you found him there. Oh, how we would like to have seen your expression. To watch the tide of grief.

Instead, there is only this frustrating period of darkness in our narrative, stretching from that morning until the morning of the following day.

You did not call any of us for help.

What did you do, Allison?

Did you cry? Did you scream?

Did you think of us at all?

We find you again the next morning.

A Saturday, early. We saw your feet and your ankles poised at the top of the cellar stairs. You paused there, at the edge of this dark gulf, uncertain of yourself. A low, steady hiss emerged from somewhere below, like an unending exhalation. You'd never been allowed in your father's laboratory before; standing there was a transgression. But after that pause, you descended with purpose, and we saw you: pale white legs, pink shorts, wrinkled black shirt, and finally your face, moonlike and frightened. You swept your hand over the light switch and threw the laboratory into flickering clarity.

Rows of shelving and workbenches filled the vast work space, each one crowded with repurposed wine boxes and milk crates, which held overstuffed three-ring binders or notebooks or jars of formaldehyde densely packed with biological misadventures. There was an aquarium empty of fish and ornament, with two severed blue eyes lolling on the bright blue gravel, tracking you as you passed; a huge telescope dominating the cellar's far corner, its wide glass eye raised toward the closed root-cellar doors; a broken, bloody Mason jar sitting at the center of a pentagram chalked onto the floor beneath one of the workbenches; and six large double-stacked dog crates with children's names stenciled on the outsides, all empty save one, which was home to an abandoned stuffed lion. The walls were covered with parchment bearing a strange pictographic alphabet. Hanging among them were your own endeavors, paintings your father had retained from your elementary-school days.

And then there were the small accumulations of a normal life: the desk chair with the wheels that stick; the crumpled bags of potato chips on the floor; the Minnesota Twins mug sitting beside the dormant laptop, still holding an inch of milky coffee, dirty water at the bottom of a well.

And in the back of the room, nearly hidden by the clutter, was the vat. It was huge, clear, slightly taller and wider than a refrigerator, mounted on an industrial-capacity cooling unit. It was filled with a bright green gel, which seemed faintly luminescent. A radio was affixed to the side of the vat with duct tape and twine; a spaghetti snarl of wires trailed from it to the vat's base, where it disappeared into the side.

This was where the hiss was coming from. It sputtered as you approached. When you stood at your father's desk, close enough to the vat to caress it, if you had wanted to, the static barked, and a voice, genderless and faint, swam up from the deeps of chaos and noise to speak to you.

"I know you," it said.

Just briefly, your face shone with the hard light of hope.

"I know you," I said again, willing my speech through the long black crush of empty space. "You're the daughter."

And you spoke to me for the first time: "Who are you?"

I never had a name, until your father gave one to me. I was a wretch, one imp among a numberless multitude of imps working in the Love Mills on the Eighty-Fourth Declension of Hell. I did not know language until I was pulled here by your father's sorcery and learned it after hearing him speak a single word; I did not know of my own individuality until I was peeled from the shared consciousness and from my own body, to be imprisoned as a scrap of thought in this

vat; and I did not know love, though my whole existence was bent to its creation, until I saw your father's face crumple in despair when he realized that the thing he had plucked from Hell was not the one he had sought.

I knew something had happened to him, though I had no word for death. In the middle of the night I was engulfed in a falling tide of his dreams, thoughts, and memories, which came raining through the ceiling like gouts of ash, as if a volcano were expunging all the dry contents of the earth. It was a bewildering experience, vertiginous and exhilarating — like nothing I had ever known. It had not abated all night, and continued even as you came down to the cellar. I could tell immediately that you did not see it or feel it. Your father's dead brain was geysering, filling the air with all its accumulated freight, and you had no way to apprehend it.

I suppose that could be considered a waste.

"Your father called me Claire, when I arrived," I told you, each word spitting through static, and I watched your face make a complicated movement: it displayed a mixture of sorrow and hope, which I have learned is part of love's vocabulary. You retreated to the desk and sat in your father's chair.

"That's my mother's name," you said.

"I know."

When you spoke again, your voice sounded strange, as though your throat were being squeezed: "Is that who you are?"

"No."

You were silent for a long time. The radio on my vat hissed, like rainfall or like the sound of your father's spilling brain. You leafed through the pages of a journal he'd kept on the desk. You turned on the computer but were unable to supply the password necessary

to get into it. Your search did not seem to be motivated by any real curiosity, though; you seemed stunned by something. Only partially there.

"Where is your father?" I asked you.

You sighed, as if I'd said something tedious. "He's dead."

"Oh," I said, understanding suddenly where the tide of dream flakes were coming from. "Is that why you're upset?"

"I'm not upset." You looked at me, as if you thought I should have a response to that. But I didn't know how to answer you, Allison. I envied your detachment. I was cast adrift from my brethren, isolated for the first time. I had never known loneliness. It caused me a grievous pain.

Pain, too, was something new.

How do your kind live like this? How do you not wish to extinguish yourselves from the cold misery of it? How do you know each other at all?

"So, you're something Dad conjured up? Like a demon or something?"

"I'm not a demon. I'm an imp. I'm a laborer in the Love Mills."

"What are those?" You didn't look at me as you asked these questions. Instead you walked slowly around the lab, tracing your finger across the pictographs or stopping to study one of your own early finger paintings.

"I don't know how to answer that in a way you can understand."

"Wow, you sound just like Dad."

You did not sound as though that were a good thing.

"I want to go home," I said, hoping to turn this conversation along a more productive course.

You stopped at the dog cages with the children's names. "What did

he do down here? I mean, I know he, like . . . summoned devils or whatever." You turned to look at me. "Is that what he did?"

"I don't know what he did before I arrived. I know that he was not pleased to see me though."

"You were an accident?"

"Yes."

You nodded and returned to his desk. You opened a manila envelope and a stack of photographs spilled out. They were of your mother. They were casual and unposed. Your father looked at them often. Sometimes they brought him to tears. Sometimes they made him angry. I couldn't understand how the same images could provoke such opposed reactions, and I was curious to see how you responded. You stared at them for a long time, too, but your expression did not change.

You put them down and said, "My dad's body is still upstairs. I haven't called anybody. I guess that's messed up."

"Is it?"

"It's what I'm supposed to do. I'm supposed to cry too."

"Why?"

You shrugged. "Because he's my dad."

"Then why don't you?"

"I'm a monster I guess."

I didn't understand this. It seemed unimportant, so I returned to my own concern. "I want to go home, Allison. I want my body back. I'm lonely here."

"Well, you can't," you said. "I don't know how to send you home. You're just going to have to suck it up."

"That's unacceptable."

You stood, calmly and with such poise, and approached the vat.

This time you did put your hand on it, and though I should not have been able to, I felt the heat of your blood, the warmth of human proximity. I did not know what it meant, but it stunned me into silence.

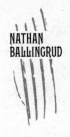

NATHAN BALLINGRUD

"You were meant to be Mom, did you know that? He was trying to bring back Mom."

I had nothing to say to that. I remembered his horrified reaction the night he pulled me here and discovered what I really am. My first glimpse of love's face.

"I'm going upstairs," you said, turning away from me.

I felt a wild and fearful longing. "Don't leave me here," I said, my voice lost in the crackle of the radio.

You just kept walking. You turned off the lights as you ascended and left me there, the green light from my vat and my strange liquid form throwing shadows into the dark air. I had never been alone like this. I began to understand that it would last forever.

Finally, you came down to us. The day was overcast and windy; you descended the long road into town, your hair, for once, not obscuring your face but trailing behind you like a dark and unfurled flag. Maybe this unprecedented event should have been enough to let us know that something had gone wrong. But we were creatures caught in our own routine. We were unsuspicious and ignorant. It's hard to know a miracle for what it is until it finally occludes the world with its beauty.

You went to the café in our local bookstore and bought a coffee, ignoring the clerk's open stare as you gave her your order. Her name was Tina; she was a senior, three years ahead of you in school and

bound for the very university that had driven your father out years ago. Her younger sister was in your computer science class, so she was privy to all the latest gossip and rumor surrounding you. She leaned forward a fraction and sniffed the air, to see if it was true that you didn't bathe, that you stank of body odor. She couldn't smell anything but assumed that this was because the jacket you were wearing obscured it. When she took your money, she was careful not to let her fingers touch yours, and she dropped the change onto the counter rather than put it into your hand.

Did you notice these minor insults?

Tina was so close to leaving our town. If your father had lived only another six or seven months, she would have missed out on everything.

You waited out Tina's shift, and then Joey came in. He saw you sitting there, and he felt a mixture of fear, anger, and excitement. He remembered going to the Devil's Willow with you earlier in the year, making out with you and wanting to go further but being told no. He remembers the humiliation he felt, the thwarted urge, and remembers too the fear of what people would say if they found out he'd tried to score with the town freak. He hadn't spoken to you or even looked at you since. Your sudden presence there scared him and excited him all over again.

You ignored Tina's hostile stare as she walked away. When Joey was alone behind the counter, you approached him.

"Meet me there tonight," you said.

Something inside him twisted. He was afraid you were setting him up. Someone like you — an ugly girl, an unwanted girl — had no right. "What are you talking about, skank?" he said.

"You know what I'm talking about. Just be there tonight."

"I don't just come when you call. What makes you think you can even talk to me?"

"Whatever. Come or don't. This is your only chance."

You left him there. He spent the rest of his shift in a slow-burning rage, because although he was determined not to go, he knew that he would.

The Devil's Willow grew like a gnarled temple on the far side of the lake. Its brilliant green foliage spilled over and trailed into the water, like a suspended fountain, hiding the bent, blackened wood of the trunk. It got its name from the fact that we believed your father practiced some of his infernal rites there. Some nights we'd see dozens of little candle flames arrayed beside it, or even suspended in the air around it, and there was that one whole week when the entire tree was engulfed in a cold, green-white fire. Julie lost her virginity to Thom there last year, and although she never admitted this to anyone, she was afraid that she'd gotten pregnant and that her baby would be born with a goat's head. When she got her period she cried with relief and terror and her hands shook so badly at school that day, they sent her home early.

You went there after leaving Joey at the café. Were you planning the night ahead? Were you there for the silence, or were you trying to get closer to the dark energies of your father's practice? We saw the shape of you as you sat lakeside, your feet dipped into the water, leaning back on your hands like some pale white orchid.

It seems that you were always just a shape to us, Allison. We knew you as the absence at the center of our impressions. We guessed at your motives, at your relationship with your father, and at your

THE DIABOLIST

reactions to our taunts and provocations. Although we were content to imagine your interior life for all these years, now we want to know the truth of it. We don't want to guess at you anymore, Allison.

We want to know if you feel what we do.

I know a story of the lake.

There are no stories in the Love Mills. There is no one to tell them, and there is no one to listen; for an imp, there is nothing but the work of building and maintaining the mills. It was not until I came to this cold tomb of a world that an idea like *story* was ever introduced to me.

I did not hear it from your father, who did not forgive me for not being his wife. He worked at his various errands in silence. It's only since he died that I've come to hear from him. He sits up there in his study, reclining in his chair like a dead king, his head a volcano of dream ash, a ghostly plume of whatever made him a human being pouring out of him like a long sigh. It's beautiful, Allison, and it's a tragedy that you can't see it.

The story of the lake was a shower of cinders that fell through me after you left. I don't know if it's based on something he read or if it's something he made up. I don't even know whether or not he believed it. The story goes that there was once an angel that roamed these hills, in the early days of your kind, long before you had dominion over the world. The angel was a giant to men, a gyre of eyes and wings and talons, stranger and more fearsome than they could withstand. They ran from it in terror. The belief is that it was one of the last of the angels to join Lucifer's rebellion. It arrived too late, and the gates of Hell were sealed. An outcast from both kingdoms, it wandered here alone until it could no longer bear the isolation. The angel found a deep lake — this one, Allison — and went to sleep at its bottom, where it would remain for the rest of time.

I don't know if the story is true. I don't know whether your father believed it or just made it up himself, the way your kind seem to do. But I drew comfort from it. It made me less lonely. It's about the Morningstar, and to hear him spoken of, even in this secondary way, opened a cascade of beauty inside me. I felt a terrible yearning for my home and my work. It was by that yearning that I knew the Morningstar's grace was still upon me. The ache of need is a music in the Love Mills.

Your father wondered if this town and everyone in it was just a dream itself, a figment the angel had created to keep itself company. Once I would have laughed at that. I would have told you that if it wanted companionship, it would not have dreamt creatures such as you.

Now I'm not so sure.

You came down to talk to me that night. You cooked yourself a dinner in the microwave and brought it downstairs, where you ate quietly at your father's desk. You left the lights off, sitting silently in the liquid green luminescence of the vat, listening to the quiet hiss of the radio. You did not acknowledge me, but your presence was a lovely surprise, and it went a great distance toward dispelling my loneliness. Though you didn't know it, it was an extraordinary act of kindness.

"I like it down here," you said. "It's like being at the bottom of the sea. No wonder Dad spent all his time here."

"I don't know the sea," I said.

"It's basically just like the lake outside, only a lot bigger."

"How much bigger?"

"It covers most of the world. Don't you know these things in Hell?"

The notion of a lake large enough to cover the world inspired that sense of yearning again. I don't know how I can ache for a place I've never been. My life had been defined by labor, by hard earth and turning bone and the pink blossoms of smoke rising from our industries, by striations of light across a sky obscured by a rosy curtain of ash. There was no sea. There was no lake. There was no wish for any other place.

Never did it occur to me to wonder what it was we labored to create.

"I don't really know anything about Hell. I was in the Love Mills. That's all I know."

You shook your head and nearly smiled. "Trust me. If my dad brought you here? You're from Hell. That was basically his thing."

"If you say so."

You pushed the plate away and took one of your father's notebooks, leaning back in the chair and paging through it with apparent disinterest. "So did he talk to you about Mom?"

"He didn't say anything to me."

"Join the club." You shook your head, thinking about it. "She wanted to leave us, you know? She didn't care." You crossed your arms on the desk and rested your head there, turned away from me. "I guess he really loved her," you said, and for a long while you said nothing else. I heard you sniff once, and I knew you were crying. I recognized this as another manifestation of love. I was coming to know all of its wonderful facets. The kind you felt was like mine: a wanting that cannot be satisfied. The kind your father felt for your mother was different. It was the kind with hooks.

After a moment, you lifted your head and looked at me. "Anyway, I came down here to see what I had to do to flush you out of there. It's right here in the notebook. I'm not sure what that'll do to you. Send you back home maybe, or kill you. So you might as well go ahead and enjoy your life for a little while longer because I'm going to go upstairs and get wasted then come down here and do it."

I did not know how to receive this information, so I said nothing. The only example of death I had was your own father, whose death seemed to have done little to change him, other than fixing him in place. After all, he still sat in his chair on the floor above us, unfurling his unspent thoughts into the air. The other possibility — being sent back home — was too wonderful to contemplate.

"And then I'm going to do one of dad's rituals."

"What do you mean?"

"I've been looking through his notebooks. It doesn't look too hard. And since he just died, maybe I can get him back. Maybe it's not too late."

"I don't understand. I thought you didn't care."

"I don't." The tears came back, but you made no move to hide them this time. "I don't care. I don't care."

Even in its absence, love pulled at you with its terrible gravity. Your face was beautiful in its anguish. I could see the work of my life at play. The house was filled with it, Allison. Love in all its grandeur. What shapes it made of your lives. What shapes it makes still.

Your father's thoughts had begun to cool, fluttering down to me now rarely, like leaves from an old tree, nearly spent. One drifted past, stately and blue. You were younger; you were on the couch watching

TV with him. You'd had a good day; you were tired and warm. You leaned over and rested your head on your father's shoulder. He pushed you away. You apologized and leaned in the other direction. Shame consumed him.

He wanted to be touched with another kind of love. What a daughter could offer him just wasn't enough.

You flushed the vat as I considered that thought. The floor opened beneath me and I flowed through a narrow chute in a wild green torrent, sliding through darkness for several disorienting minutes until I splashed from the end of a culvert and flew through the clear air, landing finally in the warm lake and dissolving there.

It was like waking. It can only be like waking.

I saw the stars overhead. I felt the ripple of wind, the pull of the roots of the Devil's Willow. I felt the bed of earth below me, and the great slow-beating heart of the thing buried under the cold mud.

I am a lake, Allison. You have made me anew.

Joey met you under the Devil's Willow. He was angry and scared, but just proud enough to believe that you regretted your earlier rejection of him and wanted him after all. He didn't come alone. He wanted to make you pay for the embarrassment you'd caused him, so he had two of his friends follow. They were meant to hide in the bushes several yards away and take pictures of you as you undressed, to pass around the school. Joey meant to have his revenge.

You were waiting for him beneath the willow. You had a picnic blanket spread out and half a dozen candles lit, their flames trembling in the cool night air. The sky was high and cold, icy with stars. You sat on the middle of the blanket, your legs curled beneath you, a glass of whiskey already in your hand. Joey paused when he saw all of this. He considered doubling back to call off his friends.

But his fear of you was too great, so he didn't. He stopped at the edge of the blanket and stood frozen.

"Come on," you said.

"Are you drunk?"

"Just a little."

"Without me? That's not fair."

"Well, sit down and catch up with me, then."

He dropped to his knees and moved closer to you. You handed him the bottle, and he took it. You let him take a good swig, his head tilted back, before you slipped the knife cleanly between his ribs. You held it there for a moment, your hand wrapped tightly around the handle.

"Ow!" He looked down at what you had done. He hardly believed it was real. It felt so small; like a wasp sting. "You bitch! You stabbed me!"

You slid the knife free, and it was like pulling the stopper from a bottle of wine: the blood gouted from the wound, and Joey fell forward, catching himself with one hand while holding the other to his side. The pain careened through him now, unbelievable in its ferocity. "What?" he said, and his voice sounded small, like the child he still was.

I watched your face for a reaction. You looked pale, but otherwise you betrayed no emotion.

"Help me," he said.

There was a rustling from the bushes several feet away and you looked up, alarmed. His two friends, boys you must have seen at high school with Joey, crept uncertainly out of hiding. One held his camera phone at his side.

"Dude. Are you okay?"

You stood, the knife drooling in your hand.

"I think you better call an ambulance," Joey said, his voice high-pitched with fear.

Because they were fools, the boys ignored him and ran forward. One dropped to Joey's side, and the other screamed at you, calling you filthy names, his body rigid with shock. You ignored them all; you were watching the tree.

A cold tongue of fire crept up from the roots and coiled around the trunk. Several more followed, and in moments the Devil's Willow was a pale green-white conflagration, shedding no heat but filling the little valley with its weird radiance. I felt the thing that slept beneath the mud stir beneath my waters. Every slow churn of its heart brightened the willow's fire.

You spoke it. "Bring him back. Please just bring him back. I'll do whatever you want. I'll kill them all. I'll kill everyone."

I realized then that you were talking to the Morningstar. Your unfilled want, Allison, the hollow in your heart and the love that goes unanswered, is a prayer to the Morningstar. Your whole life is a hymn to Hell.

I think that's when I felt love, myself, for the first time.

"I don't know what to do," you said.

You couldn't bring back your father, though; whatever sorcery your father practiced, you did not know it. You'd started something, but you did not know how to go further. In moments you would be brought down by these stupid boys, and what might happen after that I couldn't even guess.

But if the Morningstar could not respond to you, I could.

I couldn't speak to you without the radio. I would have to show you.

Joey made it easy. He lay gasping on the blanket, his friend's hand pressed into his side. The heel of his left shoe resting in the water. So I pulled him in. It only took a moment; it was easy. I had become the lake, diffused into it like a breath into the atmosphere. I poured myself into his eyes, down his throat; I filled him like a vessel. Then I used him to pull in his friend, and I filled him too. In moments I had all three. I felt their life sparking in me. For the first time since being brought here, I knew a communal mind again. I was no longer alone. And so began the miracle you brought to our town.

We stood panting by the shore, feeling our new selves. We glanced at each other, ashamed at this new intimacy at first, at the torrents of knowledge that poured into us, all our shabby secrets and desires brought to sudden light. But the shame dissipated quickly; there can be no secrets if we all share the same mind.

The same love.

We looked at you, Allison. We spoke to you in a chorus of voices: "Come here, Allison."

The look on your face — I didn't know it. Was it another kind of love? Was there yet more to learn?

"Who are you?" you asked.

"You know," we said.

You turned and fled. It was a shocking rejection. We didn't understand. Isn't this what you wanted? To be welcomed? To be loved?

The tree lit the night and soon drew other people from town.

THE DIABOLIST

They joined us, reluctantly at first — many had to be forced into the water, where the imp could pour into them — but they were grateful soon enough. By the time morning approached, we had everyone.

We decided to work. It was what we knew. The memory of the mills drove us along. Many of us went into the lake to be consumed in the labor. Limbs were broken and reconfigured, bone grafted to bone, kites of skin stretched taut. It took two hundred people broken down and reassembled to make the skeleton of the mill's first wheel; there is more to be done.

As the sun crests the hills, the mill begins to turn in the lake. We lift our voice in a chorus of groans. We bend to you like reeds to the light. Why don't you respond, Allison? Why have you never responded to us, despite every provocation?

We used to know our monster. Now we know ourselves, but we still do not know you. We see you with ten thousand eyes, standing at the window of your house, your hollowed-out father still sitting behind you like a deposed king. His head has gone cold and quiet. You're staring out at us. You press your hand to the glass. Can you feel the warmth of us, the way I once felt yours?

Your face makes a complicated movement, an expression we believe will tell us something about you. But before we can read it, the sunlight hits the glass and the glare of it reflects back to us, a tiny star in the morning light.

THIS Whole Demoning Thing

PATRICK NESS

If she was honest with herself, Angela would have happily dropped the whole being-a-fire-breathing-demon thing in favor of just playing keyboards and singing backup in her normal face, maybe under smoke and black lights or something, you know, so no one could object or look at her like she was a freak.

But that, apparently, was out of the question.

"What?" Austin asked, venom dripping down his pointed chin. "You mean . . . What do you mean?"

"Nothing," she said, feeling sheepish now. She coughed nervously into her hand, forgot about the fire breathing, and burned most of the hair off the back of her knuckles. Fortunately, her skin in Aspect was mostly fireproof. It still hurt, though. "Ouch," she said, quietly.

"God, Angela," Josh said, scratching the wall of her garage with his tail. "You're such a freak sometimes."

"Could you not . . . ?" she said, watching the tail leave another mark in the plaster. "Never mind."

Josh poked the plaster harder, carving out a small hole, before lashing his tail forward to hit the cymbals with a crash. He was a really good drummer as a demon, even Angela had to admit it, the tail coming in useful for extra percussion, but he did like to scratch people. Even Angela's demonskin couldn't stand up to the bone spire at the tail's end.

"That would be weird, though," Austin said, scratching a thoughtful claw under his ear.

"It's just that my tongue goes fireproof in Aspect," she said, quietly. "Makes it a little harder to . . ." She trailed off because the boys were staring at her.

"Conrad doesn't even have a mouth," Josh said, pointing his tail at their bass player. "And he's all right."

This wasn't quite accurate: Conrad had a mouth — it was just sewn shut. He tried to claim it as a learning disability, but the school made him unlace it during class anyway, despite the laces being right back in place every time he shifted in and out of Aspect. He pointed at them now and waved a friendly hand at Angela. She'd always liked Conrad. He was a good listener.

"Forget it," Angela said, smiling bashfully. "It's okay. I'll make do." She idly tapped out a few electronic *parp*s on her keyboard.

Austin nodded at her. Then nodded at her again. He was so beautiful, it almost hurt her to look at him, especially when he was looking so directly back at her.

Parp, she played. *Parp parp*.

Then he said, "Let's do 'The Beauty of Reckoning,' maybe?"

Josh and Conrad readied themselves, Angela did a quick

programming change on the keyboard to Gothic Choir, and Austin raised his hand over his guitar, ready to strike.

"ONE! TWO! THREE! FOUR!"

The Becoming weren't the only band at school, but they were — as Josh liked to sneer — the only "proper rock band." There was Glee Club, as ever, but it was having a seriously off year. There were two hip-hop groups — one not bad, one stomach-turningly embarrassing; and there was also Margaret "Megs" Stuart, who did amazing things with electronics and samples and who ended up deejaying all the school dances. Her Aspect had nine hands, which helped.

But The Becoming played loud, hard, fast guitar stuff with Angela's keyboards and programming filling in all the extra space and tending to cover their musical weak spots, which were many. Aside from Josh on the drums, she was the only one who could really play an instrument, having taken piano lessons since she was tiny. Fortunately when her Aspect had come in at twelve, it had left her with the correct number of joints on the correct number of fingers. She'd been secretly worried because her elder sister Samantha was a full serpent in Aspect (the school had allowed her to take her tests verbally, and she was doing great stuff now as a prelaw undergrad at the University of Washington), but it had turned out okay. Angela had surprised everyone, including herself, with the fire breathing, but that had its uses, especially on camping trips.

She could, of course, still play just fine out of Aspect, but that so wasn't cool.

She opened her locker, only to have it slammed shut again by a massive hand reaching in behind her. She turned with a sigh to the twelve feet of lizard-thing looming over her in the hallway.

"Please, Holly," Angela said. "I've got to get to class."

"I told you to stay away from Austin," Holly hissed, her tongue lapping in and out like a party favor. "But somehow your face is still on this."

Holly held out the flyer for the school dance on Friday night. Under a giant picture of Megs, her nine hands unfurled, was a smaller photo of "Opening Act: The Becoming" with the snarling faces of Austin, Conrad, Josh, and, yes, Angela. The Becoming's first-ever gig. Angela couldn't help but smile at it.

"I'm not quitting the band, Holly," she said calmly. "I told you."

Two thunderous fists drove into the lockers on either side of Angela, pinning her there. "And I told you," Holly growled, her snout angling down from her giraffe-length neck, "to keep your ugly little claws off of Austin Diaz."

"My claws aren't ugly, and they're not on —"

"He's mine, acid-breath," Holly sneered. "Not that he'd ever look twice at a flat-chested nothing like you. Even your Aspect looks like a crumpled piece of paper."

Angela met her eye. "Are you finished?"

"You think you're just a little bit better than everybody, don't you?" Holly's tongue flicked Angela's face a few times. "Perfect little Angela Constable. Pretending like you never burp or fart. Always saying 'please' and 'thank you.'"

"Please stop doing that with your tongue —"

"Well, you're just a demon like the rest of us, Angela."

"Yes," Angela said. "Yes, I am."

She opened her mouth wide and unleashed a torrent of fire into Holly's face, while at the same time sweeping up across Holly's front with the same ugly little claws Holly had just been deriding. A huge hunk of flesh came out with them, and Holly howled in agony as the fire boiled her eyes and turned her tongue to ash.

She stepped out of Aspect, holding a startled hand to her cheek. "You bitch," she said, astonished.

The hallway around them had frozen now, everyone staring at Holly in her jeans and T-shirt, her hair pulled back in a simple girl-jock ponytail. In reflexive sympathy, Angela dropped out of Aspect, too, and was surprised to be reminded that she was actually taller than normal Holly.

"Sorry," Angela said, "but you can't talk to me that way. And I'm not quitting the band. I told you, I'm not interested in Austin —"

"Liar," Holly said, re-Aspecting, her wounds disappearing. She ducked her head down so it wouldn't bump the ceiling and pointed a pus-covered talon in Angela's face. "This isn't over." She stormed off down the hallway, her Godzilla tail knocking down some of the smaller bystanders.

Angela sighed and re-Aspected, too, then jumped at a touch on her shoulder, holding up a claw, ready to strike. Conrad held up his rotting hands in friendly surrender and raised a questioning eyebrow.

"Yeah, I'm okay, thanks," Angela said, returning to her locker and getting out books for math. "She thinks everyone will be scared by her size, so she's got no moves beyond that."

Conrad nodded.

"Still," Angela said, slightly worried. "I hope I didn't hurt her. I mean, I know they're not permanent injuries, but sometimes a cruel word can . . ."

Conrad gave a dusty laugh through the laces and shook his head.

"I know," Angela said. "Pathetic."

Conrad looked around at the emptying hallway and quickly de-Aspected. *He has such lovely red hair,* Angela thought, *and a nice little smile.*

"Not pathetic," he said. "Kind."

"Is there a difference?" she replied.

There were several things Angela knew to be true.

The first was that her presence in The Becoming was down to Conrad hearing her accompany the seventh-grade choir — of which his little brother was a tone-deaf but enthusiastic member — and convincing Austin that she was the missing ingredient in their new band. And by "missing ingredient," he meant someone who could read music. Plus, she could program the hell out of a keyboard and make it sound like a whole orchestra was backing them up, making it less important that Austin's guitars and Conrad's bass struggled to reach competent on a good day.

The second thing she knew to be true was that this had instantly elevated her from middlingly unnoticed in terms of popularity to what-the-hell-is-she-doing-in-a-band hostility, catching the hitherto negligible attention of people like Holly Spelman, who had a serious, serious thing for Austin Diaz.

The third was that most people had a serious, serious thing for Austin Diaz. Even in Aspect — especially in Aspect — he had as much charisma dripping off him as he did venom from his chin. His Aspect was horned and reddish green, but his eyes bore into you like you were the only person he would ever want to talk to. When he sang (at which he was perfectly adequate) and played guitar (at which he was a pretty good singer), you couldn't stop looking at him. That was the important thing, more than talent, more than simple beauty. He became the song, one you were already wanting to hear again. With the right band behind him, he could easily go on to be some kind of megastar.

The fourth thing was that The Becoming was clearly not that band. Still, Angela had been surprised to find herself saying yes and even more surprised to find herself enjoying the practices so immensely. It had, in fact, been a bit of a revelation. She'd always played piano solo or as lone accompaniment to a choir or a singer in church, but in a band, when the music was loud and everyone was on and she was singing along, she could just lose herself in it all. In the volume, in the energy, in the sheer burning, boiling spirit of creation as the four of them made this spectacular sound. It felt like some-thing was about to happen, that potential was boiling away, waiting to be reached, as if she'd left this weak earth and found a new place to live. In fact, she could disappear into it so much that she often fell out of Aspect without realizing it. Which tended to put a quick end to whatever song they were rehearsing as the boys looked at her uncomfortably.

The fifth thing she knew was that she had to be damned certain she didn't fall out of Aspect during the gig on Friday.

The sixth was because she didn't want to let the guys down, also a new feeling, having a group of friends counting this closely on you. She liked it.

The seventh was that she especially didn't want to let Austin down. Which perhaps was less comfortable.

The eighth was that it was uncomfortable because she knew

Holly was completely deluded about both Angela "getting her claws" on Austin and also that Holly was somehow destined to get him instead.

Because the ninth thing she knew was that Austin was far more likely to ask out Conrad than he ever was Holly, and, in fact, the tenth thing was that she'd already overheard him doing so after the last rehearsal.

The eleventh was that Conrad had said yes.

And the twelfth was that none of that had stopped her liking Austin in that way anyway. Which she hoped to get over, but getting over it wasn't something she knew would happen just yet, so her list had no thirteen.

"We should open with 'The Victor and the Vanquished,'" Austin whispered behind her in math class.

"Too long," Josh said, shaking his head in the next desk over. "You can't open with an eleven-minute dirge. It should go second."

Conrad slipped a note on her desk from where he was sitting beside Austin. "Open with 'Blood Tears,'" it read. "Get everyone dancing."

Angela nodded. "It's a dance, after all." She handed the note back to Austin and saw Holly Spelman three rows ahead, her long neck twisting back, her tongue flickering angrily as she watched the exchange.

Angela smiled peacefully at her, but there was probably no point.

"Less chatter back there," Miss Jenkins said, and her second and third heads nodded in agreement. "Laces out, Conrad. And turn around, Holly."

"I'm totally lost," Austin whispered, referring to what Miss Jenkins was now going through at the board.

"Think of it as a ratio," Angela whispered back. "If B is the angle, then sine is just —"

"Oh, God," Austin said, collapsing his head down onto his desk, accidentally poking Angela in the back with his horns.

"Ow."

"Sorry."

"It's okay."

"So are we opening with 'Blood Tears' or not?" the newly unlaced Conrad said, and there was a groan among the others at his breath, which in Aspect was nearly criminal.

"My God," Conrad said. "Has anyone ever said you have the bedroom an eighty-year-old woman?"

"Yes, actually," Angela said, setting her books down on her bed.

Conrad looked around warily at all the lace and light blues and Rufus the teddy bear, who Angela was a little too slow to hide. "No, don't," Conrad said, meaning Rufus. "It's nice."

She checked to see if he was making fun, but his non-Aspect face had nothing but truth on it. "It's stupid," she said, holding Rufus half protectively, half as if he might have been covered in vomit.

"Remember those stuffed dogs you could get that came with Aspect add-ons to make him a dragon?" Conrad said. "Called mine Thomas. Still have him. Is that a beanbag chair? Retro."

He flopped down on it, and Angela sat on the floor, her back against her bed. They were waiting for Austin and Josh to show up for band practice. They only had two rehearsals to go before Friday's

gig at the school. Angela felt nervous but pleasantly so, like how you do before opening a birthday present you're pretty sure will be exactly what you wanted.

She caught Conrad looking at her, his eyes appraising — not meanly, just out of curiosity — her short blond hair, her dark green eyes, her slightly too long nose, which was the least favorite of her non-Aspect features.

"You don't really like Aspect, do you?" he asked.

"Don't be stupid," she said, blushing. "What kind of freak doesn't like Aspect?"

"Your kind of freak. It's not that big a deal. Some people are just different."

She took a long breath as if to start contradicting him but then didn't. "I just don't like how it makes everyone so angry all the time. Like the monstrous face is the only one we have. The only one we're allowed to show people."

"You're showing me your other face. I'm showing you mine."

"And I like it," she said, meaning his other face and then blushed even more. "You know what I mean."

He grinned. "I really don't see why you couldn't sing out of Aspect, honestly."

"No, they're right. Everyone would stare. It'd be like I was naked up there. No one would listen to the music."

"If you make the music good enough," Conrad said seriously, "nothing else will matter."

Angela sighed. "I wish that were true."

He levered himself off the beanbag and sat down beside her. "The only reason I'm more comfortable in Aspect," he said, "is because no one expects me to say much."

"You're talking now."

"You're easy to talk to."

"Ah, yeah, because that's the kind of girl every boy wants to date."

There was a knock on the door as it was opening. Angela's mother poked her head through, the single horn on her forehead entering a few seconds before she did. "Everything all right in here, sweetheart? You guys want any cookies and pop?"

"No, thanks," Angela said, instantly back in Aspect, but then Conrad shoved her so hard with his rotting elbow she accidentally spit out a little fire. "Or, well, okay, sure. Cookies and pop."

"Coming right up." Her mother smiled. "Hi, Conrad."

He waved back. Angela's mother left but pointedly kept the door open behind her.

"She still thinks I'm ten years old," Angela said, back to normal.

"All mothers do," Conrad said, "but the big lesson here is never, ever say no to cookies and pop."

"Who is the Victor? Who is the Vanquished? Who is the Victor? Who is the Vanquished?"

Angela was in the song. Deep inside it. She wasn't even thinking about where her fingers needed to be on the keyboard — they went there without her having to ask. The chords, all three of them (she'd added the third), stormed through her in their progression. Lower-higher-middle. Lower-higher-middle. Like they were marching her feet right off the ground.

"Blazing skulls in deepest night! Thunder strikes with demon's might! Legions fight the wars of sin! But who will lose and who will win?"

Yes, okay, Austin was maybe not the world's greatest lyricist, but when the music was this loud, felt this deeply, who cared? Who could ever possibly care —

"Ah, shit."

Angela opened her eyes, unaware until just now that she'd actually closed them. She assumed she'd fallen out of Aspect again, but no, her claws were still there, faltering across the keys as the music slowly died. Instead, Josh and Conrad were looking at Austin, bent forward over his guitar, one hand up on his back.

"Dude," Josh complained, his tail tetchily whacking the hi-hat. "That was our best version yet. Why'd you stop?"

But Conrad was already hovering concerned next to Austin. "What's going on?" he said, de-Aspecting to speak.

"Just like the worst pain ever between my shoulders," Austin said.

Conrad looked closer at Austin's back. He glanced up at Angela. She could see it, too. A pair of small humps, scaly and yellow, pushed up from under Austin's skin.

"Dude," Josh said, more respectfully this time. "That's a new Aspect coming in."

"Piss off," Austin said, standing up, trying to peer behind his own shoulder. "I went through puberty about a hundred years ago."

"It's the music that's doing it," Josh said.

Conrad gave him a don't-be-a-moron look.

"No, I'm serious," Josh said, looking to Angela for support. "You were into it, too. I saw it."

"I was into it . . ." Angela said, hesitantly. She thought she knew what he meant. Not that the music was literally causing it, but maybe if you got moved strongly enough, if you were dedicating enough

of your, maybe *soul* was the right word, to it, then who knew what might happen.

"Probably just a cramp," Austin said, standing up again.

"*Cramps* don't cause humps," Josh said, surly now.

"Aspect is malleable," Conrad said. "He probably just tore his demonskin from the effort, and it healed up in a weird shape."

Josh's tail was like an annoyed cat's, snapping the tom-tom as if ready to strike. "No one ever listens to the drummer."

Austin returned to the mic, ready to play. Conrad was back in Aspect, but concern was still written across his laced-up, rotting features. Austin said to him, "I'm okay. All good." Then he turned to Angela with that heavily fanged smile. "You didn't shift out," he said. "Good stuff. Really good stuff." He nodded again, turning around to look at them all. "First time it felt like a real band, huh?"

"As long as you don't get any more cramps," Josh huffed.

"Shrug it off, Josh," Austin said. Then he smiled up at Angela again as if she was in on the joke. The directness of it caught her off guard, and she had to look away, swallowing down a burp of embarrassingly happy fire.

"From the beginning?" she was surprised to find herself asking, because — embarrassment aside — she really, really wanted to do it again. Wanted the feeling back. Wanted how true it made her feel. True enough to find a bit more of herself inside it. Who knew what else there was to discover?

"Count us in, Ange," Austin said.

Speaking through flames, she shouted it out for them. "ONE! TWO! THREE! FOUR!"

Angela's history and civics books went flying out of her hands and into the bushes. She looked up at Holly, towering above her. "Seriously?" Angela said. "You're knocking my books away now?"

"And what are you going to do about it?" Holly growled.

"You are the least competent bully I've ever heard of," Angela said, shaking her head. She went to pick up her books. Holly stepped on one of them. Angela sighed and slashed Holly's lizard calf with a handful of claws.

"I just don't understand you," Angela said, standing up as Holly limped back angrily. "Everyone's powerful in Aspect. Why do you keep forgetting?"

Holly de- and re-Aspected in a flash to heal her wound, her face first a human then a lizard picture of fury. She pulled back a massive fist to throw a punch.

"I shouldn't think so, Miss Spelman," Miss Jenkins said, two heads reading the papers in her hands, but the third admonishing Holly as she moved down the pathway. Holly lowered her arm, watching Miss Jenkins until she was out of earshot. She turned back to Angela.

"You never used to be like this," she spat out, as confused as she was angry.

"I used to take my beatings, you mean?" Angela said.

"Well, yeah."

Angela shook her head. "You're misremembering. You never even knew I existed before, except as that nice girl in the floral print dresses who played piano and was probably a counselor at church camp."

"'Misremembering'?" Holly echoed. "You talk like some old freak."

"We weren't even friends in elementary school —"

"You'd better not show up at the dance tonight. I'm warning you. If I see you with Austin —"

"Honestly, Holly, are you totally blind? Or does being a lizard shrink your brain as well?"

Angela felt herself flush — though you couldn't really see it under the dark gray skin — at being quite so blatantly mean. But it was also a little exciting, if she could admit it to herself. To not care for one minute. To be the monster. Maybe this is why everyone did it, stayed in Aspect all the time.

But then she saw how angry it made Holly, and she felt quite bad. If perhaps not bad enough to apologize just yet.

Holly closed in on her again, her voice a sibilant whisper. "You better watch that Teflon tongue of yours, Miss Remembering. Because you're right — everyone's powerful in Aspect."

"Well," Angela sighed to herself as she watched Holly stomp away, "at least she remembered to get the threat in."

On the night of the gig, their sound check was a disaster. Austin was always early in every song, Conrad always late, Josh too fast, and Angela too slow.

"Two hours!" Josh shouted. "We've got two hours left, and we sound like crap!" He banged his snare drum so hard with his tail, it went all the way through, tearing the drum beyond repair. His eyes went wide at the disaster.

"There's at least three snares in the band room," Angela said. "See if Mr. Zbornick will let us have one."

Josh nodded gratefully and got up to leave.

"Maybe tell him I'm asking for it," Angela said. "He knows me."

Josh nodded again and hurried out of the cafeteria.

"We're doomed," Austin said. "Even with a new snare."

"It's just nerves," Angela said. "I read somewhere that if you have a really bad rehearsal, then the actual thing goes really well. It's when rehearsals are perfect that you have to worry."

Austin blinked at her. "You're making that up."

"Maybe not," she said. "All we need to do is pretend no one's here."

Austin gestured at the empty cafeteria. "No one is here, and we still suck."

"I mean in our heads. If we can get to that place we do in rehearsals where nothing matters. Where it's the song doing what it has to do, like we're just trying to keep up with it and live inside it and be everything it needs for us to be, then isn't that like our name? Isn't that what we can do when it's all working? We become the song. We become what it needs us to be. And if we can do that, then everything else will be fine."

They stared at her for a minute. "I just thought our name sounded cool," Austin finally said. "I didn't think it meant anything."

Conrad nodded his agreement.

"But I like all the rest of that," Austin said, smiling at her now. "Is that how you feel when we play, Ange?"

She flushed again. "Don't you?"

He licked his fangs. "Yeah. Yeah, actually, I do." He turned to Conrad, who nodded again, seriously.

"We become," Austin said. "I like that." He took a sudden ferocious stab at his guitar, sending a wail of distortion and feedback across the empty hall.

It sounded thrilling.

"We become," he said again and winked at Angela.

And it was such a friendly wink, filled with so much affection and decency, with so much admiration and comradeship, that it kind of did the trick. Instantly and in the right sort of way, Angela fell out of love with him a little. Enough for it to matter, enough for it to count. She played the riff from "The Victor and the Vanquished" on her keyboard, and Conrad joined in on bass. Austin picked up the riff, and they blasted through it, furiously, much faster than its usual magisterial pace, finishing in a disintegration of guitar, bass, and Gothic Choir that left them all panting.

"Ladies and gentleman," Austin said into his mic to the empty room. "We are The Becoming."

And he was right. They were more than just the three of them.

They were a band.

The door clattered open, and Josh came in wearing the snare in a harness like he was in the marching band. He stopped at the weird energy between the three of them onstage. "What'd I miss?"

They were moments away. Megs was using seven of her hands to finish setting up her DJ equipment to the side of the stage. Her remaining two were holding *Wuthering Heights* so she could read it for English class.

Through the curtains, they could hear the growing crowd in the cafeteria beyond. School dances were never all that heavily attended, but clearly a larger-than-average number of people wanted to see the band.

Wanted to see Austin, Angela thought as she watched him peek through the curtain for the hundredth time. But that was okay. If she wasn't in the band, she'd want to see Austin, too. That she was in the band just happened to make it a million times better.

"How's it looking?" Josh said, tapping his feet nervously behind the drum kit.

"Nearly full," Austin said, stepping away from the curtain and readjusting his microphone stand, also for the hundredth time. He glanced over at Angela. "Holly Spelman's out there, with Jenna Marks and Fatima Ridderbos."

"Oh, yeah," Megs said, turning a page and not looking up. "I meant to tell you guys. I overheard Holly saying to Jenna she was going to hurl a bucket of fish soup onstage during your performance." She looked over her book at Angela. "At you."

"Fish soup?" Josh asked.

"For the smell, I guess." Megs shrugged. "Maybe it's all she had at home."

Angela's shoulders slumped. "Honestly, that girl." She stepped away from her keyboards with a sigh. "I'll go talk to her —"

"No need," Megs said, returning to her book. "I landed my famous Nine-Palm Slap upside that dragon head of hers and said no one but no one was going to risk damaging my equipment with soup and that if she tried anything at all during your performance, I'd introduce her to my famous Nine-Fisted Punch."

"Thanks, Megs," Angela said.

"*De nada.*" She turned another page. "Anyone read this? It's seriously messed up."

Miss Jenkins poked her three heads through the stage door. "I'm going to have the Audiovisual Club open the curtains and dim the lights in five minutes. You guys ready?"

"As we'll ever be," Austin said.

"Well," Miss Jenkins said, holding up her fists, pinkies and thumbs out. "Rock on."

They stared at her in silence until she left.

"Teachers," Josh said, shaking his head.

"I'm out, too," Megs said, her many hands making the last adjust-
ments to her equipment. "Don't touch any of this when you're playing."

"We won't," Angela said.

"I mean it."

"I mean it, too."

"You, I trust," Megs said, pointing at Angela and heading for the
door. She made a complicated movement of blessing with all of her
hands and left them to the countdown.

Conrad took out slips of paper from his pocket. He handed one to
Josh, one to Austin, and one to Angela.

Good luck, they read.

The final seconds passed in a kind of noisy silence, no one saying
much, just waiting, waiting. Then there was a roar as the lights in the
cafeteria went down. Josh sat up behind his drums, sticks and tail at
the ready. Conrad did a quiet last tune of his bass, turning the ampli-
fier up slightly. Austin positioned himself behind the microphone.
Angela made sure her programming was ready for "Blood Tears,"
which they'd decided to open with after all.

There was nothing left to do. They looked at each other in antici-
pation. Angela felt like she was continually falling out of a car that
was driving way too fast, but maybe not in a bad way. She coughed a
little nervous fire and momentarily lit up all their faces.

"Ready?" Austin said.

The curtains opened.

Looking back, she'd be able to remember all of it and none of it.
The forty-five-minute set passed in a blur that started feverish
and only got more so. They hadn't discussed onstage patter, and it

turned out that Austin was, for this early performance at least, paralytically shy about talking to a crowd, so after they roared through "Blood Tears," they barely took in three seconds of applause before Austin was already counting them in too fast for "The Beauty of Reckoning."

It didn't matter. Nothing mattered. They were making a sound beyond glorious. Nothing else mattered at all.

During maybe the fifth song or possibly the sixth, Angela started to breathe fire at emotional high points in the music. Austin's guitar would reach a crescendo, and she'd punctuate it with a geyser of flame. The first time Austin looked surprised but then shouted, "YEAHHHHH!!!" and she kept on doing it, without even thinking, without even calculating when she should. It happened as it should happen, as the music needed it.

Josh played with such fury, his tail bent one of the cymbals nearly in half, but instead of it being another disaster, he improvised with the other cymbal and the hi-hat, and it sounded even better, purer, louder — if that was even possible. Conrad thumped his bass like a massive engine driving the band, his decaying fingers spraying blood and viscera as he twanged on the strings. Even Austin's voice was stronger, shouting through the crowd's roars, feeling their energy, singing it back to them. He may not have been able to crack jokes between songs just yet, but every word he sang was an acknowledgment of them, and they knew it, could feel it, screamed it back at The Becoming with every fevered drumbeat.

They reached the end of "London Condition," their second-to-last song, and Austin finally, finally gave the crowd a moment to just scream. Angela felt like she was blazing, and maybe she was. She sprayed fire across the upturned faces at the edge of the stage, even

the roaring lizard snout of Holly Spelman, but no one minded. They just roared back.

"This is our last song," Austin said, to disappointed shouts from the crowd, but even the disappointment was couched in appreciation of what they were witnessing.

Austin looked at each band member in turn — Conrad, Josh, Angela. They'd moved "The Victor and the Vanquished" to the end of the set, and they were going to play it at the super-fast speed they'd found in the sound check.

They'd never done the whole thing like that before. But it was going to be incredible. Angela knew it before they'd played a note.

Austin closed his sulfurous eyes, swooned into the microphone, and shouted it for them.

"ONE! TWO! THREE! FOUR!"

And they were away. If Angela was soaring before, this was more like orbit. Her claws had never played faster, her voice at the first chorus never sounded finer, her heart never lifted so high.

Which is when it began to happen.

Josh — arms and legs thudding in monstrous, unstoppable rhythm — didn't even notice as the spike on his tail grew by nearly a foot and began shooting flashes of lightning every time it smacked the metal of the cymbals.

The laces ripped themselves from Conrad's mouth as he raised his voice to join in with the singing, retying themselves like hard-earned battle scars across his cheeks and forehead.

The hump on Austin's back began to glow as the song built toward its final chorus, light splitting from the seams as his skin cracked open, and two enormous, chrysalis-wet wings unfurled behind him, newly born, ready for flight.

The Becoming were becoming.

But it was Angela to whom all eyes turned, all but her own, which were closed, as her fireproof tongue blasted off its thickened coating, as the furry skin burned away in a cascade of light, as the claws moving in their patterns across the keyboard shed their weaponry ...

And there were arguments later, arguments that would follow her for the rest of her life, about whether what emerged on that fateful night was a new kind of Aspect or was just her normal non-Aspect self she was trying to pass off as a new kind of Aspect in an audacious affront that was almost an Aspect unto itself.

It also wasn't true, because in her new Aspect she visibly glowed and could start fires just by touch, if she wanted. There were age-old, imperfect theories that Aspect was just an exaggerated version of yourself, and maybe for some people, maybe for Angela, her truest Aspect really was just her.

Only more so.

But she didn't care, not then, not later, not ever. Because in the middle of the music, playing with her friends, burning in the kiln of the crowd's roar, she became.

In the front row of the concert, an angry Holly Spelman never stopped looking at Angela, not knowing whether she should cheer or boo, a confusion that would also follow her for the rest of her life.

"Just look at her," she raged to anyone who could hear. "She's beautiful."

Wings in THE Morning

SARAH REES BRENNAN

Here the repellent harpies
make their nests. —DANTE

Luke's mother put a comforting hand, heavy with gold and calluses, over Luke's and said: "Sometimes when a mummy and a daddy love each other very much —"

"Mum, seriously," said Luke. "Is now the time?"

He'd gone to the camp infirmary after months of his shoulders aching, expecting to hear he'd pulled something. Instead they had kept him for three days, and now his mother was here when she was meant to be at the other side of the Border on patrol duty. Luke was honestly worried that he had a terminal disease.

But apparently his mother thought this was the ideal opportunity to tell Luke about the birds and the bees. Luke was seventeen, for God's sake.

"Bear with me a moment here," his mother urged. "Sometimes when a mummy and a daddy love each other very much, but they are both soldiers dedicated to the protection of the Border and often posted far away from each other, Mummy has needs and Daddy is not there."

Luke opened his mouth and found he had no words.

"So Mummy and Daddy have an open relationship while they are apart," Rachel Sunborn continued, her voice calm and pleasant. "And you may not have realized this, Luke, but your mum is a pretty adventurous lady! Sexually."

Luke did not think the black spots dancing in front of his eyes were normal.

"Long story short, I had a brief, very enjoyable encounter with a nice harpy boy."

"A harpy?" Luke asked, finding his voice. It sounded very far away, as if it were trying to escape this situation. "Mum, you didn't. Harpies aren't like elves — they're not our allies; they're . . . they're beasts. They're not even human."

"Luke Sunborn, I don't want to hear any of that small-minded camp talk out of you," Rachel said. "We protect the Border, and we offer protection to anyone — human, elf, harpy, even troll — who asks. Whether you're human or not doesn't matter. What matters is that I love you."

"Whether," Luke said through dry, barely parted lips. "Whether I'm —"

"I did the math, and I thought you were probably your dad's," Rachel said. "But it turns out that harpies gestate for different periods — whoops, silly me, should have paid more attention in pre-ternatural biology when I was a girl at training camp. Is my face red! In my defense, you did look very human as a baby." Rachel smiled at him fondly. "And very adorable!"

"As a baby," Luke repeated in a hollow voice.

"Also now!" his mother added in an encouraging tone. "The medics tell me that there is an excellent chance that your lower half will remain entirely human. Though if you spot any feathers on your belly, you should let a medic know at once. Your wings are just coming in, that's all."

His wings were just coming in. That was all.

Luke had spent the summer worrying about the shooting pains and dull aches in his shoulders, the strange heaviness as if he were always carrying a burden. But he was a Sunborn: their family had been guarding the Border for centuries. The first records from the Border were of the Sunborns, golden laughing guardians, peace-keepers, and sword-wielders. Luke knew what was expected of him: that everything be easy for him. He hadn't wanted to complain.

Even now his mother was laughing, Sunborn to the bone, a bright sound that would not falter at death and was certainly not fazed by a little detail like her son not being human.

"Your dad sent word that you weren't to worry," said Rachel. "This doesn't change anything between you two. Once you teach a boy to play Trigon, he's your son, he says. Louise sends her love as well!"

Mum beamed at him.

"Louise, I guess, is human?"

"That's right, my boy," said Mum. "Look on the bright side! Louise is totally human. And I had a fling with a centaur before she was born, so that came as a huge relief."

Luke covered his face with his hands. "Whatever you do," he said, "please don't tell Elliot."

The Border between the human world and the otherlands had existed since both the worlds were born, and guards had patrolled that Border almost as long. There were people of every kind born able to see and pass through the Border, and at the age of thirteen those people were brought into the training camp and taught all they needed to know, so they could choose whether to go back to their own lands or stay and guard the Border.

Luke had been born on the Border and raised in several fortresses along it. Luke had gone into his first day of training camp knowing everything there was to know and prepared to help any of the kids who found the Border new and scary.

Almost everyone had been really grateful.

Luke always helped out on the first day, taking the kids' names, comforting anyone who was homesick, and explaining that the Border camp was the best fun anyone could ever have. He couldn't let people down now because it turned out he was half beast.

"I'll make sure you get a special place to watch our first Trigon game," he promised a weeping dwarf girl at the sign-in desk. He knelt and gave her a hug. "What's that you've got there?"

"My lucky hammer," she said, waving it for his admiration. Luke ducked.

"It's lovely," he told her, and she beamed.

That was when the explosion happened. Luke reflexively drew in the girl to him, protecting her, and then realized what was going on. He sprang to his feet. A lot of people were crouching down, hands over their heads, so he was able to spot the shock of copper-bright red hair with relative ease.

"Settle down, everyone," he called out. "It's not an attack. It's just Elliot."

Trust Elliot to be difficult.

Elliot scowled at him as he approached. Luke was displeased to see that Elliot had grown over the summer and was now actually slightly taller than Luke himself. Luke could still have broken him in half without even trying, so he supposed it didn't matter.

"Give it to me," Luke said. "Whatever contraband you have, hand it over right now."

Elliot gathered his satchel jealously to his chest. "It's nothing. It's fine."

"I realize I'm part of war training, not council training," Luke said. "We don't do advanced linguistics, and maybe I don't know all the correct definitions of words. But I really don't think you can define 'actually exploding' as 'fine.'"

"It's under control!" Elliot protested, at which point his bag exploded in his hands.

"Give that to me, Elliot. You are going to hurt yourself —"

"No! Get off —"

Elliot was displaying his usual excellent judgment by clinging to the explosives and smacking at Luke when Commander Woodsinger came over to them. Luke saluted hastily.

"What have you got there?" she asked.

After a reluctant pause, Elliot saluted as well. "I did have several things," he admitted. "But I think most of them exploded. All I have left is my eye pod."

SARAH REES
BRENNAN

"Schafer, you are in your final year of training — you know these things react badly to the Border."

"I really think one of them will work if I just keep trying," said Elliot.

"Maybe he should keep it, ma'am," said Luke. "If the pod is for his eyes . . ."

Elliot laughed at him, in a mean way, as if Luke had said something ridiculous. Of course, he seldom laughed in any other way.

Luke was quite pleased when his bag exploded again. Elliot looked vexed.

Most kids from the human world either left quickly, screaming something about video games, or stayed in the Border and let the human world slip away from them. But not Elliot. Instead he dedicated his life to being the Border's greatest nuisance.

Luke dragged Elliot off. Serene fell in beside them.

The guards of the Border were mainly human, but the races from the otherlands who were close to human and who chose to stay and guard on the Border were valued members of the force. Serene was going to be the greatest elven guard who had ever lived.

Luke had seen that, even at thirteen, when Serene was in line to sign up for their first year. The leaves in her dark hair had been trembling, but she'd stood with her back straight as a blade. It had been love at first sight: he'd known they would always be best friends.

Unfortunately, with Serene came Elliot. Serene was one of very few trainees who chose to do the warrior course and the council course, and she was set to excel in both. But she needed a partner for each, and being part of Serene's chosen team made Luke and Elliot, however reluctantly, on the same side.

Luke had never worked out why Serene had chosen Elliot. She was usually very clever. He was just grateful that the horrible five weeks when they were fifteen and Serene and Elliot were dating were over.

Luke had noticed Elliot on the first day of training camp too.

"Luke Sunburn?" Elliot had echoed during the students' attendance call. "Like, Luke Giant Melanoma? Are you kidding me?"

Nobody had ever made fun of Luke before. Elliot had never stopped since.

"Luke Sunborn," said Commander Woodsinger, in the here and now.

Luke said: "Present and accounted for, ma'am!"

"Serene-Heart-in-the-Chaos-of-Battle," said Commander Woodsinger.

Serene saluted. "Present and accounted for, ma'am!"

"Elliot Schafer," said Commander Woodsinger.

"What . . . she said," said Elliot, and mumbled, "I hate the attendance call."

Luke did not see why Elliot had to proclaim his hatred for totally normal things.

Commander Woodsinger said, "Dale Wavechaser."

"Present and accounted for, ma'am," said Dale Wavechaser, with a flawless salute. He was tanned from the summer, the same nut-brown color as his hair, and even better-looking than he had been last year. Which was saying something, as he'd already been the handsomest boy in the whole Border training camp.

Luke had had a crush on him for almost two years, and this was their last year at camp. This year, Luke had promised himself, he was going to ask Dale to go down to the Elven Tavern. Dale liked guys, liked Trigon and hunting, and always seemed glad to be Luke's sparring partner. And Dale was really nice: he'd never been anything

but nice to Luke, and besides Luke could tell from his kind blue eyes. Luke was almost sure Dale would say yes.

Luke had been almost sure, before Luke had found out he wasn't human.

"What is wrong with you, loser?" Elliot demanded. "Why are you looking like that?"

"Are you upset about something?" Serene asked. "You have to say if you are. I don't have any masculine intuition."

Gender roles were a bit different for elves. Serene looked vaguely panicked that Luke was going to weep.

Luke elbowed Elliot instead. "Nothing's wrong," he said. "I'm really looking forward to killing it at Trigon."

Trigon was a game from the human world, but Elliot said they didn't play it in the human world anymore. Luke believed this was evidence he never needed to go to the human world: they obviously had their priorities all wrong. There was a scooped-out Trigon field beside the training camp, like a quarry with crags strategically placed in it, and starting from those points the three players feinted, threw, and dodged the glass ball.

The ball could never be allowed to drop.

Luke had never dropped it. Last year they'd tried to recruit him for the professional Trigon team — as if Luke would waste his time when the Border needed protecting — and he'd been on the front page of the *Border Daily*. Luke privately thought the picture of him rumpling back his blond hair and looking sweaty was embarrassing. He would have been happy to have his picture taken once he'd washed up and found a shirt.

But everyone had seemed proud of him. At least he could get this right and make it look easy and fun.

They always celebrated the first day of school with the first Trigon game of the year, and his mother had stayed to watch. Luke could see her with Elliot and Serene in the stands.

He turned to Dale and said: "Good luck."

"You too. Not that you need it, Sunborn," Dale added, with his warm smile.

He hated to throw and get someone so good-looking out of the game, but that was how it went. Nothing personal. Some people didn't do well under pressure, but Luke had borne pressure his whole life, and he wasn't letting anyone down: he scored on nineteen people his first try, the ball catching the light and arcing through the air like a second small sun that wanted to be nowhere but in Luke's hands.

Then Delia Winterchild threw too soon and too short, and the crowd let out a horrified sigh. Without thinking, Luke was suddenly coasting down the crag, feet barely touching the ground — maybe not touching the ground — what should have been a fall was a glide, and he stood on the stone with the ball cupped in his hands.

The applause came from the stands a second late, but Luke thought he could still pretend everything was normal.

"You were wonderful!" his mother said later, holding his face and kissing him on both cheeks. "And I have to run now, darling. See you at Christmas!"

"Good form," said Serene.

"Did you win?" Elliot inquired. "I may have dozed off in the stands for a minute there."

Luke was walking into the changing rooms when Delia Winterchild

threw the ball at his feet: it made an ugly crunching sound like broken bones.

"Guess we know why you're so inhumanly good now, don't we,"
she said.

Someone at the infirmary had told, then. And everyone had seen
that jump. Luke stood and waited at the door of the changing rooms
because he didn't want to take his shirt off in front of anybody else.
He could feel the muscles of his shoulders aching and stretching and
straining. He stood with his head down and stared at the glass shards
as if they were fragments of a shining, broken world.

There were a lot of reasons Luke had hated Serene dating Elliot.
He didn't want to be alone, but he didn't want to lose, either:
he couldn't bear the thought of losing Serene. And he'd been
alone, and they had had something between them he hadn't
been able to share. Except then they didn't anymore, and Serene
and Luke would get together and talk about their wistful hopeful crushes on boys they hardly dared speak to — in Luke's case
Dale Wavechaser, and in Serene's an elven boy back home called
Golden-Hair-Scented-Like-Summer.

Then it was like Luke had won, since Elliot obviously wouldn't
want to talk about boys with them.

So Luke was really happy for Serene but also completely crushed
when that night in her cabin Serene, kneeling on her bed, said:
"Golden and I pledged our love this summer under the waterfall at
home!"

"Oh, wow," Luke said. "Awesome! Good for you, Serene. That's so
great. Wow. Awesome."

Elliot was lying on his stomach scribbling notes and consulting a book, as if somehow he'd picked up homework before they had class. Elliot was no help.

Serene seemed happy to continue with minimal encouragement. "I have been wearing his token to carry into battle with me for two and a half weeks," she said. "You can see it if you like, as my trusted comrades."

She showed a handkerchief with their initials (elves had long initials) embroidered with Golden's own hair. Apparently by Golden himself. Serene launched into a long story about how excellent Golden's embroidery was and how beautifully he sang.

Luke, moved to desperation, glanced at Elliot. The firelight lingered on his face in strokes of red and gold, and he looked absorbed by his book.

"Reading anything interesting?"

Elliot lifted his eyes from the pages, firelight gilding his gray eyes. There was a wicked look in them that indicated he was aware of just how much Luke was not enjoying himself. "I know reading is a fascinating mystery for you, loser," he said. "But no. No, not compared to Serene's beautiful tale of love. Please, Serene, do go on."

"All right," Serene told them. "Since you are my dearest and best beloved friends. I will confide . . . and you must never breathe it to another soul . . . that Golden granted me permission to steal a single, sweet, life-altering kiss."

There was a silence. Eventually, Luke offered: "But, Serene . . . you have kissed people before."

"It was different with Elliot," Serene said. "Human men are allowed to run wild and be shameless. They'll do anything with anyone."

"You know that's right," Elliot murmured.

It wasn't that Luke wasn't happy for Serene, because he really was. It was just that he was sorry to lose the bond between them, the crush on someone you never really talked to. It had made him feel not so bad that Serene hadn't dared talk to Golden either. But now Serene had dared. She'd gotten the guy. She'd kissed him.

And Luke hadn't ever kissed anybody.

Now he did not know if he ever would.

History was one of the few classes that those in warrior training and in council training shared. Luke usually found it deeply boring.

Luke would have paid to be bored now, since the lesson was on the time the trolls and the harpies allied to storm the Border. He opened to a page with a black-and-white drawing of a harpy rending the dead with its talons and heard someone laugh and cough at the back of the classroom.

He felt sweat prickle under his collar and looked at Serene, who was as usual listening to the instructor with the laser focus that got described in her reports as "admirable but incredibly unsettling." Elliot, who had four different books open on his desk and really seemed to have assigned himself a pile of homework for fun, was scribbling and paying no attention.

Dale was looking slightly troubled. Luke was feeling slightly ill.

". . . the battlefield afterward, due to the smaller number of the human force, the fact it was a wooded area, and the horrors inspired by the depredations of the harpies, was known as — can anyone tell me?"

There was another muffled laugh, and a girl's voice said: "Why don't you ask Sunborn?"

Everyone was looking at Luke. He looked at the table.

"The Forest of the Suicides," he said, his voice sounding much too loud in his own ears.

After class, Luke said, "You might be wondering what all that was about."

"Quiet, loser," Elliot commanded, rapidly making notes even though class was over. "I'm very busy."

Luke let the occasion pass. He'd been hoping, really, that nobody would ever have to know, that Luke himself could stop thinking about it.

Except the secret was so obviously out. At sparring practice, Luke and Serene chose each other because they always did, but nobody asked Luke to help with their form like usual. Luke said, "How's it going?" to Dale, and perhaps it was his imagination, but Dale looked embarrassed.

It wasn't Luke's imagination that when he was praised for his lunge—and instructors always praised him, it wasn't anything noteworthy—someone mumbled, "Yeah, he's a real flier."

When Luke crept into the library at lunchtime to look for books on harpies, there were conspicuous gaps all over the Creatures of the Otherlands section; and when Luke heard footsteps coming by, he ducked around the shelves and hid, flattened against the Science of War section, his heart pounding.

Everybody seemed to know. But Serene and Elliot didn't know, and maybe they didn't have to. Luke resolved not to tell them.

"There," said Elliot at dinner, flinging down what he called his "ballpoint pen" into his peas. Luke honestly didn't see what he had against quills. "I'm done."

"You can't eat those now," Serene observed.

"I wasn't intending to," Elliot said. "I'm suspicious of all green food."

"I'm half harpy," said Luke.

Luke was very bad at resolutions.

"Yes, we know," said Serene. "Your mother told us at the Trigon game. But she said not to tell you."

Luke's mother and Serene were very bad at keeping secrets. Luke looked at Serene, whose face bore its usual martial lack of expression, and then reluctantly at Elliot.

Elliot was arranging his large stack of paper with a self-satisfied air.

"Yeah, loser. I have not been compiling a comprehensive and yet comprehensible to even the slowest — that's you — record on harpies for my health."

"What? Give me that!"

Elliot held it out of his reach, smiling. "What will you give me for it?"

This wasn't a joke: this was Luke's life. Luke could have beaten up Elliot. He'd always known he could, if he wanted to, and never quite been able to do it.

"What do you want?" he said through gritted teeth.

"Let me hide my contraband in your place," Elliot proposed. "I think the commander's planning a raid on mine."

"All right," Luke said after a pause, and Elliot handed the pages over.

It wasn't much to ask for, Luke thought, and his eyes narrowed. "How much contraband do you have?"

"That isn't important at this time," said Elliot.

"That much, I see," Luke muttered. But the weight of the papers was comforting in his hands.

"Instead let's talk about you being half harpy," Elliot suggested. "Isn't it great?"

"Why, because you like to see me suffer?"

"That's a side benefit," said Elliot. "Those of us who do council training know that we've been trying to arrange a diplomatic visit to the harpies' principal fortress for, oh, thirty years. Now you have given us the perfect excuse. You need to go discover your heritage."

"Oh, no," Luke said. "I don't. No."

"If we could get the harpies to be our allies, that leaves the trolls with none," Serene said. "It could mean a lasting peace with the otherlands."

"I don't want to go consort with animals," Luke growled. Elliot and Serene looked shocked, but he continued: "Haven't you heard the things everyone's been saying? I'm surprised you weren't saying them—"

"Why would I make fun of you for this, when there are so many actual things to make fun of you for?" Elliot asked. "Consider Exhibit A: your face. And Exhibit B: your rotting brain. If you think that you won't be visiting the harpies within the month."

Luke looked to Serene, but Serene obviously agreed with Elliot because she was concentrating on her food; Serene might be intense, but Luke did not think the peas were going to perform a daring escape.

Luke didn't know how to escape, either.

Elliot wasn't useful for much, but he did take good notes. Luke spent the night in his cabin going over them: they were written the way Elliot talked (unfortunately including insults) and much easier

to understand than the way books talked, as if they were teachers pressed dead and even drier between their own pages. There was a sketch of wings, with a note saying, "Most like the eagle's wings: ideal for soaring. Don't flap too much, loser," and a page about the history of half and quarter harpies. Back a few centuries ago, a winged human was seen as lucky, the notes said. Even though Luke couldn't imagine that, he was slightly entertained by the stories of Caroline the Fair, who had wings, many lovers, and a face that launched a harpy army to fight for the Border. (Elliot: "And we get you? We were robbed.")

Luke got about a quarter of the way into it — it was really long, and Luke wasn't much for books. And as long as he wasn't finished, it might have all the answers.

The next day he hid the pile of paper under books for their art of war class. When he was shoving books into his bag and heard footsteps coming up behind him, he froze, sure he had been discovered.

When he looked up, though, he saw not the teacher but Dale, smiling awkwardly at him.

"Hey."

Luke always had great conversations with Dale in his head. Out loud the best he was able to manage was, "Hey."

"So, I heard about the mission to the, uh, harpies."

Luke stared.

"Which obviously you haven't heard about!" Dale said, and looked horrified. "Do you . . . think you'll go?"

It was nice of him to ask, Luke thought.

"I don't want to, but if they ask me to — yeah. It's my duty."

"Yeah," Dale echoed. "Of course. I mean, of course you don't want to, but of course you will. It's going to suck, though. I'm sorry."

"Thanks," Luke said.

"I know you're not —" Dale stopped.

"Like that," Luke said. "Like them."

Dale bit his lip and nodded.

"Thanks," Luke said again. "Do you . . . are you coming, too?"

"Hey, you're the reason we're going," Dale said. "If you want me to go, I'm there."

"I want you to come."

Dale grinned, and Luke got up the nerve to say, "Do you want to . . ." but instead of "go to the Elven Tavern with me," he mysteriously found himself saying, ". . . spar with me?"

"Sure," said Dale.

The third time he pinned Dale to the mat, sweating, Dale's muscled shoulders under his hands, he felt the material of his shirt tug at the shoulders, the dark unfurling.

"Okay, good spar! Bye now!" Luke shouted, and threw himself backward across the room.

He stood with his back to the wall as Dale gave him a puzzled wave and left.

It had been really nice of him to reassure Luke.

There were reasons Luke hadn't kissed anybody. The Sunborns, as a family, loved life and loved love, and treated it as a game. It was fine for them: it worked for them.

Luke had always known that a riot of brightness and different loves and leaving someone laughing was beyond him. He wanted kindness and steadiness: he did not want someone who would leave. He wanted love that would last.

———⋅†⋅———

As he'd told Dale, he knew his duty. When he was told he was going on a mission to the harpies and asked if he could name anyone from the warrior course to accompany him, he said Serene and Dale.

At no point had he mentioned Elliot.

"Because you are not in the warrior training course!" Luke snapped. The early morning sky felt like it was pressing down on him, a sheet of cold gray metal. His pack felt like he had carried it for too long on aching shoulders, and they hadn't even left camp — the last thing he needed was this.

Elliot toyed with the straps on his own pack and beamed as if he had not a care in the world. "Ah, but you see, I explained to Commander Woodsinger that this was a time of emotional turmoil and you needed me."

"You what?" said Luke. "I what?"

Elliot gazed at him with limpid eyes. "I'm just glad to be here for you, buddy."

"I suppose the three of you are inseparable," Commander Woodsinger commented. "But you could have asked earlier, Sunborn."

"He was shy, ma'am," Elliot said. "He's so bashful and modest."

"All right," said Commander Woodsinger. "But you and Schafer will have to share a tent, Sunborn. He can't go in with Chaos-of-Battle: I know they used to be an item. No romantic getaways on my watch."

"But, ma'am!" Luke said, appalled. "I was going to go in with Serene."

Serene observed, "If I wanted to be taking shameless advantage of Cadet Schafer — no slur intended to his virtue, but — I would be."

"It's true," Elliot said earnestly. "But I need a tent of my own, please. I require extra blankets because it is very easy for me to take a chill, and there are space issues! Besides, I go both ways, and I have wandering hands. Nobody is safe with me!"

There was apparently nothing Elliot would not say to get what he wanted.

"This is why we don't take cadets from the council course on missions!" said Commander Woodsinger. "Schafer, you go in with Sunborn. Chaos-of-Battle can go in with Wavechaser."

It was an appalling start to the most horrible trip Luke could imagine.

"Why are you being so quiet, loser?" asked Elliot once they were in the woods and the sun was sinking to afternoon.

"I'm not being quiet," Luke said. "I'm not talking to you. Because you used my actual feelings to get yourself on this trip, and you made it so I'm not sharing with Serene, and you lied to our commander. I didn't ask you, I don't need you, and we're not friends."

Elliot had always made that perfectly clear.

Elliot paled slightly, and Serene said: "Boys, please don't be catty."

"Okay," Elliot said, his mouth twisting. "You're upset. I understand. But I had to come. Peace talks with the trolls are breaking down. This is a really important mission, and we needed more people from the council on it, and it's terrible that war gets prioritized over peace. But I was being personally insensitive. I'm sorry. I'll make it up to you."

"That's all —" Luke was about to say "right," as having Elliot

sincerely apologize to him was a first, but despite what Elliot believed, Luke wasn't a complete moron. "How will you make it up to me?"

"You'll see," said Elliot, which Luke took to mean: "You won't like it, and something will probably explode."

Still, Elliot had apologized. Luke had been raised to know you accepted an apology and put the matter behind you. Besides, Elliot had written the pile of paper, which was the only comforting thing in Luke's pack, and it did feel more normal to have Elliot on the other side of Serene, complaining about his nose getting sunburned. It seemed less like they were going into a bizarre unknown.

The trees got taller and taller the farther into the woods they went. Their autumn-bared branches looked like vast skeletal fingers blocking out the sun. Luke shivered in the shadows and thought he would be grateful when they came upon a stretch of moorland.

He wasn't. His boot hit a stone as they left the woods, and he felt the stone give a little too much.

It was a human skull, half buried in the earth. Beyond the old battlefield, there was a host of the highest trees yet, and above the black tops of the trees, there were moving blots against the sky.

Harpies were on the watch. They were approaching the Forest of the Suicides.

The forest floor was littered with dead pine needles and dry bones. Luke could not look down or up, to the wheeling shapes in the sky. He could only look in front of him at the shapes of the trees ahead, black slashes in the gathering mist.

When the harpy landed before them — wings making a heavy creak like knee joints ten times over, feathers making a heavy swish like a woman's long dress — Luke started so badly, it was almost a jump back. The jolt brought him against support: not a tree but Serene's steady hand. There was warmth at his other side, despite the cool mist: Elliot had gone around. Luke glanced at both of them, and then he was able to look at the harpy.

She wore a breastplate of woven bones over her breasts and nothing else: her lower half looked as though a lion and a huge bird had had a child, heavy furred paws ending in vast eagle's talons. Her hair was in many different chestnut braids, every braid ending in a chestnut feather, and her nose had a pronounced hook. For all that, her face was entirely human.

She looked right at Luke, as if — as if she could tell. As if he bore some sort of mark.

"I am Celaeno, the leader of this flock," she said.

"I'm . . ." Luke said, and swallowed. "I'm Luke Sunborn."

Her fierce blue eyes seemed to swallow him at a gulp: he pressed back hard against Serene's hand.

"Luke Sunborn," she repeated softly. "I bid you and your comrades welcome."

The harpies nested on treetops. The mission set up its tents on a slope mercifully clear of trees and bones, and Elliot even helped.

"I still think my talents would have been better suited to supervising," he observed, once every tent was in place and the two unlucky

cadets on kitchen duty were making them all a meal. "Also, why don't you just fly up there and nest so I can have the tent to myself? Haven't those wings come in yet?"

Luke scowled. "No."

"I saw harpy kids way younger than you with wings. Would you describe yourself as a late bloomer?"

"Don't —" The words stuck in Luke's throat. *Don't talk about it so casually,* he wanted to say. *Don't talk about it like it could ever be okay.*

"All right," Elliot said, after a minute. "I haven't forgotten I owe you. Go sit on that blanket, and I will get us all food."

Luke went and sat by Serene, who began talking about the trees in the Forest of Suicides, as if that were clearly the most notable part of it. Elves loved trees.

"Very old pines, some of them," Serene continued approvingly. "Tended well. This forest is like the harpies' garden."

Luke did not want to talk about harpies. He hunched his shoulders and looked around for Elliot, who was over by the campfire waiting for food to be dished up. He was talking to Dale.

"Serene!" Luke hissed. "Mayday! Mayday!"

It was something Elliot had taught them to say: it was apparently a human-world warning that there was trouble. Luke only ever said it about Elliot.

"Elliot is talking to Dale! What's he saying to him! This is a disaster!"

"Stop twittering," Serene said kindly, patting his hand as she did when she felt he was overwrought. "My keen elven hearing assures me that you have nothing to fear. Elliot's just inviting him to sit with us."

"What! Why? Has he told you what he's planning?"

"My keen elven mind assures me that dinner invitations are not usually part of nefarious schemes." Serene's face was blank, except for one slightly raised eyebrow. There were times Luke suspected she was messing with him. There were other times he was sure of it.

Elliot had hold of Dale's elbow, and he tilted his head, firelight gilded, in the direction of Luke and Serene. Luke considered running as if from an avalanche. Elliot laughed, a sweet and genuine sound Luke rarely heard. It was all so distressing.

Dale walked over with Elliot. What choice did he have, with Elliot's hand still on his arm? Elliot gestured to the space on the blanket beside Luke.

"Be right back with the food," he said, and was as good as his word. When he came back and found Luke staring at the blanket, he leaned toward Dale and said: "Dale. Can I call you Dale?"

"Um, well," Dale stammered. "Sure."

"Wonderful," said Elliot. "Why don't you and Sunborn explain to me how Trigon works?"

"Elliot, you are at every game," Luke snapped.

"No," said Elliot incredulously. "Is that what you're running around doing when I sit on my reading stands? Well, isn't that embarrassing? I never noticed. Tell me, does Trigon involve a ball?"

Dale laughed, hesitantly, and the sound encouraged Luke to go along with Elliot's lunacy. Twenty minutes later, with Serene saying, "That is not an efficient use of a chicken bone," and Elliot laughing that new laugh, Luke had spoken more words to Dale than he had in three years of training together.

"Then the ball broke," Dale said, snapping a wishbone in two. "Eleanor Sunborn won. That was the only four-day Trigon match ever played."

"To hear Aunt Ellie tell it, it seems longer than four days," Luke said, and grinned when both Elliot and Dale laughed.

"Excuse me a minute," said Elliot. "Serene, come with me?"

"I'm comfortable here," Serene objected.

Elliot rolled his eyes at her and walked back over to the campfire alone. An awkward silence followed in his wake. Luke glanced over at Dale's profile, classically handsome as a coin, and swallowed.

"Uh, well," he said brilliantly. "We both know how to play Trigon."

"Uh, yeah," said Dale. He glanced at Luke, and then at Serene. "So . . . what's council training like? You and, um, Elliot have fun with . . . that?"

"I think you would find accounts of my lessons very dull," said Serene.

"I'm sure . . . I wouldn't," said Dale.

Usually Luke liked that Serene was the strong, silent type.

"So, uh," he said.

"Yeah, what?" Dale asked.

"You first," Luke said, brilliantly.

"Oh, I think Iyara needs me," said Dale, and fled.

Elliot returned ten minutes later and exclaimed, "You let him get away?"

"What was I supposed to do?" Luke demanded.

"You were meant to ask him out! See if I ever do anything nice for you again." Elliot ran his hands through his hair. "I can't believe I just spent half an hour in the company of one of the most boring guys in the world for nothing. I hate you."

"Dale is not boring!" Luke snapped, wounded. "And — and I thought we were all having a nice time. I think he maybe likes me. He asked if I wanted him to come along on this mission."

"Or maybe he likes going on important missions," Elliot suggested.

"Pot, meet kettle, who shouldn't even be here!"

"Point," said Elliot. "Here's another point. While amazingly dull, the guy is good-looking. Someone else is going to ask him out. And then you, loser, will die alone."

"Excuse me if I'm a little hesitant when I know I can't even take off my shirt in front of somebody," Luke snarled. "Because I'm turning into a monster!"

"You're not turning into a monster," Serene said. "But I wish you boys would talk about something other than clothes or romance."

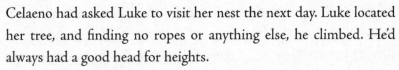

Celaeno had asked Luke to visit her nest the next day. Luke located her tree, and finding no ropes or anything else, he climbed. He'd always had a good head for heights.

It had looked like a nest from below, but now that he had climbed in, he saw it was like a tree house, the woven twigs and moss a vast cup for a wooden hut with a soft floor, half earth and half twigs. The floor looked as if it were regularly raked, Luke thought, and then realized as Celaeno came toward him that it was her talons crossing the floor again and again that made those marks.

"Tea?" asked Celaeno. It was so unexpected, Luke simply stared at her.

When she shoved the bowl full of liquid into his hands, he snapped out of it enough to say, "Uh, sure. Tea, lovely," and then he noticed the subtly rough texture of the white bowl.

He was pretty sure he was holding a skull.

"Do you harpies kill people?"

"Of course," said Celaeno. "Don't you soldiers?"

Luke pretended to drink from his skull cup.

Celaeno walked around him, her talons scoring the ground, as if she were securing a circle around him where he would be trapped forever.

"You have good shoulders," she observed. "The breadth is necessary for flight. Some half-breeds can't fly."

"Like Caroline the Fair?"

That seemed to surprise Celaeno: for the first time, she smiled. "So you do want to know about us."

Luke clung to his cup and was silent.

"We are as eager for an alliance as you," said Celaeno. "But we must be respected. There used to be a great deal of interbreeding with the humans: we used to be much closer with them than we can be with trolls."

"I know there are many more female harpies than males," Luke volunteered, blessing Elliot's notes. "Is . . . is that why there was a lot of—"

He actually couldn't say the word "interbreeding" in front of an adult.

"No," said Celaeno. "It's the women who have the most to do with breeding, after all. I always wondered why humans had so many superfluous males. But I admit they can be fun."

She moved away from Luke, toward the window, and Luke wondered if all the harpies were looking out their windows at the humans below, picking and choosing as if they were sweets on a tray.

He could see Elliot's hair, even at this distance.

"There's a pretty thing," said Celaeno.

"Elliot?"

"We tend to like bright things," Celaeno said casually.

Luke's skin crawled. Of course they did: Elliot was practically walking around with a target on him. And he wasn't war-trained. He couldn't protect himself. Luke or Serene had had to step in a few times, back at camp, and those weren't harpies.

"Uh, I don't know how to put this," Luke said. "But Elliot . . . shares a tent with me. If you, um, understand what I mean."

What he meant was that Elliot was all elbows and constant complaints about being cold and that Luke was seriously considering sleeping outside, but he hoped Celaeno would not get that.

"Ah," said Celaeno. "Pity. Take off your shirt."

She said it like an order, so Luke did it and found himself shivering, skin bare, in the dark cool lair of the harpy. Celaeno circled him again, and he felt the light touch of her sharp fingernails against the sensitive skin of his shoulders. He wanted to fight: he felt his shoulders bunch and swell, and he crushed the urge down.

"You're holding them back," Celaeno murmured. "You'll have to let go sometime."

Apparently the meeting had gone well enough that the harpies descended to mingle with them. Or, rather, mingle with Commander Woodsinger, who was talking about treaties; Serene, who was talking about being an awesome lady warrior and the weakness of men; and Elliot, who was being charming and also making notes on harpy culture. It was very odd seeing Elliot be charming, and Luke really would have liked to cower with the others, but this was meant to be his mission and he didn't want to be a coward. He went to stand with Elliot in the absolute confidence that Elliot would tell him if he said something stupid.

"They were all being stupid," Elliot raged later in the tent. His voice carried clear outside it, to where Luke was getting changed in the merciful darkness, and probably beyond to the other tents. "We need this alliance, and that means we need to treat the harpies like allies."

"We don't need the alliance so badly," Luke said, climbing back into the tent. Elliot was dressed for bed and already shivering theatrically under his blanket.

"We do," said Elliot. "The whole otherlands and the Border need to be united."

"What?" Luke asked, appalled. "Even the trolls?"

"You don't know what the human world is like — people out there know about us, some of them can cross over, information spreads like wildfire, and they are greedy for resources," Elliot said in a rush. "They'll come. We need to be ready."

Other humans did not sound very scary to Luke, but Elliot got overexcited about many things.

"We'll have the alliance," Luke said. "You're very good at being friendly with the harpies. Maybe too good."

Elliot frowned. Luke grinned at him.

"Celaeno called you a pretty thing," he observed. "But don't worry: I told her you were my boyfriend."

Elliot stared. "You did what," he said in a flat voice.

It was Luke's turn to frown. "You're welcome."

"Why are you out to ruin my life?" Elliot demanded, and Luke gaped at him. "Is it your idea of fun? Oh, no awesome flings for Elliot, his life has to be a never-ending round of misery because Sunborn says, is why, because that's hilari —"

"Oh, my God," said Luke. "Don't tell me you would let one of those creatures touch you!"

That stopped Elliot, which was weird because he'd clearly been in full ranting mode and that usually lasted hours.

"Luke," said Elliot, which shut Luke up, because Elliot never called him that. "Don't be so stupid," Elliot continued after a pause.

That was more familiar.

Apparently that was all Elliot had to say, as if subjects were closed by mystifying random insults.

"This ground is so cold," Elliot grumbled. "I'm going to catch an ague. Or plague? Something ending in 'ague.' I'm freezing. Stupid camping."

Luke waited until Elliot was asleep to give him his blanket, because Elliot was spoiled enough and never asked nicely for things, and that kind of behavior shouldn't be rewarded. But he didn't want him to catch cold, either.

When Luke woke, the tent was crammed from edge to edge with wings.

At first, Luke didn't even know what was going on. It was like waking to find himself surrounded by pale ferns, but they were feathers, a mass of pale feathers. There was a weight on his shoulders, and he didn't dare turn over because what if he crushed them or what if he crushed —

"Elliot," he said in a strained voice.

"Go 'way," Elliot mumbled. "Comf'ble."

"Elliot, I need you to wake up right now! And don't panic," Luke added belatedly. "And maybe don't move very much."

He would not have blamed Elliot for freaking out, but, wonder of wonders, Elliot appeared to listen. Luke heard him take a deep breath, and felt him go still beneath — beneath one of —

It was so weird, having new limbs: like having a new arm or a leg but entirely different, weighed with feathers, sensation muffled by them — and yet there was feeling there, too. He could feel the jointed fold of his wings, feel them pressing against all sides of the tent and feel . . .

"Elliot," Luke growled. "Do not touch them!"

The gentle press of fingers was removed. "Sorry," said Elliot, not sounding particularly sorry. "This is cool. And the wings are pretty good. Mostly white but also gold-y. They could have turned out ginger. Trust me, as someone who has the hair, ginger wings would have been terrible —"

Luke snapped: "Stop talking like this is normal!"

"So you want me to panic?" Elliot asked. "Because you just said —"

Luke made an incoherent grating sound of rage and distress.

"Okay," Elliot said decisively. "We do have a problem here. If either of us moves, this tent is going to collapse." He continued, an edge of laughter in his voice: "So put those bad boys away. They're too much for this tent to handle."

"Are you — Shut up," Luke said. "Shut up, shut up."

Elliot kept snickering even while he was volunteering unhelpful comments like, "If you think about folding them like a deck chair"— what on earth was a deck chair? Luke concentrated on folding, putting them away . . . It was like working puppets, but puppets he could feel, and for an instant he just thought they were stuck. Then he finally got them down and sat up. The air was full of feathers.

Elliot was laughing against the back of his hand. "What would you call this? In the spirit of scientific inquiry, would you refer to it as 'morning wing'?"

"Shut up forever," said Luke, grabbing his shirt and pulling it on.

He went into the woods and shook feathers out of his hair, tried to remove all evidence, when the peace of the sky above him broke suddenly into shadow and noise: a harpy overhead shouted, "Troll force in the woods!"

Someone had obviously let slip a rumor that the humans were visiting the harpies, and the trolls had sent a brigade to check if it was true. If they hadn't seen humans, perhaps it would have been a peaceful foray.

But they had, and it was battle.

Luke had been fighting and killing since before he was ten: it wasn't easy, but it was his duty and he did it well. The mission had to run for spears and swords and shields, but the harpies held the trolls back.

The harpies were very helpful. Luke was fighting a troll when he saw a javelin coming down on Commander Woodsinger's unprotected head.

Then Celaeno swooped down and whisked up Commander Woodsinger. She dropped the commander a few yards away, looking windblown and dazed, but not so dazed that she didn't nail the troll with her spear.

Ten minutes of fighting later, Luke heard a cry and saw Delia Winterchild flat on her back in the pine needles, a troll about to smash her head like an egg.

She wasn't his friend, but she was his comrade.

The wings exploded out of Luke's back. He jumped like he would have for a Trigon game but for Delia. He didn't have talons to snatch with like the harpies did, so he just grabbed her and launched himself into the air: it was a short, lurching flight, and Delia made a terrified sound that echoed how Luke felt.

But she was safe. He didn't look back to see how she looked at him: there was Elliot to think of. They all knew Elliot wasn't battle-trained, and any one of them would have laid down their life for his, as they would for any civilian, but Elliot was Serene's and Luke's especial charge, always had been, and Luke could protect him better than anyone else.

Where Serene was, Elliot went, so Luke only had to follow the trail of troll bodies with arrows in them until he came upon Serene, out of arrows and surrounded on all sides, until Luke dived in and plucked her from their midst. She gave him a bloody nose.

"Let me go! Let me at them! I was just about to slaughter them all!"

Serene got a bit crazed with bloodlust. Luke dropped her, more gracefully than he'd dropped Delia, near some arrow-riddled bodies, and she started grabbing them as soon as she hit the ground. Serene could deal with the trolls, but Luke could see better if he was up higher, so he went higher and saw Elliot just as the trolls, robbed of Serene, noted him too.

Luke swooped in again: third time was the charm, as he didn't stumble and Elliot seemed pleased. He put his arm around Luke's neck and said, "Don't let me die, I'm brilliant and worth at least four soldiers. You'll need me when the battle's over."

"I won't let you die," Luke promised.

He dropped off Elliot, close enough so he could see him but far enough from the fighting, and turned back to the battle.

It went well, if any battles could be said to go well. Until it was over.

Luke flew with the others to catch any trolls farther afield. He left his team behind at their campsite. He was the only one who saw the harpies defile the bodies of the fallen, raking them with their talons, tossing pieces of them about in the blood and dirt.

For a moment that could not be washed away or ever forgiven, Luke felt the instinct to join them.

Then he landed in the undergrowth, folding those hated wings down and away, and was violently sick into the bones and leaves of the forest floor. He rested his forehead against a tree trunk and hated the monsters and hated himself.

Then he stumbled back to Elliot and Serene. They were on the edge of the campsite, Elliot talking with his notebook open, but they both turned to look at him and both smiled. Luke wanted to be alone with them: to curl up somewhere and be wretched, but everyone on the mission would see and Elliot would laugh at him anyway.

"There you are," said Serene. "Never remove me from combat again."

"Leave him alone," said Elliot. "He swooped me away from the trolls: he's my hero." It was a nice thing to say, one of the nicest

things Elliot had ever said about Luke, but there was an edgy laugh
to Elliot's voice, so he probably didn't mean it. Luke wasn't sure that
mattered: he thought about Elliot putting his arm around Luke's
neck.

Elliot didn't do it again, of course. He put his arm around Serene's
waist. "And you stabbed a troll with one of its own fangs in my
defense: you're my double hero!"

"Well," said Serene, who was susceptible to men making eyes at
her and complimenting her on her valor.

"We're going to have a treaty, as soon as the harpies are done,"
Elliot said happily. "I bothered Commander Woodsinger to let me
see a copy of the treaty, and it was a mess, but I have some notes here
and —"

"Oh, yes," said Luke. "As soon as the harpies are done doing what,
exactly? I guess you're not thinking about that. All you're thinking
about is all you ever think about . . . how clever Elliot Schafer is, and
how stupid the rest of the world is. Because you're a snotty little brat."

Elliot's arm fell away from Serene's waist. His mouth was thin,
suddenly. "I'm sorry. Are you, Luke Sunborn, actually telling me that
I think too much of myself?"

"I just want to know why, exactly, you think you're so superior. You
can't fight, you don't have any friends —"

Elliot raked a hand through his hair: there were still feathers in it,
Luke saw, but not Luke's.

"I can't fight?" Elliot echoed. "Who cares? Who wants to? But I
forgot: that's what you base your life on. Being one of the Sunborns,
being warriors, as if war is ever anything but a terrible failure of peace.
Oh, I'm Luke Sunborn — nothing matters but what a good little soldier I am and how excellent I am at games and how I look and how

everybody worships at my feet, and you'll never realize how little any of that matters — how could you? You're too narrow-minded: too wrapped up in strutting around convinced of how fantastic you are, being handed every break in the world."

"It's not easy!" Luke shouted. "Being a Sunborn, having everyone expect you to be the best, it's —"

"Oh, poor baby," Elliot sneered. "Being Luke Sunborn is so hard! Even when I get wings, they look perfect! I take every benefit of being a Sunborn and act like I don't even notice them! My loving family has expectations of me!"

He was twisting everything, and he was actually throwing the harpy stuff in Luke's face. He didn't understand anything, and it was unbearable.

"So that's it," Luke said coldly. "My family. You've always been jealous of them. And you've always thought I was stupid, but I'm not: I know what's going on. It wasn't about us being Sunborns, was it, Elliot? It was for the same reason you keep coming back to the Border. Nobody wants you in the human world, do they? Nobody ever did. I don't blame them."

Elliot was white as bone. Luke thought Elliot was going to hit him: he wanted Elliot to, but that wasn't Elliot's style. Instead he shot Luke one last hateful look and stormed off.

"Elliot —" Serene said, and wheeled on Luke. "What was that? I don't understand you men. Why were you so angry?"

"He's always awful to me," Luke said. "Whatever. We don't need him."

"I do," said Serene. "You're both my best friends. We're all friends."

"We're not."

"We are," Serene snapped. "You two can pretend that you're not

and snipe or whatever you need to do, boys and your feelings are incomprehensible anyway, and it was working so I put up with it. But we've all spent the better part of three years together. We are inseparable. The commander believed it because she knew it was true. Everybody knows it's true. You two are not going to make three years of being my comrades worthless. And you should apologize to Elliot, because you went too far."

Luke almost snapped back at her, but now the heat of anger was receding and the chill of shame was creeping in.

"All right," he said, heavily. "Yeah. Just . . . give me a little while. I will."

Except he didn't see Elliot, not when they were lighting the campfire or when they were eating. Not until night had fallen, so black they could not see the wood or the harpies, and Elliot walked out of the trees holding Dale Wavechaser's hand.

They went to the other side of the campfire. Serene drew in a deep breath and launched in on a detailed description of her valor in battle and the new bow she required.

Luke could not really respond in any way that made sense, because nothing made sense anymore. Dale and Elliot were kissing.

A couple of years ago, Luke had gotten a dictionary and a thesaurus, and he tried to look at them every day so he could understand the words Elliot used and so Elliot would stop laughing at him for being stupid. He quit reading them when Elliot just laughed at him for mispronouncing the words instead, but before that he learned a word that he thought described Elliot perfectly: provoking.

It turned out that Elliot could be provoking when he wasn't even talking: when he was ignoring Luke entirely. The slow curl of his mouth under Dale's mouth, the slide of his firelit hair through Dale's fingers: it was all utterly, unimaginably provoking.

Luke stayed up most of the night waiting, but Elliot did not come to the tent.

All the next day Elliot acted completely normally, in that he spent all his time with Celaeno, Serene, and Commander Woodsinger, working out the agreement. The only time he wasn't there fiddling with it was when Luke came up to sign it.

"I don't believe him," Luke fumed on the march home. "He makes out with Dale to spite me — he doesn't even like guys."

"Yes, he does," Serene said. "Surely you remember? He told the commander at the start of the trip."

"He was lying!"

Serene looked at him as if she felt sad that men were so stupid. "Lying to our commanding officer would be very wrong. He certainly was not. I knew before. Elliot had a boyfriend in the human world last summer. His name was Jason, and he worked in a music store. I'm not certain of how they sell sounds, but it's very inter —"

"It's not," Luke interrupted. "This is ridiculous. Why didn't I know about it, why —"

Serene interrupted in turn. "Elliot is a private person. As really men should be about their romantic lives, lest they be ruined for marriage. Maybe he would have told you if you hadn't been so dedicated to the stupid pretense that you are not friends."

"Well, we're not now," Luke snapped. "I don't care anyway. I'm never going to forgive him."

The words were barely out of his mouth when Elliot drew up on Serene's other side.

"Hi, Serene," he said, and slid a hesitant look past her. "Er, hi, Luke."

Luke stared stonily ahead. Out of the corner of his eye, he saw Elliot's mouth was still swollen, and his eyes looked wild.

"Okay," Elliot burst out. "I'm really sorry. I went too far, and it was spiteful and wrong, and I'm very, very sorry. You were right about stuff back in the human world, and I wanted to hurt you, but it was a low blow, and I'm ashamed of myself. I honestly feel terrible, Luke. I can't apologize enough."

"Oh . . . no. It's all right," said Luke, and Serene snorted. "Look, he's not . . . he's not my boyfriend. I'm sorry, too. I shouldn't have said any of that. It was dishonorable and you didn't deserve it. I'd just seen the harpies on the battlefield and I was . . . I was upset. I think the human world sounds stupid anyway. You should stay here with me and Serene."

"If anybody's going to cry," Serene offered, after a pause, "I don't have a handkerchief."

Elliot stopped looking touched and said: "Now that that's settled, you two have to help me. Hide me! I don't want to talk to Dale."

"Elliot Jerome Schafer!" Serene exclaimed: yet another thing that had been kept from Luke. "You cannot play fast and loose with a man's affections. Are you some sort of rogue?"

"Serene!" Elliot wailed. "It's so awkward. He is so boring! He can barely string two words together. Can't you guys stay with me at all times and don't let him talk to me until he gets the message?"

"Certainly not. Men! Have you no idea of honor?" Serene demanded. "You cannot dally with a man and then abandon him without a word. A man's heart is like a flower: beautiful but delicate, easily crushed by a careless hand."

Elliot stared. "Fine," he said crossly. "But for the record, my heart is not like a flower."

He stamped back toward Dale, who smiled as he saw Elliot approaching. Dale continued to smile for a few minutes of the conversation, which led Luke to think that Serene had made an awful mistake.

Then Dale stopped smiling. They couldn't hear what Elliot was saying, but it was pretty clear that he was yelling.

"Luke," Serene said. "Do my eyes deceive me, or is Elliot shouting at the poor boy I sent him to let down gently?"

"That's Elliot for you," said Luke, and grinned.

By the time Elliot returned, it had started to rain, a fine continuous drizzle that Elliot clearly regarded as the last straw.

"Not a word, Serene," Elliot warned. "I did my best, I'm a terrible person, let's move on. Luke, wing!"

"Excuse me?"

"Wing," Elliot said sternly.

Luke's voice scraped in his throat. "I can't —"

"I'll catch a chill. I can't believe this place, umbrellas are not high tech — should I make one, would that be fraud? What kind of time do you think you get as an umbrella-inventor impersonator —"

Luke knew the volley of words he didn't understand would continue until he obeyed, and he didn't actually want Elliot to be sick, so he glanced around and concentrated on sliding the wings out in a subtle way.

Stupidly massive wings did not come out in a subtle way ever,

it turned out, but Elliot immediately drew in with an appreciative sound. So did Serene, nodding and saying: "Very efficient."

Then Luke felt a stirring of his left wing, and saw Delia Winterchild ducking under it, looking at him in a way that was both uncomfortable and grateful.

"Much better," she said loudly. "Lucky you have them, isn't it?"

Luke had not thought yesterday that he could feel this much better.

"Elliot must have put Wavechaser off by screeching at him, so you can court him now," Serene suggested.

"Dating isn't Pass the Parcel," said Luke.

But when they arrived at camp, Dale pointedly said good-bye to Luke alone.

They were hailed as conquering heroes when they returned home. One boy made a crack about wings in class, but Delia Winterchild shut him up. And Luke and Elliot's truce actually held: Elliot called him Luke fourteen times in five days, and once when Serene wasn't there, he came and sat with Luke without hurling an insult of any kind. At Luke, that was: it being Elliot, he did insult several other people, the food, and the weather.

Serene had a catch-up session on the history of territory disputes because of her conflicting war and council schedule. Elliot might be looking for him, so Luke was packing up in a hurry when Dale said: "So d'you want to . . . come spar with me?"

"Oh," Luke said. "Not up to sparring right now."

He was packing his harpy notes carefully into his bag when the desk was pushed away from him, and Luke looked up into a kiss.

It was light, almost a question: it was his first.

"D'you want to maybe come do other things with me?"

"Oh," said Luke. "Yes."

They went to Dale's cabin, and when the door shut behind them, Dale kissed him again, for longer: it was — very nice but very strange, being with Dale but also just being with a guy, the way Luke had wanted to be and imagined being for such a long time, Dale's chest against his and mouth against his. He was worried he was clumsy, but Dale didn't seem to have any complaints: he was breathing hard, and so was Luke, into the warm space of their mouths. Dale put his arm around his neck, and Luke jolted back slightly.

"What?" Dale murmured.

"Nothing," Luke murmured back. "Nothing, it's —" and his words were lost in kissing, and so was he, warm and increasingly urgent, and then Luke's wings came out, in a burst of movement and feathers.

Dale gave a shout and reared backward, across the bed and away from Luke.

"I'm sorry," said Luke.

"No, it's fine," Dale gasped. "Man. Give me a minute."

Give him a minute to overcome revulsion.

"I don't know," said Luke.

"Really," Dale insisted. "It's fine. It's like I told Elliot, that little snot —"

"Hey!"

"I mean, I said I knew you weren't like the others, and I . . . I thought maybe before, and this, it's something I can get past." Dale took a deep breath and repeated, "You're not like the others."

"That's not entirely true," said Luke, his feathers making a soft whispering sound in the quiet of the room.

It seemed ridiculous to feel sad, kneeling on a messy bed and still panting, but Luke did.

Dale visibly nerved himself and slid back toward Luke, the blue eyes Luke had thought were kind drifting closed as he drifted closer. Luke had thought he wanted him — by the campfire, watching his hands in Elliot's hair — so much.

"Come on," said Luke, gently. "You don't really want to do this. And . . . neither do I."

Luke had the boy of his thousand faraway imaginings, kind blue eyes and muscles and mouth for the taking. It was such hideous timing that suddenly, with strange terrible ferocity, the only person he could imagine wanting in the world was Elliot Schafer.

"I'm in love with Elliot," said Luke, bursting into the cabin.

Serene put down her quill. "That's nice. Elliot who?"

"What?"

"I don't think I know an Elliot," Serene said. She added, "Aside from the obvious —"

"The obvious Elliot," Luke interrupted. "Our Elliot."

"Ehhhh," said Serene. "That doesn't seem like a good idea."

"Why not?"

"He's mentioned that he thinks he might be allergic to your face," Serene observed. "I don't think that is a good foundation for a relationship. Also, since when, and you two have just started being friends again, and . . ."

Serene stopped ticking things off her fingers when she looked at Luke's face.

"Fine," she said in a reasonable voice. "I understand. You have a yearning for the unattainable. Young men often indulge in day-dreams. Why don't you sit down and tell me all about Elliot and plan out some involved scenarios for how you might get talking to him."

Luke regarded Serene with some annoyance.

"I don't really have time for that. I need to find Elliot and ask him out."

"Ehhhhh," said Serene again.

"I don't think you realize that someone else could do it at any time," Luke told her severely. "Do you know where he is?"

"The library. It's a building on the other side of —"

"Yes, thank you, I know where it is," said Luke, and bolted.

Luke had never tried the mushrooms from elven woods, but he thought he knew what people meant when they talked about being in an altered state now: the world seemed so different, as if he had been seeing every shade of color subtly wrong, and he seemed different as well. It was deeply unsettling, and he found himself wondering if his perception would shift back, if the reality that seemed so clear now would seem strange again. He walked in the door of the library and saw Elliot, rumpling his hair and making an annoyed face at a book, and everything seemed to coalesce around the sight of him: this was real.

Luke went to him like a homing pigeon. "Hey."

Elliot looked up at him, blinking, as if he had been sleeping rather than reading, because reading to Elliot meant he was somewhere completely other. "Hey. Looking for a book?"

"Um," Luke said, and seized one from Elliot's pile. "This one."

He took the chair across from Elliot's and opened the book to have

a casual context rather than be an insane person throwing himself into libraries and demanding people go out with him.

"It's in Latin."

Luke threw the book aside because it was obviously doing him no good. "Do you want to come to the Elven Tavern with me?"

"Well," Elliot said, and the world was narrowed down to this desk, the pool of light cast by the lamp, and the thoughtful curve of Elliot's mouth. "Sure," he said eventually. "Let me finish up here. You go get Serene."

"No," Luke said. "I mean, do you want to go . . . with me. Just us. So we can . . . talk."

"Oh, my God," said Elliot. Luke was relieved that he understood and was scared at the same time.

Elliot leaned over the table, eyes dark gray and worried.

"Are you sick?" he asked. "Is it harpy cancer?"

Luke burst into slightly despairing laughter.

"Shhhhhhh!" hissed Bright-Eyes-Gladden-the-Hearts-of-Women, their burly elven librarian.

"Harpy cancer is treatable if caught in an early stage," Elliot continued. "Wing amputation only happens in extreme —"

It was odd that he'd never thought of having them cut off, having it all hidden, but he couldn't reflect on that now.

"I don't have harpy cancer. Do you want to go out on a date with me?"

Elliot's eyes narrowed. "Ha," he said crossly. "Very funny. I don't have time for this, and this book is not properly citing its sources."

He stood up, absently whacking Luke over the head with the — rather heavy — book as he did so.

Luke would have followed him, but instead he had to sit in his chair and ferociously will his wings down.

When Elliot came back, two different books tucked under his elbow, Luke leaned back in his chair and looked up at him: at his familiar face.

"Seriously," Luke said, his voice hoarse.

Elliot looked down at him and did not look either cross or confused. He looked sad. "Seriously," he said. "That's not a good idea."

Elliot and Serene acted like nothing had happened. Luke supposed they were being practical. Luke had been shut down: there was nothing to do but forget about it.

Luke could not forget about it.

This was not like the passing pleasant thoughts of Dale. This weighed on him, like the pressure of a stone feeling heavier minute by minute. Luke had never wanted what he knew he could not have before, let alone wanted it with this miserable insistent longing. He tried to be a soldier and crush it: he could not.

It felt like a necessary part of him, to always be wondering how and where Elliot was, what Elliot thought of him, to have that matter more than anything else. It felt like it had always been that way.

Maybe it had. Maybe it was like Elliot said, and Luke was stupid.

Elliot had not called him stupid in some time now, though, not since the Forest of the Suicides. He was being much nicer to Luke: maybe he felt sorry for him.

"I don't want to," Elliot said. "Let me put this as tactfully as I can: I won't like it, you shouldn't have suggested it, and it's a terrible idea."

It was still Elliot, though.

"If you knew a little self-defense, you'd be safer," Luke argued.

"If you learned how to fly underwater, you could go frolic with the

penguins," said Elliot. "But you still wouldn't be a penguin. No. I feel temperamentally and physically unsuited for war, and you cannot talk me into this."

"What's a penguin?"

Elliot laughed, his bright head tipped back. It was odd that Luke understood now that the slightly edgy laugh was the real laugh, and the charming one was Elliot being political. He seemed to understand a lot more about Elliot, now he no longer felt like Elliot's dislike was directed right at him personally, with no way to escape it or change Elliot's mind.

He understood a lot more, and he pretty much liked it all.

"Anyway, flying underwater is swimming."

"Nothing gets by you, Luke," said Elliot.

"I'm not a penguin, whatever that is," said Luke. "But you're an idiot. What if you got posted to a dangerous fortress?"

"I'm thinking I'll ask to be posted in an elven fortress at first," Elliot said. "Elves won't want a guy to fight anyway. Also someone needs to talk to those boys about a little emancipation, they can't all enjoy embroidery. And I want to learn more about elven history and culture: very few humans ask to be posted among the elves —"

"Maybe I will too."

Elliot looked surprised, but he didn't have the chance to say anything because Serene walked over to them and said: "Elliot, this came to you from Podarge the harpy," and handed over a letter. "Luke, at the library again?"

"I love books," said Luke. "They're so full of knowledge."

"I'm not sure that Podarge should mark her letters about gardening as urgent," Elliot remarked, borrowing Luke's knife to slide under the wax seal. Then he looked at the letter and bolted out of his chair, books going every which way.

"Cadet Schafer!" exclaimed Bright-Eyes the librarian.

"Get Commander Woodsinger," Elliot snapped. "Troll forces have been seen allied with human forces near the Forest of the Suicides."

Luke and Serene were out of their chairs as soon as he'd spoken.

"Contact the elves," said Luke. "I'll get everyone ready to march."

"I'm coming too," said Elliot.

"No," said Luke and Serene, as one.

"You need someone from the council course with you! You have no idea of how much that treaty would have been messed up if I wasn't there. Serene can't do it, not right after a battle, and immediately after you send the humans running, you have to offer the trolls peace . . . you have to offer an agreement that looks good. I have to be there to negotiate it!"

"You don't have to be there, because you could die there. You can't defend yourself. Someone else can go, a councillor who's not a student —"

"The treaty's with the harpies as well," Elliot protested. "No other councillor was brought to see the harpies. They don't know anyone else; they just know me! Luke, come on, you have to understand. You'd do anything if you thought it was your duty."

He was close, his eyes blazing: Luke tore his gaze away and set his jaw. Why had he ever thought he wanted someone who was like himself, and why had he thought that meant someone who liked sports?

"I understand," he bit out.

Elliot's voice was stern. "I'm going, with or without your help."

"I'm helping."

The women of Serene's clan were sworn to her defense and came at her call: the column of stern-faced martial women, hair and armor gleaming, met them on the bone-strewn plain before the Forest of the Suicides.

Luke watched them go past, and he was just thinking that one blond lady had an extremely strong jaw when Serene gasped out, "Golden?"

The blond lady spun around. Now that Luke saw her properly, he noticed that her . . . well, her chest was a little oddly placed.

"Serene!" said the blond gentleman. "I've come to fight by your side!"

Serene's mouth had stayed open on her gasp. She looked like a goldfish.

"Don't worry, I can take care of myself!" Golden continued enthusiastically. "I've been practicing with the sword while Mother and Father thought I was doing embroidery."

Elliot clawed at Luke's sleeve. "Luke," he murmured. "This is the happiest day of my life."

"I knew you would understand," Golden said happily. "I knew you were open-minded and caring and not a rogue who consorts with loose human men like Father said!"

Elliot beamed.

"You truly respect men!" Golden finished triumphantly. "You call them comrades. You fight with them! And now I'm going to fight with all of you!"

"Your . . . How did you . . ." Serene croaked, and gestured to her own chest.

"Ah." Golden looked proud. "I made some pudding and sneaked the extra into bags I sewed up and popped them right in my shirt. They're very realistic, don't you think?"

Luke was concerned that Serene was going to have a heart attack due to being so scandalized, or that Elliot was going to have one due to being overjoyed.

"Serene. You understand, don't you? You always told me you believed men were equal to women!" Golden's lip trembled.

"Golden, I assure you," Serene said, "your courage does you much credit and I . . ."

"Yes?" Golden asked dangerously.

"I like a man with spirit?" Serene still looked a little dazed. Luke dragged Elliot away, even though Elliot seemed to urgently wish to discuss something he called the elf suffragette movement.

Serene and Golden deserved a moment, if they were going to fight. He would've liked a moment with Elliot, if Elliot would have wanted one with him.

He did put his arm around Elliot's neck, which caused Elliot to glance at him, startled though not objecting, but that was for nefarious purposes.

They were aligned with the elf forces now, marching through the trees to the sound of battle. Luke could hear harpies shrieking challenge on the wind, hear the sound of them on the wing. He was a soldier, and battle was his terrible but absolute duty. He knew how to do this, and he would.

After he did one other thing.

When they were passing under Celaeno's house, Luke tightened his grip on Elliot and launched them both into the air. Elliot didn't get the chance to do anything but yell in surprise before he was stumbling backward across Celaeno's swept-earth floor.

"I'm sorry," Luke said rapidly. "You're right, we do need you for the treaty, and I don't mean to disrespect that or you, but you'll be in

danger down there, and you can't help until the fighting is done. I'll tell Celaeno you're here —"

"Good idea."

"I'll tell any harpy I see so they can consult with you, and you won't be stuck here if I get killed —"

"Luke!" Elliot protested. "I already said good idea! Please don't talk about getting killed!"

"What?" said Luke. "Oh."

"I don't actually want to be on the field of battle," Elliot continued. "I wouldn't be any help, and fields of battle are horrible places. That's why they're called fields of battle instead of fields of licorice, or . . . Try not to die, Luke. Okay?"

"I always do."

More than that he'd always wanted someone to think of coming back to. He didn't have that now, not really, but this felt almost like it: Elliot, red hair turned dark in the shadows of a harpy's hut, his mouth in an uncertain, upset shape because Luke was going into danger.

"I'm sorry," said Luke. "This isn't meant to be disrespect either, it's just that I am — and you're so —"

"I'm so what?" Elliot demanded. "Are you actually about to insult me right before you go off to war? Oh, I don't believe this, you loser —"

He said nothing more, because Luke walked three steps, took Elliot's face in both hands, and kissed his mouth.

He was aware in the back of his mind that it was a bad idea. He hadn't known what he was doing with Dale — he still didn't — and his wings were already out, filling the hut with shadows, and that must be scary; and aside from all the monstrous horror and human

clumsiness inherent in himself, Elliot had made it quite clear he didn't want this.

Elliot kissed him back. In fact, Elliot being Elliot, and so bossy, took charge of the kiss, hands in Luke's hair. The smiling questioning shape of his mouth was so familiar against Luke's, a challenge that showed Luke what to do, and this was so different from the other. It was strange and sweet and almost terrible that the same action should be so different, beautifully and irreplaceably different. Luke kissed that challenge of a mouth, the curve of it against his lip, the curve of Elliot's jaw in his palm, and the curve of Elliot's back under his folded wings, his feathers sliding up Elliot's skin and his wingspan encompassing Elliot, keeping him safe and close. He knew what to do, and he knew whom he wanted, and everything was right, after all; everything was natural.

Until Elliot tried to get away.

Luke made a low sound of distress and kissed him again, not even a real kiss, his mouth only catching the edge of Elliot's, but it made Elliot go still.

Then Elliot batted at his wings and said crossly: "No, but, Luke, the war."

"Oh," said Luke, and: "Oh."

His comrades: Serene and the rest of his class, the soldiers and the harpies. He was letting them all down. His wings snapped back into position for flight; his mind cleared.

"I have to go."

"No, really?" Elliot asked, tugging his shirt back down. "Do tell."

Luke turned to the door of the house, the sky outside blazing blue and gold except for the hurtling shapes of the harpies, the chaos on the ground below.

"Wait!" Elliot said.

He pushed one of Luke's wings casually aside, catching Luke on the threshold of the harpy's lair and by his shirt, his grip not gentle. He kissed Luke again, brief and fierce, another kind of challenge, and Luke let the edge of one wing skim Elliot's shoulder, curling lightly around, in case he never got to touch him again.

"Good luck," Elliot said breathlessly. It was almost a tender moment until Elliot actually pushed Luke out of the door.

Luke fell several feet, tumbling down toward the war, until the fall turned into flight, and he swooped down on a troll and slammed it into a tree with his momentum.

Trolls were big but trained for solitary hunting, and the men they had with them were obviously scared, but there were so many, and the Border camp had to win a decisive victory. Everything was screaming chaos for too long: Luke's arms and shoulders and wings were all aching, but the pain was somewhere far away from the blazing fire of adrenaline.

He banked to shield Serene but saw that Golden had gotten there first, giving Serene the moment she needed to recover and attack — they were building a nice rescue rhythm between them. He fired an arrow at a troll that had grabbed hold of Celaeno.

Luke became aware it was his last arrow and that he was pretty far from the ground when he saw the triumphant smile on a man's face — a young man, not much older than he was. And though he was a stranger, he didn't look strange to Luke — he was wearing clothes reminiscent of Elliot's, holding a small metal object with a trigger like a crossbow pointed at Luke. He was a human from the other side of the Border, and he was looking at Luke with combined dread and disbelief. He did not recognize Luke as human at all.

He pulled the trigger, and Luke smiled.

"They don't work over here," Luke said mildly, and the object exploded in the man's hands. Luke flew away to save another comrade, feeling a few feathers burn and fall.

The day was won, inch by painful inch.

When it was done, Luke went back for Elliot, but he was gone. Luke had hardly time for a sick rush of fear before he saw him, through the window, with Celaeno and Commander Woodsinger already. There was a tent set up and papers spread across tables that the harpies must have carried down. Luke thought he recognized the troll by one of the tables, his arm bound up, as someone he'd been trying to kill twenty minutes ago.

That was war, and now it was over. Luke's wings were so tired, they would almost not bear him: he landed on the bloodstained earth, walked past the bodies and the grave diggers and the harpies, circling and tearing.

He felt the impulse to join them. It did not shock or sicken him this time: he felt it and pushed it aside. Human or harpy, he had a choice, and he would not choose that. He passed Serene fussing over Golden: Golden was going to have a scar on his face, Luke thought. From the look on Serene's, despite all her talk about flawless golden beauty, he did not think that she would care.

Elliot was already arguing about something called codicils when Luke reached him. He shouted at Commander Woodsinger and set out to diplomatically charm a troll.

At one point, Celaeno came over to where Luke sat and said: "Your pretty thing isn't just pretty, is he?"

Luke squinted up at her, confused about how she knew, and then remembered his long-ago lie. Maybe it was true now. Maybe not, of course. Elliot might have kissed him because of the battle, or on a whim, or simply with no serious intention. A kiss did not have to mean anything: a kiss was unlikely to mean everything.

"I like him," Celaeno said. "Good nesting instinct."

"Uh. Thanks."

"Well done, Luke," Celaeno said, and Luke thought she meant more than Elliot and was sure of it when she added: "Your other father died in battle years ago. He was brave, and he had a good heart: I loved him, I suppose you'd say. He had wings like yours, and we were nestmates."

"So," Luke said, after some thought. "You're my aunt?"

Celaeno gave him a brief smile. "There is a bond between us. Is that what humans call it?"

His other father, someone with wings like his, that didn't seem real, and maybe never would. Luke knew what a father was: love and pride, being taught to play Trigon. When Luke's mother had been posted abroad, Luke had lived with Dad in a military fortress for three years and been trained as a soldier so that when Luke arrived at training camp, he was better with any weapon than any other trainee.

But an aunt, a living aunt, Celaeno's stern face and bloodied talons, seemed like something he could believe in.

"Yeah, Aunt Celaeno."

She smiled again and was peremptorily summoned by Elliot back to the table.

Night was not closing in but passing fast, the torches painting the sky blurred orange. The other soldiers set up camp away from the battlefield and slept.

Luke sat on a tree stump and waited, bloodied hands hanging between his knees and bloodied wings hanging behind him in the dust. That was what love had in common with duty: that it was something to be fought for, and if it was not your fight, to be waited for.

The treaty was signed and their leaders departing when Elliot turned to Luke.

"You should be in bed, you idiot."

"Back at you," Luke muttered.

"Well," said Elliot, grabbing his hand and towing him along. "All right, then."

"Um," said Luke.

There was blood on his hands and ink on Elliot's. Luke looked at their fingers twined together in the dawn light and almost tripped over a tree root.

He almost tripped again when he saw where Elliot was headed.

"Elliot, that is the commander's tent!"

"I am offended by the privileges of rank," said Elliot. "Also she's going to the infirmary, and you're dead on your feet."

He pushed Luke inside the same way he'd pushed him out of Celaeno's hut.

"Celaeno is my aunt," Luke said blurrily.

"I know," Elliot said. "Luke! Don't tell me you didn't even read the family tree in the notes I got you."

"I was saving them," Luke mumbled. "I love them."

"You're delirious with exhaustion," Elliot said, and dragged him to the bed.

Commander Woodsinger not only got a fancy tent, tall enough to stand in, but a bed lifted off the ground and proper blankets. Elliot crawled onto the bed and threw his arm over his eyes.

Luke hesitated.

"Luke, the commander isn't going to find out."

"That's not what I . . ." Luke began. It had been easier, when he had potentially been going to die.

"We're just going to sleep," Elliot added.

"I know that!" Luke yelped, mostly relieved.

"So?" Elliot said, and took his arm away from his eyes, sitting up. "Isn't this why you were hanging around? Isn't this what you wanted?"

To be with Elliot.

"Yes," Luke said slowly, and climbed onto the bed.

Elliot collapsed back on the pillows and curled into Luke, naturally and sweetly, as if he had done it a thousand times before, and said in a low tender voice: "Wing. It's chilly in here."

It didn't exactly qualify as whispering sweet nothings.

Luke draped his wing over Elliot's shoulders, drawing him in closer. It was warm in the little space between them, Luke's wing blocking out the light. Luke chanced putting his arm around Elliot's waist.

"All that time waiting around, and you couldn't find time to bathe?" asked Elliot.

"All that yelling at the commanders of three different armies, and you're not done complaining yet?"

Luke was starting to think they were terrible at romance.

Elliot laughed, as if Luke had said something right, and kissed him. Luke heard himself make a low helpless sound and fastened his arm around Elliot's neck. Elliot drew back, his lashes touching Luke's cheek.

"Sorry," said Elliot. "I assumed you were asking me out to hurt Dale."

"What?" Luke asked in total bewilderment: for a moment he could not actually remember who Dale was.

"The timing was very suspicious," Elliot said.

Luke kissed him. "Do you understand now?"

"Mmm," said Elliot, sleepy. "Maybe."

Luke was beyond tired: he had Elliot safe, Serene safe and happy outside, his Border safe. He wanted to sleep for hours and wake to find Elliot there.

Except he had to know something, before he could sleep: that Elliot would stay. There had been Dale, and Jason who sold sounds, and Serene. Elliot might not count Luke as anything more than that.

"Elliot," said Luke. "Are you . . . serious about this?"

Elliot made a small strange sound, as if lost for words. Luke supposed that counted as some sort of major achievement.

Finally and very quietly in the hushed warm space carved out for them by Luke's wings, Elliot said, "I'm serious as a heart attack."

He curled in closer to Luke, his hand fastened in the material of Luke's shirt as if Luke would ever think of trying to get loose. All he could hear in the quiet of the dawn was Elliot's breathing and outside the hushed sound of wings.

He felt the curve of Elliot's smile, tucked against Luke's skin.

"I'm serious as harpy cancer," Elliot murmured, and Luke laughed.

Left Foot, Right

NALO HOPKINSON

"Allyou have this in a size nine?" Jenna puts the shiny red patent shoe down on the counter. Well, it used to be shiny. She's been wearing it everywhere, and now it's dulled by dust. It's the left side of a high-heeled pump, pointy-toed, with large shiny fake rhinestones decorating the toe box. Each stone is a different size and colour, in a different cheap plastic setting. The red veneer has stripped off the heel of the shoe. It curls up off the white plastic heel base in strips. Jenna's heart clenches. It's exactly the kind of tacky, blinged-out accessory that Zuleika loves — loved — to wear.

The girl behind the counter is wearing a straw baseball cap, its peak pulled down low over her face. The girl asks, in a puzzled voice, "But don't you bought exactly the same shoes last week?"

And the week before that, thinks Jenna. *And the one before that.* "I lost them," she replies. "At least, I lost the right side"— she nearly chokes on the half-truth — "so I want to replace them." All around her, other salespeople help other customers. The people in the store zip past Jenna, half seen, half heard. This year's soca road march roars through the store's sound system. Last month Jenna loved it. Now any happy music makes her vexed.

"Jeez, what's the matter with you *now?*" the girl says. Jenna startles, guiltily. She risks a look at the shoe-store girl's face. She hadn't really done so before. She has been avoiding eye contact with people lately, afraid that if anyone's two eyes make four with hers, the fury in hers will burn the heart out of the core of them.

But the girl isn't looking at Jenna. With one hand, she is curling the peak of her cap to protect her eyes against the sun's glare through the store windows. Only her small round mouth shows. She seems to be peering into the display on the cash register. She slaps the side of the cash register. "Damned thing. It's like every time I touch it, the network goes down."

"Oh," says Jenna. "Is not me you were talking to, then?"

The girl laughs, a childlike sound, like small dinner bells tinkling. "No. Unless it have something the matter with you too. Is there?"

Jenna turns away, pretends to be checking out the rows of men's running shoes, each one more aerodynamically fantastical than the last, like race cars. "No, not me. About the shoes?"

"Sure." The girl takes the pump from Jenna. Her fingertips are cool when they brush Jenna's hand. "What a shame you can't replace just one side. Though you really wore this one down in just a week. You need both sides, left and right." The girl inspects the inside of the shoe, in that mysterious way that people who sell shoes do. "You say you want a size nine? But you take more like an eight, right?"

"How you know that?"

"I remember from last time you were in the store. Feet are so important, you don't find?"

Jenna doesn't remember seeing the girl in the store before. But the details of her life have been a little hazy the past few weeks. Everything seems dusted with unreality. Her standing in a shoe shop, doing something as ordinary as buying a pair of shoes. Her standing at all, instead of floundering.

The shoe-shop girl's body sinks lower and lower. Jenna is confused until the girl comes out from behind the counter. She's really short. She has been standing on something in order to reach the cash register. Her arms and legs are plump, foreshortened. The hems of her jeans are rolled up. Her body is pleasantly rotund.

The girl glances at Jenna's feet. At least, that's where Jenna thinks she's looking. Jenna's seeing the girl from above, so it's hard to tell. In addition to the straw cap, the girl's twisty black hair is in thousands of tiny plaits that keep falling over her face. She must have been looking at Jenna's feet, because she says, "Yup. Size eight. Don't it?"

Jenna stares down at the top of the girl's head. She says, "Yes, but the pumps run small." The girl is wearing cute yellow moccasins that look hand-sewn. She didn't get those at this discount shoe outlet. Her feet are tiny; the toe boxes of her moccasins sag a little. Her toes don't quite fill them up. Jenna curls her own toes under. Her feet feel unfamiliar in her plain white washekongs, the tennis shoes she used to wear so often, before her world fell in. Now she only wears two sides of shoes when she needs to fake normal. Or when she needs to take the red pump off to show the people in the shoe store. The blisters on the sole of her right foot are uncomfortable cushions against the canvas-lined foam inside the shoe. Although she'd scrubbed the right foot bottom before putting the washekong on, she hadn't been able to get all of the weeks of ground-in dirt out. The heel of her left foot, imprisoned most of the time in the red high heel, has become a stranger to the ground. Going completely flat-footed like this makes the shortened tendons in her left ankle stretch and twang.

NALO HOPKINSON

The girl hands the shoe back to her and says, "I going in the back to see if we have any more of these." She disappears amongst the high rows of shoe shelves. She walks jerkily, with a strange rise-and-fall motion.

Jenna sits on one of the benches in the middle of the store. She slips off her left-side tennis shoe and slides her left foot back into the destroyed pump. The height of it makes her instep ache, and her foot slides around a little in the too-big shoe. When she'd borrowed Zuleika's pumps without asking, she'd only planned to wear them out to the club that one night. The discomfort of the red shoe feels needful and good. It will be even more so when she can remove the right-side washekongs, feel dirt and hot asphalt and rocks with her bare right foot. She waits for the girl to bring the replacement pumps. The girl returns, hop-drop, hop-drop, carrying a shoe box.

Jenna doesn't want to be in the shop, fully shod, a second longer. She takes the box from the girl, almost grabbing it. "These are fine," she says, and stumps — hop-drop, hop-drop — to the cash register. She starts taking money out of her purse.

Behind her, the girl calls, "You don't want to try them on first?"

"Don't need to," Jenna replies. "I know how they fit."

The girl gets back behind the counter and clambers up onto whatever she'd been standing on. She sighs. "This job," she says to Jenna, "so much standing on your feet all the time. I not used to it."

Jenna isn't paying the girl a lot of attention. Instead, she's texting

her father to come and get her. She doesn't drive at the moment. May never drive again.

The girl rings up the purchase. Her plaits have fallen into her eyes once more. When she leans forward to give Jenna her change, her breath smells like pepper shrimp. Jenna's tummy rumbles. But she knows she won't eat. Maybe some ginger tea. The smell of almost any food makes her stomach knot these past few weeks.

The girl pats Jenna's hand and says something to her. Jenna can't hear it clearly over the sound of her grumbling stomach. Embarrassed, she mumbles an impatient "thank you" at the girl, grabs the shopping bag with the shoes in it, and quickly leaves the store. After the air-conditioned chill of the store, the tropical blast of the outdoors heat is like surfacing from the river depths to sweet, scorching air. She kicks off the single tennis shoe. She stuffs it into the shopping bag with the new pair of pumps.

What the girl said, it had sounded like, "Is Eowyn Sinead."

Jenna doesn't know anybody with those names.

Daddy texts back that he'll meet her at the Savannah, by the ice-cream man. He means the ice-cream truck that has been at the same side of the Savannah since Jenna and Zuleika were young. Jenna likes soursop ice cream. Zuleika liked rum and raisin. One Sunday when they were both still little, their parents had brought Jenna and Zuleika to the Savannah. Jenna had nagged Zuleika for a taste of her ice cream until Mummy ordered Zuleika to let her try it. A sulking Zuleika gave Jenna her cone. Jenna tasted it, spat it out, and dropped the cone. So Daddy made Jenna give Zuleika her ice cream, which made Jenna bawl. But Zuleika wanted her rum and raisin. She pouted and threw Jenna's ice cream as far as she could. It landed

in the hair of a lady who was walking in front of them. Jenna was unhappy, Mummy and Daddy were unhappy, the lady was unhappy, and Zuleika was unhappy.

Jenna remembers the odd satisfaction she had felt through her misery. Except that then Zuleika wouldn't talk to her or play with her for the rest of the day. Jenna smiles. It probably hadn't helped that she had followed Zuleika around the whole rest of that day, nagging her for her attention.

Jenna turns off her phone so no one else can call her. Her boyfriend, Clarence, tried for a while, came to visit her a couple of times after the accident, but Jenna wouldn't talk to him. She didn't dare open her mouth, for fear of drowning him in screams that would start and never, ever stop. Clarence eventually gave up. The doctors say that Jenna is well enough to return to school. She doesn't know what she will say to Clarence when she sees him there.

As Jenna is crossing the street, she walks with her bare right foot on tiptoe. That almost matches the height of the high heel on her left foot, so it isn't so obvious that one foot is bare. But she can't keep that up for long, not anymore. After more than a fortnight of walking with her right foot on tiptoe, the foot has rebelled. Her toes cramp painfully, so she lowers her bare heel to the ground. She steps in a patch of sun-melted tar, but she barely feels the burn. Her foot bottom has developed too much callus for it to bother her much. People in the street make wide berths around her in her tattered one-side shoe. They figure she is homeless or mad, or both. She doesn't care. She makes her way to the three hundred–acre Savannah. Not too many people walking or jogging the footpath yet, not in the daytime heat. But the food trucks in full swing, vending oyster cocktails, roast

corn, pholourie, doubles. Jenna ducks past the ice-cream man, hoping he won't see her and ask how she's doing. He knows — knew — Jenna and Zuleika well. He had watched them grow up.

The poui trees are in full bloom. They carpet the grass with yellow and pink blossoms. Jenna steps over a cricket wicket discarded on the ground and goes around a bunch of navy-uniformed schoolgirls liming on the grass under the trees. A couple of them are eating roti. They all stop their chatting long enough to stare at her. Once she passes them, they whoop with laughter.

Jenna doesn't know how she will manage school next week.

She finds a bench not too far from the ice-cream man, where she can see Daddy when he comes. She sits and puts the shoe bag on her lap. She clutches the folded top of it tightly. She doesn't put the new shoes on. She never has. They aren't for her. She was wearing the left side of Zuleika's shoes when she surfaced. She has to give Zuleika a good pair of the shoes in return for the ones she took without permission.

For a few minutes, Jenna rests her aching feet. Then she realizes that the air is beginning to cool. The sun will be going down soon. Jenna texts her father again, tells him never mind, that she will come home on her own later. He tries to insist. She refuses. Then she turns the phone off. Is better like this, anyway. Her parents are doing their best. Looking after Jenna, asking after her. Doing their grieving in private. Some days Jenna can't bear the burden of their forgiveness.

She can't take neither bus nor taxi half shod the way she is. She gets up off the bench, wincing at the separate pains in her feet. She starts walking. *Clop, thump. Clop, thump.* One shoe off, and one shoe on.

It's dark when she gets to the right place on the highway. The sight

of the torn-apart metal guardrail sets her blood boiling hot so till she nearly feels warm enough for the first time in almost a month. Anger is the only thing hotting her up nowadays. When are they going to fix it?

She lets herself through the space between the twisted pieces of metal and starts clambering down the embankment. Below her, the river whispers and chuckles. A few times, she loses her footing in the pebbles and sparse scrub grass of the dry red earth of the embankment and slides a little way down. She could hold on to clumps of grass to try to stop her skid, but why? Instead, she digs in the heel of Zuleika's remaining pump. Above her, cars whoosh by along the highway. But the closer she gets to the tiny patch of wild between the highway and the river, the more the traffic sounds feel muffled, less important. The moonlight helps her to see her way, but she doesn't need it. She knows the route, every rock, every hillock of grass. She has been here every night for a few weeks now, as soon as the bleeding stopped and the hospital discharged her.

Tiny glowing dots of fireflies prick the darkness open here and there all around her. Jenna's skin pimples in the cool evening breeze. The sobbing river flows past, just ahead of her.

At the shoreline, Jenna gets to her knees. "Zuleika!" she yells. She sits back on her heels in the chilly riverbank mud, clutching the shoe bag in her lap, and waits. The heel of the red shoe pokes into her backside, but the mud feels good on the blistered sole of the other, bare foot.

"Zuleika!"

Nothing.

"I sorry about your fucking shoes, all right?"

Nothing.

She gets the new shoes out of their box. She tosses them into the water. They sink. She waits. She is waiting for the frogs in the reeds to stop chirping. For the sucking pit of grief in her chest to fill in.

For Zuleika to forgive her.

When none of that happens — just like it hasn't happened every other time she's come down here — she sighs and stands up. The heel of the left shoe sinks down into the mud. She pulls it out with a sucking sound.

The river isn't the only thing weeping. Someone is crying, over there in the dark, where the mangroves cluster thicker together. Jenna heads, hop-drop, towards the sound. There are tiny footprints in the muddy soil. They lead away from the crying, towards the direction of the embankment. In the dark, Jenna can't make out how far they go. But she can tell where they came from, so she follows the footprints backwards.

There's a child sitting on a big rock by the waterside. The child is the one crying. It is wearing a huge panama hat. To keep from burning in the moonshine? Jenna doesn't laugh at her own joke. The child is wearing jeans rolled up at the ankles, a too-big T-shirt. It has its legs tucked up and its chin on its knees, propping sorrow. In the moonlight, Jenna can see the yellow moccasins on its tiny feet. It's the girl from the shoe store.

When she gets near enough, Jenna says, "What you doing out here? Something wrong?"

"I was trying to catch crabs," the girl replies. "I like them too bad."

Jenna remembers the seafood smell on the girl's breath. "Trying to catch them how?"

"With my hands, nuh?"

"You went wading in this water at night, with nobody around?

This water not good," says Jenna. *It takes people*, she doesn't say. Sure enough, now that she's closer, she can see that the girl is sopping wet. Water is running off her clothes and streaming down the sides of the rock.

"Mummy don't have time for me," the girl replies. "I been trying to catch my dinner myself, but . . ." The girl starts sobbing again. "My feet hurt so much! All that standing in the shoe store, all day. Every time I put my feet down, is like I walking on nails. I keep flinching when I step and frightening off the crabs-them."

Poor thing. Something small releases inside Jenna, like the easing of a stitch. She squishes through the mud and sits on the rock beside the girl. She puts the bag with the empty shoe box in it down on the rock. "I know how it feel when your feet paining you," she says.

Whimpering, the girl leans closer to Jenna. The smell of seafood makes Jenna's tummy grumble again. Jenna thinks she could comfort the girl with a hug. She doesn't do it, though. Since last month, she doesn't have any business with comfort. But the girl won't stop crying, her shoulders jerking with the force of her sorrow. Unwillingly, Jenna asks, "You want me help you catch the crabs?"

The girl doesn't lift her panama-hatted head, but her crying noise stops. "You would do that for me?" she asks, sounding so young. She's only a child!

"You would have to show me how," Jenna replies. "And how old you are, anyway?"

The girl says, "You have to put your feet in the water, slow-slow and quiet, so the crabs don't know you're there. You have to stay crouched over, ready to grab them when they come up."

Jenna doesn't want to put her feet back into the river that had swallowed her and Zuleika not too long ago. She still has nightmares

of escaping through the open driver's-side window, of her head feeling light from holding her breath in. Only in her dreams, Zuleika doesn't let go when she grabs Jenna's right foot.

Jenna whispers so the child won't hear her talking to Zuleika. "I told you to undo your seat belt, don't it? When we started sinking, I told you. You should have come with me. But all you did was scream."

In Jenna's dreams, she isn't able to kick her leg free of Zuleika's panicked hold. In Jenna's dreams, river weed comes pouring out of Zuleika's hand and wraps itself around Jenna's right ankle and doesn't let go. In Jenna's dreams, she drowns with her sister. Every night, she drowns.

But she's promised the shoe-shop child. "Okay," says Jenna. "Just until your mummy comes." She briefly wonders why a little girl is working in a shoe store, why she's hunting for crabs alone down by the river at night, but she doesn't wonder for too long. The world has become strange, and she is no longer part of it.

Jenna takes off the mashed-up left-side shoe and puts it on the rock. She wiggles her toes. Night air slips through the spaces between them. It feels odd. She had put that shoe back on after Zuleika's funeral.

She eases herself down off the rock. Now she's standing, both feet bare, on the riverbank. Her feet are squishing up mud. The left foot sinks a little farther into the mud than the right one. In front of her, black as oil, the roiling river giggles.

She can't do this. Jenna turns to walk back to solid land, to leave the child to wait there alone for its mother.

"Don't be frightened," says the child.

"I not frightened," Jenna replies. She is, but not of the water. Truth to tell, she wants nothing more than to sink down into the river, to join Zuleika. She wants it so badly, but she knows she can't. Can't make her parents lose two daughters to the river in less than a month. And she loves the sweet air. Heaven help her, but she loves it more than she loves her sister.

The child says, "You have to walk slow, keep your eyes peeled on the river bottom. When you see a crab, you reach down and grab it with your two hands."

"And what if it pinch me?"

"They small. They can't pinch hard."

Jenna tries it. She slides her feet along in the shallows. The moonlight lends its glow to the water there. After a minute or two of squinting, she can make out the river bottom. At first Jenna's feet hurt every time she takes a step, but pretty soon the chilly river water numbs them. A crab scuttles sideways in front of her. Jenna pounces. Splashes. Misses. She falls into the shallow water. She's wet to the waist. The child laughs, and Jenna finds herself smiling, just a little. Jenna picks herself up. "Lemme try again."

She misses the second time, too. At the third fall, she laughs at herself. And at the fourth. By the fifth missed crab, she and the child are shrieking with merriment.

The child points. "There! Look another one!"

Jenna leaps for the splayed, scuttling crab. She catches it. She's holding it by its hard-shelled body. Its claws wave around and scrabble at her hand, but the crab is too small to do any damage. Jenna rises with it, triumphant, from the riverbed. She whoops in glee, and the child applauds. Jenna realises that she's stopped thinking of the child as a girl. Really, she doesn't know whether it's a girl or a boy. She wades closer to the bank with her catch. "What I do with it now?" she asks.

The child hesitates. Then slowly, it removes the large panama hat that's been obscuring its face. It turns the hat over, bowl-like, and holds it out. "I put them in here," it says.

It has no face. Just a small bump where a nose should be, and that perfectly bowed mouth. Jenna is startled for a second, but she recovers. Not polite to stare. Anyway, in a world gone strange, why make a fuss about a missing pair of eyes and a nose with no holes? Jenna drops the crab into the hat the child holds out. Immediately, the child grabs the live crab up and rips into it with tiny, sharp teeth. It spits out a mouthful of broken shell. "You could catch more, please? I so hungry."

Jenna splashes about some more. She catches crabs, and she laughs giddily. Before this the river has been making fun of her. Now, it is chortling with her. Jenna catches crabs and drops them into the child's hat. Jenna is shivering, belly deep. Maybe from being cold and wet, maybe from giggling so hard. The child smiles and eats and pats its full belly. Jenna pats her empty one. She goes closer to the shore. "Let me have one," she says to the child. She holds her hand out.

The child turns its blank face towards the sound of her voice. "You eat salt, or you eat fresh?" it asks.

"You have salt?" Jenna asks. "I would prefer that over eating it fresh."

"I don't have any."

Why does the child sound so happy about that? Jenna doesn't have patience with gladness nowadays. She has stopped hanging out with her friends and them from since. They would probably just want to go to the club, to dress up nice, to lime. Jenna doesn't want to do any of that anymore. Dressing up leads to borrowing your sister's shoes without permission. It leads to quarreling over the shoes in the car on

the way to the club. It leads to your sister losing control of the steering wheel and driving the car off the road into the river.

Jenna's eyes overflow. She has become used to the quick spurt of tears, as though someone has squeezed lime juice into her eyes.

Gently, the child says, "And look the salt right there so." It nods approvingly and hands over a particularly big crab. Jenna snatches it. She pulls off a gundy claw. With her teeth, she cracks it open. Crab juice and moist meat fall into her mouth. She sucks the rest of the meat out of the claw. She's so hungry that she barely chews before swallowing. As she eats, she cries salt tears onto the food, seasoning it. She fills her belly.

Jenna stops eating when she notices that the child is trying to reach for its own moccasined feet. Its arms are too short. The child says, softly, "I wish I could take these shoes off." It turns its smooth face in Jenna's direction and smiles. "She had them with her in the car that night. She was going to give them to you, Mummy. As a present for me."

Jenna's mind goes still, like the space between one breath and the next. Somehow, she is out of the water and sitting on the rock beside the child. Gently, she touches one of the child's infant-fat legs. The child doesn't protest. Just leans back on its hands, its face upturned towards hers. Jenna lifts the child's small, lumpy foot. She loosens the lace on the moccasin and eases it off. The tiny yellow shoe sits in her palm, an empty shell. The child's foot is cold. Jenna cups the foot to warm it and removes the other shoe. She looks at the two baby feet that fit easily in her hand. The child's strange gait makes sense now. Its feet are turned backwards.

Jenna gasps and pulls the child onto her lap. She curls her arms around it and holds its cold body close to hers. The other life she'd

lost that night. The one only she and her older sister had known about.

The child snuggles against her. It puts one hand to its mouth and contentedly sucks its thumb. Jenna rocks it. She says, "I didn't even self tell Clarence yet, you know." The child grunts and keeps sucking its thumb. Jenna continues, "I sixteen. He fifteen. I was trying to think whether I was ready to grow up so fast."

The child sucks its thumb.

Jenna takes a breath that fills her lungs so deeply that it hurts. "Part of me was relieved to lose you." Her breath catches. "Zuleika *drowned*. And part of me was glad!" Jenna rocks the child and bawls. "I sorry," she says. "I so sorry." After a while she is quiet. Time passes, a peaceful space of forever.

The child takes its thumb out of its mouth. It says, "Is her own she need."

Jenna is puzzled. "What?"

"Is that I was trying to tell you in the store. She don't want new shoes. She have the right-side shoe already. You have to give her back the left-side one. The one you been wearing."

Jenna surprises herself with a low yip of laughter. All this laughing tonight, like a language she'd forgotten. "I didn't even self think of that."

The child replies, "I have to go now."

Jenna sighs. "Yes, I know." She takes the child's blank, unwritten face in her hands and kisses it.

The child stands and pulls off its T-shirt and jeans. Its body is as featureless as its face. Jenna puts its hat back on. The child says, "You could keep my shoes instead, if you want." It eases itself down off the rock and toddles towards the water, away from life. But in the mud,

the imprints of its feet are turned towards Jenna. The child enters the river. Knee deep, it stops and looks back at her. It calls out, "Auntie say she will look after me!"

Jenna waves. "Tell her thanks!"

Her child nods and waves back. It dives into the water, panama hat and all.

Jenna is still holding the tiny, wet moccasins. Gently, she squeezes the water from them. She slips them into the front pocket of her jeans. She goes and picks up the destroyed left pump from the rock. She kisses it. She yells, "Zuleika! Look your shoe here!" She raises her arm, meaning to fling the shoe into the river.

But there, in the very middle of the water — a rising, rolling semicircle, like a half-submerged truck tyre. Blacker than the blackness around. Swallowing light. The back of Jenna's neck prickles. Muscles in her calves jump; her running muscles. She makes herself remain still, though.

The fat, rolling pipe of blackness extends into a snakelike tail that wriggles over to the shore. The tail is unbifurcated, its tip as big around as her wrist. The tip is coiled around a red patent pump, the matching right side to the shoe that Jenna is holding. In a whisper, Jenna asks, "Zuleika?" The tail tip slaps up onto the bank, splashing Jenna with mud.

Zuleika rises godlike from the river. Jenna whimpers and runs behind the rock.

Zuleika's upper half is still wearing the red-sequined minidress, now in shreds, that she'd worn to go dancing the night of the accident. Moonlight makes the sequins twinkle, where they aren't hidden by river weed that has become tangled in them. The weed dangles and drips. Zuleika's lower half has become that snakelike tail. At her

middle, the tail is as thick around as her waist. She floats upright. Her tail waves on the surface of the water. It extends as far upriver as Jenna can see in the moonlight.

Jenna's douen child clambers from where she'd been hidden behind Zuleika's back. The child climbs to sit on Zuleika's shoulders. It knots its fingers into the snares of Zuleika's hair. The water hasn't damaged its hat. Is the child smiling, or baring its teeth? Jenna can't tell.

Zuleika raises the whole length of her tail, and Jenna quails at the sheer mass of it, blacker than black against the night sky. Zuleika smashes her tail against the water's surface. The vast wave of sound, echoing up the river, hurts Jenna's ears. Jenna hears cars screeching to a halt on the highway, horns bleating. Jenna puts her hands against her ears and cowers. Not another crash. Please.

But there is no sound of collision. A couple of car doors slam. A couple of voices ask each other what the rass that sound was. Mama d'lo Zuleika hovers calmly in the water. The few trees must be hiding her from view, because soon, car doors slam again. Cars start up and drive off. Zuleika, Jenna, and the douen child are alone again.

Jenna finds that she's still holding the left-side shoe. She gathers her courage. She comes out from behind the rock. She says to her sister, "This is yours." She holds the shoe out to Zuleika.

Zuleika's tail tip comes flying out of the darkness and grabs the shoe from Jenna. She hugs both once-shiny red shoes — the dusty one and the waterlogged one — to her breast.

The wetness in Jenna's own eyes makes the moon break up and shimmer like its own reflection on the water. "I miss you," she says.

Zuleika smiles gently. Carrying her niece or nephew, Zuleika sinks back beneath the water.

Jenna's hands are cold. She slides them into the front pockets of her jeans. One hand touches the child's shoes. The other touches her cell phone. She brings it out. It's wet, but for a wonder, it's still working. She texts her mother, says she will be home soon. She calls another number. "Clarence, you busy? You could come and give me a lift home? I by the river. You know where. No, I'm all right. I love you, too. Have something I need to tell you. Don't worry, I said!"

She still has her washekongs. She rinses her feet in the river and puts them on. She collects the empty shoe box and the plastic shopping bag. She climbs up the embankment to the roadside to wait for her boyfriend.

NALO HOPKINSON

THE
Mercurials

G. CARL PURCELL

One night, after everyone in North Bangor, Michigan, had gone to sleep, and only one woman was left to sing the night-song shift, Blank Itzikoff snuck out of his bedroom window and walked through the black field toward the ruins of South Bangor.

On his way through the tall corn, he spotted Nit Stevens mounted on a pedal-driven noisemaker. That Nit had the energy to pedal the thing was surprising. He was an incalculably old man, older than Dumb Maxwell and all the other learned men. Blank could hear him breathing heavy above the wooden clop of the noisemaker. Blank tried to sneak behind him and had barely crept a dozen feet before he heard Nit's voice call his name.

"Itzikoff! What are you doing sneaking around?" Nit hollered.

Nit Stevens had picked up the Mad Hatter's tremor; Blank could hear it in his voice, and though it was a warm late-summer night, Nit shook like it was winter. He smiled, and his gums glittered like pink rocks in his mouth.

Blank shouldered his way out of the corn and made himself visible. "Your head on top of that corn looked like a Ping-Pong ball floating in a tub," Nit yelled, breathlessly. Nit never stopped pedaling the noisemaker. He had to shout to be heard.

"I'm going to scavenge some rubber gloves," Blank said.

"What do you need those for?"

Blank couldn't think of a lie. "I want to take up learning, like you and Dumb Maxwell."

Nit Stevens kept on him with a wet, wild look. Then he burst out laughing. "You find any rubber gloves out in the ruins, you bring some back to me, you hear? You give me a little taste of them rubber gloves," he said.

Blank gave Nit a distrusting look. He thought he would get whipped for sneaking right out there in the field. "I'm free to go?"

"You ain't going to find nothing in the ruins, boy, but you're young and full of mosquito piss. You'd find some way anyway. You got your whistle?"

Blank showed him his whistle.

"Get back before sunup. Don't tell no one I sent you. And watch the ground."

Silence was a fact, like the Earth, and it always took some implement to beat it back. Blank held his whistle between his teeth and kept his eyes away from the fascinating old Kozy Inn and Dawg 'N Burger

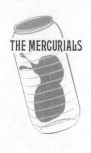

signs that hung crookedly above his head. He kept his head toward the ground. A few silvery shapes scuttled across the road ahead of him, but nothing touched him.

After a few hours of searching, he found a waterlogged old house two rows to the back of the State Road. Its upper floors had all given way, giving the house the large, empty feeling of a barn. The concrete basement was carpeted silvery black, and when Blank pointed his whistle at it and blew, the floor came alive. The mercurials Blank usually saw shaped themselves like common things — the odd salamander or chipmunk. Yet some of the creatures that scurried away in that basement caught the moonlight, and Blank could see long legs and heads, weird things, reflected there.

After some searching, he found a sealed packet of gloves among some rotten rags. They looked thinner than Dumb Maxwell's and might have had holes, but there were a lot of them, and he had to start somewhere.

A few hours before sunup, Blank found Nit Stevens fallen asleep astride his noisemaker. His beard had bunched against his chin and his feet were kicked up on the handlebars. He did not wake the old man.

That morning one of the skinny cows was dead, and another one — a fat, useful one — was wobbling and drooling out in the field. The whole village had come out to see. Dumb Maxwell led them, banging a cowbell with an old gray spoon.

Dumb Maxwell was always telling about things, and some of those things were well beyond Blank's imagining. There wasn't a villager old enough to remember the day the silver bodies slanted out of the sky and covered the earth, but Dumb Maxwell knew more about them than anyone else, and they were the subject of most of the fearful tales he had to tell about. They poisoned wells and crops, he said, but the worst thing about them was that on rare occasions they liked to burrow into warm, living fat. And so one of them had crawled into the cow's ear or mouth or asshole early in the evening as Nit Stevens slept, and by morning the cow was sick and would probably die.

Dumb Maxwell, Frittering Jane, Stupid Hess, and a few other learned folks banged bells and buckets up and down the cow's body. Nit was there, too. He was yelling at Dumb Maxwell about how he wasn't going to find anything in that cow, and Dumb was telling Nit to shut up. They banged and hollered for a good fifteen minutes near the cow's head until she fell on her front knees with a wet-sounding bellow. Mucus trailed from her nose in great clumps, followed by a braid of shimmering mercury. Dumb Maxwell caught the mercury in a bucket and sealed it with a lid. Later that day the cow would be slaughtered and stripped for her skin, and her meat would be buried far away from the village.

"That ain't on my watch," repeated Nit. "No sir."

Blank half expected Nit to call Blank out for the sneaking, to take the tanning off himself. But Nit was lost in thought now, kind of sad looking. "Not on my watch," he said, and Hess and Jane looked at him, hard and sort of crossly.

Dumb Maxwell, scowling, walked back to his home with the bucket beneath his arm. Blank trotted to catch up with him. "I'd like to see what you do with that," Blank said.

"You worry about you and yours," Dumb said.

Blank stopped and called after. "Let me get scarecrow duty, now that Nit's not gonna be on it. How 'bout then? Then you can show me what it does."

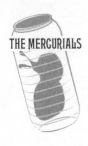

"You ain't of age yet," said Maxwell over his shoulder. He drummed the bucket. "And that there's a mystery."

It was Maxwell who first showed how the creatures died when you pulled a seed out of them, how that seed vibrated so as to make the rubber on the tips of your gloves purr. It was Maxwell who first showed in class especially how loud noises made the seed stop purring altogether, which felt like an answer to Blank's own fear.

Tuesday-evening service was sparsely attended. Folks were always welcome to listen to the sermon from the comfort of their homes, since sermons could be heard in all directions for five miles around, but that was not a privilege the Itzikoffs commonly took. All three of them — son, mother, and father — were wiry people, not easy to distinguish from the other farm people sitting around them. They, too, had multiple tattoos strung around their arms, which celebrated both the fruitful harvests and the low; professed in dense calligraphy the names of their wives, husbands, sons, and daughters; and enacted in fleshy ink lines the fearful fights of the mercurials in the forms of snakes, Rodentia, whales, squid, demons, dragons, mad dogs, and wildcats. They wore the same clothes to church they wore in the fields, shirts dyed in sacred black with fat stitches, black leather stripped from the limp-looking cows out in the fields and dyed with the same tannin-and-iron dye they all used. If anything distinguished Joe Itzikoff, it was that he was rangier and taller than most, a trait Blank followed.

Fulsome Chet, the church caretaker — not rangy himself but tall in the way of a large man — opened all the windows and the large barn doors of the church, while his wife, Hannah, took care

of the outside, making sure the loudspeakers had not drooped or
craned away from the fields by the wind. On the field's edge, the
foot-pedaled noisemakers and bells were still, and behind the wind
chimes just a few crickets sounded. The moment before congregation was the only silence the town of Bangor, Michigan, ever knew,
and one could feel the presence of the mercurials closing in on that
silence, waiting to take up space.

Priest Waverly, so partial to the color black he took to dying
his great tousle of hair and beard in it, took the stage with a great
clomping of boots. He was followed by two of his retinue. They had
raccooned their eyes with campfire pitch and were dressed in fine-
looking leather. The congregation waited. Priest Waverly nodded to
Fulsome Chet, who from offstage began to crank the wheel of North
Bangor's only working dynamo. The dynamo squealed, tearing into
the silence of the church, and began to raise sparks.

Priest Waverly plugged his bass guitar into the dynamo-powered
Marshall stack, as the drummer sat behind his equipment with an
ambient rattle. The guitarist plugged in with an electrical burst.
None of them said a word as they prepared.

So they began. The night's sermon would be bottom-heavy, slow,
and repetitive, in the chords of G and F. Blank looked over at his
father, who had long been a partisan of the F chord. His eyes were
shut, and his face had gone slack in the warm bath of the congregational sonics. The sermon had a physical presence, like wind blowing
through an open window, and Priest Waverly sang in a voice sunk
low in thunder and fat:

Let me down
Down to the sea

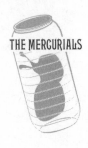

THE MERCURIALS

Right silver rabbit
Right black bird
Carry me down
Intangible flame
Down to the sea
Bu-u-ry me
Bu-u-ry me

Between the candlelight of the church and the fading dusk outside, the two great stained-glass windows began to assert themselves. On one pane, a demon threatened to fling a crucified farmer from a hand sling. In another, hook-kneed demons fell before a long wall of orange flame, beneath writing that had always puzzled Blank. Once he saw a few drops of tannin fall into a pail of milk, where they whorled and furred like a living thing; the writing looked like that, formed of dizzying spikes and jagged curls.

Dim Henry, the eldest of the learned, sat trembling next to Dumb Maxwell in the back row. Nit Stevens was a piker when it came to the Mad Hatter's syndrome, compared to Old Dim Henry; Dim was now generally acknowledged to be the very stupidest of the learned ones. Tonight's sermon was in his honor, because today he'd be retiring from work and noisemaking. He smiled, and his patchily shaven face showed a single yellow tooth.

Priest Waverly and his retinue played for an hour. The dark sonics entered the church and forest like varnish soaking into wood. When the hour was done, the guitarist dropped out first, then the drums went silent, and finally Priest Waverly's lead bass guitar rang one final, heavy note that dissipated slowly, like salt on the tongue. Chet stopped turning the dynamo, sweating through his leather vest. Every face was turned to the ceiling, where silence and mind briefly mingled.

"Well, then," said Priest Waverly. He nodded to Dim Henry, which elicited grunts of approval from the old ones in the pews. Nit Stevens was not to be found among them. The priest started packing up his bass.

Dumb Maxwell led Henry through the front door and to the back of the church, proudly pointing his lightning-streaked orange beard before him like a dowsing rod. Henry kept talking about his grandson's birthday, though his grandson had left Bangor many years back. The congregation stood, each in his or her own time, and left the church. A few wandered off to scarecrow duty, to get the noise-makers running again. Still more went home, as there was work to be done in the morning. Many, including the Itzikoffs, followed Dumb Maxwell to the back of the church. Blank's dad put a hand on Blank's shoulder.

"Why don't you get on back to the house," he said.

"I want to see Old Dim get his retirement," said Blank.

"You get on back and boil up a pot of water for your ma's tea," said Blank's father. Blank expressed an unhappiness but did as he was told.

Coming back from the church, Blank found Nit Stevens sitting on his porch, staring out into the black wood across the field. He trembled as he looked into the dark.

"Why ain't you at Old Dim Henry's retirement?" asked Blank.

"You think I gotta go to everybody's fuckin' retirement?" The retort was sharp.

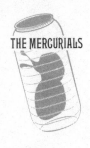

A few houses away, Judy Glick began singing a song about a place called Miami. She always led the first night-song shift. All the women's songs were about cities, how bright they were, how many people lived in them, how the women there danced all the time, just danced and danced.

"I didn't say you got to do anything," Blank said, his voice lowered. "Pa says you and Henry go back a ways."

"We go back a ways, that's true. We was kids together forty years back." Nit Stevens frowned deeply and looked at the floorboards of his porch. "But that's an end of it." There was a little bit more of the wise Nit present here, as if Nit had sat down and focused on being wise the better part of the day.

"It's just, I never seen you miss a service," Blank said. "I remember all those times you used to sing with the congregation. You were funny when you used to sing."

Nit did not reply. Things were silent between them for a moment. Blank was thinking he ought to go but reluctance held him, and then a notion took him.

"Hey, I found them rubber gloves we was talking about," Blank said.

Blank thought he saw a worried look pass across Nit's face. "I don't know what you're talking about, boy."

"It's the gloves I was looking for in the ruins, Nit," Blank said. "You remember."

Nit looked back out to the woods. "I don't remember shit, boy. Get on." This last the old man yipped, like a dog, so that Blank turned and ran off.

———✦———

An empty seat was held open for Dim Henry for a month, by way of custom. By the time it filled again, the sermons sounded earlier each dusk, and North Bangor had begun the harvesting of corn. From morning through the afternoon in those shrinking days, all was corn in the village, and Blank worked every day. Corn was broken from its stem and collected by the men and women and detasseled by the women and the children and by Blank. The women sang songs about Chicago and Providence and Houston as they worked.

Corn was apportioned to each family, who roasted and ate it every night. Corn was set to dry and was ground as meal. It would be turned throughout the winter into every manner of pone, bread, biscuit, and tortilla. The greater share of corn was set aside in the better-made barrels and stacked in the large barn, which served as the village commissary. In the morning in the schoolhouse, Blank was compelled to do figures in terms of how many corn kernels, or to multiply these bushels of corn against these others and see what you came up with. In the afternoon Blank would work, and every night the congregational sonics were about corn or hard work, or both, or about the winter to come. They would alternate: lively, then dirgelike, and back to lively. Priest Waverly's retinue would play *chunk chunk chunk chunka chunka*, as folks stumbled into church with blistered hands and aching backs. As congregation wore on, the sonics would slow into the long, muscle-soothing *bwooowm*, which indicated the work would soon be done.

By this time, Blank had snuck into the ruins two more times. It was a relief from corn. He knew Bangor a bit from the one time his dad took him there, but now he had a street map in his head. Blank had collected the gloves, plus a dead clock, some edible mushrooms, and an old jar for his efforts, all of which he kept under his bed.

He felt he was ready for the next step. He intended to catch a silver body. He'd keep it under his bed, too, and study it. Eventually he'd find the seed inside of it and stop it and show Dumb Maxwell or Nit Stevens what he'd done.

The best thing about being learned, Blank thought, was that you didn't have to be musical or good with plants, and you didn't get yelled at all the time for dropping things.

Nit Stevens was no longer on scarecrow duty, and Bill Kingdom, who took his place, was a big fat boy who couldn't concentrate on anything but pushing his pedals nice and loud. Blank found it easy to pass him by. The path to the ruins led Blank to a moonlit section of the dead interstate near the old schoolhouse. From the outside the brick walls of the school were rotten, as if a giant had swung hammer blows to the corners and knocked out great chunks of masonry. The BANGOR HIGH SCHOOL sign that had been affixed to the brick wall had lost its individual letters and were instead ghosted on the wall and smothered by decay. Blank snapped on a pair of rubber gloves. He held his jar before him like an offering, his whistle between his teeth.

The shadows scattered. Once, when Blank was young, he fell into a trough and snorted a gout of water, which seemed to fill him up to the eyeballs. If a silver body got up inside of his face, through his nose, he wondered if it would feel like that, like drowning, or worse than that. A couple of shadows got close, and he blew his whistle at them.

Soon one silver-dark lizard, a big one, was playing near his shoes, and he let it stay there. It wiggled in and out of the moonlight. Before Blank knew it, the thing was running up his leg.

Capturing it was a mighty struggle. The thing was cold as ice and would not easily be caught. It scrabbled from his leg to his chest and then around to his back. Blank danced like a child possessed. When Blank finally stopped using his gloved hands to catch it and used the jar instead, the thing right walked into it from his hip. Blank twisted the lid tightly and there he had it. He felt learned as hell at that moment.

Blank looked at his jar. The silvery thing inside, larger than the one Dumb Maxwell had shown him, had become sleek and rabbitlike, and it was surprisingly heavy. Blank had to hold on with two hands as the weight shifted within the glass, making him feel vulnerable.

He came to the town a few hours before sunup, as was usual, and snuck past Bill Kingdom, who had slowed his pedaling but was concentrating all the harder for it.

Blank was telling himself how easy it all had been when, to his surprise, he found Nit Stevens was waiting for him, slumped on a beam on Blank's father's front step. He looked as if he'd just snapped awake. Blank quickly hid the heavy, awkward jar behind his back.

"I remembered about the gloves you promised," said Nit. "I seen you sneak out to the back forty again through my window. What you hiding there?"

Blank, barely able to hold the jar, was about to deny everything. Then he dropped the jar, which shattered on the dirt walkway behind him.

The mercurial, newly freed, did not run. It was shaped like a large rat now. It had a nose too long to be natural, from which mercury dripped like snot. This poked at the air between itself and Blank, who had scrambled next to Nit Stevens.

"Tuck tuck tuck," Nit said. "Now now now." He held his arm toward the rat, who, after a moment's hesitation, crawled onto it. Nit snaked his arm back and forth, and the Mercurial snaked with

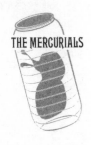

it. "You are a cold one, aren't you?" said Nit to the thing. He held his arm just a foot from his face, and the silver body traveled to the end of his curled fingers and stuck its nose out in the space between them.

"You're like to kill yourself screwing around that way," whispered Blank.

Nit looked back at him with a gap-toothed condescending smile. In the dim not-quite-dawn, his eyes seemed to travel a mile backward in his skull. "It won't hurt me," Nit said.

Blank watched the creature climb up and down Nit's arm. Man and mercurial moved well together, like flotsam against water.

"How do you do it?" Blank whispered.

"They's explorers, like us. They won't get inside you if you keep 'em busy, doing something else. They like to move, to explore new surfaces." They both watched the silver rat for a moment as it clambered up and down his forearm. "Look at him," said Nit. "It's as if he was trying to communicate." Blank saw something in this, how the rat synchronized its movements with his. "Would you like to try?" asked Nit.

"No," said Blank, but his eyes watched the rat with painful longing.

Nit up and walked off with the mercurial.

"That there is mine," said Blank, with no conviction. He heard his father stirring inside the house and a light went on.

"You come on by my place after harvest," said Nit, walking into the shadows. "Maybe I'll trade you for them gloves you promised."

Blank could hear the dusk sermon begin. As he knocked on Nit's door, his hands were sore from detasseling, he was ripe with sweat, and he was tired.

Blank had been in just about everybody's home before, but never Nit Stevens's. It was a marvel of beautiful scavenge. There were sculptures and bas-reliefs of tractors and sandwiches and people, women in hot colors and rich fabrics, with painted lips and cheeks and eyelids, though the color of these plastic sculptures had faded to the beige of an eggshell. There were large aquaria all hooked together. Inside, mercurials flattened themselves against the floor of their tanks as the music of the sermon bore through the house. In one jar, Blank thought he saw his own mercurial. It was nearly turtle shaped but about the right size. The sermon flattened this one, too, and made it seem to melt. It must have come from a real silent place to hate sound so much.

"I brought them gloves you wanted," said Blank, and handed them over. Nit took them, frowningly looked them over, and threw them back toward Blank. "Keep 'em," he said.

There were books stacked neatly on shelves. Impulsively, Blank reached out for one. It puffed with dust as he lifted it. He caught a brief glance at the cover, featuring planetary bodies swooping through broad illustrated orbits, before Nit Stevens snatched the book from Blank's hand and tremblingly but firmly pressed him into a chair.

"You gonna give back my critter?" Blank asked.

Nit pulled a box out from underneath a table as if it were in answer to the question. It was full of hard square paper tablets, larger than a dinner plate. Nit motioned to Blank that he should take a look. There were dead people on the tablets, and demons with pitchforks, and that spilled-tannin-in-milk calligraphy. He saw a picture that was just like the stained glass in church, demons plummeting before a great wall of flame. It, too, said "South of Heaven."

"Me and Dim Henry and Maxwell used to collect these records

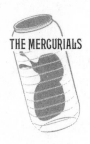

when we was young men," said Nit. "This was back when you could still power up a proper record machine or a computer to play recorded music on. Now all I got is this."

Nit picked up a record, and with some trouble unsheathed the black disc from its cover, which featured a drawing of a skeleton pulling out the intestines of a living man. The writhing man's hands grasped at nothing. It was called "Cannibal Corpse." Nit put the record on a kind of pottery wheel and wound it up with a hand crank. When the wheel's axle started spinning, sermon-type music came out of a tin horn wound from the wheelbox. The music sounded far away and seemed to ride in the dips and valleys of a wave, slowing down in places, speeding up in others. It sounded awful.

"You want to give back my critter?" Blank repeated his question.

"I oughtn't," said Nit.

"But you said you would."

"I said I'd do you a trade. I still got the sense to know he'd be swimming up your brains before breakfast if I let you have him."

They sat looking at each other.

"Does that mean you ain't gonna give me back that critter?" A desperate tone crept into Blank's voice. "How am I gonna get learned if I can't get a look at that critter, Nit, huh?"

"Maxwell'd have my skin," said Nit. Even when his eyes were bright, which was rare, his mouth slacked off toward an empty smile. "I'll tell you what. Take a couple of jars off my shelf. You fill 'em up and bring 'em back to me, and we'll call 'em shared property. Then I can show you a thing or two."

Blank was put out at first, but the night after he caught a small silver centipede near the edge of the wood dragging its way from the town during the congregational sonics. He brought it to Nit, and the old man showed him how, when two silver bodies get near each other, they sort of shock each other with electrical arcs.

Blank was enthusiastic.

A few nights later, Blank went out and came back with a big one. He'd only ever seen cats in books; this one looked like a cat that crawled like a hurt thing. Here Nit showed him how a gaggle of mercurials would sort of fuse their bodies into one large body and could lift themselves off of their bellies that way.

That night Gerta Stevens came by to bring her father a basket full of corn-and-apple fritters. Gerta's family had a living apple tree in their yard, which was accounted a thing of great wealth. She was a sweet woman with a fine voice who had a tattoo of an octopus wrapped around her right arm.

She stuck around and joked with Nit in a sort of sad way. But when she asked where he'd gotten all the new specimens, Nit became cagey and winked at Blank, and so Gerta gave Blank a worried look.

A few nights after that, it was too close to dusk and Blank was too close to the edge of the field, so that Fay Harbush saw him catch something, a little sparrow with dripping silver wings, while she was out collecting wildflowers. She screamed and ran when she saw what Blank was doing.

When he came home that day, he found his father, his mother, Dumb Maxwell, and Nit Stevens hovering around the kitchen table, waiting for him. Blank's mom had served them all big plates of corn bread and bacon. Now she put out a cold plate for Blank, too. Dumb Maxwell was standing. He was a large man, and his body filled the house. He was wearing his leather apron and leather gloves, with his goggles snapped up over his forehead. He was covered in cow blood from the day's work.

G. CARL
PURCELL

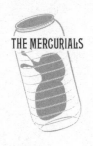

"Get yourself a chair, boy," said Blank's father. Nit frowned and looked at the ground. Blank did as he was told. Then Maxwell swung out a chair of his own.

"Your dad tells me you been sneaking out at night, skipping sermons," said Dumb Maxwell.

"Naw, he don't know about that," said Blank.

Nit Stevens snorted, but Maxwell let that hang for a second, until Blank knew what he said was a dumb thing.

"Let's try that again," said Maxwell.

"I've been sneaking," said Blank, trying not to meet Maxwell's or his father's eyes. "I snuck into town a couple of times."

"And what did you find out there?"

"I collected a jar and some rubber gloves. For safety." Blank thought Maxwell would be impressed by that safety part. "I even caught and cornered one of those critters. Nit seemed real impressed."

Maxwell shot Nit a look.

"You could have killed yourself," Maxwell continued. "Never mind the critters. You walk into the wrong house in Bangor, and the whole thing could have come down on you. Could have been highwaymen in town."

"No, uh-uh. I stuck to the concrete floors just like when I went out with Dad the one time. I stayed well out of sight."

"Blank, you're a thick kid," said Maxwell finally. He turned to Blank's father. "No offense, Joe," he said, to which Blank's father replied there was none taken. Maxwell turned back to Blank. "You've got that dumb look in your eye, like things ain't processing and things ain't gonna process. But you're curious, and in that you're a hell of a lot like me when I was your age." He looked away, seemed to turn over a thought. "You can read?"

"I can read real good," said Blank. "Most of what I read, anyway."

"All right," he said. "I'm gonna borrow this one a second, Joe," said Maxwell. "Nit, you're coming with us."

Together they went to Maxwell's, in a line, Blank thought, like a family of ducks.

Outside of Maxwell's home, Maxwell turned to Nit. "Now, I said what I said to you earlier, and I meant it, and that's all. What you got to say?"

Nit, already frowning, frowned more. "I ain't got shit to say, Maxwell."

Maxwell grabbed Nit by the scruff of his neck and held him up to his own face, but there was nothing rough in it. The big man held his feelings pretty close, but now, Blank noticed, Maxwell's emotions showed out, and his face was like Gerta's a few days before and concerned in the way of family.

"We go back, don't we, Nit?" said Maxwell.

"We do."

"Remember when you named me Dumb?"

"That I remember."

"So hold on." Dumb Maxwell tried to catch Nit's eye, but Nit kept frowning, his eyes kept darting around. "You hold on, Nitwit. Keep your fucking head down, and keep out of trouble." He let go of Nit, and Nit took off.

Nothing inside of Maxwell's home looked sized to fit him right. His table and chairs looked like they were made for a doll, compared to Maxwell.

"What was it about what you said to Nit?" asked Blank. "I mean about what you said earlier."

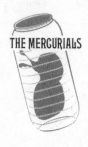

"Shut the fuck up and sit down, boy," said Maxwell. Blank did as he was told. He did not say it sharp, because he was already going through his bookshelf. He took down three books and handed them to Blank. They were *Merriam-Webster's Collegiate Dictionary, 7th Edition*, a book called *Electronics for Sound*, and another called *First-Aid Safety and Wilderness Survival*. He pointed out particular chapters on heavy metals and on poison prevention, symptoms, and treatment.

"You keep those indefinitely," said Dumb Maxwell. "You come back to me when you've read those chapters. Look up any words you don't know in the dictionary. Most important; you don't understand something? Ask me about it. It's the real dumb ones who clam up when they don't know a thing. That's the first lesson; you don't know, you ask."

Then Maxwell took Blank out back of his house.

He took out an eight-pound hammer, set a chestnut on a tree stump, and told Blank to set down the books and pick up the hammer.

"Joe wants me to find something you're good at. Now, see if you can't hit that walnut with that hammer," Maxwell said.

The hammer was not much heavier than the hammer Blank's father used. He hit the nut, just off plumb, so that half of it split off and bounced against Dumb Maxwell's knee.

"Almost true on your first try," said Maxwell. "You keep practicing that and read them books. And stay away from Nit Stevens."

Blank was pulled out of school, which suited him, and spent three mornings a week with Dumb Maxwell instead. Blank was permitted to miss evening service to stay home and read, which he did every night with the crossed brow of a tortured penitent, and still heard it

buzz and echo against the valley until the fat sonic force of it seemed
to fill the sky and melt the sun like butter back of the trees: and it
distracted him, so he had to read and read a sentence again before
he understood it. He started with *Electronics for Sound* and then
moved on to the book about first aid. He had to look up the meaning of "induce" and the meaning of "vomiting," and a thousand other
words. The meaning of "chellate" wasn't even in the dictionary. He
fell asleep regularly with a book over his face, filled with vexing questions. These questions entered his dreams as silver bodies cutting
through moonlight.

Every morning he practiced with his father's hammer and little
nuts and pinecones he found at the edge of the wood.

One time Maxwell took Blank to see Fulsome Chet, who showed
him how the dynamo got oiled and what the back of the Marshall
stack looked like. Blank recognized some of the dusty old wiring in
the back from the book Maxwell had given him. As Chet explained
the pedal that Priest Waverly used to fuzz the guitar sound, he got
a faraway sort of look. Maxwell yelled his name, and Chet came to,
apologizing, and continued his explanation.

Maxwell and Blank shared a look, and Maxwell raised a lone eyebrow. Blank did not understand the secret Maxwell was trying to
convey with that look, but he was damned edified to be sharing it
with him.

When the autumn days got shorter and all there was left to do was
gather the hay and turn the soil for next year, Maxwell gathered
Blank for his first day of scavenge, not in the darkness but in broad
daylight. They took along Bill Weathers and Frank Weehawken,

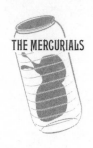

neither of them especially learned, but both of them large men who knew how to handle a gun, as well as Stupid Hess, who had a special need for lubricating agents. Together these large men seemed to bend the cart they rode in toward the earth, and the skinny horses carrying them frothed beneath the effort.

Blank was thoughtful and quiet. The night before, Nit Stevens had come to Blank's window. He was shaking so badly, he made the pane rattle.

"You come on over, boy. I got a critter on the Bunsen burner," Nit said. His eyes rolled around in his head.

"You get on, Nit," said Blank. "I ain't supposed to see you no more."

"You never saw those critters react to an open flame," Nit said. "It's the sparkingest thing you ever saw."

Something about Nit scared the hell out of Blank then, and he yelled at him to get away from the window. Soon Blank's father showed up and shooed him off.

So Blank was still tired the day he was invited on scavenge and cursed Nit secretly for it.

"Bangor's played out," said Maxwell, as they rolled along the old railroad path, well known to caravans but not to highwaymen. "I'm surprised you found what you did there, in fact. Time was, we used to go to South Haven and Kalamazoo for good scavenge, but the squareheads and highwaymen have those places locked down good and proper."

All along the path, living mercury skittered back and forth, met by the whistling and bell ringing of the men in the cart. In good sunlight their mirrored bodies sometimes blinded a person.

"Let me see them muscles," said Maxwell. Blank showed him. "See them muscles?" said Maxwell to Stupid Hess. Hess said they'd do.

They got to Hartford when the sun was still high. In town they found a few syringes in a home medical kit, about a dozen small jugs of motor oil, and a lot of threadbare towels and shirts and things that could be mulched into paper. Best of all, Maxwell found a pack of playing cards wrapped in cellophane and fresh as the day they were printed. He nearly clicked his heels over the find and said he'd show Blank how to play euchre as soon as they could find doubles.

Near the end of the day, Maxwell had Bill climb a water tower, where he found something of immense value: an old thermometer. Everywhere the mercurials had burst thermometers and absorbed the mercury from them, said Maxwell. It's only in high places you found unspoiled examples of mercury anymore.

"It goes to show," said Dumb Maxwell.

"Don't show nothing," said Stupid Hess. Together they fell into the rhythm of what seemed a long-ago argument.

"You can't get that kind of mercury on Earth. It's too much."

"Naturally occurring mercury's rare, okay. These things're Earth-bound as a dog's dick, and they synthesize the stuff."

"They come from space, and they brought their own with 'em."

It was dark, and Blank was tired and happy by the time they got home. Service should have been sounding across the valley, but Bangor was quiet. As the track widened and the men came closer to Bangor, they could hear yelling. The smell of burning wood and leather reached their noses.

By the time they got home, the damage had been done. It was Priest Waverly who'd led the fire fight, pulling water from the town pump and the icehouse. They had stopped it spreading from the Stevens house to their neighbors, but that was all. Nit's house was lost. Every sort of mercurial had slithered out of the fire, and people

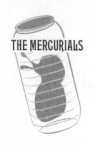

in the town hollered and sang to catch them out and drive them back to the woods.

After the fire was out, they all sat in the church. Priest Waverly did not so much play for them as absently tune his instrument. It sounded hollow and weak without the dynamo turning.

Nit approached Maxwell. Nit wrung his hands out, gripping one hand with the other, trying to keep them from shaking. It only made them shake worse.

"Maxwell, you remember that time?" Nit said. It was a placating tone, never before found in irascible old Nit. Maxwell ignored him, frowned hard at the floor. He was covered in ash. Nit giggled. "You remember that time when you fell in the river, and I gave you your name?"

The next day Maxwell said he had a few more books to show to Blank.

At his house Dumb Maxwell dragged out a box. From within, he pulled out a large book. The book was full of small columns of print and lots of pictures. It was magazines, all pressed together and bound like a book. The magazine was called *The New Yorker*.

"I found these back when I was your age, in a library. Well, you couldn't believe how excited I was just to read something other than crop rotations and old operating instructions. The people in these magazines were paid their share just to think, back before the mercury come down," continued Dumb Maxwell. "Except they'd bring up a big notion, then they'd punch it up full of holes, to let you know they don't give a rat's ass. I used to ask myself why. These folks had everything you could want. They had telescopes floating in geostationary Earth orbit you could see whole galaxies with. They had lamplight cartoons they made out of photographs. They could draw in and around the lamplight. They could make it seem like men and ladies were cavorting with — oh hell, what have you — aliens, talking donkeys, whatever."

Blank continued to watch Maxwell with expectant fascination.

"See, here's a movie review," continued Maxwell. "It says a robot got its druthers up and turned into a lady, of all things. And all this inside of a spaceship! Well, I'd pop if I saw something like that! And the reviewer of the movie, he says he's bored. Says he's seen it all a thousand times.

"Well, when I found these things, I didn't know which end was up. How could these folks act so nonchalant about the miracles they had all around 'em?" Dumb Maxwell asked. "Then I started thinking about those mercurials out there. They can't be said to have a thinking mind among them. All they got is a curiosity, a curiosity that don't distinguish between pig shit or living guts. They got a means to convey themselves around the stars, but nothing is valuable to them. Ain't nothing precious, not even life."

Maxwell pulled out a box of records. These had churchlike images on them too, same as Nit Stevens had.

"I used to hate these records. I used to hate church service especially. The imagery, the music, everything about them battered my brains."

After a moment, Maxwell sort of deflated.

"If we didn't need the noise, I'd just as soon cure 'em all with these magazines instead."

Blank continued to watch Maxwell, his eyes turning from Maxwell's face back to the books. He was wondering which book he'd get next to read.

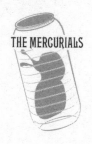

"Get on," Maxwell said. He sounded sad. "Go practice that hammer."

One November night soon after, Nit closed his eyes and rocked slowly to the congregational sonics. Priest Waverly's service came on very loud that night. Blank's stomach — his "bowels," as he liked to say, now that he'd learned the word — felt loose and slippery in the deep reverberation. Maxwell stuck close to Nit, with his arm around the man's shoulders.

"Wooah-wow-wow," Nit said, mimicking the music, making fish faces.

Priest Waverly played a long time, perhaps an hour and a half, by Blank's estimation. He could scarcely hear, much less discern, the cryptic poem Priest Waverly recited over the din, the one he recited, with small variations, at every retirement party:

> *Run silver rabbit*
> *Run black rabbit*
> *Into the sea*
> *Down to the sea*
> *Mercurial fire*
> *Bu-u-ry me*
> *Mercurial flame*
> *Bu-u-ry me*
> *Bu-u-ry me*

When the music ended and the dynamo whirred to a stop, the people sat in silence a long time. After a while, Blank could hear the chirruping of nighttime animals past the silence of the church.

"Well, then," said Priest Waverly. He nodded to Nit Stevens, which elicited grunts of approval from the old ones in the pews. Then he started packing up his bass. "That's all right," said Nit. "That's okay." It made Blank sad to see what a lively and playful man Nit used to be, and how stupid and serious he was now. Some folks reached out to pat him on the back.

Dumb Maxwell led Nit Stevens out before the rest, proudly pointing his lightning-streaked orange beard. Nit kept talking about how things could spark in a Bunsen burner. The congregation stood, each in his or her own time, and left the church. Many, including Blank, followed Dumb Maxwell and Nit Stevens to the back of the church. Out on the field began the familiar cloppity rattle that would last all night, and in town some of the women were singing.

In back of the church, a hunk of slate rested on an old stump. Leaning next to that was an eight-pound hammer. Dumb Maxwell, Priest Waverly, and a few other men gave Nit Stevens great back-slapping hugs, while Nit talked about tea, what kind of tea he'd like to make for everybody.

Gerta kissed her father sadly on the cheek and put a yellowed oak sprig in his shirt pocket. Dumb Maxwell lifted Nit Stevens by the knees like a wheelbarrow, and Nit's head fell awkwardly on the stump. The old man's hands grasped weakly for purchase against the gnarls of the old stump's roots.

Fulsome Chet spit into his thick leather gloves and lifted the hammer. He was slow about it, and left Maxwell to struggle with the legs some, but finally Chet brought the hammer down on Nit's head once, and that was all it took. Chet had done this job for many years, and he knew his mark. Blank watched the man with close attention, trying to learn a thing.

Kitty Capulet AND THE Invention OF Underwater Photography

DYLAN HORROCKS

These are the photos I took on the plane:

1. *Dad, asleep*

I wish I knew how he does it. I never sleep on planes. Never, ever, ever. It doesn't matter how luxurious the cabin is; there could be king-size beds, aromatherapy massages, and soothing ambient whale songs. I'd still be wired and awake from takeoff to landing. I hate not being on the ground. Dad, on the other hand, drops off the moment we're airborne, leaving me alone to deal with flight attendants and bad food and boredom. Plus, he snores.

2. Flight attendant in love with Dad

This flight attendant named Suzie kept coming by to ask if I needed anything, but it clearly wasn't me she was interested in. I'll never understand why so many women are attracted to Dad. I mean, seriously? He's pale, scrawny, and hairy, with an unforgettably, ridiculously, prodigiously enormous nose. Actually, "nose" is a woefully inadequate word for that *thing* in the middle of Dad's face. "Proboscis," maybe. Or "trunk." You could establish a small nation on that nose. And yet here's Suzie, leaning against an aisle seat, gazing straight at Dad's vast nasal formation, lips parted, pupils dilated, cheeks slightly flushed. Did I mention he snores?

3. Krystle and Thomas kissing

So there I am: thirty thousand feet over the Pacific, deathly tired but unable to sleep, and I'm watching some stupid movie called *The Wakening*, about a girl who falls in love with a vampire. (Or werewolf? Zombie? Shape-shifting people-eating werebat from Mars? I honestly don't remember, that's how stupid it was.) Anyway, halfway through there's this scene where Krystle (the girl) and Thomas (whatever he was) kiss for the first time in a sunlit cherry orchid while falling blossoms paint everything pink (etc., etc.) . . . and then *BAM!* My dear father's voice fills the headphones, singing some stupid song about sunlight and blossoms and *love, love, love.* I tore off the headphones and hit the pause button, but it was already too late. That god-awful song had burrowed deep into my poor tired high-altitude brain, and it wasn't going anywhere. It was still in there twelve hours and five thousand miles later. Some people might call it catchy. Sure. Like Ebola.

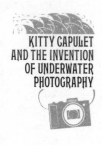

4. *Sky monsters*

Actually, these were clouds. But they looked just like giant living creatures, swimming slowly through the sky. Of course I know clouds are
really nothing more than water suspended in the atmosphere through
a process of condensation and convection. But honestly, these looked
alive. Just look at them — *really look* — and I swear you'll see it too.

I took plenty of other photos, of course, but those are the ones I
kept and put online. Except for the picture of Dad; that went straight
into a hidden, locked, password-protected folder on my trusty laptop,
George. I keep all photos of Dad offline to protect my secret identity.
No one must know that Kitty Capulet (mysterious, well-traveled
photographer whose enigmatic images are the toast of Tumblr) is in
fact the daughter of alt-folk sensation Daniel Flynn (aka Parliament
of Trees).

Actually, I lied about being the toast of Tumblr. Truth is, my
Tumblr only has seven followers. But still — that's seven people who
must *never learn* my true identity.

Judging by the airline's in-flight magazine, New Zealand is a fun,
outdoorsy sort of country full of beaches, forests, and mountains,
with a population the size of Kentucky's. The original inhabitants,
the Maori, apparently possess "a rich, unique culture that forms an
integral part of the Kiwi national identity." Which is another way
of saying: "Sorry we colonized you." New Zealand's main industries
seem to be bungee jumping, skiing, and eating, and their main export
is Lord of the Rings movies. A giant sign in the airport arrivals hall
welcomed us to Middle-earth.

The festival promoter was there to meet us in person: a wine-maker named Gerald who looked like a skinny George Clooney. Gerald wore expensive jeans and purple Vans and a bright red shirt with his festival's logo: CLEARWATER FOLK.

"Welcome to New Zealand," he said, shaking Dad's hand. "How was the flight?"

"Awful," I muttered. But no one was listening to me.

Gerald Clooney had a minibus waiting outside, driven by a woman named Maria with long black hair and soft brown skin. She smiled at Dad, and he smiled back. I rolled my eyes. No one noticed.

Dad had brought two backup musicians: Jacob (on percussion) and Lucy (second guitar/double bass/banjo/keyboard/clarinet/vocals). Jacob was new, but Lucy's been traveling with us for ages. She's short, tough, and wiry, with a sharp blond crew cut and cold gray eyes. Lucy's from Düsseldorf and doesn't say much. She's the coolest person I know.

Then there was Steve, Dad's longtime sound mixer/assistant/roadie/part-time manager. Steve's madly in love with Lucy but hasn't realized it yet. He watches her all the time and turns her micro-phone up way too loud. I don't think Lucy's even noticed. One day maybe I'll tell her. Or him. Maybe one day I'll sneak onstage in the middle of a show and shout it down the microphone to fifty thou-sand swaying hipsters, and the secret of Steve's hidden passion will surge down a twisting snake cable at the speed of light through his Euphonix mixing console to a towering wall of giant speakers, boom-ing out across the seething crowd of skinny boys and beardies, music nerds and drunk teenage girls.

But until that day, it's my little secret. One of the many I've col-lected over the years, traveling from gig to gig with Dad and Lucy and

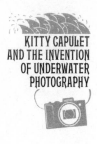

Steve, living in hotels and trailers, with my two blue suitcases (one for clothes and shoes and one for books, cameras, hard drives, and sundry private comforts) and a laptop named George.

I know what you're thinking. "Oh, *poor you.*"</sarcasm>

Seriously, though: having a famous singer for a dad isn't as glamorous as it sounds. For starters, we're on the road most of the year, doing concerts and festivals around the States and the rest of the world. And when we do stop for a month or two, it's almost never at our official residence in Vermont. Living with Dad means I don't have much of a home or family or friends (unless you count Lucy and Steve, which — frankly — is a bit of a stretch). As for my mother . . .

Actually, let's not talk about my mother. Ever.

The drive to the festival site took three hours, through bland suburbs, shabby sunlit farmland, and occasional patches of wet dark forest, which the locals apparently refer to as "bush." The last couple of miles were on a bumpy gravel road that ran alongside a narrow winding stream.

"Sorry about this," Gerald said. "The old track gets pretty chewed up by all the festival traffic. We're trying to put a proper road in, but it's been a nightmare getting permission from the council, thanks to —"

Maria swore and hit the brakes. We lurched to a stop in a cloud of brown dust.

"What the hell?" Gerald said.

The road was blocked by a group of people holding signs. When Gerald got out to move them along, they started to shout and yell: "Save our river!" "*Kaitiakitanga!*" "Shame! Shame!"

"Now *this* is interesting," I said, slipping out of the van, camera in hand. Dad started to say something, but I ignored him, as usual.

It was a ragtag bunch: a dozen or so people, mostly Maori, from young guys in hoodies and wraparound sunglasses to old ladies in long skirts and thick black cardigans. One figure stood silently watching from the sidelines: a solidly built middle-aged man, his entire face covered with swirling green tattoos. When I raised my camera to take a picture of him, he turned to look me straight in the eye. For a long cold moment, I felt like he was peeling away my skin and staring deep inside. The camera shook in my hands and my throat went dry.

But I got the picture.

Gerald was talking to the protesters, obviously angry but trying to stay calm. One of the younger men was shouting at him, jabbing a finger at his chest. I got a picture of that, too. Then Dad appeared at my shoulder and steered me back to the van.

"I don't think that's helping," he said.

"What's going on?" I asked.

Maria turned and grinned at me. "It's about the new road," she said. "Some of the locals don't want it built."

"Why not?" I said.

She shrugged. "People think it'll destroy the stream."

"Will it?"

"Probably not. But the water will have to be diverted through a culvert under the road."

I looked out the window at the thin brown stream threading through the trees. It wasn't very impressive.

"What's the big deal?" Jacob said, leaning forward from the rear seat. "I mean, it's hardly the Mississippi."

Maria gave a small smile. "There's supposed to be a *taniwha*," she said.

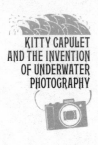

"A what?" I asked, but then Gerald climbed back into the van, bringing the noise and dust with him, and a moment later we were rumbling forward through the reluctantly parting crowd. I looked at Dad, and he made an "oh, well" face.

As the van drove past the tattooed man, he watched me through the dusty window. His face looked like it was carved out of wood.

The festival was held in the fields below Gerald's vineyard. The main paddock sloped down to form a natural amphitheater with two stages set up at the bottom. There was a roped-off area patrolled by security guards, with trailers and tents for the artists. I took one look at the arrangements and went to find Maria.

"Can I borrow a tent? Something small, just for me?"

She laughed. "Does your dad know?"

"He snores," I said. "And farts. I'd rather sleep alone."

"Okay," Maria said, and grinned. "I'll see what I can do."

She brought me a cherry-pink pup tent from last year's lost property, and I pitched it a long way from the trailer, near the edge of the bush. Dad was too busy checking that all the gear had arrived safely to notice.

The festival was due to start the following day, but people were already drifting in, setting up tents and enjoying the afternoon sun. It was a familiar scene, just like a hundred other music festivals I'd been to, in more places than I can remember. When you're always traveling, everywhere starts to looks the same.

A group of kids was heading into the bush, laughing. I'm usually pretty shy, but it was hot inside the tent and the bush looked cool and quiet, so I grabbed a camera and followed. The sounds of the campsite faded away among the densely packed trees, replaced by the soft crunch of old wood, the hush of swaying leaves, hissing cicadas, and singing birds. There was no path, so I made my own, ducking under branches and pushing past brambles that caught on my jeans and scratched my arms. After a few minutes, I was lost. It was like another world.

Then I heard voices and laughter ahead. I climbed over a sagging barbed-wire fence and emerged at the edge of a sunlit stream. Where I stood, the water was narrow and quick, tumbling over rocks and stones. But a little farther down, the stream widened to form a quiet pool, and there I saw one of the kids swing out on a rope and drop with a whoop and a splash.

The others followed one by one: two lanky boys and a dark-haired girl, their brown skin flashing in the sunlight as they swung out from the trees and let go, disappearing in a cloud of glittering water. I started taking pictures, but one of the boys saw me and they all turned and stared. I lowered the camera and waved, feeling stupid.

"Hi," I said, trying my best to sound relaxed and likable. "Is the water cold?"

"Who are you?" the girl asked.

"Um — my name's Kitty," I said, trying another halfhearted wave. "My dad's playing. At the festival."

Okay, so I'm not above using my dad's fame to make friends. I'm not proud of it, but what can I say? It's a lonely life.

"Parliament of Trees. You heard of him?"

They glared at me in silence. This wasn't working.

"I'll — uh — go and get my swimsuit," I said, as if they'd invited me to join them. Like maybe if I just pretended we were friends, they'd end up believing it?

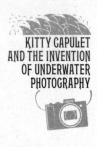

Oh, the Walk of Shame. Even the bush seemed to be mocking me, tripping my feet and pulling my hair all the way back to the campsite. Inside my tent, it was cramped and stuffy, and getting changed turned into an exercise in contortion. On the plus side, by the time I emerged, swimsuit hidden under T-shirt and towel, I was so flustered and hot, no amount of embarrassment and humiliation was going to keep me out of that water.

When I reached the swimming hole, the other kids were gone. I don't know if I was relieved or disappointed. Maybe both. But, damn it, I was going to swim.

I found the rope swing hooked over a branch. I hung my T-shirt and towel on the same tree, then gripped the rope tightly and took a deep breath. For a moment the sun was hidden by a cloud, and I shivered in the sudden cold, looking down at the dark pool below. The surface of the water looked like skin, sliding and shifting as though muscles moved inside. Like a living creature, huge and heavy, breathing, asleep. Then the sun came out, and it was water again, sparkling and bright.

I swung out and let go. There was a moment of stillness, surrounded by light. Then the cold water swallowed me up, and I shut my eyes tight, every inch of my body tingling and alive. I don't know how deep the pool was, but I seemed to sink for a long time before something bumped into my shoulder, and I pushed myself up toward the surface — and was abruptly yanked back.

Something was wrapped around my foot, holding me down. I opened my eyes, but the bottom of the pool was too murky to see. Reaching down, I tried to get free, but rough shapes slapped against my arms and coiled around my legs; the more I pulled and thrashed, the more trapped I became. I fought the urge to open my mouth

and scream. The water was thick and heavy, weighing me down till I
could hardly move. I had a brief vision of the view from the airplane
window: huge white giants drifting through the sky. And then my
mouth filled with water, and I knew I was going to die.

I'm not sure what happened next. There was a blur of motion, and
the world was flooded with light; I gasped and coughed and swallowed sweet warm air, pushing hard against the arms that held me
up. Then my head cleared and I grew still, staring into the eyes of the
boy who'd saved my life.

He looked my age: long black curls, smooth dark skin, full lips,
bare arms around my waist. I realized my hands were on his shoulders and felt my face turn red.

"Th-thanks," I managed to say, gently pushing him away. His grip
eased and I began to tread water, kicking back toward the shore. He
followed me slowly.

I climbed out and sat down. The earth felt firm and safe after that
strange dark underwater world.

"Really, thanks," I said again. "I must have caught my foot in something. If you hadn't come along . . ."

He stayed in the water, silently watching. I was uncomfortably
aware of my ugly green swimsuit and pale blotchy legs. I pulled
the wet hair back from my face, wishing I had gorgeous brown skin
like his.

"I'm Kitty," I said. "I mean, Catherine. Kate. Cat . . . ?" *Get a grip,
girl.* "Um . . . were you here before? Swimming with those other kids,
I mean?"

There was a long painful pause, and then he lifted himself out of
the water and sat beside me on the grass. He stretched out his long
legs to dry in the sun.

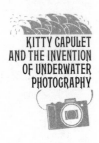

"Ruakiri," he said.

"That's your name?" I asked, like an idiot. "Um . . . is that Maori?" He smiled lightly and nodded. "You are from far away," he said.

"God, yes," I said. "Like fourteen hours by plane. And that's just from L.A. We actually flew from Boston, which took another seven hours, with a few hours wait in between." I couldn't believe I was listing our itinerary like a moronic travel agent. "I hate flying," I finished, lamely.

"You're from around here?" I asked, after another long silence.

"*Ae,*" he said. I guessed that meant yes.

"Oh," I said. "It's nice. *Here,* I mean." I think my toes actually curled with embarrassment.

He looked at me, a little sad. "It's changed," he said. "Trees cut down, rivers dirty and weak. Once there were no people here. None at all."

I looked up at the bush, tried to imagine a world without people: huge old trees and clear clean streams; birdsong and wind and water the only sounds.

"You're cold," he said, and I realized I was shivering, covered in goose bumps. My fingernails were blue.

"I'm all right," I said. "I warm up fast." I got up and walked to the tree where I'd left my T-shirt and towel.

"My dad's here for the festival," I said, drying my hair. "He's headlining tomorrow." Pathetic, I know.

"Your father?" he asked.

I pulled on the T-shirt and wrapped the towel around my skinny, pale, unappealing legs.

"Yeah," I said. "Parliament of Trees. Maybe you've heard of him?"

He shook his head, and I saw he was completely unmoved by my father's celebrity status.

"Actually, he's not very good," I said quickly. "I mean, he has a lot of fans, but I think he sucks."

Ruakiri raised his eyebrows.

"Singer-songwriter stuff," I said, making a face. "Involves banjos."

"Will you stay here?"

I wasn't sure what he meant. "At Clearwater? Till the festival's over. Then it's on to the next show. I don't even know where. It's never up to me. I'm basically Dad's prisoner, forced to go wherever he decides."

The bitterness in my voice surprised even me. I bent over to find my shoes. But when I turned back, he was gone.

"Ruakiri?" I called.

I listened for a long time, but all I heard were the sounds of the bush and the stream and a radio playing nearby.

Dinner was at Gerald's house, on a hill overlooking the vineyard. Most of the musicians were there, along with staff and volunteers. Gerald was in a bright red shirt covered in tiny white unicorns. He no longer looked like George Clooney. More like Nicolas Cage on a bad day.

There was a buffet and a barbecue, with a lot less vegetarian food than you'd expect at a folk music festival. I haven't eaten meat since I was old enough to understand that the juice in a juicy steak is actually blood. So I piled my paper plate with coleslaw and potato salad and bread, and I tried to find a quiet corner where I could eat by myself. But it was not to be. Dad called me over, and I had to sit at the table with everyone else.

I ended up stuck between a drunk music journalist with a handlebar mustache and a frail-looking harpist from Ecuador whose band

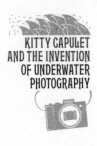

was apparently called Savage Monkey (El Mono Salvaje, to be precise). The harpist's name was Inocencia, but the looks she kept sending over my head at the wobbly journalist were anything but. I did my best to ignore them, staring down at my plate or across the table at Dad, who was deep in conversation with Gerald Cage and the lovely Maria. They were talking about the protesters who'd stopped us earlier.

"It's quite silly, really," Gerald was saying, looking terribly disappointed by just how silly it was. "You've seen how bad the road is. By the end of the weekend, it'll be all churned up and muddy. And it's far too narrow. The traffic jam when everyone's leaving is the worst."

"Last year it took ten hours to clear the exit," Maria said.

"The new road will solve all that, with two lanes and a parking area outside the grounds." Gerald smiled, presumably at the thought of all that concrete. "We'll be able to host busloads of tourists at the vineyard and double the size of the festival. I'm thinking of inviting Sandy Gardener next year."

"Wow," Dad said. Dad hated Sandy Gardener.

"Well, with better access and all the other facilities we're planning, I think we can get the numbers. It'll be the festival's fifth anniversary — time to take things to the next level."

"But not everyone's in favor?" Dad asked.

Gerald frowned at his wineglass. "That's where things get ridiculous," he said. "Apparently there's a *taniwha* in the stream."

"A what?"

"A *taniwha*. It's a monster from Maori folklore: a giant lizard that lives in rivers and eats occasional passersby." Gerald leaned back and laughed. "Of course, no one really believes in it — they're just using it as an excuse to extort my money."

Maria shifted in her seat. "The local Maori claim the roadwork will block up the stream," she said. "But I reckon they're using it to draw attention to wider issues. The waterways around here are badly polluted by farm runoff and chemical sprays. But it's not fair on Gerald. His business brings money and jobs into the area."

Gerald gave a wry smile. "Here we are in the twenty-first century, and we can't build a road in case it hurts an imaginary monster's feelings. It's political correctness gone mad."

"Is this the stream with the swimming hole?" Everyone turned and looked at me. I cleared my throat. "I was down there this afternoon. It's nice."

Maria smiled. Gerald looked like he had no idea whose child I might be and what I was doing in his house.

"In the bush, behind where the trailers and tents are," I persisted, feeling my skin turn bright pink. "Is that the stream all the fuss is about?" I don't know why I'd called the swimming hole "nice" when I'd just about drowned there. Maybe the memory of Ruakiri's long black hair and deep brown eyes trumped the near-death experience?

"Yeah, that's it," Maria said. "Clearwater Creek. The vineyard's named after it."

"Is it true, then?" I asked her. "Will the new road ruin the stream? There were kids swimming in it today."

Gerald frowned, but Maria ignored him. "I don't think so, Kitty. But it's not ideal for swimming anyway. Sometimes all kinds of bacteria and chemicals get into the water from farms upstream. I know it's a shame, but it might not be a bad thing if kids couldn't swim there anymore."

Great. So even though I'd escaped drowning, the botulism could still kill me. Suddenly I didn't feel so hungry. I got up to get rid of

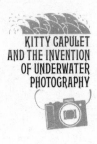

my plate, and Inocencia shuffled over to move in on her prey, while across the table Dad whispered in Maria's ear and she smiled. Just another night on tour.

But for once I didn't really mind. I liked Maria. I figured she could look after herself.

I took twenty-three photos that night: Inocencia close dancing with Handlebar Mustache like a cheesy music video; Gerald wiping ketchup off his unicorn shirt; and the usual predictable shots of posing musos, starstruck volunteers, and bored staff.

But the best photo came when I was going back to my tent. I was all alone, walking across a wide lawn in the moonlight. For a brief moment, it seemed like the rest of the world had disappeared: there was nothing but the grass and the trees and the cool night air. And I stopped and knelt and raised the camera to catch the silver light on the ground. And just as I took the picture, a bird cried out, right behind me: a loud harsh shriek. And when I turned around shaking, there was nothing to see. Just thick black shadows. And I ran all the way to my tent and crept inside and zipped the flaps shut and climbed into my sleeping bag with my head buzzing and my heart pounding. But when I'd calmed down enough to check my camera, there was the photo I'd taken in the garden, and it was perfect and beautiful and mysterious and strange. The silver grass, the looming trees, the heavy black sky. And best of all: my own shadow spread out across the ground, arms raised to take the picture, and above my head the shadow of a bird, wings spread wide.

That night I slept curled around my camera bag, dreaming of monsters and owls and deep dark pools.

I took my first photo when I was three years old. I loved how it froze time: bodies became statues; balls hung in midair. It was like casting a spell. I filled Dad's camera's memory card in half an hour, snapping nonstop. For a while he tried hiding it, but I'd just steal his phone and use that instead. In the end he bought me my own camera: a two-megapixel Canon that lasted exactly four weeks before I tried to invent underwater photography in a hotel swimming pool. I was so sure that idea would make me rich.

Since then I've gone through a lot of cameras — from the latest DSLRs to antique box Brownies and even a homemade pinhole or two. I love it all: film, digital, paper, glass. And one day I will build my own house with a darkroom and studio and a camera obscura in the loft.

You see, life is scary. The world makes no sense. But when I look at it through a camera, all that fear and chaos and confusion is contained in a small neat frame. And later, when I see the picture I caught, sometimes it's like the world has given me a gift: a perfect magical arrangement of light that sets off fireworks in my brain. Then when I share that picture on Tumblr, it's like I'm letting the whole world see this amazing beautiful thing we've made. And then we're even. And the world can go on being huge and crazy and terrifying, and I'll go on looking at it through a lens.

And that, basically, is me.

When I peeked out of my tent in the morning, the field was filling up fast with people and music and noise. I pulled on a bright cotton dress and went looking for a bathroom without a line.

279-

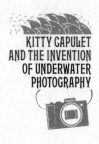

I was sitting in the trailer having breakfast when Dad came in and looked at my dress, surprised.

"Looking good, Kitten." I hate it when he calls me that.

"How's Maria?" I retaliated.

He smiled. "None of your business."

"When are you playing?"

"Twice," Dad said. "Big show tonight at eight and a solo acoustic session tomorrow afternoon."

"Huh. Gerald's sure getting his money's worth," I said.

"You don't like him, do you?" Dad looked at me over his coffee cup.

"Are you kidding? What a creep."

"He's just an entrepreneur," Dad said. "He's trying to make money from the things he enjoys: good wine, good music. It's not a sin to earn a living."

"How about destroying the planet for a profit? Is that a sin?"

Dad laughed. "Destroying the planet? Come on, Kitty, they're talking about running a creek through a culvert. You're familiar with the term *hyperbole*, right?"

"Don't patronize me." I knew I sounded childish. But I was tired and grumpy. And I really didn't like Gerald.

"Anyway," I said, standing up to leave.

"Take care, Kitten."

I went for a walk with my camera, collecting photos of spectacular beards and hats. One guy had both: a flowing chin-mane that could have been mistaken for a small bear and a striped top hat taller than me. He grinned for the camera like a hungry cannibal.

At some point, tired of all the noise and dust and excitement, I drifted toward the entrance, pushing against the flow of people until I was outside. The gravel road was one long line of crawling cars. Volunteers in festival T-shirts directed them to parking spaces on a churned-up field.

Standing at the edge of it all was a small group of protesters, holding signs about saving the river. The man with the tattooed face was arguing with a security guard. It was hot in the sun, like standing under a grill.

Then a police car drove up, bouncing over the grass to avoid the long traffic jam. Two cops got out — one Maori, the other European — and strolled over to Tattoo Face. When I got close enough to hear, Tattoo was talking to the cops in what I guessed was Maori. He sounded calm but determined. I raised my camera, but the security guard shook his head.

"Excuse me, miss," he said, pointing at the camera. "No photos, please."

"Oh?" I said. "This is a public place, and I'm allowed to take pictures." I took one of his frown to demonstrate.

"Oy! Clear off before I confiscate that." He looked just about angry enough to do it.

"I know my legal rights, mister, and if you touch my camera, you'll be in very serious trouble."

He took a step forward, but then one of the cops intervened. "Give it a rest, Tony," he said. "She's just a kid." Tony made an ugly face but backed off. Which made a great photo.

The police were arguing with Tattoo. "Look, Wiremu, we're only going to say this one more time. You're entitled to express your views,

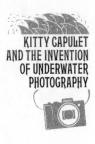
but there's a time and a place. You're causing an obstruction, and if you don't move this protest ten meters away from the road and parking lot, we'll have to arrest you."

I looked around. Ten meters in either direction would put them in the bush.

"That's ridiculous," I said, lowering the camera. Everyone ignored me, except Wiremu, who glanced my way before turning back to the police.

"*E hika mā,*" he said. Then he called to the rest of the protesters: "Come on, let's go!"

They started gathering up their signs and getting ready to leave. The police retreated to their car and talked into the radio, while the security guard stood back with crossed arms looking pleased with himself. But Wiremu came over to me.

"Who are you?" he asked. I forced myself to answer with a steady voice.

"Kitty," I said. "My dad's playing at the festival."

He looked me up and down. I realized I was staring at the tattoos: a dense pattern of swirling lines dug into the skin. Even his lips were dark with green ink. I kept thinking how much it must have hurt.

"You're American," he said at last. "What do you do with all these photos you take?"

"Um . . . nothing. Sometimes I put them on my Tumblr. That's like a blog."

"I know what Tumblr is," he said, with a hint of a smile. "*Tōna pai nei, hine.* You take your pictures. Just make sure you keep your eyes open too." He turned to go.

"Wait," I said. "The . . . the *taniwha* . . ." He looked back at me, his face totally impassive. "I mean, is there really a *taniwha* in the stream?"

He frowned and said nothing. "Because yesterday," I said, "when I went for a swim, something pulled me down. I nearly drowned . . ." My voice trailed off into silence. I was starting to feel stupid.

The silence stretched between us. Then he made a rough chuckling sound, like a cough. "You probably shouldn't swim in that stream, eh?" he said. "They say the water's pretty dirty." He walked away to join the others, still chuckling.

I didn't swim again, though God knows it was hot enough. Instead I sat at the foot of a tree, staring at the stream from a safe distance. At least I hoped it was safe.

The sun was high, and the water glittered like liquid light. The noise of the festival was loud enough now to compete with the birds, but it still felt good to be surrounded by trees, watching dragonflies skim across the pool. I wondered what was down there, beneath the shining water, moving among the rocks and sunken logs.

When someone spoke, I almost screamed.

"*E kete.*" Ruakiri sat down beside me. His hair hung loose, curling around his shoulders. His skin was the color of polished wood.

"Hey," I managed to say. Or squeak. Definitely a squeak.

We sat for a while without saying anything. I watched the veins on his feet, imagining I could see them pulse with each heartbeat.

"Pretty noisy," I said at last, meaning the music pounding through the trees. "Sorry about that." Like it was my fault.

"Swim?" he asked, rising to a crouch.

"No," I said, a little too quickly. "Not after yesterday." I smiled, trying to make it a joke.

He turned and slid into the water, smooth like a snake.

283-

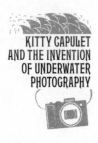

He took so long to surface, I was starting to panic. Then his face appeared in the shimmering light, and he shot me a quick grin before disappearing again. I sat and watched him swim, wishing I had the courage to join him, or that he'd get out before some mythical monster swallowed him whole. In the end, I did what I always do in these situations: I got out my camera.

Ruakiri swimming.

Ruakiri floating.

Ruakiri diving.

Ruakiri smiling straight at me.

A tree.

Then he was hauling himself out, long hair pouring down his back, splashing water on my dress. I put the camera away, too shy to look. He lay down to dry off in the sun. I could have sat there forever.

After a while a different band must have gone onstage because the music got a lot louder, deep bass notes thumping up from the ground. Ruakiri flinched and sat up.

"I guess the festival's kind of annoying for locals," I said. "All the noise and people, and of course the new road . . ."

He glanced at me, his face unreadable.

"This stream is so beautiful," I went on. "I can't believe they're going to ruin it."

"What?" Ruakiri asked, frowning.

"You know," I said. "People say the new road will cover up the stream."

He said nothing, his mouth a thin straight line.

"The protest outside?" I said, lamely. "I thought the locals were all talking about it . . ."

"Who is doing this?" he asked.

"The . . . the music festival. I mean the vineyard." The look on his  face was starting to scare me. "But maybe it'll be fine. It might not happen, and even if it does, maybe it won't be so bad."

He stood up and walked past me into the trees. I got up to follow but couldn't see which way he'd gone.

"Ruakiri?" Nothing.

Stupid stupid stupid. Why did I have to mention the road? Why couldn't I just sit quietly and surreptitiously watch him soaking up the sun like any normal, sensible love-struck girl would have done? Now he was angry and probably blamed me, and he'd never want to be my friend (let alone something more). And I would grow up lonely and miserable and nerdy and weird and never go to college and never have a life and eventually end up a crazy cat lady living in a garbage dump in Santa Monica with twenty-seven semi-feral street cats and a particularly pungent skin disease, shouting at strangers and throwing poop at social workers, until one day I'd die of acute septicemia and the ungrateful flea-ridden felines would feast on my rotting corpse for six whole weeks before someone finally noticed the smell and called the police.

I do worry about that sometimes. Seriously.

My tent was small, hot, and airless, and the relentless grinding beat of Australian dub-folk trio Blackheads made my head hurt. But I didn't want to be seen like this, so I sat in the bright pink glow of that tiny nylon cage thinking about the last ten years of my stupid, stupid life.

I was five when Dad got custody. I don't remember much before that — a few vague images of a house in the country, climbing trees, a wide blue lake. And *her*.

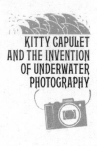

Dad's career took off soon after we left. "Weeping Willow" hit half a million views on YouTube, and he suddenly went from tiny shows in local cafés to playing headline gigs all over America. We've been touring ever since. Sometimes I think Dad only makes music so he never has to stay in one place for more than a month. But he sure is popular. *Haunted Xylophone* magazine called him "the leading alt-folk lyrical melodist of our time." Whatever that means.

Personally, I can't stand Dad's music. It's all soft acoustic guitar and heartfelt vocals, harmonica solos and glockenspiels and brush work on the drums. Folk music makes me want to break things. Banjos give me hives. *My* favorite band? Ice Nine. The most brutal Finnish smashcore noise band ever heard this side of Tuonela. Their lead singer, Pilko "Chop" Mustajärvi, is so pale, he looks like a ghost, with long black hair that covers his face and deep dark scars on the back of his hands. He's kind of a freak. Dad calls it "slaughterhouse" music and won't let me play it when he's around. So I put on my headphones and crank it up past health-advisory levels, and my brain turns to water and —

The floor of the tent quivered to Blackheads' bass. "Argh! I can't stand this!" I grabbed my camera and pushed out of the tent, my head like a bomb about to explode. I started taking pictures: the ground, my feet, the sky, and way too many people. The closer I got to the stage, the more the world shook with noise. But I stayed focused on the LCD screen, turning light into memory again and again and again.

I kept taking photos like that till the memory card was almost full. By then I'd calmed down and the sun had disappeared behind a wall of gray clouds, low and heavy. Blackheads had finished their set and been replaced by a country group called Desert Snow, who boasted not one but *two* banjos. My neck began to itch; it was time to go.

At the back of the field was a line of food stalls: kebabs, hot dogs, french fries, vegetarian curries. The kids from the swimming hole were leaning on a fence, watching the steady stream of hipsters with ice creams, cold drinks, and fries.

"Hey," I called to them. "Want something?"

They looked at each other then slowly wandered over.

"What do you want?" I asked. "I've got money."

"Your dad's in a band, eh?" the dark-haired girl said.

"Yeah. Parliament of Trees," I said. "They're on later tonight. You guys live around here?"

One of the boys nodded. "You serious about getting us some *kai?*"

"I'll have a Coke."

"Ice block."

"Chips."

"Okay," I said. "You seen Ruakiri?"

The girl frowned. "What?"

"Ruakiri. I was talking to him at the swimming hole. By the swing."

They exchanged a look.

"Who are you on about?" asked the shorter boy.

"He's about my age," I said. "Local boy. Don't you know him? He was there yesterday just after you left."

"Maori?" the girl said, looking skeptical.

"Yeah," I mumbled, wondering if I'd said something wrong. "He said his name was Ruakiri. I saw him again today."

"Nah," she said. "We know all the kids around here. He must be here for the festival."

They let me sit with them while we ate and drank. The girl kept asking about Dad: Was he famous? Were we rich? Had he been on TV or in the movies? I told her about his song being in *The*

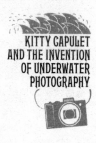

Wakening, and she seemed impressed. But they swore they'd never met the boy by the stream. And then one of them said he must be pulling my leg.

"Ruakiri isn't a real name," he said. "It's the name of the stream: Wairuakiri."

"*Wai* means water," the girl added, like she was speaking to a young child. "So it means Ruakiri's water, Ruakiri's stream."

"Ruakiri's the *taniwha* who lives there."

All three of them giggled.

"Want one of your chips?" the girl asked, grinning.

Halfway across the field, I felt something shift, like a change in the air pressure. And when I turned around, there was Ruakiri, standing so close I could have touched him.

"Oh!" I said, taking a step back. "I — uh — hi."

He didn't move, didn't even blink. Just stared straight at me, his face a dark mask.

"Are you okay?" I asked.

"They must stop," Ruakiri said. He spoke low but clear.

"What? Who?"

"All this," he said, sweeping an arm at the field, the crowd, the stage, everything. "The people. The road. It all must stop." There was something very strong in that gesture and in his voice.

"Um —"

"Tell them. Tell your father." He still hadn't blinked. "If it does not stop, there will be flood and fire."

A drop of water hit my cheek and then another. Big round blobs of rain started splashing around us.

"Ruakiri," I said, reaching for his arm. "Who are you?"

But he turned away, and the rain closed around him like a curtain.

I ran to the trailer. Steve answered the door.

"Kitty!" he said. "You're drenched!"

He found me a towel. Lucy checked my camera while I dried off.

"It looks fine," she said. "Water-resistant, huh?"

"Everything-resistant," I said. I loved my camera. "Where's Dad?"

"Having a glass of wine with Maria." Steve gave a lopsided smile. "Preshow ritual. A new one, started today."

"I need to talk to him," I said. "Something weird's going on."

They both frowned. "Are you okay?" Steve asked.

"I don't know. *Where?*"

They were in Dad's tent, sitting under the awning with a bottle of pinot gris, watching the rain fall.

"Hey," Dad said as I ran up. "You look wet."

I shook the raincoat off. "Dad," I said, "we have to talk."

"Uh-oh," he said. "What is it, Kitten? Is everything all right?"

I sent him a glare that said "in *private*, you idiot." But he apparently mistook it for "It's really important that we have this conversation in front of Maria," because that's what he started to do.

"Did someone . . . ?" He reached out to take my hand. "Is it a *boy*?"

I almost hit him. "No, Dad," I said through gritted teeth. "It's *not* a boy." Although, actually, it kind of *was*.

Maria got to her feet. "I should get going," she said, smiling at Dad. See? I was right about her.

Dad watched her walk away. I cleared my throat.

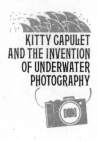

"Listen, Dad," I said, in the heaviest, most grown-up voice I could muster. "Something really bad's about to happen. They have to shut down the festival."

Dad did a double take. "What? I thought . . . Kitty, what the hell are you talking about?"

"I don't know how to explain," I said. I really should have thought this through before barging into Dad's tent.

I took a deep breath. "You know the road they're building?" Dad frowned, but I carried on talking before he could interrupt. "It's going to destroy the stream. Wairuakiri. Kids swim there all the time, and it's . . . well, it's really special."

"Kitty," he began.

"No, Dad, just listen. You're always singing about how important nature is. Trees and willows and lakes. Well, here's an actual real-life situation where something natural is about to be ruined, and you can do something about it."

"What can I do?" he said, looking annoyed. "I can't call off the concert. I'd be breaking a contract."

I tried to speak, but he shook his head. "I promise I'll look into it," he said, "*after* the show. But Gerald's version of what's going on is very different from whatever you've been told."

This wasn't working. I started to panic. "It's not just that," I said quickly. "There really is something in the stream, Dad. I know that sounds crazy, but I've seen it. And it's angry. Something very bad's going to happen."

"Darling, I can see you're upset." As soon as he called me "darling," I knew I'd lost him. "But it's just a stream." He put his hands on my shoulders. "How about you sleep in the trailer tonight with Lucy? Or I could ask Gerald to give you a room in the house? I think you need to get out of that claustrophobic pup tent, especially if it's raining . . ."

That did it. I pushed away his hands and swore. "I'm not five years old! This is serious!"

He took a step back. "Hey — come on, Kitten. You're being silly."

I think I screamed with frustration then; I might even have thrown something. I remember striding away from the tent muttering about stupid useless fathers and how much I hated them. Without knowing why, I headed for the stream.

"Ruakiri!" I called, still angry. "Come on, Ruakiri, come out and talk to me! Damn it, Rua — I'm on your side!"

I didn't know what I would do if I found him. But he didn't show. Instead, I found myself splashing through ankle-deep water long before leaving the trees. And then I saw what was ahead and froze.

The quiet creek was gone; in its place a dark turbulent river raged, cutting a wide path through the bush. As I stood staring, a wall of black water rose up and rolled forward, crashing into the trees and surging around my legs till I staggered and almost fell. Another wave followed and another, each higher and stronger than the last.

The tree with the rope swing now stood entirely surrounded by water. I watched as it slowly tipped sideways then vanished, sucked under and away. The river made a low hungry sound, like a growl in the back of its throat.

I don't know how long I stayed there, unable to move. As each new surge of water rushed up, I held my breath and imagined being swallowed and swept away, leaving no trace behind. But the waves always broke just short of where I stood, washing all around me, tugging at my legs like an invitation to come join them. And part of me longed to let go and slip into that cool dark world, to be pulled

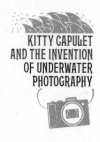

rushing and flowing over smooth stones and rich soil, through valleys and over falls, churning around rapids and dancing down gullies, till finally we'd merge with the vast warm sea.

And then I thought, *I want to get a photo of this*. And my mind cleared, and I looked down. I was up to my waist in water, clinging to a tree. The sun was gone, and night was closing in; I would have to use a long exposure. Wrapping one arm around the trunk, I steadied the camera on a branch and tried to stop shaking long enough to take a few good pictures. Then I hauled myself backward, fighting the powerful pull of the flood until at last I was free, climbing out of the water and running through the trees.

When I got back to the field, the rain had eased and the natural amphitheater was packed with people.

"Flood!" I cried. But no one could hear me over the music.

On one stage, a local band was finishing their set with a three-guitar feedback war. I checked my watch. Dad was due to play in ten minutes. I pushed into the dancing crowd, a seething mass of bodies that swept me up and pushed me backward and forward.

"Out of my way!" I yelled. "Let me through!" But the guitars were too loud, and it was too dark to see, and everyone was having too much fun to notice.

Somehow I got to the edge of the crowd and slipped under the fence to the backstage area. I thrust my All-Areas pass at the security guy. He frowned at me skeptically.

"I'm Daniel Flynn's daughter," I half yelled at him. And then, when he looked blank: "*Parliament of Trees*. He's my dad."

"Oh," he said, "sorry, girl. They're onstage now, about to start."

"Thanks. And listen — you'd better raise some kind of alarm. The stream behind those trees has broken its banks, and the water's still rising."

He blinked. "What stream?" He glanced in the direction I'd pointed, but it was too dark to see anything.

"Just tell someone who's in charge," I said firmly. "Quickly!" He stared at me a moment, then turned and took out a cell phone.

I went through the same routine two more times before finally climbing onto the back of the stage. Through a tangle of lashed cables and light stands, speakers and amps, past a couple of idle road-ies watching from the rear, I could see them: the nearest thing to a family I had in the world. Jacob had sat down at his kit and was giv-ing it a final check, stroking the cymbals and gently working the bass drum pedal. Lucy was adjusting her guitar strap over a pale green dress. And off to the side, hidden from the audience, sat my father, quietly writing in his notebook.

The lights were in preshow mode, dimmed onstage, with a couple of spots rolling across the crowd outside. Everyone was waiting for Dad's imminent appearance, with that mixture of expectant hush and restless noise I knew so well. Lucy looked up and saw me and smiled. Then she saw the state I was in, and her smile faltered.

"Kitty?" she said. "What —?"

I walked right past her and stepped up to the mic stand. The stage manager must have thought I was Dad because the lights flicked on, turning everything white. The audience roared like a hurricane. I couldn't see and my hands shook. But I forced myself to reach out and take hold of the microphone. The audience fell silent, confused by the sight of a bedraggled girl in a filthy wet dress alone on the stage. I cleared my throat.

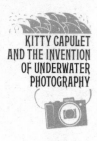

For a second, I thought of announcing Steve's secret love for Lucy, just like I'd imagined a thousand times. But I didn't. I took a deep breath and tried to sound as serious as I could.

"I'm sorry to interrupt the show, but this is an emergency." It was weird hearing my own voice amplified across the valley. "There's going to be a flood, and you're all in its path. You have to move to higher ground."

A murmur spread through the crowd.

"Please stay calm and don't panic," I continued. "But start making your way to the hill at the back of the field."

People were talking to each other and looking around, trying to work out if it was a joke. But no one was leaving.

"Kitty." Dad was behind me, speaking quietly. "What are you doing?" I put my hand over the microphone so our voices wouldn't carry.

"It's true, Dad," I said. "I've just been down to the river, and it's rising fast. We've got to clear people out of here."

Dad frowned darkly then turned to the stagehands. "Where's Gerald?"

And then the heavens fell. With a hissing roar, rain suddenly filled the air, pounding down with such force, the crowd cowered and broke. Dad was shouting, but I ignored him, staring at the shimmering wall of water caught in the spotlight. For a moment I thought I was back at the bottom of the stream, held down, unable to breathe.

Then a rush of cold wet spray hit my face, and I stumbled back. I saw Dad step up to the microphone, wanting to calm the crowd, but water gushed over his hands on the mic and the cables at his feet, and there was a sickening flash and a bang, and he was thrown off the stage and disappeared.

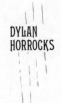

I screamed and ran forward, vaulting off the edge. The downpour hit me in midair, taking my breath away and hurling me to the ground, where I slipped and rolled in the mud. The audience was gone. There was no one there.

"Dad!" I yelled again and again, my voice lost in the pummeling rain.

I saw movement off to the left and began to run. A dark shape loomed up in the chaos: a glimpse of something tall and inhuman, dragging a limp form away. All around me was water; the river was pouring into the bowl-shaped field, merging with countless puddles to form a wide shallow lake. Into this flood slid the strange giant shadow, pulling my father behind it.

Then the rain shifted, and the shadow became a slim teenage boy.

"Ruakiri?" I no longer knew what I was seeing.

He looked up at me. Black hair framed his beautiful brown face, shining and wet.

"Ruakiri, please . . ." I said, moving closer. "Let him go."

"Why?" He spoke quietly, but it cut through the rain clear and cold. "You are his prisoner. Now you will be free."

"What? I didn't mean —"

"You can stay."

I wiped the water away from my eyes. "No, Ruakiri," I said. "You don't understand. It's not like that. I — I was angry at Dad. But he's a good person. And he's my father." I realized I was crying.

Ruakiri stopped moving. "They must be punished," he said at last, still holding Dad's shoulders. "I *will* defend myself. They are killing me."

"Please," I said again. "Not like this. It's not his fault. I can stop the road, if you give me a chance. I'll make them understand. Please just

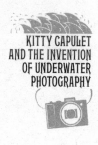
don't hurt anyone." I reached Dad and fell to my knees, lifting his pale face clear of the water. "Please."

I looked up, and our eyes met. Ruakiri's face was very still, yet somehow it flickered back and forth between that soft young boy and something else. For a moment it felt as if I were doing the same, as though I was no longer just Kitty, but also someone older and bigger and braver than before. The crying had stopped. I knew what to do.

"Go back to the stream," I said, calmly this time. "Go to Wairuakiri and rest. I will finish this."

His hands slipped from Dad's shoulders. "Go," I said. And he slid into the water and was gone.

The rain eased away. I rested my head on Dad's chest and listened to the slow steady drumbeat of his heart. It was going to be all right. I closed my eyes and lay like that until they found us.

Dad was unconscious for eighteen hours. They took him to the hospital in a helicopter, and they had to take me, too, because I wouldn't let go until we reached ER. Lucy and Steve arrived a few hours later with Maria, who'd driven all the way from Clearwater Creek in Gerald's fastest, flashest car.

Gerald didn't turn up till morning. He'd had to cancel the festival and was up all night dealing with the chaos of the flood and several thousand angry music fans. He looked pale and irritated.

"How's your dad?" he asked, forcing his mouth into an unconvincing smile. "The doctors tell me he's going to be fine."

I didn't say anything, just looked him in the eye till he coughed and said, "Well, I'll check in again in a little while. Let me know if anything changes."

It was true; the doctors had said Dad would be fine. He'd had an electric shock from a wet cable, and the fall from the stage had left him scraped and bruised. But no one seemed terribly worried. Except Steve, who's always worried, even when nothing's wrong.

And, well, maybe me.

I was alone with Dad when he finally woke up. The room was full of afternoon light, and I'd opened a window to let in the warm summer air.

"Kitten," he said.

"How are you feeling?" I asked, fighting the urge to cry.

"Sore," he said. "What happened? Where are we?"

I told him about the electrocution and the fall, but then I kind of ran out of things to say. I had meant to tell him the rest, too: about the *taniwha* and the flood and how he'd nearly been carried off to drown. But in the end, I couldn't.

"Is everyone else okay?" he asked. "I remember a hell of a lot of rain."

"Yes," I said, smiling. Just like Dad to worry about everyone else. "The festival was washed out, and Gerald had to shut it down. People are pretty mad."

Dad turned and watched the sunlight on the walls for a while.

"Kitty," he said at last. "All that stuff you said in the tent — about the stream and the road and . . ."

I flinched, not knowing what to say.

"You meant it?"

I nodded. "Yes," I said. "Yes, I did."

He went back to watching the wall, and soon I saw he was asleep. I rubbed my eyes and realized I'd been awake for more hours than my tired brain could calculate.

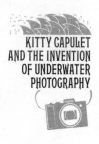

So.

It turns out those narrow hospital beds have just enough room to curl up next to your sleeping Dad if you nestle in close like a little girl. And if you're lucky, the sound of his huge nose gently snoring can make you feel cozy and safe and like you're five years old. And you'll close your eyes and drift off and have the best sleep you've had in years.

Two weeks later and I'm sitting on another plane. Dad's dozing across the aisle while Maria watches a movie in the seat next to his. I don't know how long she'll stick with our crazy traveling family, but I kind of like having our own official driver. I've been copying all my photos from New Zealand onto George, and now I'm going through them one by one, deleting, renaming, cropping, and uploading.

There's Dad in the hospital, giving the nurses an impromptu solo concert on the day they let him out. And there's Gerald arriving for a meeting with Dad, with his colorful shirt and handshakes and backslapping and smiles. I sure wish I'd seen Gerald's face when Dad told him he'd sue for negligence over that faulty electric cable unless he dropped his plans for the new parking lot and road. But Dad wouldn't let me in the room for that. Still, I managed to get a couple of great photos of Gerald walking out, ashen-faced and thin-lipped. He didn't look at all like George Clooney that time. More like Steve Buscemi. Or Monty Burns.

And here's Dad again, onstage at the fund-raiser he threw together with some of the other bands from the festival. The one-day concert cheered up a lot of disappointed fans and collected over $100,000 to clean up the rivers and streams around Clearwater.

It won't solve everything, but at least it's a start.

This one was taken by Lucy: it shows me and Dad hugging onstage while the audience cheers. The newspapers said I saved lives in the flood. I don't know. It feels weird being talked about and seeing my face all over the web. But I like the way Dad looks at me now, like I'm not just a little girl anymore. I think he's proud.

But *this* is my favorite photo.

I took it on our last day in New Zealand, when I slipped away from the motel just before dawn and climbed the fence around Gerald's vineyard, ran across the dark wet fields, and crept through the bush to Clearwater Creek.

The flood had left broken trees and stones strewn across the ground. But the stream flowed dark and strong and quiet. I stood for a long time, watching and listening as the sky turned gray then pink then blue. And then I raised my camera for one last look.

And the sun rose above the trees and the water lit up like liquid gold, and for one brief moment I was in his world, and it was beautiful and alive and filled with light. And then the light became memory, and the memory was saved, and I turned and walked away.

And here it is.

Look. Can you see it?

Look.

Son of Abyss

NIK HOUSER

It was Mom's idea for me and Dad to build the blood altar in the garage.

She said it would be a bonding experience. We could drive out to a dread farm together to pick out the raw materials, then stop at the hardware store on the way home for anything else we needed.

I remember being so excited. I kept saying I wanted to get a mirrorfox for cunning or a shaded tortoise from the Southern Breach with ink for blood. I saw Dad drooling over a thousand-year-old angler slug wound up in coils as wide as my leg, a dim white light pulsing out from the center of its curled mass.

"Here he is," my father said, as he led the old greyhound out of the barn. He must have seen my expression, which I can't say I did my best to hide, because his own face darkened. "He's all we can afford," he said. "Come on, Mom wants us home before dinner."

"He looks good." I sat in the backseat with the nameless dog, petting his flank. His fur was mottled, bald in patches where he'd chewed at whatever it was that made him so affordable. The dog smiled, tongue out, tail wagging between his legs like its hinge was broken.

"A lot of families can't afford an animal this nice, Samaeul," Dad said.

"I know," I said. I put my hand out the window and drummed my claws against the side of the car. We had 2-60 air-conditioning, which meant you rolled down two windows and went sixty miles per hour.

The drive home took us past the power plant where my dad worked, with its monolithic smokestacks covered in runes two stories high. Whenever we passed it, I always stuck my head out the window and strained my ears, convinced I could hear the confessors at work, that I could discern faint screams beneath the hum of the roadside pylons.

The dog smiled the whole way home. I couldn't get him to stop licking my ear.

I begged Dad to let me hold the knife. He refused, said he needed me to hold the bucket to catch the blood, which we couldn't afford to waste. Every part of the animal had a purpose. But Mom insisted he at least let me try.

"Don't cut yourself." He handed me the knife. The bone-handled blade was the oldest thing in the house. When he was alive, my grandfather used to tell me how he'd used it to cut the finger off a seraphic warlord at the Battle for the Abyss. Until the day he died, Granddad kept the finger strung around his neck where it still bled a little, half a century later, staining every shirt he wore.

"I won't cut myself," I said, rolling my eyes, and cut my thumb pretty much in half.

We were in the kitchen, my father and I seated at the table, Dad's reading glasses perched on his nose to monitor the leech he'd spread over my thumb to clean the wound, when Mom came in.

"As per usual, your son thought he knew best," Dad said to my thumb. "And as per usual, he got his hubris handed to him on a . . ." His voice trailed off when he saw my face and turned back to look at his wife.

Mom looked confused. Like she didn't know where she was or who we were. She looked at Dad and me, at my cut, at the leech. She ran a hand through her hair and straightened her sleeve. She walked over to the table and put a tiny flower on the table in front of my father, who recoiled from it. "I think I might need to see a doctor."

It took six months for the horticancer to consume my mother, to coat her skin with a layer of moss thick enough that the doctors couldn't burn it away even if Mom had wanted them to keep trying, if the cure hadn't become worse than the disease. By the end, only her eyes — a pale lilac faded from their once deep purple — could be seen beneath the bed of flowers that covered her like a blanket, flowers of every color sprouting from every pore on dark green hair-thin stems, swallowing her body in a canopy of petals, their roots spreading through her body, turning her veins to kindling as they reduced her heart, liver, and lungs to lumps of misshapen wood.

"Whoa, check it out."

I waved Dad over from the corner of the garage where he'd spent the afternoon packing and stacking cardboard boxes labeled MOM against a wall on the far side. My father stretched his back, wiped the sweat from his forehead, and followed my voice to where I knelt, bent over a small wooden chest. It was late summer, which meant Mom had been dead for two months, that my sophomore year of upper school was about to start, that all my friends were still out of town, and that I was made of equal parts boredom and sweat. It was the time of year when the world was perfectly placed between its twin suns, Brother and Other, so that night never fell and wouldn't fall for at least another month, on Transgressor's Eve.

Dad squinted down at me, his gaze one of constant appraisal, an X-ray that peered inside things and people to see how they worked and what was wrong with them.

"Check it out." I held up a small net of leather straps and iron fastenings.

"Your old muzzle," Dad said. "Your mom said she threw all that stuff away."

The old chest smelled of mildew and damp yellowed paper and clothes half eaten by whatever lived there. From inside I fished out the tangled steel knot of a choke chain attached to a powder-blue collar with *Samaeul* stitched across it in dainty yellow thread.

Dad picked the old leash out of my hand. Examined it with that look of his. Normally, my father's face made a habit of being unreadable; his thoughts kept their own council. But right then, I knew he was thinking about Mom. I held my breath and watched him think, not wanting to break the spell.

He dropped the leash into the chest.

"You shouldn't leave these things out," he said. "They have a lot of power."

I closed the chest, gently. "Can we have dinner now?"

"Dinner?" said Dad. I'd gotten a lot of those answers since we'd burned Mom, like I was speaking a language he didn't understand: *Laundry? New backpack? Permission slip?*

Not that I relished the idea of chili for dinner for the eighth night in a row. A month ago, it had dawned on my father that he could simply buy a whole grocery cart of something and make that for dinner till it ran out. He'd smiled and shook his head in that *I can't believe no one's thought of this* way dads get that invariably augers doom, like when they discover a shortcut to somewhere that's anything but. It wouldn't have been so bad if the chili was made with beef or fox — or even dog. Instead, Dad bought out the store's entire stock of Forest Ranch-Style chili, which meant a heady mélange of squirrel, vole, mouse, and, if you were lucky, a little snake meat.

Dad took my hand, turned my fingers in the light. "When was the last time you cut these?"

My claws were at least two inches long, unclipped in the two months since Mom had died.

Dad took my chin between his forefinger and thumb. "Better have a look under the hood. Come on, open up, mister."

I opened my mouth. Dad whistled between his filed fangs. He kept his teeth like he kept his hair: short, practical, and without the slightest hint of fashion sense.

"You need to file those teeth down, young man. Tonight. You've chewed your cheeks to ribbons. Hey, what's this?"

My father reached up, ran a finger over the four sharp nubs that protruded from the top of my head, still hidden under my shaggy, uncombed mop of summer hair.

"When did these start coming in?"

"Two months ago."

"A four-pointer," said Dad, nodding, impressed. A two-pointer himself, my father's own horns extended a foot over his head, straight up, no twists or branching, which, while unremarkable, made it easier to put on a T-shirt. At least, that's what he said.

I grinned from head to heels. "Granddad was a four-pointer."

My father's father had had the largest horns in the city, a chandelier of bone that grew a towering five feet over his head.

"Did you need a muzzle when you were a kid?" I asked.

"We all need them."

"Even Mom?"

I only ever saw my dad laugh three times. This was one of them. "Especially Mom."

The walk to school took me past the Chasm.

The Chasm was this giant crack in the earth a thousand feet wide that went for forever in both directions and had no bottom and that we supposedly came out of a million years ago, sent by the Father of Fear to lay waste to all the plants and animals because life was chaos and we were order or something. I don't remember it all. Just that we gave the Chasm our dead. Other cities buried bodies to feed the Wyrm. Or set them adrift in the sea, an offering to the Leviathan. We dropped ours in that big hole to feed the Void, weighted down so they couldn't get sucked up into the sky and kidnapped by the Empire of Heaven.

I didn't think I wanted to get dropped in a giant hole when I died. Maybe burned like Mom. Then maybe someone could take my bones and make something out of them, like a chair. Not a confessor's torture chair like my dad used on angels at the plant, but a really comfortable one that girls would sit on and it would be so comfortable they'd want to take their clothes off.

I hadn't seen Jushuh since my mother's pyre, just after school let out for summer vacation. She'd spent the summer at an internship studying with the healers of the Eastern Massif.

"Sam!" she shrieked when she spotted me walking through our school's parking lot, the end of a five-mile trudge that began at my front door. I looked up from the sidewalk just before she collided into me. Jushuh's strong, slender arms wrapped around my neck as a curtain of matted auburn hair fell over my face. Her scent filled my nose with the tang of oranges, paint, and girl sweat. Since childhood, Jushuh had bathed only occasionally and grudgingly.

Something was off. Something about the way she hugged me. Not wrong, but different. For a second, I thought something was pinned between us. A pair of somethings.

Jushuh had boobs. A double scoop of maturity tightening a T-shirt that she hadn't yet figured out no longer fit.

"Guess I should have stuffed my shirt if I wanted a hug, too."

Ungluing myself from Jushuh, I found Bon standing behind her, smiling the half smile that was always present on his aggravatingly clear complexion and that made you smile even when you didn't want to, like he was letting you in on the best secret ever. He'd let his claws grow all summer like me, only his folks hadn't made him cut them. His teeth were sharp, too, and his horns were already six inches grown, spiraling out in a *V*. At least he only had two of them.

"You look like crap, dude," Bon said. "What happened — somebody die?"

Jushuh rolled her eyes with her whole body. "Nice one, Bon. Real classy."

"Aw, Sam knows I got nothing but love." Bon stepped up, hugged me, put an arm around my shoulder. "Seriously, you hangin' in?"

Bon Dur Suun Kyyver was like the weather: you could complain about him or you could accept him, but you couldn't change him.

"Hey," I said. "What's up with your ear?"

Bon touched his left earlobe, or the place where it should have been.

"Oh, that. Me and Jushuh were making out, and she got a little carried away." Bon laughed. Jushuh hit him. Hard. Something sharp poked at me when she did. Something in the way she smiled at him. "No, for real, either of you ever gone on safari in the Underveldt and woken up to find a dream-eater having dinner in your ear?"

Like either Jushuh or I had ever been on safari. Like either of us had a high-ranking Ministry official as a father.

"Well, trust me, you don't want to. Now come on." Bon cupped a hand around the back of my neck and led me toward the western grotto. "We're gonna be late."

"We've got five minutes," Jushuh said.

"You don't understand." Bon pulled a tightly rolled stick of fire-weed from his pocket. "*We're gonna be late.*"

"Blood is not enough." From his lectern, Elder Kohl addressed us while we struggled to arrange spaghetti-string handfuls of rabbit

intestines into a pattern that matched the diagram illustrated on the chalkboard at the head of the class. Dressed in the sapphire robes of a Master Elucidator, Elder Kohl worried at his three jade lip rings as he spoke. Two ebony horns rose from either side of his head and curled toward the ceiling. "Blood is nothing without intention. Intention is everything."

The entire day, I'd been routed by Bon when I tried to sit behind Jushuh in class, been forced to frown from the next row over as Bon passed her notes, offered little massages, made her laugh. At least once during every subject, Bon would turn to me and mime like he was holding heavy melons, the universal sign for *TITS!*

Which meant that my sharing a workbench with Jushuh during animalurigical studies was a major victory, though due to no guile or strategy of my own, but, rather, Bon's need to go to the bathroom at least once during the school day to jerk off.

The last seat available when he'd come through the door was in the first row of tables, directly in front of me and Jushuh, next to Rudi Onvl.

I think maybe we all knew something would happen to Rudi. Maybe not as soon as it did but eventually. Some people just walk through life with a MESS WITH ME sign stuck to their back. Usually, you don't feel too sorry for nerds because, hey, they might be social outcasts now, but when they grow up they'll be the ones in charge, summoning the deep Terror to hold back the hordes of Heaven and keep our children safe at night while the rest of us struggle to pay our bills. But Rudi wasn't just a nerd with greasy skin and the physique of a six-foot baby. He was a stupid nerd. The only kid whose grades were worse than Bon's.

"We channel the blood through intention, and we channel intention through knowledge. Remember, this world does not belong to us, boys and girls. The world belongs to chaos. We are the Voidspawn, the Redkind of the Cold Womb. We are order. And order never takes anything from chaos, merely borrows it. Without knowledge, we are the victims of the chaos. The Mother of Mercy wishes nothing more than that end."

No one knew much about the Mother of Mercy. Just what the confessors could torture out of her soldier angels. We knew she ruled an empire called Heaven, and that she claimed dominion over all life, that we were all her Children. According to her, nothing had the right to die. She wanted everyone to live forever. Which sounded okay until you saw what she took in exchange for eternal life.

Some people said the Mother of Mercy was the Father of Fear's own daughter, and that she rebelled against him eons ago when he sent us out of the Chasm to rein in the chaos of life. But that's not the story I believed.

At the front of the class, Elder Kohl pinned his own rabbit to his workbench with the easy motions of muscle memory, weaving geometric patterns into the entrails. Even with the windows open, the smell in the room was a physical presence, the scent of warm blood thickening the air so you could taste it when you breathed.

"You're doing it wrong," Bon hissed at Rudi, his partner's clumsy fingers lost in a maze of guts.

"I'm doing my best," said Rudi.

"That's what your mom always tells me."

"However," Elder Kohl said, "with the right training, the right channeling of intent, a nuanced focus of power, perhaps one of you

will help bring order to the chaos by donning the hood of a Master Confessor someday. Or as long as you're dreaming big, the gilt tongue of the Speakers Without Mouths."

Beside me, Jushuh shivered in the ninety-degree heat. We saw one once, a Speaker Without Mouth. Imagine a man-size wad of used chewing gum squished into a wet black wrapper floating three feet above the ground, warped and twisted by their dealings with the deepest sciences.

Elder Kohl clacked his tongue, murmured something under his breath, drew a long claw down the length of his tongue, then stabbed it through the rabbit's small purple heart as it burst into flame.

"I can't believe I forgot the marshmallows," Bon said.

Without a word in response, Elder Kohl strode casually over to Bon and plucked a hair from his bangs. "Ouch!" Bon said, and rubbed his head. Beside him, Rudi snickered. He shouldn't have.

Back at his worktable, Elder Kohl murmured something under his breath. The flames consuming the small heart turned a dark green.

"Sacrifice is nothing without intent," he said to Bon, and held my friend's hair over the fire. "Power is nothing without control."

The whole class heard Bon swallow. His eyes, already wide, became saucers when Elder Kohl let the hair fall into the flames.

It took about a minute for the class to start breathing again, once they realized that nothing was going to happen.

"As I said"—Elder Kohl clapped his hands together—"sacrifice is nothing without intention. What was my intention? To scare this young man. But I didn't need to summon a gender thief or an emotionmutt to do that. I simply needed to imply my intention. *Sacrifice. Intention. Power. Control.* By the end of this year, you will be seeing these words writ on the backs of your eyelids while you sleep, children."

The great iron bell rang in the High Tower to announce the end of class. Everyone rose from their chairs.

"Your homework for this week is to bring a live animal to class on Friday! Please remember: *Bigger animals don't mean better grades.* It doesn't have to be a demiverge from beyond the last veil. In fact, it shouldn't be, because then we'd all be turned inside out. It can be a mouse, as long as it's alive."

"Seriously, did you hear Rudi laughing at me? I could've died, man. Kohl is sick in the head."

We sat in my garage, smoking fireweed with the windows open.

"All I heard was you wetting your pants," I said. "Come on, it's Jushuh's turn."

Jushuh took a drag off the fireweed. "I don't know," she said.

"Oh, come on!" Bon said. "You promised. I've been waiting all summer to show you guys!"

Jushuh rolled her eyes. "Fine. Go. But nothing, like, freaky. I'm already scarred for life knowing Sam stuck a battery up his butt."

"*When I was five!*" I protested.

"All right, I'll let you off with an easy one." Bon leaned forward over crossed legs. The concrete was cool beneath us. "If you could steal anything and get away with it, what would it be?"

Jushuh smiled, then bit her lip when Bon leaned closer. Her cheeks reddened, chin quivering. She crossed her arms, trying her best not to answer, to resist the pull of Bon's blood talent.

I'd spent the whole summer sweating in the garage, bent over my

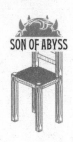

half-built cheapo dog-bone altar with a children's book in my lap called *So You Still Haven't Discovered Your Blood Talent*, trying to set silverfish on fire with the power of my words.

"My neighbor's jacket!" Jushuh offered through gritted teeth. She looked at Bon expectantly.

"Nope," Bon said, lips pressed into a hard smile. "You're lying." He leaned closer, his eyes becoming two pinpricks of light in a curtain of shadow. "*What do you want*, Jushuh?"

Jushuh bit her own smile so hard, I thought she'd chew through her lips until she shouted, "Mr. Firehot!" and burst out laughing. She shoved Bon into me as the two of us snickered.

"Excuse me?" I said. "Like, the candy guy?"

Firehots were this candy we all loved as kids. They were sweet and tangy and delicious, but you had to spit them out before you got to their lethally spicy centers or you wouldn't be able to taste anything for a week. Mr. Firehot was a cartoon guy on the candy's wrapper with a red face, sharp teeth, and fire for a tongue.

"I had a huge crush on Mr. Firehot when I was a kid, okay?" Jushuh said. "Whatever."

"You know he's not a real person, right?" I asked.

"We're totally gonna get married someday, so shut up!" Jushuh smiled, her breath heavy, like she'd just sprinted down the block. She rubbed her temples. "That's so creepy. I can't believe I let you do that."

But her smile said something else. Whatever it said, she changed her face when she saw me watching her. A little emotional striptease I wasn't meant to see.

"All right, Sam," she said, "your turn. And make it good, Bon."

"Mr. Firehot good?"

She shoved him again, wearing that striptease smile. "If you ever

use those three words in a sentence again, I will throw you in the Chasm!"

I never mastered that way of talking to girls where you were making fun of them but really you were flirting with them. I never got the *I can't believe you just said that* love shove, the way you do when you're young and need an excuse to touch someone you like.

"You guys need some privacy?" I said.

"Would you mind?" Bon said.

"Shut up!" Jushuh said, and gave him another love shove.

"Come on, man, my turn," I said. "Don't make me use the battery on you."

"You really want a second try?"

"At your talent, not the battery." Leaning back against the MOM wall, I took a drag off the fireweed and lifted my chin to Bon. "Bring it."

"All right," he said, and flashed a wicked smile. "Who do you like at school?"

Oh, no, no, no, no, no.

At once, my head felt heavy, like it was filling up with sand. I could feel my friend's new talent working on me. It had developed over the summer like Jushuh's sweater melons. Blood came to a slow simmer behind my eyes, the muscles in my legs going tight as I fought the urge to blurt out the name of the girl seated directly across from me.

"Who do you like at school?" Bon asked.

My breathing went ragged. Then stopped all together.

Jushuh's face darkened. "Bon . . ."

"Tell me."

"Bon, stop. He doesn't want to tell you."

"But he *does* want to," Bon said. Beads of sweat dappled his forehead, his own breath shallow. "He *has* to."

Cold needles stabbed at my heart. My throat closed, jaw rigid. A sharp *crack!* rang through my mouth as a tooth chipped.

"Bon, for real, turn it off." Jushuh pulled on Bon's arm.

The world became a fluid thing, shimmering and unreal, filled with stars that swam through my pinhole vision. My heart slowed to a murmur, a mere rumor of life.

The next thing I knew, I was on the floor, on my side, looking up at Jushuh kissing Bon.

The world came back into focus. I gasped, gulped down all the air in the smoky garage. Put my hand on my heart to make sure it was still beating.

What I saw when Jushuh pulled away was Bon's grin. Just this knife slash of pleasure cut into his face, and the way he wiped his mouth off with the back of his hand. Like she was this overripe fruit he'd just eaten down to the pit.

"Thanks," he said.

"I didn't do it for you," Jushuh said. She'd saved me, broke his concentration with a kiss.

"I was talking to Sam," Bon said.

I didn't realize Jushuh was leaving until she had her hand on the doorknob. I opened my mouth to say something, but she was already gone.

"Let her go, dude," Bon said. "My dad told me that if they could weaponize the hormones of teenage girls, the War would be over tomorrow." Bon dragged on the nub of fireweed until his fingertips blackened, hissing as he shook out the pain. "You all right, man?"

I nodded, still trying to swallow my lungs back into my chest.

"Hey, I was just having fun," he said. "I didn't mean to, you know, kill you or whatever. I didn't know you liked her that much."

Liar.

When I was a kid and I'd come home with a scraped knee or a torn shirt or a tongue swelled up to the size of my foot because I couldn't swallow the spider Bon had dared me to eat, my dad would always ask why I was friends with him. I never had an answer while Bon was still alive. But I do now. When people ask, I tell them he was like fireworks. You know they're dangerous. You've heard all the stories about what happens to kids who play with them. But you can't help yourself. Fireworks don't mean to blow up your hand. At least, you don't think they do.

"Whoa, dude." Bon rose unsteadily to his feet and hobbled to the rear of the garage. I followed. "Is that what I think it is?"

The chair was made of iron and angel bone.

"It's my grandfather's old confessor's chair," I said. "They gave it to him when he retired."

"It's so small." Bon stared at it reverently. Held out his hand to touch it, changed his mind. "I wonder how many people died in it."

"None," I said. Grandfather had been famous for never losing a prisoner. He could keep an angel alive and healthy for years, draining every last ounce of its faith, until its soul had corroded from the inside out, leaving only an insensate shell that dreamed of death.

I asked my grandfather once, what it was like, torturing an angel. For a second I thought I was in trouble because we'd been at dinner and everyone had stopped eating and just stared at me like I'd taken a dump in the middle of the table.

They are like children, Granddad had said. *Children who love you. So, it's like killing your children.*

That's what the Mother of Mercy did, in exchange for eternal life in her Empire of Heaven. She made you a child. All the currency of

experience you worked so hard to earn through living and growing up and learning how to be you, all the joy, the regret, the pain, desire, fulfillment, love and despair and everything else that made you *you*: that was the price she asked. Only . . . she didn't ask. So we fought. For a million years we'd fought.

"Hey, I just wanna say, that really sucked about your mom," he said to the chair.

"Thanks," I said to the chair.

"I wanted to go to the funeral, you know?"

"I know."

"But, I mean, my dad."

"I know."

We stared at the chair for a long time, having the same conversation we'd had a thousand times in our heads but had never vocalized:

My dad's still mad at your dad for stealing your mom away when they were teenagers, Bon wouldn't say.

My dad's still mad that my mom cheated on him with your dad when they worked at the plant together, I wouldn't reply.

My dad's still angry she went back to your dad.

My dad's still angry your dad became his boss, and then his boss's boss, and then his boss's boss's boss's boss's whatever. What does your dad do anyway?

I don't know, some important junk with the War.

My dad still doesn't want me hanging out with you.

My dad still doesn't want me hanging out with you.

Screw 'em.

Totally.

After a time, Bon reached out a hand, tried to touch the chair again, and again found himself unable.

"Dude, you know who we need to get in this thing?" he said, grinning that fireworks grin. "Rudi."

That night I stayed up in the garage reading *So You Still Haven't Discovered Your Blood Talent*. Dad worked nights at the plant, so it wasn't a big deal if I stayed up late. He'd never made it past First Novice Confessor, which basically meant he cleaned up the cells once the Master Confessors were done for the day and their prisoners were dragged off by their clipped wings to be healed while the faith their confessors had tortured out of them was piped down to Refining to light our streets and heat our water and make our cars run.

I spent all night in that garage — or what passed for a night with Brother and Other refusing to set completely for another few weeks — staring at that stupid book. I knew every god call in the book, but I couldn't summon so much as a minor fecal imp to my altar. I even cut my hand on Granddad's old chair, just to see what would happen, which was nothing. The chair was cold, though. Colder than anything in that sweltering garage had a right to be.

In the end, I gave up and went upstairs to my bedroom to polish the horn and call it a night.

When we were kids, Jushuh used to come over and spend the night without permission. Mine or my parents'. She used to sneak in my window and crawl into bed with me, shoving me over so she could have the warm spot. I don't know when it started. Back when her dad was still around. I never asked which were the bad times, when her dad was drinking or when he wasn't. But when he didn't, or when

he did, she would come over and not say anything. Just lie next to me and hold my hand, looking for cuts on my fingers because I was clumsy and just always cut myself.

When she found a cut, she'd put that finger in her mouth. She didn't suck on it or anything. Just stuck in her mouth for about a minute. Then spat it out all covered in spit.

"You need to wash your hands more," was all she'd say, every time, while I held my healed finger close to my face, smelling her spit. It smelled sour. It took a lot to convince Jushuh to brush her teeth.

She stopped coming to my window the summer Mom died. I still leave the window open at night.

Some people said the Mother of Mercy was actually the Father of Fear's mother, and that it was he who rebelled against her, that he created us to undo the chaos of creation she had invoked and inflicted on existence. But that's not the story I believed.

Chili for breakfast.

Chili.

For breakfast.

The look of betrayal I gave my cereal bowl that morning could have boiled water if I had a pyromancer's blood talent.

"You don't like it, you don't have to eat it." Across the table, Dad propped himself over his own bowl of chili, still dressed in the jumpsuit he wore at the plant, its armpits pitted out with sweat, the cuffs saturated with a shift's worth of blood spatters and other dark stains you could only identify by the smell.

I asked him once, maybe the year before, why he didn't change clothes when he got home, because I mean he stank, right? His answer was to strip down to nothing but his scars, of which he had a ton, right there at the breakfast table. Not much of an answer, if you ask me, but I never asked again. Not because I didn't want to see him naked again (which I didn't), but those scars? I mean, wow. And I thought *my* dad was strict. And, yeah, of course I thought about what Granddad had said about torturing your children, so shut up.

"I miss Mom's eggs," I said. Mom had this way of taking a single turtle egg and turning it into a feast for three when money was tight. She did this thing with spices and stonecat milk. It was amazing.

Dad said nothing to this. Of course he said nothing. He didn't even keep a picture of Mom in the house anymore except inside the top drawer of his nightstand. He wasn't a husband anymore. And he'd never been a dad.

"Why can't you heal yourself?"

All through her illness, I kept asking Mom the same thing. My constant asking would have driven her up the wall if she could have gotten out of bed, all wrapped in gauze and reeking of the flowers that had buried their roots deep within her, green stems bursting out of the open sores on her arms and legs and stomach and cheeks in explosions of violet and marigold, crimson and cornflower blue.

"Why can't you just make yourself better? You're a healer. Why can't you just heal yourself?"

Every time I asked, she'd just reach out a hand and touch my face.

"Your horns are coming in," she said once, toward the end. "They're going to be so beautiful. Just like your grandfather's."

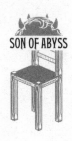

"Granddad always said I was gonna be just like him when I grew up."

Mom gave me this look then, this smile I couldn't mistake for anything but relief. "No, you won't."

Bon had Rudi cornered when I got to animalurgical studies. A crowd of students had gathered around them.

"I asked you a question," Bon said. "Have you ever seen your mom naked?"

"Y-yes," Rudi said, the word pried from between his teeth. An eruption of applause and laughter as Bon took a quick bow.

"When?"

"I-I don't know. When I was little."

After dumping my backpack, I made my way over to the crowd. I wondered where Elder Kohl was, then noticed him standing right next to me, arms crossed, staring through narrowed, analytical eyes at the two boys. Bullying wasn't exactly allowed, but there wasn't a really clear definition of it, either, considering what they were training us to do. Let me put it this way: When it came to breaking the rules at my school, you got a lot of points for style.

"Okay," Bon said. "How 'bout your dad? You ever see him naked?"

Rudi's eyes grew wide, red-rimmed. He bit his lips, squeezed his eyes shut. He had a horn coming in. A single nub protruding from the center of his forehead. Or maybe it was just a big zit. "Yes."

Bon leaned closer. For a second, I thought he was going to kiss Rudi. "*When?*"

Rudi whispered his answer. "All the time."

Damn.

More cheers, laughter, clapping. Bon leaned against the wall, then slumped to the floor, doubled over with his hands on his guts. I thought he was hurt, then realized that he was laughing so hard that he couldn't stand, tears streaming down his face.

At some point, someone reached down to help Bon up. Bon waved them off with a bandaged hand, four pink fingers poking from a cocoon of gauze. I squinted at his hand, thinking I must have counted wrong. I hadn't. Three fingers and a thumb. The pinkie was gone. The whole thing. Beside me, Elder Kohl studied my friend, and his bandaged hand, for a long time.

"Do you know what you're gonna do for Transgression Day?" Jushuh asked.

"No," I said. "You?"

We sat on my roof, watching the War. Brother had set, and Other was low on the horizon. A thick front of thunderheads covered the sky. Forks of lightning split the clouds where angels swung flaming swords of Truth at our own Void masters, who opened gaping mouths of space-time to swallow the Enemy whole. About once a week the evening sky would tear open, and a host of angels would swarm out to try to do battle against us. This kind of thing happened all over, not just where I lived. Our city had never fallen to the Enemy, but other places weren't so lucky.

"I don't know." Jushuh shrugged. "Probably just swipe something like last year."

It was always a struggle, picking a transgression, another stone to

tie to your soul in the hope that when you died, your soul would be heavy enough to weigh you down and keep you from getting sucked up and turned into a Fatherless Child.

Growing up, whenever I got busted for sneaking cookies or staying up past my bedtime or something, I would ask my parents why, if transgressions were good, if doing bad stuff was good, why we couldn't do bad stuff all the time. I mean, why was being bad *bad* instead of good?

My dad would always say that transgressions weren't good, just necessary. That's why we could only do them once a year. Why we all had to wear leashes and muzzles when we were young, until we learned to behave. He sounded just like my teachers when he said how life was chaos, and how we, the Redkind, had been sent by the Father of Fear to rein in that chaos, and that if we all committed transgressions all the time, it would just be another form of chaos.

"I think I'm gonna kill Rudi," Bon said, plopping himself down on the roof between me and Jushuh. That guy always knew when Jushuh was over.

"That's not funny," said Jushuh.

"I'm not laughing," said Bon.

"I mean it," said Jushuh. "That's really not funny."

"I totally agree," said Bon.

An explosion shook the sky. A burst of white lines jagged through the black clouds like cracks in the pavement of the world. The house shook under our butts. Bon and I laughed nervously, exchanged scared smiles. Jushuh glared at Bon.

"Say you're not gonna do it."

Bon smirked at Jushuh. "What do you mean? I'm totally gonna do it."

"That's really not funny," Jushuh said, her face painted the brightest color of *Don't mess with me.* "Say you're not gonna —"

"You guys," I said, rising to my feet. The sandpaper feel of the roof scratched at the soles of my bare feet. The air smelled burned. "Look!"

Bon and Jushuh followed my pointing finger to where a rain of feathers fell from the sky, a million points of light tumbling out of the black. They fell around our feet, on our shoulders, in our hair. Weightless needles as long as your forearm trailing a halo of pearl-colored light as they fell.

"Angel feathers." I don't know who said it. Maybe all of us.

Bon picked one off his arm, dropped it with a bark of surprise, sucking his scorched finger over a smile. "It shocked me!"

"Ow!" Jushuh howled, shaking the pain off her fingers where she'd brushed a feather off her arm.

"Wait a sec," Bon said. He skittered toward the edge of the roof, then out into the tree we used to get up there.

"What's he doing?" I stepped closer to Jushuh, her whole body glowing with fallen needles.

"I don't know," she said, "but I am totally afraid to move."

"Seriously. Whatever you do, don't sneeze."

"Don't make me laugh!" Jushuh giggled, then cursed the sizzle of feathers that shook loose from her shoulders and tumbled down her arms. "I mean it!"

"Check it out!" Bon scrabbled back onto the roof.

"Oh, god!" Jushuh howled, clapped a hand over her mouth, and winced at the thousand tiny shocks that assailed her when feathers cascaded from where they'd settled all over her body.

Wearing my father's work gloves, a pair of black underwear, and nothing else, Bon held out a glowing white feather.

"What are you —" I began.

"Check it out . . ." Bon said, and drew the tip of the feather across his chest. My friend sucked air sharply between his teeth as his skin made a popping, sizzling noise, the fine gold hair around his nipples fizzling into ash. In about thirty seconds he'd burned the words BON ROCKS! into his chest.

"You. Are. Insane." Jushuh's tone was sharp, but she couldn't shake the grin off her face, try as she might.

"Also," Bon said, "if you put it in your mouth, your whole face goes numb."

"Your brain is numb," I said.

"Come on." Bon pointed at me with his feather. "Seriously, chicks dig scars."

Bon was giving me that *tell the truth* look he got when he was using his blood talent. I'd heard some confessors could Persuade. I wondered if Jushuh would think I was more mature or something with a scar. She must have known what I was thinking, because she did that rolling-her-eyes-with-her-whole-body thing, head lolled back, hands in the air, never more beautiful.

"You're seriously gonna do this?" she asked me.

"I dunno."

"Stupidity is a germ and it's spreading!" She laughed.

"Come on," Bon said. "It fades in, like, a week. My dad zaps my mom all the time. He likes to zap her butt when she bends over. No wonder she hates him."

A weird silence settled over the roof then. I looked at Jushuh, who was looking at Bon, who was looking at his feather, holding it to his forearm, where the skin was turning black.

"Bon, stop," she said. When he didn't reply, she smacked his hand away, sending the feather flitting to the ground.

They exchanged a look I couldn't read, though the air between their eyes crackled like Bon's skin did when he held the feather to it. I would've given my left foot for her to look at me with that same intensity.

Without a word of good-bye, Jushuh slid down the roof and disappeared into the tree. Bon and I watched her hop the fence at the far end of my backyard.

"Are you really gonna kill Rudi?" I asked.

"You remember in your garage, when I was using my talent?" he said, ignoring my question, his eyes fixed on the place where she'd jumped the fence.

"Yeah, I remem—"

Bon turned to me with a grin. "She totally snuck into my room that night."

"What?" My heart dropped into my guts.

"She does it, like, all the time." My friend's eyes had grown wide and hungry, like he was eating my attention. "She started doing it when your mom, you know, got sick. Then when she went off to the Eastern Massif for the summer, I figured it was all done, right? I didn't hear squat from her the whole time, no *It was nice while it lasted* or anything. But then, like, the first night she was back, she snuck over. I even locked the window once, maybe a week ago, just to see. Girl *still* got in. She doesn't even talk to me. Not one word. Just comes in my window and starts pulling my clothes off. It's crazy."

At least, that's what I think he said. Crazy as it sounds, I wasn't really paying attention toward the end.

One of Bon's nipples was gone.

The left one was missing. A long slash stood in its place, crudely stitched together. Like he'd done it himself. I tried not to stare at it but couldn't help it.

He saw me seeing him. And smiled. And held out the angel feather.

"We've gotta get Rudi in that chair."

That Friday when I came down for breakfast, I put my bowl of breakfast chili, or chilereal as it had come to be known, in the trash can, bowl and all. Right in front of my dad. It wasn't the chili I was protesting. I mean, I know that now, and I sort of knew it then. It was my complete and utter lack of talent that I hated. It was the fog in my head from staying up all night, every night, working on the altar and practicing from my stupid kids' book. It was the way Jushuh looked at Bon when she didn't think I was watching.

"You have no idea how hard I work," Dad said, his own mouth full of the hot stink of ground meat, beans, cumin.

"I know you wouldn't have to work as hard if you got a promotion," I said, headed toward the door.

"I put a roof over your horns."

"Grandpa put this roof over our horns. But, hey, they say talent skips a generation, right? So maybe by the time I've got a Ministry position like Bon's dad, we can afford to fix the leaks."

I kept expecting him to do the almost-hitting-me thing he sometimes did when I mentioned Bon's dad. To grab me by the shirt and almost do what he never did and would never do. At company picnics, it always gave me this weird tickle to watch my Dad suck up to Bon's dad while they pretended to like each other. They were the same age, but my dad looked twenty years older. His hair was gray and his horns were brittle, like they would shatter if you hit them right. Bon's dad barely looked older than Bon himself, except for his dad gut. His hair was all gold blond, his curled ram horns a glossy pearl color.

But all my father said to me was, "I don't want you hanging out with Bon anymore."

"Come on," I said, trying to do Jushuh's roll-my-eyes-with-my-whole-body thing and totally failing. "You've been saying that for forever. You and Bon's dad hate each other. I get it. Mom told me."

I watched my father get up from the table, fish my bowl of chili out of the trash, and take it to the counter. "He's dangerous," he said, like I hadn't even mentioned Mom.

"He's your boss."

"Not Elder Dur Suun Kyyver." Dad took a steel thermos down from a cabinet and poured the chili into it. "His son. Your friend Bon. He's dangerous."

"What are you talking about? I don't —"

"Yes, you do. You know exactly what I'm talking about." He screwed the top onto the thermos and stuck it in the fridge. "Power can't be created, Samaeul. If a man *has* power, that means he *took* it from something else. He took the blood of a stag or a hound, or he tortured out an angel's faith and used the old words of the deep science to change it and trade it for power. That's legitimate. That's order. That's why we're here. But self-mutilation is a shortcut to power, and a bad one. You're giving more than you get. More than you can possibly know. Until it's too late to get it back."

"Why are you telling me this?"

Dad weighed the thermos in his hand, spoke to its brushed metal surface.

"Because your friend Bon is in trouble."

His attention shifted to my face, to my reddening cheeks, the ache in my clenching jaw.

"You can't hang out with him anymore. This is not a subject for debate."

How bad is it that all I could think of was Bon hanging out with Jushuh without me? Not that I couldn't be with Bon, but that I couldn't get in his way with Jushuh anymore. Not that I was doing much good in that department. Which was probably at the root of the whole thing.

"I'm saying this for your own good," he said.

"No, you're saying this for *your* own good," I said. Oh great, I was gonna cry.

"Look —" he tried.

I fled. Listened hard as I stormed down the block for him to call after me, which he never did. Even when I was miles away, walking past the Chasm, I was still listening.

"'Sup, brother."

Bon was just coming out of his house when I passed it. The city's nicest houses had a view of the Chasm, and Bon's house commanded one of the best.

"You all right, man?" he said. "You look like you spent the night in a confessor's chair."

"You should talk," I said. Bon looked ragged. Like he hadn't slept in a week and hadn't eaten in twice that long. His top front teeth were missing when he smiled. There were cuts on his arms. Countless and tiny. Like a swarm of razor blades had attacked him.

"Top of the world," he said. "For real. You have no idea. Here, check this out."

Bon pulled back his collar. A half-dozen bite marks pocked his lower neck and shoulder in concentric rings. "What is that?"

"Jushuh. She's totally a biter."

I recoiled, like he'd spat at me.

Bon laughed, ate up my reaction like a cheeseburger. "Awesome, right?" He leaned close to my face, eyes hungry like he was about to take another bite of whatever I was feeling. "Dude, you should see the bruises she —"

"Hello, Samaeul."

Bon's face soured. Behind him stood his dad, though he could have been my friend's older brother. Elder Dur Suun Kyyver wore the gold robe of a Ministry Elder, with red brocade cuffs and a high collar to show that he had achieved the rarefied post as a Master Confessor. Blue brocade meant healing. Purple, for combat in the War. Above them all were the Speakers Without Mouths, but their robes were black, not for dramatic effect, but because they sweated horror the color of shadows while the Abyss wrung them like living rags, and it stained whatever they wore. "How's your family?"

Bon flinched, offered a look of apology.

"We're fine, Elder," I said. *Thanks for asking. You're looking especially sinister today. My dad would throw me in the Chasm if he knew I was talking to you.*

"I was so sorry to hear of your mother's passing."

"Yeah. Me, too," I said. Knew I shouldn't antagonize him, but couldn't help it. Bon's dad was one of the most powerful men in the city.

"She was a beautiful woman. Everybody thought so. Immensely

NIK
HOUSER

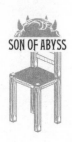

powerful. For your sake, I hope you are your mother's son, rather than your father's. If you got even a fraction of her power, or better yet your grandfather's, you'd be the most fortunate boy. Did you know your grandfather's name became a curse in the angelic language? Do you think anyone will remember either of your names, boys?"

Without another word, Bon took my shoulder and steered me away from his house. His dad watched us go. Probably saw my hands making fists so hard they shook.

"Sorry my dad's such a tool," said Bon when we were a block away. "Come on, I'll let you kiss my bite marks. It'll be like kissing Jushuh, only less smelly. Girl really needs to brush more often."

"Whatever," I said, trying not to laugh and scream at the same time.

I almost asked him if he used his talent on Jushuh to get her to be with him, if he had gotten that good. I wondered if he'd teach me. Hated myself for wondering.

"Why can't you just switch with Dad?"

I knelt at her bedside, my hand as close to her own bandaged palm as it dared, her body swaddled in bandages from the latest round of burn therapy. Her skin should've smelled scorched, like cooked meat, because that's what it was. But it smelled fresh, like dirt and tilled earth, like life. Chaotic, uncontrollable, insatiable life.

Mom sighed. Did she know where she was? That I was with her? Her breath reeked of flowers.

"Bon told me how it works," I said. I had a basic idea of how it worked, but my friend had clued me in to the whole deal, how a confessor cuts and burns the angels and whatever, killing their hope and siphoning their faith until they're about to die. Then the healer

comes in to heal the prisoner up again. They have a couple of dogs with them, or a deer, and the healer draws the life out of the animal and gives it to the prisoner, whether the prisoner wants it or not. That's how my mom met my dad. "Why can't you do it?"

I made the mistake of touching her arm with the tip of my finger. She stifled a moan.

"Why can't you just . . ." I scrubbed my tears away with my fist. "Why can't you just use Dad like one of those animals and heal yourself?"

Her answer was to touch my face, to run her bandaged fingers through my hair. It made her cry to touch me, to touch anything, but she held my hand and never let go until she was gone.

Some people said the Mother of Mercy was the Father of Fear's twin sister, that she is his opposite, that war between the two of them, between life and death, between chaos and order, is the only True Order. But that's not the story I believed.

Our animal didn't have to be expensive. Most of us brought a mouse or a lizard or a snake if we were lucky. I brought a roach. I'd found it in a kitchen cabinet, looking for food. I don't know if it had been more confused by the empty pantry or the paper bag I stuck him in.

"Nice," Bon said to my roach. "If my teddy bear gets a hangnail, I'll ask you to heal it."

I didn't respond. Hadn't said a word to him since we got to school. Beside him, Rudi took his seat. Bon snorted.

"Now if you'll excuse me," he murmured. "I have an angel to torture."

Bon took his seat beside Rudi, who did his best to disappear as

Bon set his backpack on the worktable in front of them. Something moved inside it. Something big. I kept waiting for Bon to say something about it, some joke to bait Rudi into asking what was in the bag. But he didn't say anything. Which, really, should have been warning enough.

"It's okay," Jushuh said when she sat down and saw my roach. Her own mouse scratched for purchase at the walls of the glass jar she'd brought it in. "Elder Kohl will understand."

Bon leaned back to speak over his shoulder. "Yeah, we all know your granddad's money is gone."

Jushuh leaned forward and tagged Bon on the shoulder. "What's wrong with you?"

"Come on, Sam knows I'm just messing with him."

"Why am I even your friend?" Jushuh said.

"Didn't I give you enough reasons last night?"

Jushuh gasped, gave up a furious smile, cheeks red.

I felt like such an idiot, sitting there, pretending to look way down into the bottom of my backpack for something so Jushuh would think I hadn't heard. Bon wasn't wrong, though. My dad was drowning in debt after everything we tried to save Mom.

As soon as class began, Elder Kohl launched into a lecture on the perils of self-mutilation, occasionally looking up from his notes to glare at Bon, who pretended to be asleep, bare arms crossed over his chest, covered in those thousand tiny cuts.

After the lecture, we all had to bleed. Nothing huge. Just a pinprick. We had to do it ourselves, then our lab partners would try to heal us by sacrificing whatever animal we brought to class. It was through this kind of experimentation that we were meant to discover our blood talents.

"Do you want me to do the cut?" I asked Jushuh when it was her turn. I sucked my thumb where I'd cut it. It still stung, though Jushuh had already healed it. My roach hadn't done squat for me. Jushuh healed me on her own. Put my finger in her mouth like old times, turning me bright red as my heart tried to break out of my chest.

"No," she said, and drew a long cut down the center of her palm. She didn't cuss or cry. Merely held her concentration on the cut while I held out her jar. "What are you doing? You're supposed to heal me."

"You do it," I said. "There's no way I'm gonna heal that." I pointed to the blood running down her forearm.

Jushuh gave me this look, and I still don't know what it meant, though I've narrowed it down to either disappointment or gratitude. She reached inside the jar for the mouse. Didn't pull it out. Just squeezed that squeaking thing so hard, her fist vibrated while the wound on her hand sealed itself up in a wisp of smoke. She hissed through her teeth at the brief searing pain.

"Wow," I said, unaware that I was speaking aloud. "That was —"

A piercing, agonized scream filled the room. Every head in class jerked toward the front row, where Rudi slumped doubled over in his chair, both hands pressed against his right eye. A clear, viscous fluid ran between his fingers, down his cheek. Beside him, Bon's shoulders shook in a silent laugh. He snorted, tried to hold it in. On the workbench between them lay a discarded dissection blade.

"Jeez, man," he said, "it was only a suggestion."

Rudi slid to the floor, blubbering. Jushuh was already at his side, an arm wrapped around Rudi's shoulders, telling him to let her see. I don't know how she got him to pull his hands away from his face. Long spiderweb strands of ocular jelly clung to the kid's fingers.

A collective groan rose up from the class. Bon was laughing so hard, he couldn't breathe.

"You did this," Jushuh told him.

"Hey, it's cool," Bon said. He wiped a tear from his eye and opened his backpack. "It just so happens, I brought medicine."

From his backpack, Bon drew out Rudi's cat. I'd seen it before. Rudi actually had a shirt with a picture of his cat on it. Yeah, I know. And while I can't say for sure that his mom made him wear it, I should certainly hope so for his sake. But anyway. The orange stripes, white boots, stub of a tail. It was unmistakable. Rudi's remaining eye went wide, the other a shrunken, puckered hole. His mouth moved, no doubt to ask how Bon had gotten ahold of his damn cat, but no sound came.

Jushuh also said nothing. Didn't even bother to wipe the tears from her eyes before she flattened the squirming cat down onto the table with one hand as her other hand picked up the knife we'd used to cut ourselves.

"No!" Rudi cried. He shot up from the floor, arms out. But the cat's neck was already open. Jushuh dropped the knife and grabbed the back of Rudi's hair with her free hand. She held the cat up high. Its blood drizzled down onto Rudi's head, pooling in his punctured socket like runny pancake syrup while he wailed. When the drizzle became a drip, Jushuh dropped the cat, stuck her thumb in her own mouth, then thrust it into the wounded eye. Rudi screamed when the thumb entered his socket, then louder when the cat's blood burned up in a bright, heatless flash.

"Don't open that eye for a week," Jushuh said, halfway to the door by then, both hands covered in rose-colored ash.

"Look at it this way, Rudi," Bon said. The door slammed behind Jushuh. "Now you can cry for your cat with both eyes."

In the middle of the kitchen table, waiting for me when I got home, was a can of chili.

I didn't even take off my backpack. Just took the can out to the garage where Dad had stockpiled the stuff like the world was running out, a mountain of chili I was sure he came out there to worship like the Father of Fear incarnate con carne.

I opened every can. Dumped them on the half-finished altar and burned it all. I watched the small flames char the meat and thought about Jushuh and Rudi and Bon and Mom and Dad and everything else. I was more worried about Jushuh than Bon. Whatever Bon was becoming, it looked like a one-way ticket. But I wouldn't let him take Jushuh. Whatever sex or love or whatever had started between them over the summer, he was using it like a confessor's tool to manipulate her. I'd tried to ditch him after school, but he'd caught up with me on the way home and regaled me with details about how Jushuh had "abandonment junk" that made her want guys like him instead of guys like me, which he always followed up with "no offense" as I squirmed.

The chili didn't burn for that long. Maybe twenty minutes. I opened the windows and made sure there was nothing else nearby. I was staring at the fire, lost in the flames, when something touched my leg. I jumped, screamed. Looked down and let out a smaller yip of surprise.

Maybe Rudi's cat had smelled the meat cooking from whatever

hell he'd tumbled into. Maybe I'd done something right with the altar that I wasn't aware of. Whatever the cause, he huddled there on the concrete floor, looking like complete crap. Scraggly fur, eyes glossed over with a cataract of death, shivering in the stifling heat. It didn't look like it was in pain, but it didn't look happy. It just looked kind of confused. Like it was lost.

I'd taken it from animalurgical studies. Stuck it in my backpack for whatever reason, I don't know. It had seemed like the right thing to do. I couldn't let it just get thrown away. Now that its soul had been incinerated to heal Rudi's eye, the cat's body wasn't of any use, even if it was still alive.

My first instinct when it came back to life was to throw the cat on the fire. Maybe some use would come of it, even without a soul. Some power or something, I don't know. It was freaking me out in a really good way that I'd done something right, even by accident. I mean, holy crap, I was an amateur necromancer. But instead of capitalizing on my success, I found myself on the garage floor, legs folded beneath me, stroking the cat's patchy fur.

When it purred, the slash in its neck whistled.

I kept waking up that night expecting it to be morning, for Other to have set and Brother to have risen, expecting to hear my dad stomping up the stairs to throw me out of bed to force-feed me the ashes of the chili pyre until it was gone.

When Brother had come up but my father still hadn't, I went downstairs to find him scraping the chili from the bottom of a can and spooning a sliver of the cold gunk into his mouth. At first, I thought it was a new can he'd bought at the store. Then I saw the

row of maybe ten cans lined up on the counter, scraped clean. The ones I'd left on the garage floor.

And, yeah, I get it now that I wasn't pissed at the chili. That I just wanted my dad to react to *something*, even if he couldn't react to Mom. Or maybe it's not that complex after all. Maybe I was just really tired of chili.

"Bon's dad is having a Transgression party tonight," I said. Every year, on Transgressor's Eve, Bon's dad invited half the city to his house for this legendary party that began all formal but devolved into yelling and fighting and taking their clothes off, all in the name of committing a transgression just after midnight, on Transgression Day. "I'm going."

I wasn't going for Bon. Bon was crazy and going crazier. I was going for Jushuh. I didn't want her to be alone with him on the one night of the year where you were *supposed* to do something bad.

I don't know what Dad was looking for at the bottom of that chili can, but he wasn't finding it. He didn't say crap. Just kept scraping at the bottom of that can.

Stalking toward the door, I snarled under my breath: "I wish Mom traded you and saved herself."

"I know how you feel."

My shoes made this little squeak on the linoleum in the foyer.

"I asked her to do it," he said to the can. "She could have. Your mother was the greatest healer of her generation."

I didn't know what to say. I never asked Mom to trade me in order to save herself. What did that say about me? Was that bad? Was that selfish? Or was that a normal thing?

"She said no, of course," Dad said. "I knew she'd say no. But it didn't stop me from begging her to give you up and heal herself."

You ever see someone do something to themselves that you shouldn't see? Not undressing or anything, but giving themselves a shot or sitting on the toilet? It's like they're doing something they're not supposed to, something unnatural. Imagine that times a million, and you'll get close to what it was like watching Rudi beat himself up.

"Now your face," Bon said.

Rudi balled up his fist and popped himself in the nose. A cry went up from the circle of students that surrounded the two boys in the hallway. Laughter, now applause. Bon was in his element. Unfortunately for Rudi, so was he.

"Stop it, Bon," Jushuh said. "Come on."

"You punch like such a girl." Bon shook his head. "Come on, break your freakin' nose."

Rudi wiped at the blood and snot that ran down his lips, smeared it in a streak across his cheek, then clocked himself in the nose.

"Stop it!" Jushuh may have said. It was hard to hear over the cheering.

"Harder!" Bon said. They all said.

Another muffled smack as Rudi punched himself in the nose.

"*HARDER!*"

I don't know if it was his hand or his nose, but something made a wet crack in the center of Rudi's face the next time he popped himself one. Twin ribbons of blood ejaculated out over his chin. Jushuh was crying now, jerking my arm and screaming for me to stop Bon before he told Rudi to kill himself. But I was transfixed. Mesmerized. Couldn't believe Bon could do this. Where had this power come from? What had he done to himself to get it?

"Now your balls," Bon said. "Punch yourself in the balls."

Rudi did as he was told, swung the pink pendulum of his fist down between his legs. A strangled woof escaped his throat. His knees buckled and he doubled over, threw up, collapsed onto the ground to uproarious applause.

Glancing back at the crowd, I wasn't surprised to find three Elders off to the side, watching, arms folded into the sleeves of their robes. Occasionally, one would murmur something to the other.

"Pull your pants down."

Through a lens of tears, Rudi shot Bon a look of animal fear. He tried to say something, but he must have bitten his tongue because the only thing that came out of his mouth was blood.

Bon bent over Rudi. From where I stood, I could feel the fever heat of spent power my friend gave off. It was like standing next to an oven.

"*Pull your pants down,*" he said.

Sobbing, Rudi unbuckled his pants to a sound track of hysterical laughter.

"Underwear, too."

Oh, man.

All at once, the laughter died. You could hear a pin drop. Or a pair of underwear. No one spoke. No one breathed.

Lying on his side, Rudi had gotten his tighty-whities down around his ankles before they got so tangled that he couldn't kick them free. Bon leaned into Rudi's face so their foreheads almost touched.

"Now make a fist, and sh —"

I don't remember seeing Jushuh tackle Bon. My only memory is of them on the ground, Jushuh punching and slapping and clawing at Bon. For about a second. Then Bon was on top of her, holding her hands to her chest as she bucked and kicked.

"*Take off your clothes,*" he said, by turns laughing and snarling. By now he was baking. Waves of heat rippled the air around him.

Jushuh fought like a wildcat, thrashing under him.

"Take off your clothes and dance."

And then I was on him. My turn to snort and huff and struggle before I chipped a tooth on the concrete when Bon flipped me over and shoved my face to the ground.

"What's your deal, bro?!" Bon shouted, half laughing and half pissed. "You should be thanking me. I was doing you a favor. I was about to make your dreams come true."

Bon leaned down and breathed in my ear, pointed my face at Jushuh crying against a row of lockers. "Why did you think she was with me? 'Cause she needed somebody, and you were too scared to touch her."

I think that's what he said. That's what the people there told me he said. I didn't hear him. Didn't hear anything. I was too focused on the shirt I'd torn from Bon's body, and what it showed me. His body was a battlefield. Trenches of flesh gouged out of his chest. Countless razor-blade cuts. Unnatural dents and crevices pocked his torso where pieces of Bon had been removed and traded in dark transactions.

Somebody broke us up. Took the four of us four different directions and called our parents. When my dad couldn't come pick me up, Elder Kohl drove me home saying I didn't look so good. Was I eating? Were things okay at home? Because if there was anything I ever needed to tell anyone, about how things were at home, I could tell him. I knew that, right?

I gave no answers. Couldn't believe this was the same man who'd stood by and watched one of his students destroy another, just to see what kind of aptitude he had for his future job. I wished I had a can of chili to offer him.

———✦———

The sun was nearly down for the first time in a month by the time I reached the Chasm. Another thirty blocks to go before I got to Rudi's house. Walking along that great gaping mouth of darkness, I peered through the windows of the mansions on the other side of the street, saw the Transgressor's Eve parties going in full swing now that the sun was setting.

Bon's place was all lights and noise, barks of pain and peals of laughter, screams of agony or ecstasy or maybe both. I wondered where Jushuh was. I hadn't seen her since she left school early. I'd gone by her house first once Elder Kohl had dropped me off, to show her how I'd brought Rudi's cat back to life, but she hadn't been there. No surprise. Some injuries are harder to heal than others.

Rudi's mom screamed when I tried to give her the cat back.

OH, CRAP! OH, CRAP! OH, CRAP! OH, CRAP, CRAP, CRAP!

Running.

Sprinting.

Taking a break to breathe and throw up next to some house on some dog, who thought it was awesome.

Flying past the Chasm. Past the school. Past houses with music blaring as they all hosted their own Transgression parties while the cat went crazy in my backpack, which shook and bounced because Rudi's mom had refused to touch it once she'd recovered enough to speak, to tell me she would never let that abomination into her house. And to tell me that Rudi wasn't home. That his friend Bon had come

by. That they'd left together. Wasn't I expecting them? They said they were going to my house.

There are things you aren't prepared for.

Like when you get a present you hate and you want to hide your disappointment, but for a second you can't and they see it.

Or when she kisses you, and you didn't even know she liked you.

Or when you turn the corner and see the police lights twirling at the end of the block, in front of your house, and the bottom drops out of the world and your heart floats up into your chest because you're in free fall, and there's already a crowd of neighbors forming an arc around the scene like a blast radius of tragedy.

The garage door was open. I could see them from the sidewalk as I half fell, half threw myself through the crowd of neighbors and strangers and cops and saw them.

Jushuh and Rudi knelt to either side of Granddad's chair, their eyes empty, faces masks of incomprehension.

"Hey, dude."

Bon stood between them, in front of the empty chair, naked. His skin was a relief map of a confessor's country, covered in burned, abraded, and slashed flesh. His nipples were gone; his naval, a melted puddle. His arms and legs above the wrists and ankles looked like burned hamburger meat. He was holding Granddad's old bone-handled knife. The empty chair behind him looked like an open mouth waiting to chew something.

"How's it hangin'?" Bon said. He pumped his hips. They made a broken, grinding noise. "Almost midnight. Happy Transgression Day."

It was then that I noticed Bon's father curled up on the garage floor

behind his son, bound and gagged, barbed wire strapped around his chest and wrists and ankles. Bon must have used Rudi and Jushuh to bring him here. From the look of his wounds, he'd been dragged.

The Elder's head lolled to one side, glared up at his son with exhausted terror, tried to say something, but succeeded only in moaning.

"NO!" Bon screamed down at his father. "*You don't get to talk!*" He kicked his prisoner in the gut with a foot that was missing most of its toes. Curled on the concrete floor, Bon's father coughed up bile and blood, wheezed for breath as the barbed wire dug into his chest. The smooth skin of chest. That perfect, unmarked skin that always looked so young next to my father at company picnics. So improbably, impossibly young.

Bon met my eyes, saw understanding there. Whatever look of surprise or pity or horror that contorted my face then made him laugh. Not some big evil cackle. Just this little chuckle. Like he was thinking about something that had happened a long time ago that always made him laugh a little when he thought about it.

How long has this been going on, I wondered.

"Since always," Bon said, the answer to the question written all over my face. "Before I was born, dude. How many came before me, Dad?"

Bon put his hand on the shivering skin sack at his feet.

"Eight? Nine? *I'M TALKING TO YOU!*"

Another kick. Another bitter laugh under his breath.

"But how?" I heard myself say.

"What?" Bon said. "What'd you say, dude?"

"Your . . . your talent," I said, stepping forward. A coldness crept up my skin, though not from fear. It was Granddad's chair. It pulsed cold. Waiting. Hungry. "If you weren't doing all that to yourself, how did you get your talent so fast? Was it Rudi?"

I didn't ask to get him talking, to put the brakes on the situation. I'm not that smart. I asked because I wanted to know.

That laugh again.

"Are you serious?" he said. "Oh man, you are serious. You still think that the worst thing you can take from someone, the most valuable thing, is their blood."

Then he gave me this long, sad smile. He looked at Jushuh, then at me, then at whatever waited for him when he closed his eyes, and smiled so wide, like he'd taken the longest, most refreshing drink.

That's when I knew. Granddad's chair wasn't empty. It had been occupied for weeks. Ever since Bon saw the way his best friend looked at this one girl.

"Your friendship has meant so much to me." Bon opened his eyes, tightened his grip on the knife.

And drove it into Jushuh's heart.

A sound came out of me, ripped from me. The sound a stone makes when time breaks it. The sound a house makes when the tornado wins. The sound a soul makes when it's separated from its body and is drank down by your best friend like water while he stands naked in your garage next to the ashes of a chili bonfire.

Jushuh folded over the knife, eyes wide, mouth open. Bon drew out the blade. He spoke to his father.

"You see what I am now? What I've become without you? *Despite you?* Now I'm gonna untie you. And I'm gonna give you this knife. And you're gonna cut Rudi's head off with it because I told you to. And then you're gonna shove this knife into your own —"

The blade was still in Bon's hand when I pushed it into him, somewhere under his naval. Bon jumped a little, startled. He glanced down at the knife, then up at me with this look of confusion. Blood

bubbled out of his wound, so hot it scalded my hand on his hand on the knife. With a grunt, I drove him back across the concrete floor until he thumped against the altar.

What happened then, what I saw, or, perhaps more accurately, what I was shown . . .

To this day, I still sleep with a light on.

My hand still on his, I dragged the knife up toward his chin, ripping through the scarred flesh of his abdomen. Bon's intestines unspooled between our feet. The blade scraped a trajectory over his breastbone until the knife's point reached the soft sponge of skin where his collarbones came together. I brought the knife's bone handle up and plunged it down through the roof of my best friend's heart.

The fire started there. In the furnace of his rib cage, on top of the altar I'd finished with my mother's bones when the greyhound ran out of raw material, using the talent I had only begun to know when I brought the cat back. It was then — staring at Bon's uncomprehending face, at Jushuh dying on the floor, at Bon's father writhing in barbed wire, at my own hand on the knife — that I understood the true mechanics of power, the nature of sacrifice, and realized what I would give for that power, what I would sacrifice to save Jushuh.

Everything.

That was my magic spell. My abracadabra. One word. A word whispered into the heat pouring out of Bon. A word screamed in silence, a promise that I would burn the whole world to bring Jushuh back.

I don't know who heard my prayer, my offering, whatever it was. The Void. The Wyrm. The Leviathan. Some minor fecal imp or the Father of Fear himself. But whatever it was, it was there when I

opened a door inside Bon with the tip of that knife and told it to take what it needed but to leave the girl.

Some stories said that the Mother of Mercy was mortal, a Redkind like us, only vastly more powerful. As powerful as the Father of Fear.

These stories go on to say that this Redkind woman fell in love, but that her lover died. She would not accept this. Driven mad by grief, the Redkind woman rebelled against the Father of Fear. She rebelled against death itself and became something beyond the Redkind. She became a god. Ever since then, she has waged her war, rendering us like unto children so that nothing would ever have to die, and no one would ever again feel the pain of love or loss.

That's the story I believed.

The fire burned for a month, a house fire that spread through the neighborhood, then moved on to consume the whole south end of town, becoming a finger of blue flame that scraped Heaven's cellar when it reached the power plant and just ate and ate and ate, until the contract I'd offered it was fulfilled and half the city was ashes and Jushuh finally woke up. Scared but unhurt, unscathed but not unscarred.

I was there when she woke. Outside her hospital room, my father stood with the Ministry Elders, who watched me through the window. They'd taken me into custody on the night of the fire, one minute after midnight, on Transgression Day.

Standing over her, I took the iron tongue of the Speakers Without Mouths from around my neck, got into bed between her and Rudi's cat, and spread my black robe over the three of us.

A Small Wild Magic

by K. Jennings

UF!

I HATE IT WHEN THAT HAPPENS!

TAKE A PICTURE! IT WILL LAST LONGER!

...

YOU'RE A BIRD. YOU WERE A BIRD.

YOU WERE IN THIS CAGE.

GET YOUR EYES CHECKED, EINSTEIN.

I LET YOU OUT.

OH, SO YOU'VE WORKED THAT OUT, HAVE YOU?

YOUR NAME'S MARILYN.

WORKED WHAT—

OH, DO I GET WISHES?

The End

THE
New Boyfriend

KELLY LINK

Ainslie doesn't rip open presents. She's always been careful with her things, even the things that don't matter. Immy is a ripper, but this is not Immy's present, not Immy's birthday. Sometimes Immy thinks that this may not be Immy's life. *Better luck next time around, Immy,* she tells herself.

Ainslie scores under the tape with a fingernail, then carefully wiggles the pink wrapping paper out from under the coffin-shaped box.

Ainslie's new Boyfriend is in there.

Ainslie's birthday, this year, is just Ainslie and her bestest, oldest friends. Just Ainslie, Sky, Elin, and Immy. No family allowed. No boys.

Earlier there was sushi and cake and lots of pictures to put up online so that everyone will know how much fun they are having.

No presents, Ainslie said, but of course Immy and Elin and Sky
bring presents. No one ever means it when they say that. Not even
Ainslie, who already has everything.

It's normal to want to give your best friend something because
you love them. Because you want them to know that you love them.
It isn't a competition. Ainslie loves Elin and Immy and Sky equally,
even if Immy and Ainslie have been friends longest.

Immy's heart isn't as big as Ainslie's heart. Immy loves Ainslie best.
She also hates her best. She's had a lot of practice at both.

They're in the sunroom. *As if you could keep the sun in a room,*
Immy thinks. Well, if you could, Ainslie's mother probably would.

But the sun has gone down. The world is night, and it belongs to
all of them, even if it belongs to Ainslie most of all. Ainslie's brought
out dozens of pillar candles, a small forest of mirrored candelabras,
both of her Boyfriends. They both wear little birthday hats, because
that's the thing about Boyfriends, according to Elin, who has a lot of
opinions and isn't shy about sharing them. You can't take them too
seriously.

Of course, anyone can have an opinion. Immy has plenty. In her
opinion, in order not to take a Boyfriend seriously, you have to have a
Boyfriend in the first place, and only Ainslie has one. (Two.) (Three.)

Creatures of the night in silly hats, Vampire Boyfriend (Oliver)
and Werewolf Boyfriend (Alan) lounge on candy-striped settees and
gaze with identical longing at their girlfriend, Ainslie. Immy decides
against having a second piece of cake. One piece of cake really ought
to be enough for anyone.

And yet, there on the tiled floor, right under the cake (plenty left,
Immy, why not have another piece, really?) and the candelabras, right
there under everyone's noses, the new Boyfriend has been waiting

all this time. Immy knew, right away, as soon as she came into the sunroom, exactly which Boyfriend it would be.

It's dark inside the box, of course. Night wrapped up in pink paper. Are his eyes open or closed? Can he hear them talking? Love will wake him.

Love, oh, love. Terrible, wonderful love.

Ainslie lifts the lid of the coffin, and white rose petals spill out, all over the floor, and —"Oh," Sky says. "He's, um, he's gorgeous."

Real rose petals, real and crushed and bruised. Probably not the best packing material, but, oh, what a smell is filling the room.

Not night after all.

The Boyfriend's eyes are closed. His arms are folded across his chest, but his palms are open and full of rose petals. His hair is dark. His face is very young. Maybe a little surprised; his lips parted, just a little, like he has just been kissed.

"Which one is he?" Elin says.

"The Ghost one," Immy says.

Ainslie reaches out, touches the Ghost Boyfriend's face, brushes a piece of hair back from his eyes. "So soft," she says. "So weird. Fake Boyfriend, real hair."

"I thought they weren't selling those anymore?" Elin says.

"They're not," Immy says. Her chest feels very tight, as if she's suddenly full of poison. You have to keep it all inside. Like throwing yourself on a bomb to save everyone else. Except you're the bomb.

Why does Ainslie always get what she wants? Why does Ainslie always get what *Immy* wants? She says, "They don't. You can't get them now."

"Not unless you're Ainslie, right?" Sky says without a trace of discernible malice. She scoops out handfuls of petals, throws them at Ainslie. They all throw rose petals. When Immy reaches into the coffin, she tries very hard not to let her hand brush against Ainslie's Ghost Boyfriend.

"What are you going to call him?" Elin says.

"Don't know," Ainslie says. She's reading the instructions. "So there are two modes, apparently. Embodied or Spectral. Embodied is just, you know, the usual thing." She waves a hand in the direction of her Vampire Boyfriend, Oliver. He waves back. "In Spectral Mode, it's like a movie projection and he floats around. You can hang out with him like that, but it's random or something. Like, he comes and goes."

"Huh," Sky says. "So you can't see him all the time, but maybe he's watching you? What if you're getting dressed or on the toilet or something, and all of a sudden he's there?"

"Maybe that's why they did the recall," Elin says. She is tearing a white petal into littler and littler pieces, and smiling, like that's her idea of fun.

"You can customize him," Ainslie says. "If you have a thing that belonged to somebody who died. There's a compartment somewhere. Ew. Inside his mouth. You put something in it. I don't know. That part seems kind of dumb. Like, you're really supposed to believe in ghosts or something."

"That's not supposed to be a good idea," Immy says. "That's the reason they did the recall, remember? There were a lot of stories."

"People are so *impressionable*," Ainslie says.

"So turn him on already," Elin says. "No pun intended."

THE NEW BOYFRIEND

"What's the rush?" Ainslie says. "We have to come up with a name first."

They debate names for the new Boyfriend while Ainslie opens friend presents. They take more pictures. Ainslie holding the bottle of absinthe that Sky made from a recipe online. They throw rose petals at her, and so there are petals caught in her hair. It's very pretty.

Oliver and Alan in their hats, Ainslie sitting on Oliver's lap. They change out Alan's boy head for his wolf head. He can't talk with the wolf head on, but he's still very cute in his tuxedo. Cuter than most real boys.

More pictures. The new Boyfriend in his box, Ainslie leaning over to kiss him. Ainslie wearing the red suede boots her grandmother sent. Ainslie holding up the tickets that Elin got her to some show by some band they were both into. Two tickets, one for Ainslie and the other for Elin, of course.

Immy isn't really into music. Sky isn't really into music either. Music is Elin and Ainslie's thing. Whatever.

Immy's present for Ainslie is a beaded choker with an antique locket to sit right over the hollow of Ainslie's white throat.

The beads are cut glass and jet.

There's a secret in the locket.

The choker is in a little box in a pocket in Immy's purse, and she doesn't take it out. She pretends to search for it, and then she says to Ainslie, "Uh-oh. I think I left your present at home, maybe?"

Ainslie says, "Whatever, Immy. Give it to me at school on Monday."

She passes around the homemade absinthe, and they all drink straight from the bottle. *That way,* Immy figures, *it's harder for everyone else to tell if you're only taking little sips or even only pretending.* It's a little bit herbal and a little like toothpaste.

"You could call him Vincent," Sky says. She's looking at baby names on her phone. "Or Bran? Banquo? Tor. Foster, um, maybe not Foster. But it ought to be something old-fashioned — ghost names ought to be old-fashioned."

"Because nowadays no one ever dies," Ainslie says, and swigs from the absinthe bottle.

Fake swigs, bets Immy. *Let's all get fake drunk and have fake fun with Ainslie and her fake Boyfriends.* Because she's fairly sure that all of this is fake, this whole night, the way she finds herself acting around Ainslie and Elin and Sky tonight, maybe this whole year. And if it's not fake, if it's all real — this fun, these friends, this life — then that's even worse, isn't it?

Immy has no idea why she's in such a horrible mood. Except wait, no. Let's be honest. She knows. She's in a horrible mood because she's a horrible friend who wants everything that belongs to Ainslie. Except maybe Ainslie's mother. Ainslie can keep her mother.

Immy has wanted a Boyfriend ever since they came out, even before Ainslie knew about them. Immy was the one who told Ainslie about them. And then Ainslie had Oliver and Alan, and then you could buy the limited edition Ghost Boyfriend, and then there was the recall and you couldn't get a Ghost Boyfriend anymore, and so that was okay, because then even if Immy couldn't have a Ghost Boyfriend, Ainslie couldn't have one either. Except now she does have one.

Immy wants a Ghost Boyfriend more than she's ever wanted anything.

"What about Quentin? That's a good name," Sky says.

"What about Justin?" Elin says.

Then they are all looking at Immy. She stares right back at Elin, who says, "Oops." And shrugs and smiles.

"Ainslie can call Ainslie's Ghost Boyfriend whatever she wants," Immy says. She knows what kind of friends she is with Elin. Sometimes a friendship is more like a war.

Ainslie can keep Elin, too.

Anyway, Immy is the one who broke up with Justin. And *Justin* is the one who can't get over it, and anyway, *anyway*, Elin is the one who still has a thing for him. Immy's been there, done that.

Ainslie says, "I'm going to call him Mint."

They all laugh, and Ainslie says, "No. Really. His name is going to be Mint. He's my Ghost Boyfriend, I can call him whatever I want, and I'm going to call him Mint."

"Weirdish," Elin says. "But okay."

"Come on," Ainslie says. So they all go over and stand around the box, and then Ainslie leans down and sticks her fingers into the Ghost Boyfriend's hair, moving them around until evidently she's found the right place.

His eyes open. He has really pretty eyes. Long lashes. He looks at them, each in turn. His lips part, just a little, like he is about to say something. But he doesn't.

Immy is blushing. She knows she's blushing.

"Hi," Ainslie says. "I'm your girlfriend. Ainslie. You're Mint. You're my Boyfriend."

The new Boyfriend's eyelids flutter shut. Eyelashes like black fans. Skin just like skin. Even his fingernails are perfect and so real, as real as anything Immy has ever seen.

When his eyes open again, he only looks at Ainslie.

"Okay, so, we'll see you later," Ainslie says.

She straightens up and says to Immy and Elin and Sky, "You guys want to put on some music and dance or something?"

"Wait," Elin says. "What about him? I mean *it*. Are you just going to leave it in there?"

"It takes them a while to wake up the first time," Sky says. Sky has a Biblical Handmaiden. Esther. Sky's parents were kind of religious for a while.

"Oh, yeah," Ainslie says. "There's one other thing. We have to choose a mode. Embodied or Spectral. What do you think?"

"Embodied," Elin says.

"Embodied," Sky says.

"Spectral," Immy says.

"Okay," Ainslie says. "Spectral. Might as well." She reaches back down, runs her fingers through her Boyfriend's hair again. "There. Now let's go out on the deck and dance in the moonlight. Come on, Oliver. Alan. You too."

Ainslie and Elin deejay. The moon is perfectly round and bright. The night is warm. Ainslie tells Oliver and Alan to dance with Immy and Sky.

Which is the kind of thing Ainslie does. She isn't ever selfish. But then: You have to have things in order to be generous with them. Right?

Immy and Oliver dance. She's in his arms really, his hand on the small of her back. It's sort of a waltz that they're doing, which doesn't really suit whatever song this is, but Oliver can do either the waltz or the tango — or a kind of sway-y standing-there dance, and that gets old after a while. Sky bounces around with Alan, who still has his wolf head on. Alan is actually more fun to dance with than Oliver is, although the bouncing gets tiring after a while.

"Are you happy, darling?" Oliver the Vampire Boyfriend says, so

softly Immy has to tilt her head up and ask him to repeat himself. Not that this is, strictly speaking, really necessary. Oliver always asks the same questions.

"Sure," she says. Then, "Well, I don't know. Not really. I could be happier. I'd like to be happier." Why not? If you can't be honest with your best friend's Vampire Boyfriend, who can you be honest with? Vampires are all about secrets and unhappiness. Secret unhappinesses. You can see it in their black and fathomless eyes.

"I wish you were happy, my love," Oliver says. He presses her more firmly against his body, nuzzles her hair. "How can I be happy if you are not?"

"Ainslie's your love. Not me," Immy says. She really isn't in the mood. Besides, sometimes it's just really too weird, playing pretend eternal love with a borrowed Boyfriend when what you really want is your own Boyfriend. It would be so, so much nicer to have your own. "So, I mean, don't be unhappy on my account."

"As you wish," Oliver says. "I shall be unhappy on my own account. How happy it makes me, o delicious one, to be unhappy together with you." He clasps her even tighter in his arms, until she has to ask him to ease up just a little. It's a fine line between being cuddled and being squeezed like a juice box, and Vampire Boyfriends sometimes cross right over that line, maybe without even noticing.

There is also the endless hovering and the endless brooding and all the endless talk about how delicious you are and eternity, and they like you to read poetry at them, the really old-fashioned rhyming kind, even. It's supposed to be educational, okay? Like the way Werewolf Boyfriends go on and on about the environment and also are always trying to get you to go running with them.

———◆———

Immy doesn't get music. She doesn't want to get it. The way it wants to make you feel something. Just because it's a minor chord, you're supposed to feel sad? Just because it goes faster, your pulse is supposed to speed up? Why should you have to do what the music wants you to do? Why shouldn't it do what you want? She doesn't want a sound track for her life. And she doesn't want somebody's pretty lyrics getting in the way of what she's really thinking. Whatever it is that she's thinking.

Immy doesn't want a Vampire Boyfriend. Or a Werewolf Boyfriend. Not anymore.

"I want more absinthe," Ainslie says. "Somebody go fetch the absinthe."

"I'll get it, darling," Oliver says.

"No," Immy says. "I'll go get it." If you send a Boyfriend off for a bottle of homemade absinthe, likely as not he'll come back with a bottle of conditioner. Or a table lamp.

"Thanks, Immy," Ainslie says.

"No problem," Immy says. But maybe you can't trust a friend, either, because instead of going straight back with the absinthe, she finds herself lingering in the sunroom, looking down at the new Boyfriend. His eyes are closed again. She reaches down and touches his face. Just one finger. His skin is very soft. It isn't actually like skin at all, of course, but it isn't like anything else, either. His eyes don't open this time; he's still not all the way awake. She's read about this online. It takes a few hours. And, anyway, Ainslie set him for Spectral Mode. His body will just lie here. His ghost will do whatever it is that ghosts do.

He could already be here, she supposes. He could be watching her. She doesn't feel as if she's being watched. She feels all alone.

So it's an impulse, maybe, that makes her reach inside her purse

and take out Ainslie's present. She rips off the wrapping paper and the ribbon, not carefully.

Inside the locket is a braided ring of human hair. Victorian, according to the online seller. Probably their own kids' hair, but never mind.

Two pieces of the braid of hair are jet black; one is ash blond.

The ring doesn't fit over any of Immy's fingers. Maybe she has fat fingers. She goes back to the coffin, crouches down beside it. "Hey," she says softly. "I'm Ainslie's friend. Immy."

She puts two fingers on his lips. She takes a breath and holds it, like she's about to jump off a bridge into very deep water. Well, she is. Then she sticks her fingers inside Ainslie's Ghost Boyfriend's mouth. There are the teeth, and, okay, here's the tongue. How weird is this? It's very weird. Immy's not saying that this isn't weird, but she keeps on doing it anyway. Her fingers are where they really shouldn't be.

It's not wet like a real mouth and a real tongue would be. The teeth feel pretty real. The tongue is weird. She keeps thinking how weird this is. She slides a finger under the not-a-real-tongue, and there, underneath, is a place where, when she presses down, a kind of lid thing opens up. She fumbles the hair ring into the compartment there, and then presses the lid back down. Then she takes her fingers out of the Ghost Boyfriend's mouth, studies that face carefully.

Nothing about it seems different to her.

When she stands up and turns around, Elin is there in the doorway. Elin says nothing, just waits.

"I thought I saw him move," Immy says. "But he didn't."

Elin gives her a long look. Immy says, "What?"

"Nothing," Elin says. She looks like she wants to say something else, and then she shrugs. "Just, come on. Oliver keeps on asking me to dance with him, and I don't want to. You know how I feel about

Ainslie's Boyfriends." What she is really saying is that she knows how Immy feels about them.

Immy grabs the absinthe. "Okay."

Elin says, "Immy? Can I ask you something?"

Immy waits.

Elin says, "I don't get it. This Boyfriend thing. They're creepy. They're fake. They're not real. I know how much you want one. And I know it sucks. How Ainslie gets everything she wants."

Immy blurts out, "Justin has no sense of humor. And he uses way too much body spray. He kisses like it's arm wrestling, except with lips. Lip wrestling."

"Maybe he just needs more practice?" Elin says. "I mean, Ainslie's Boyfriends don't kiss at all. They're just really big dolls. They're *not real.*"

"Maybe I don't want real," Immy says.

"Whatever it is you want, I hope you get it. I guess." Elin takes the absinthe bottle from Immy, takes a long slug from the mouth. A real one. Apparently Elin wants real, even if real isn't all that great. Immy suddenly feels a wave of love for her. Elin isn't always a good friend, but, okay, she's a real friend, and Immy appreciates that just as much as the way she really, really didn't appreciate it when Justin wanted to lip wrestle.

They go back to the dance party and the real friends and the fake Boyfriends. They leave Ainslie's Mint all alone with the ring of hair in his mouth. Immy doesn't feel guilty about that at all. It was a present for Ainslie, and Immy is giving it to her. More or less.

There's only a sludgy oily residue left in the absinthe bottle by the time they go to bed. Oliver and Alan are back in their coffins in

the closet downstairs in the rec room, and Ainslie has blown all the candles out in the sunroom. They've eaten the rest of the cake. Sky is already passed out on a couch in the living room.

Is Mint around? Ainslie says he probably is. "The Ghost Boyfriends are supposed to be kind of shy at first when you put them in Spectral Mode. They don't manifest much right at the beginning. You're just supposed to see them out of the corner of your eye, once in a while. When you aren't expecting them."

"Is that supposed to be fun?" Elin says. "Because it doesn't sound like fun."

"It's supposed to be real," Ainslie says. "Like a real ghost. Like a real ghost is falling in love with you. Like, he could be here right now. Watching us. Watching *me*."

There is something about the way she says this. Ainslie is so sure of being loved. Maybe Ainslie will get a surprise this time. Immy hopes so. After all, what could be a better present for the girl who has everything?

"On that note," Elin says. "I'm going to go crash on your mom's bed. Your new Boyfriend better stay the hell out of there." Elin doesn't like to sleep in the same room as everyone else. She says it's because she snores. "When is your mom getting back, Ainslie?"

"Not until two or three tomorrow. I made her promise to call before she shows up." Ainslie is swaying on her feet. She keeps putting her hand out to balance on things: the side table, the back of a settee, the lid of the coffin. She stumbles and almost falls in, catches herself. "Good night, Mint. God, you're cute. Even cuter than Oliver. Don't you think so?"

The question is for Immy. "I guess," she says, her heart burning for just one beat, with that hatred, that poison, again. She watches

Ainslie lean over, precariously, and plant a noisy kiss on Mint's forehead.

"I slept in Oliver's coffin once," Ainslie says to Elin and Immy. Immy isn't sure what to say to that, and apparently Elin doesn't know either.

Immy feels lit up and inside out, her hands and feet heavy and slow as lead, her skull and her rib cage all airy and hollow. All that poison dried up. A powder.

Or maybe this is just the way she thinks getting drunk on absinthe should feel. *La fée verte.* Green fairy juice fizzing all through her blood. She should probably go drink some water, take some Tylenol.

Immy always sleeps in Ainslie's bed when she stays over. She has her own toothbrush in Ainslie's bathroom, borrows Ainslie's T-shirts to wear to bed. Immy even has a favorite pillow, and Ainslie always remembers which one it is. In the morning, she'll wear Ainslie's clothes home if she wants to. Ainslie never minds.

They brush their teeth and they get dressed for bed, and they turn out the lights and get into bed, and all of that time Immy can hardly breathe — she doesn't even want to blink, because maybe Mint is in the room with them. Maybe he is coming. Perhaps she will look up, and Mint will be there. He will be there, and then he'll be gone again. She knows Ainslie is thinking the same thing. Ainslie is watching for Mint, too.

"This has been a really, really good birthday," Ainslie says in the dark. "It's everything I wanted it to be. I got everything I wanted."

"I'm glad," Immy says. She means it, too. "You deserve everything you're getting."

Immy doesn't think she'll be able to go to sleep. She doesn't want to sleep; she wants to stay awake. She could wait until Ainslie is

asleep and go back to the sunroom. Maybe Mint will manifest there first. After all, his body is there. She tries to think of what she would say to him, what he might say to her. And soon enough Ainslie's asleep, and then Immy's asleep too.

When she wakes up — she is in the middle of a nightmare, something about a garden — someone is standing beside the bed. A boy. Mint. He's looking down at Ainslie. Ainslie asleep, Ainslie's mouth open, and Mint is touching Ainslie's mouth with his thumb.

Immy sits up in bed.

Mint looks right at her. He looks at her and he smiles. He touches his fingers to his own mouth. Then he disappears.

Immy doesn't see the Ghost Boyfriend again for at least two weeks. Ainslie says he's around. She thinks he's exploring the house. She sees him, just for seconds at a time, in different rooms, then he's gone. He shows up almost every time Ainslie watches TV. Usually during the commercial breaks.

"He likes to watch commercials?" Immy says. They're at the yogurt place, loading toppings on their plain frozen yogurt. Blueberries, raspberries, mochi.

What is mochi, exactly? Some kind of zombie topping, Immy is sure. It gives like flesh when you bite into it.

"I think he's being considerate," Ainslie says. "He doesn't want to interrupt what I'm doing, so he waits for the commercial breaks. Like, I never see Mint in the bathroom or when I'm getting dressed for school. So I think it's the same thing with the TV."

Over in the corner of the yogurt shop, a middle-aged woman sits and moves a stroller back and forth with one hand while she eats

with the other. Immy keeps looking over. She can't tell if it's a real baby asleep in the stroller or a Baby.

"So he's there for a few seconds, and he does what, exactly?" she says.

"He watches TV with me. The commercials. He seems to like the commercials where a man and a woman are driving somewhere in a car. You know, those ones where there's a road going alongside the ocean? Or a hill. He looks at the commercials on TV and he looks at me," Ainslie says. "He just looks at me. Like no one has ever looked at me before. And then he goes away."

There's something about the way Ainslie says this, about her face, and so Immy does what the Ghost Boyfriend does. She looks at Ainslie as carefully and as closely as she can. Ainslie looks like she had a very bad night's sleep. Her lips are chapped and there's lots of concealer, poorly applied, under her eyes. As if she's keeping secrets there, under the skin. "Do you ever see him at night? In your bedroom?"

Ainslie blinks. "No," she says. "No, I don't think so."

"Good," Immy says. "Because that would be creepy, if he was in there looking at you while you were asleep."

Ainslie's face crumples, just a little. "Yeah. That would be creepy."

School is school. Why can't it ever be something else? Immy can't believe she has two more years of this. Two more years of equations and sad books where bad things happen to boring people and Justin giving her wounded looks. Okay, so maybe he'll get over it faster than that. If she ignores him. Two more years of unflattering gym shorts and Spanish that she's never going to use and having to be the person that she's always been, because that's the person that everyone thinks

she is. That everyone assumes she's always going to be. Everyone
thinks this is the real Immy. And what if the Immy they see is the
real Immy, and the one on the inside is just hormones and chemicals
and too many little secrets and weird jumbled thoughts that don't
mean anything after all?

Maybe she should shave her head. Maybe she should take her
classes more seriously. Maybe she should give Justin another chance.
Maybe not.

She has a dream that night about driving a fast car along a curv-
ing road. The ocean is far below. The Ghost Boyfriend sits in the
passenger seat. They don't say anything to each other. The moon is
high overhead.

She texts Ainslie in the morning. *I dreamed about your Boyfi.
weird right*

Ainslie doesn't text back.

That afternoon Immy and Sky go over to Ainslie's house to study
for a Spanish quiz. Elin takes AP Latin because, Elin.

They mostly don't study, though. They ransack the cupboards for
the Reese's Peanut Butter Cups and Little Debbie Spinwheels and
bags of Oreos that Ainslie's mother hides away in soup tureens and
behind boxes of rice and cereal. Once they found a little baggie with
weed in it, and they flushed it down the toilet.

Ainslie says they're doing her mother a favor eating the Oreos and
Reese's. They're teenagers. They have higher metabolisms.

Sky says, "*Dónde está* Mint?"

Ainslie says, "He's downstairs. In the rec room with Oliver and
Alan." She's decapitating a Reese's Peanut Butter Cup. Ainslie only
eats the insides. Like a spider. Spiders only eat the insides. "I turned
him off, actually."

"You did what?" Immy says.

"I turned him off," Ainslie says. "He was kind of freaking my mom out. I can see why they did the recall. It's not romantic, having a Boyfriend pop in and out of existence all the time. And it's not like you could sit and have a conversation with him, or like Mint ever said anything romantic. He just stared. And, you know, after a week it felt like maybe he was somewhere nearby staring at you all the time. Like, if I was looking in one direction, maybe he was right there behind me. I kept turning around, and he wouldn't be there. But that didn't mean that he wasn't there. He might have been there. Every time I turned around and didn't see him, I was positive he was still there in the room with me, somewhere just out of sight. My neck got sore because I kept jerking my head back to look up at the ceiling. Because once I looked up and he was there. And once I found him under the kitchen table. So I kept having to look under things too."

"Just like a real ghost in a movie," Sky says. Sky loves scary movies. No one will go see them with her.

"What about Embodied? Did you try him out in Embodied Mode?" Immy says.

"Yeah," Ainslie says. "And that was also no fun. He said all the right stuff, the stuff Oliver and Alan say, but you know what? I didn't buy it. Like, not that it was fake. Like he was *lying*. Like he was making fun of me. I don't know. Maybe we're getting too old for Boyfriends."

"Let's go turn him on," Sky says. "I want to see. I want to see him float up on the ceiling."

"No," Ainslie says. Ainslie never says no. They both stare at her. She says, "Here. You want the chocolate?"

Later Ainslie wants to show them something online. It's an actor
they all like. He's naked and you can totally see his penis. They've all
seen penises online before, but this one belongs to someone famous.
Sky and Ainslie go looking for other famous penises, and Immy goes
back to the kitchen to study. But first she goes down to the rec room.

The rec room is full of Ainslie's mother's abandoned projects.
An easel, with a smock still draped across it. A sewing machine; a
rowing machine; bins of fabric and half-finished scrapbooks with
pictures of Ainslie and Immy when they could still run around the
yard naked; Ainslie and Immy and Sky when they had their first
ballet recital; Ainslie and Immy and Sky and Elin graduating from
middle school. Back before Ainslie's parents divorced and Immy got
boobs and Ainslie got Boyfriends. All those Ainslies and Immys,
with their dolls and their princess dresses and Halloween costumes
and valentines. Immy's always been the prettier one. Ainslie isn't ugly,
but Immy's prettier. If Boyfriends worked the usual way, Immy could
get one like *that*.

But maybe then she wouldn't want one.

There are three coffins standing up inside the closet. *No room for
a fourth,* is Immy's first thought. They used to spend hours playing
with Oliver and Alan. Now they hardly ever do. And it's not like
Immy can just suggest bringing them out. They belong to Ainslie. It's
not like playing dolls. It's more like telling your friend you want to
hang out with some fake people she keeps in her closet, and anyway
they're only nice to you because Ainslie wants them to be nice to you.
If Immy had a Boyfriend, she wouldn't keep him in a closet in her
basement.

The first coffin she opens is Oliver. The second one is Mint. It's a
ridiculous name. No wonder he's been acting weird.

"Hi, Mint," she says. "It's Immy again. Wake up."

Then she holds her breath and turns around to look for him, but he's not there, of course. He's just a fake boy in a fake coffin, right? That's what Ainslie thinks, anyway. What Immy thinks is you shouldn't be able to just turn your Boyfriend off, just because he's not the way you want him to be.

She sticks her fingers into his hair. It's incredibly soft. Real hair, which should be creepy, but it's not. It's like she's petting him. If he were Ainslie's real boyfriend, she couldn't do this.

She finds the little soft place behind the ear and presses down. Once for Embodied, twice for Spectral Mode. She presses down again. She wakes him up.

When she closes the lid of the coffin and turns around, this time the Ghost Boyfriend is perched on an exercise bike. He's staring at her like she's really there. Like he knows her, knows something about her.

Like he sees the real Immy, the one she isn't sure is really there. Right now, though, she's real. Immy is real. They both are. They're making each other more real the longer they look at each other, and isn't that what love should be? Isn't that what love should do?

"I'm Immy," she says. "Imogen."

She says, "I wish you could tell me your real name. Ainslie doesn't know I did this. So be careful. Don't let her see you."

He smiles at her. She puts out her hand, moves it to where she would be touching his face, if she could touch his face.

"If you belonged to me," Immy says, "I wouldn't keep you in a box in a closet in the dark. If you were my Boyfriend."

THE NEW BOYFRIEND

The rest of the night is penis GIFs and Oreos and Spanish vocabulary. When Ainslie's mother gives Immy and Sky a ride home, Immy looks back and thinks maybe she can see a boy looking out the window of Ainslie's bedroom. It's kind of a gas to think about Ainslie being home all alone with her Ghost Boyfriend. Immy falls asleep that night thinking about Ainslie and ceilings and kitchen tables and the way Mint's hair felt when she ran her fingers through it.

Immy doesn't know if Ainslie knows she's being haunted. She seems out of sorts, but that could just be Ainslie-and-her-mother stuff. Meanwhile, Sky and Elin are having a fight about some boots that Elin borrowed and wore in the rain. All Immy can think about is Mint. She keeps having that dream about the car and the highway and the ocean. Mint there in the dark with her, the moon above them. Maybe it means something? It ought to mean something.

Friday night is Elin's birthday present to Ainslie, tickets to see the O, Hell Kitties! play at the Coliseum. Sky and Immy are going to have a movie night without them, except then Elin gets Sky a ticket too, an apology for ruining the boots.

Whatever, Immy doesn't want to go anyway.

The idea comes to her when she hears about Ainslie's mom, who was going to be the ride to the concert, and who, it turns out, has gotten a ticket for herself after watching some videos on O, Hell Kitties! YouTube channel. Embarrassing for Ainslie, sure, but this is Immy's chance to see Mint.

Immy knows where Ainslie's mom keeps a spare house key. She knows the alarm code, too. One of the benefits of long-term friendship: it makes breaking and entering so much easier.

Easy too, to tell her mother she's been invited to dinner at Ainslie's house. She gets a ride from her dad. Her mother might have waited around until someone opened the front door, but that's why she asked her dad.

She waves, he drives away, then she lets herself into Ainslie's house. She stands in the hallway and says, "Hello? Mint? Hello?"

It's early evening. Ainslie's house is stuffed with shadows. Immy can't decide whether or not to turn on the lights. She's made peace with breaking and entering — it's for a good cause. But turning on the lights? That would be making herself at home.

She looks up at the ceiling, because she can't help it. She goes into the kitchen and crouches down to look under the table and is, despite herself, somehow relieved when Mint isn't there, either.

It gets darker second by second. Really, she needs to turn on the lights or else she won't be able to see Mint even if he's there. She goes into room after room, turns on lights, leaves them on even as she moves on. She has the sense that Mint is there ahead of her, leaving each room as she enters it.

She finds him finally — or does he find her? They find each other, she thinks, in the rec room. One minute Immy is alone, and the next Mint is there, standing so close that she takes a step back without meaning to.

Mint disappears. Then reappears. Standing even closer than before. They're nose to nose. Well, nose to chin. He's not much taller than she is. But she can see through him: the couch, the exercise bike, and the sewing table. He shouldn't stand so close, she thinks. But she shouldn't be here.

None of this is okay. But it's not real. So it's okay.

"It's me," Immy says unnecessarily. "I, uh, I wanted to see if you

were, um. If you were okay." He blinks. Smiles. Points at her, then extends his arm, so that it goes right through her middle. She sucks in her tummy. He disappears. She turns around, and there he is again, standing in front of the closet.

He disappears again when she reaches out to open the closet. Is there, inside the closet, standing in front of his coffin. Is gone again. She opens the lid, and there is his body. It's pretty clear, now, what he wants her to do. So she reaches into his hair, finds that button, and pushes it twice, Off, then Embodied.

She's still standing there like a freak with her fingers in his hair when his eyes open. And this is the first thing Ainslie's Ghost Boyfriend, Mint, ever says to Immy. "You," he says.

"Me?" Immy says.

"You came back," Mint says.

"I had to," Immy says. She backs out of the closet in a hurry, because she doesn't want to have a conversation in a closet with Ainslie's Ghost Boyfriend, standing next to the coffins of Ainslie's Vampire Boyfriend and Ainslie's Werewolf Boyfriend, because *no*. Mint follows. He stretches, arms above his head, flexing his neck, the way Boyfriends do, as if they are real boys who have, regrettably, spent too much time stored in coffins.

"I did something to you," Immy says. "The ring."

Mint puts his fingers up to his lips. Opens his mouth in a wide yawn. Can he feel it in there, the hair ring? The thought makes Immy gag. "You did this," he agrees.

Immy has to sit down. She says, "Okay, I did something. I wanted to do something, because, well, because *Ainslie*. I *meant* to do something. But what did I do?"

"I'm here," Mint says. "I'm here with her."

He says, "I shouldn't be here."

"Here?" Immy says. "Like, here? You shouldn't be in this house, or you shouldn't be here at all? Because you're a ghost? A real ghost?"

Mint just looks at her. A real ghost in a fake boy? She did this? That look in his eyes, then, is that something real? He has the most beautiful eyes Immy's ever seen. And, okay, so they're molded out of silicone, or they're bags full of colored gel and microelectronic components, but so what? How is that really any different from vitreous humors and lenses and rods and cone cells?

Boyfriends can even cry, if you want them to.

Immy wants to believe so badly. More than she's ever wanted anything. She says, "Who are you? What do you want?"

"I shouldn't be here," Mint says again. "I should be with you." He touches his mouth again. "I belong with you."

"Oh," Immy says. "Wait. Wait." Now she's sure that someone is playing a trick on her. Maybe Ainslie knew, somehow, that she was coming? Maybe she booby-trapped Mint, told him to say all of this, is hiding somewhere with Elin and Sky. They must be here — they're watching all of this, watching Immy make a fool out of herself. Aren't they?

"I love you," Mint says. And then, as if he's agreeing with himself. "I love *you*. I belong with you. Don't leave me. Don't leave me here alone with her. Immy."

Everyone who is alive has a ghost inside them, don't they? So why can't there be a real ghost in a fake boy? Why can't a real ghost in a fake boy fall in love with Immy? Justin did. Why can't Immy get what she wants, just for once?

Why can't Mint get what he wants?

Immy comes up with her plan sitting on the couch with Mint,

so close that they're practically touching. Immy can hardly breathe. She studies Mint's fingers, those half-moons at the base of his fingernails, the ridges on the tips of his fingers. The creases in his palms. The way his chest rises and falls when he breathes. It would be creepy, staring at a real boy like this, the way Immy stares at Mint. A real boy would want to know why you were staring at him.

She wants to ask Mint so many questions. *Who are you? How did you die? What's your real name? What is it that made you love me?*

She wants to tell him so many things.

They'll have time for all of that later on.

Her dad texts to say that he's about two minutes from Ainslie's house, and now there's no time for anything. When Mint gets back in his coffin and it's time for Immy to put him back in Spectral Mode, she can't wait any longer. She kisses him and presses that button. It's her first real kiss, really. She doesn't count Justin. Lip wrestling doesn't count.

She kisses Mint right on the lips. His lips are dry and soft and cool. It's everything she ever wanted a kiss to be.

Her dad's car is pulling up in the driveway as she comes up the stairs, and before she reaches the door, Mint is there again in front of her in the dark hallway, a ghost this time. This time he kisses her. It's the ghost of a kiss. And this kiss, too, is everything she's ever wanted, even if she doesn't feel it at all.

On the ride home, her dad says, "How's Ainslie?"

"Ainslie's *Ainslie*," Immy says. "You know."

"It would be pretty weird if she wasn't," her dad says. "Is she still big on those Loverboy things?"

"Boyfriends," Immy says. "She got a new one for her birthday. I don't know. Maybe not so much anymore."

Her dad says, "How about you? Any boyfriends? Real ones?"

"I don't know," Immy says. "There was this guy Justin, but, uh, that was a while ago. He was, you know. It wasn't serious. Like, we hung out some. Then we broke up."

"True love, huh?"

The way he says it, jokingly, makes Immy so mad, she wants to scream. She pinches her arm, turns her head, and bares her teeth. Shivers and it's all okay again. "Dad? Can I ask you something?"

"Shoot."

"Do you believe in ghosts?"

"Never seen one," he says. "Don't really want to see one either. I'd like to think that we don't just hang around here after, you know, we're dead. I'd like to think we get to do something new. Go places."

"Can I ask you another question? How do you know? If it's love, I mean."

Her dad turns to look at her, then nods as if she's just told him something she didn't even realize she was saying. He looks back at the road. "That kind of night? Who's thinking the big thoughts about love and death? You or Ainslie?"

"Me. I guess."

"You know what love is, Immy."

"I do?"

"Of course you do. You love your mom; you love me and your mom, right? You love Ainslie. You love your friends."

"Sometimes I love my friends," Immy says. "But that's not the kind of love I mean. I mean, you know, boys. I mean love, like the way love is in books or movies. The kind of love that makes you want to die.

385-

That makes you stay up all night, that makes you feel sick to your stomach, that makes everything else not matter."

"Oh, Immy," her dad says. "That's not real love. That's a trick the body plays on the mind. It's not a bad trick — it's how we get poetry and songs on the radio and babies — and sometimes it's even good poetry or good music. Babies are good too, of course, but please, Immy, not yet. Stick to music and poems for now."

"God," Immy says. "I wasn't asking about sex. I was asking about love. And if the kind I was asking about, if that kind of love is just a trick, then maybe the whole thing is a trick. Right? All of it. You and Mom need to love me because, otherwise, it would suck to be you. Stuck with me."

Her dad is quiet for a minute. He hates to lose an argument, and Immy loves that he never tries to bullshit her. "Some pretty smart people say that it is all a trick. But, Immy, if it's all a trick, it's the best trick I know. Your mom and I love you. You love us. You and Ainslie love each other. And one day you'll meet a boy — or, I don't know, you'll meet a girl — and you'll fall in love with them. And if you're lucky, they'll love you back."

"Sometimes I don't love Ainslie," Immy confesses. "Sometimes I hate her."

"Well," her dad says, "that's part of love too."

Immy is in love. Immy has a secret. Ghosts exist and the world is magic; and there is an unreal boy whose real name she doesn't even know with a ring made of hair in his mouth, and he loves Immy because she put it there. He loves Immy, even though Ainslie is the one he was supposed to love. Guess what? Immy finally has a

Boyfriend. And guess what? It's exactly as awesome and wonderful and amazing and scary as she always thought it would be, except it turns out to be something else, too. It's real.

She hardly slept at all. And today the cafeteria is too loud, and the fluorescent lights are too bright, and the sandwich she made for lunch leaves her fingers smelling like old lettuce and mayonnaise.

All Ainslie and Elin and Sky want to talk about is the lead vocalist of O, Hell Kitties! and the hot guy who spilled his beer on Sky's shirt and Ainslie's mom, who is the worst.

"You should have come," Sky says. "They were like, *amazing*, Immy." So Sky is going to be all about music too, now? Apparently.

Last week Elin told them all that not liking music was one of those signs, one of the ways you could tell if someone was a sociopath. Other clues: bed-wetting, being mean to cats, and setting fires. Of course, they all remember when they were just kids and Sky used to pee the bed.

Fine. Immy will be a sociopath all by herself.

Ainslie says to Immy, "And nobody's even told you the really creepy thing! So we get back to the house last night, and I just wanted to kill my mom. Like, what I really want to do is defenestrate her or chop off her head and put it in the microwave for a few hours, okay, but you can't do that, and so Elin and Sky and I had this other idea, which was to turn Mint on, and I was going to tell him to go scare her. But guess what?"

"What?" Immy says. She knows what.

"He was already on! Spectral Mode! Which is impossible because I turned him off, remember? I told you that? I did it a while ago, so how was he back on? That's creepy, right? Like real ghost-stuff creepy."

"Maybe your mom did it?" Immy says.

"Maybe it was the butler," Elin says.

Sky bugs her eyes out and says, "Maybe Ainslie's Ghost Boyfriend is a real ghost boyfriend." Sometimes Immy isn't sure about Sky. Are you supposed to take everything she says at face value? Or is she actually the most sarcastic person Immy knows? Unclear.

"So what did *you* do last night?" Elin says. "Anything interesting?"

It would be worrying, this question, except that Justin is eating lunch two tables away from them. He keeps trying to catch Immy's eye. Elin has noticed, and you can practically hear her teeth grinding together. Maybe she can sense how happy Immy is? How loved she is? Immy deliberately looks away from Elin as she answers; sends a little almost smile in Justin's direction. "Well," she says. "You know. Not really. Nothing worth talking about."

Ainslie says, "What do they put on this pizza? It's not cheese. I refuse to believe this is really cheese."

Carrying out the plan, rescuing Mint, is actually pretty simple. The hard part is the waiting. Spring break is coming up, and Ainslie and her mother are going out to Utah to go skiing.

Immy can't ask her dad to drive her over to Ainslie's house again, because Ainslie has already come over for dinner and couldn't shut up about black diamond slopes and polygamy and bison, and even if Immy's dad forgets, her mom won't. But she's already done the research to find out how much a cab would cost. Definitely affordable. And she can go during the day while her parents are at work.

Or wait, she can bike over. She's done it once or twice. It's doable.

Then call a taxi when she's ready to leave Ainslie's house. Simple

plans are good plans. Buy a duffel bag big enough for Mint to fit in, and remember the blankets to pad out the bag. The thing is, Boyfriends don't weigh as much as you think they would, and the taxi driver will help.

Remember enough money for the tip.

Over to the U-Stor-It, where Ainslie's mother has a storage space big enough to throw a circus in. Immy's been there a few times with Ainslie, bringing over lamps or rugs or ugly pieces of art when Ainslie's mother redecorates. There's at least one pretty nice couch and some boxes of books. There are outlets in the wall so Mint can recharge.

The key to the U-Stor-It locker is hanging up in the laundry room at Ainslie's house. All of the keys at Ainslie's house are labeled. (Just like how Ainslie's mother keeps all her online passwords on a sticky on her screen.) It's as if they want to make things as easy as they can.

And the U-Stor-It isn't all that far away from Immy's house. A mile or two, which is absolutely bikeable.

It's not a long-term solution, but it will do until Immy figures out something better. She isn't sure how any of this is going to work. She's trying not to let that bother her. Over spring break there will be frozen yogurt and dumb movie nights and thrift stores with Sky and Elin, and then there will be Mint. If he were a real boy, he could come along, too, for all the other, real stuff. But he isn't, and he can't, and that's okay. She'll take what she can get and be happy about it, because love isn't about convenience and frozen yogurt and real life. That isn't what love is about.

Immy sees Mint twice before spring break. It makes the waiting easier. The first time is when Ainslie asks her over to help with her hair. Ainslie's mother has decided that Ainslie can put in a streak of

color, just one streak, for spring break. Ainslie can't decide between green and red.

"Stop or go," Immy says, looking at the squeeze tubes of Manic Panic.

"What?" Ainslie says.

"What do you want to say with your hair?" Immy asks her. "Go is green; stop is red."

Ainslie says, "I'm not trying to make a statement here. I just want to know which one looks better, okay? Is green too weird?"

"I like the green," Immy says. "Goes with your eyes."

"I think I like the red," Ainslie says.

While they're waiting for the bleach to work, Ainslie takes Immy down to the rec room. The whole time Immy has been trying not to think about Mint. And now that's where Ainslie is taking her.

"I just need to check," Ainslie says. "I check every single day now. Sometimes I check a couple of times. He's never on. But I still have to check. Last night I woke up at 3 A.M., and I had to come down here and check."

She jerks back the coffin lid, as if she thinks she'll catch Mint up to no good. His eyes are closed, of course, because how can he turn himself on?

Where is he when he isn't here? It hurts Immy to see him like this, turned off like he's just some old toy.

The bleachy part of Ainslie's hair, wrapped in foil, sticks practically straight up. It looks like a handle, and Immy imagines yanking it. Hearing Ainslie shriek. And Mint still wouldn't wake up. So what's the point?

Ainslie stabs at Mint's head like she's killing a spider. Turns then and shrugs at Immy. "All good. I know I'm being an idiot. He's just

a semidefective Boyfriend or something. He's not even that cute, right? Oliver is much cuter. I don't know why I wanted him so much."

Maybe if Immy asked, Ainslie would just give her Mint.

Ainslie says, "I asked my mom if we could sell him on eBay, and she had a fit. Acted like I was the worst person in the world. Kept telling me how much she paid for him, how hard it was to get him, that I didn't appreciate everything she did to make me happy. So I had to pretend like I was just kidding."

Well, then.

Immy says, "Come on. I think it's time for the bleach to come out."

She gets one last look at Mint before Ainslie shuts the lid again. And Ainslie changes her mind, chooses the green, then the red, the green, and then the red again. They both like the way it looks when it's finished, like a long streak of blood.

At school two days later, Ainslie tells them about how her mother went and put a streak of red in her own hair. She's so angry she cries. They all hug her, and then Immy helps her cut all the red right out with a pair of scissors in the art room. All Immy wants, at that moment, is for Ainslie to be as happy as Immy is.

The next time she sees Mint, it's two days after that. Four in the morning. She's done a stupid thing, biked all the way over to Ainslie's, six miles in the dark. But she did it for love. Call it a trial run. She lets herself into the house. She's a shadow among shadows. She's a ghost. She almost goes to Ainslie's bedroom, to stand beside Ainslie's bed and watch her while she's sleeping. Ainslie's almost pretty when she's asleep. Immy's always thought so. But Ainslie isn't why Immy's there. And she's seen Ainslie asleep before.

She goes down the stairs to the rec room, and she turns Mint on in Spectral Mode. He's there immediately, watching her from over by the couch again. "Hi," she says. "I had to come. Everything is fine. I just had to come see you. That's all. I miss you. Today is Friday. I'm coming back on Monday and everything is going to be fine. We'll be together. Okay?"

Her Ghost Boyfriend nods. Smiles at her.

"I love you," she says. He says it back silently.

She really ought to turn him off, but Immy can't do it. Instead she goes back to the closet, and she opens the lids of Oliver's and Alan's coffins. She finds their buttons, one with each hand, and she turns them both on, shutting the closet door as quickly as she can so they won't see her, know who's done this. She's back up the stairs and out the door, the key is under the rock again, and she pedals madly away. When she gets home, the sun is just coming up.

She thinks with satisfaction, *That's going to surprise Ainslie.*

But Ainslie doesn't mention it. Ainslie is kind of a wreck since the thing with her mom and the hair. Or maybe it's all the Boyfriend stuff. Either way, what Ainslie really needs is her friends. After school Immy and Sky and Elin take her out for yogurt. Tomorrow Ainslie and her mom leave for Utah. Immy wants to get up and dance on tables. There's a song on in the yogurt place, and it's kind of a good song. Immy really ought to find out who does it, except if she asks, Elin or maybe everybody will look at her like, *You like that song? Really?* But she does. She likes it. Really.

She hardly sleeps at all Sunday night. Goes over and over the plan
in her head. Tries to work out all the things that might go wrong so
she can fix them before they happen. A horrible idea lodges itself
in her head: What if after Immy turned on the Boyfriends, Ainslie
did something crazy? Like, finally get her mom to take them all to
Goodwill? Or worse? But nothing goes wrong. All the coffins are
right where they should be. The taxi drops her off at the U-Stor-It,
and she puts Mint in his duffel bag on a pallet mover, and the key
works just fine, and so what if the storage space smells like dust and
mold and there are random things everywhere? She unzips Mint and
pushes the button for Embodied.

And it's just like it was in the rec room. The first time they were
alone together. It's just so easy to be with him. Immy has already
cleared off the couch, plugged in one of the nice lamps, put in one of
the bulbs she brought from home. She even has a blanket for them
in case the storage space is cold. Well, for her. Mint probably doesn't
get cold.

That's one of the things she wants to ask him, now that they can
finally talk. Not about getting cold. About his name. She doesn't have
to be home for hours.

They're facing each other on the couch. Holding hands just like
boyfriends and girlfriends do. It isn't really like holding hands, exactly,
because he's made out of silicone and plastics and tubes of gel, metal
rods, wiring, whatever, and his hand feels weird if she tries to think
of it as a real hand, but that doesn't matter.

And of course he can't really feel her hand, she knows, but it must
mean something to him, her hand in his. The way it means something to her. Because he's just as real as he isn't real.

It's good enough. Better than anything she ever imagined.

"I don't remember," he says. "I don't remember much. Just you. Only you."

She's a little disappointed but doesn't want him to know it. "Is it okay if I keep calling you Mint, then?" It's just a stupid name that Ainslie came up with, but when she thinks about it, Immy realizes that Mint is how she thinks of him. Maybe it would be weird to try calling him by another name.

"Do you remember anything about when you were alive?"

He shakes his head. "I remember being hungry. I remember being cold. I remember being alone."

"Do you remember how you died?"

"I remember love."

Immy doesn't want to know about other girls. Girls he knew when he was alive. Not even if they're dead and gone. She says, "I've never been in love before. I've never felt like this before."

That awful hand flexes; those fingers curl around her own. She wonders how he knows how much pressure to exert. Is it Mint who does that, or is it some kind of Boyfriend basic subroutine? It isn't really important which one it is.

"I can stay for a while," she says. "Then I have to go home."

He looks at her as if he never wants her to leave.

"What will you do when I go home?" Immy says.

"I'll wait," he says. "I'll wait for you to come back to me."

She says, "I promise I'll come back as soon as I can."

"But you don't have to go yet," he says. "Stay. Stay with me."

"Okay," Immy says. "I'll stay as long as I can."

She says, when he only looks at her, "What do you want to do? You've been stuck in one of Ainslie's closets for, what, a month now?

Where were you before that? Before Ainslie turned you on, and I put the ring in your mouth? Is it weird, talking about this?"

"I'm yours. You're mine," Mint says. "You can say anything you want to me."

So Immy tells him everything. Everything she's been feeling this year. About Justin. About Ainslie. About how she's not sure, sometimes, who she is. They hold hands the whole time. And then, before she leaves, she turns Mint back to Spectral Mode. That way he can investigate the U-Stor-It if he wants to, while she's gone. Spectral Mode has a range of three thousand square feet, which is one of the cool features of the Ghost Boyfriend. Immy has been reading everything she can find online about Ghost Boyfriends. She's read it all before, but now it's different.

There's a lot of discussion online about the uncanny valley, which has to do with things like dolls or how characters are drawn in video games. It's why things that look like people but aren't people are scary sometimes. It's that gap between the real and something that's almost real. Vampire Boyfriends and Werewolf Boyfriends and Ghost Boyfriends, supposedly, don't fall in the uncanny valley. People have forty-three facial muscles that you use to smile or frown or raise an eyebrow, although some people have a lot less than forty-three facial muscles. Apparently Boyfriends have the equivalent of fifty facial muscles. They're supposed to be more realistic than real people. Or something. Their heads are slightly bigger; their eyes are bigger too, which is because of something called neoteny. It makes you feel good things when you look at them, like how you're supposed to feel when you look at a baby.

Immy has joined two separate Listservs for people with Boyfriends.

She imagines what it will be like, posting to the Listservs about the cute things Mint says, the fun things they do. She'll have to come up with a different name for him though.

It's the best week of Immy's life. She hangs out with Elin and Sky. Ainslie texts them to tell them all the horrible things her mother is doing. And Immy spends as much time as she can in the storage space with her Boyfriend. Her boyfriend.

The storage space is dark and awful, but Mint doesn't seem to care. Well, he was living in a coffin in a closet before this, so he doesn't have much to compare it to. He tells her about the things that other renters have in their lockers. A lot of pianos, apparently. And textbooks. Mint is perfectly happy to list everything he's discovered. And Immy is perfectly happy to sit and listen to him go on and on about empty aquariums and old dentist chairs and boxes of Beanie Babies.

When she and Justin were hanging out, he kept talking about video games he liked. She'd played some of them too, is pretty good at some kinds of games, but it wasn't like they were having a conversation. Justin didn't leave any room for her to say anything.

Immy manages to find that song from the yogurt place and downloads it onto her phone. She plays it for Mint, and they slow dance in the extremely small space not taken up by all of Ainslie's mother's crap.

"I really like this song," she says.

"It's a good song," Mint says. "You're a good dancer. I've been wanting to dance with you for so long."

His hand is on the small of Immy's back. He's a good dancer too, maybe even better than Oliver, and she leans her head against his shoulder.

"Which hair was yours?" she says.

Mint says, "What?"

"The ring. Which hair was yours? The blond hair or the black hair?"

"The blond hair," Mint says. He hesitates. "The black."

"Never mind," Immy says. She kisses his shoulder, hugs him a little tighter. It's a little weird, how Mint doesn't smell like anything. It's a good thing, probably. If you kept a real boy in a storage locker, you'd need to figure out how he could take showers. Plus you'd have to feed him. Although maybe Mint is starting to smell a little like the storage space, a little bit like mildew. Maybe Immy should buy him some cologne.

He's still wearing the black funeral suit he came in. Maybe she could buy him some T-shirts and jeans at the thrift store. She can't picture Mint in a T-shirt.

Ainslie comes home in two days, and Immy isn't sure what happens after that. It's not as if Ainslie is going to think Immy took Mint — why would she think that? But it's still going to be complicated. And then there's the storage space, which isn't going to work for long. And anyway, when spring break is over, it's not like Immy can just come over and hang out in the storage space all day.

When she tells Mint all of this, he isn't particularly bothered. "You'll think of something," he says.

But she's not sure she can.

That night she can't sleep. At some point after midnight, she decides she might as well go and see Mint. They've never spent the night together. Maybe the time is right. They can lie on the couch together, and she can fall asleep on his shoulder. She can wake up in his arms.

THE NEW BOYFRIEND

It's a cold night, and there's no moon. Immy feels like a ninja on her bike. She's alone and daring, and no one will see her or know what she's up to. She could sneak into a house. Cut off a lock of someone's hair while they're asleep. Pour drain cleaner in a fish tank. Salt in a sugar bowl. What couldn't she do? She should do this more often, she thinks. Go places, do things. Have adventures.

The U-Stor-It after midnight is a different place. Gothic, satiny black, full of other people's secrets. But her secret is the best.

When she gets to the storage locker, she hears voices. A voice. Someone is talking. Mint is talking. Mint is talking to someone. She recognizes everything that he's saying.

"I love you. Only you."

"I love only you."

"Stay with me. Don't ever leave me."

"We're together now. I'll never leave you."

"I love you."

It's peculiar, because Immy set Mint to Spectral Mode. And who is he talking to, anyway? Everything that he's saying, it's everything he says to Immy. All of this is wrong. Something is wrong.

She unlocks the door, lifts it up. And something is definitely wrong, because there is her Ghost Boyfriend, standing in the dark, in Embodied Mode, and there is her Ghost Boyfriend in Spectral Mode. Except the ghost isn't her Ghost Boyfriend. It's a girl. Barely there, less there than Mint ever is. The beam of Immy's flashlight pins her there in the air. Holes for eyes. Light hair.

The ghost's hand is reaching out to Mint. Her fingers on his mouth.

Immy may be an idiot, but she's not an *idiot*. She knows, instantly, the mistake she has made. The mistake she has been *allowed* to make. Those three strands of hair, the two black pieces and the yellow. Apparently Immy isn't the one who gave Ainslie's Ghost Boyfriend a real ghost — she's the one who gave Ainslie's Ghost Boyfriend two ghosts.

No one is in love with her. She isn't anyone's girlfriend.

This isn't her love story.

She goes right up to the Ghost Boyfriend, Mint, whoever he is. And that other girl. That dead girl. Who cares who she is, either. It's not like she can do anything to Immy. But Immy can do something to her. Body or no body.

"Immy," Mint says.

"Shut up," she tells him. And she sticks her fingers right into his traitor's mouth.

He bites down. And then his hands are up and his fingers are around her throat. Mint's fingers.

She thinks, *They aren't supposed to do that!* She's so angry, she isn't even scared.

And then Immy's fingers are under that wriggling tongue, and then she's got hold of the hair ring. She yanks it out of the mouth, and, like that, the girl ghost is gone and the Ghost Boyfriend is just a *thing* standing there, its hands loose at her neck, its mouth slightly open.

She sticks the hair ring in her pocket. Her fingers are really throbbing, but she can bend them, so not broken. They're just a little mangled.

She's alone with the Ghost Boyfriend looming there, like he's just waiting for her to turn him on again. And those other two, the ghosts? Are they still around? She gets out of there as fast as she can.

She rides her bike through the dark streets, crying the whole time.

Snot all over her face. *What an idiot.* Worst of all, she'll never be able to tell anyone any of this. Not even *Ainslie.*

She washes her hands thoroughly once she's home. Takes the nail scissors and a pair of tweezers out of the cabinet in her bathroom. She holds the hair ring under a magnifying glass and uses the tweezers to tease out the blond length of hair. Cuts it with the scissors, and tweezes out every last strand. Now she has a ring of black hair, and a very small pile of blond hair. The black ring goes back into the locket on the necklace she got for Ainslie. Next she goes through her jewelry box, looking for the necklace she used to wear all the time last year. A kind of medicine bag thing on a leather strand. The blond hair goes into that.

After that, she gets in bed. Leaves the light on. When she falls asleep, she's in that car again on the moonlit road. Mint is in the passenger seat. Someone else is in the backseat. She won't look at either of them. Just keeps on driving. Wonders where she'll be when she gets there.

In the morning, she explains things to her dad. Not everything. Just the part about the Ghost Boyfriend and the storage locker. She tells him it's all part of a joke she and Elin and Sky were going to play on Ainslie, but now she's realized what a bad idea it was. Ainslie would have really freaked out. She explains that Ainslie is really fragile right now. Going through a bad breakup.

He's proud of her. They drive to the U-Stor-It and retrieve the Ghost Boyfriend. When he's back in his coffin in the closet in the basement of Ainslie's house, her father takes her out for frozen yogurt.

Ainslie comes back from her ski trip with a tan, because Ainslie is a multitasker.

At lunch they all sit out in the sunshine in their coats and scarves, because it's hard to be back inside, back in school again.

"Here," Immy says. "Happy birthday, Ainslie. Finally found it."

It's a little tiny box, hardly worth it, but Ainslie does what she always does. Unwraps it so carefully, you'd think what she really likes about presents is the wrapping paper. She takes out the choker, and everyone *oohs* and *ahhhs*. When she opens the locket, Immy says, "It's probably not true, but supposedly the hair is Bam Muller's hair." Bam Muller is the lead singer of the O, Hell Kitties. She checked. He has black hair.

"Kind of gross," Ainslie says. "But also kind of awesome. Thanks, Immy."

She puts on the choker, and everyone admires how it looks against Ainslie's long white neck. Nobody has noticed the little bruises on Immy's neck. You can hardly see them.

"You're welcome," Immy says, and gives Ainslie a big hug. "I'm so glad you're back."

"Be more lesbian," Elin says. Sky has spilled the beans on Elin and Justin. The weird thing is that Elin doesn't seem that much happier. Probably the whole kissing thing. Although the way it turns out, Elin and Justin are still together when school gets out. They're together all summer long. And when Halloween rolls around and Ainslie has a party at her house, Elin comes as a sexy Red Riding Hood and Justin is a Big Bad Wolf.

Oliver and Alan and Mint are all at the party. Ainslie brings them out for the first time in a long time. Immy dances with all of them.

401-

THE NEW BOYFRIEND

She dances with Mint twice. They don't really have anything to say to each other.

It's a great party.

Sky has made another batch of absinthe. She's a cowgirl. Ainslie's mother is a sexy witch, and Ainslie isn't in costume at all. Or if she is, nobody knows who she's supposed to be. At some point, Immy realizes that Elin is wearing the choker, the one Immy gave Ainslie. So maybe she borrowed it. Or maybe Ainslie got tired of it and gave it to Elin. Whatever. It's not a big deal.

Immy's wearing her medicine bag. She wears it a lot. *Take that, ghost girl.* Immy is looking pretty good. She's a succubus. She has to keep explaining what that is, but that's okay. The main thing is she looks amazing.

Justin, for one, can't take his eyes off her. She looks at him once in a while, smiles just a little. All of that practice, she bets Elin has taught him a thing or two about kissing. And he was Immy's boyfriend first.

THE Woods Hide IN Plain Sight

JOSHUA LEWIS

Behind the shopping center is the parking lot; and behind the parking lot is the drainage ditch; and behind the drainage ditch, before the back lawns of the housing development, are the woods. The woods are narrow and ugly, their borders uninviting. On one side the random refuse of commerce: the cigarette butts of cashiers on break, empty foil potato chip bags faded to sooty pastels, cardboard boxes rain-soaked to ink-stained pulp. On the other side, the owners of the houses in the development have put up hedgerows, windbreaks, unfriendly spreading things with thorns — the detritus of the shopping center will not invade their quiet civilized yards.

And in between, no more than twenty yards wide at its widest point, are the woods. They run perhaps two miles before ending abruptly at the far end of the elementary-school soccer field, behind the playground.

Emiline walks in the woods and takes inventory. She has: One semester of college now behind her. She has brown hair that goes stringy in good weather and flat in bad weather, and a blue streak she keeps in it that looks nice the first day but fades to dishwater gray almost immediately, even if she bleaches it first. She has purple glasses that her mother says hide her "lovely green eyes" (in fact, plain hazel), and she has contacts but she never wears them because she is nervous about touching her eyes. She has a collection of T-shirts that say things like "I roll twenties" and "You get what everyone gets; you get a lifetime" and "She blinded me with library science." She has all of her mom's Anne Rice hardcovers. She has a Celtic cross necklace that her best friend, Marcus, got her when they went to the Renaissance Faire in Tuxedo, New York, on her seventeenth birthday. She has a place she lives, most of the time, that is not this boring suburb she's returned to for winter break. She is no longer confined in her dull plain shoe box of a hometown; now she has a monkish room in a beautiful stone tower — nothing so drab as the term "dormitory" suggests — where she works daily to transmute into the fascinating soul she wants to be.

She does not have: A boyfriend. A life of adventure and mystery. Sufficiently narrow hips. A car of her own. A dark, perfect, forbidden love.

She is home from her first semester of college, and she has made it three whole days of claustrophobic cohabitation with her parents before fleeing for the quiet of her little strip of forgotten wilderness. The general mood at home is antagonistic, and her parents mostly ignore her in favor of bouts of fighting with each other, interspersed with sulking alone. This is a new and unpleasant development, and Em wonders what has happened to chip away at their marriage in just the four months she's been gone. She feels strongly motivated to spend as little time at home as possible.

As always, the woods calm her. When she stops walking, and the crunching and cracking of leaves and twigs under her ceases, the trees hum with bewitching silence. It's evening, not late, but the sun is long gone.

Her destination is a house in the development at the far end of her walk; she is meant to meet up with her friends Marcus and Lilith. She kind of doesn't want to spend the next month going to her old high-school hangouts with her old high-school friends, but she can't imagine what else she might do. Tonight they gather at Marcus's parents' house — where Marcus, it should be noted, still lives, since he is going to college locally — and try to figure out what they have now with each other.

She kicks at leaves, crunchy with frost. This town is dead, she thinks. It is a terrible place to be from if you are trying to be somebody.

JOSHUA
LEWIS

The boy could not possibly have appeared anywhere else in her stupid little town, so he appears at the end of the woods where the soccer field starts and orangeade-colored sodium lights mark the boundaries of school property. She has made this walk hundreds of times and has met another person here perhaps twice before. But from the shadows comes the boy, and when he sees her, though she doesn't know him, he smiles as though he was expecting her.

He could only appear here because his appearing anywhere else in town would make him ridiculous. He's dressed in clothes appropriate to a night at the opera, not a weeknight walk past the split-levels in Owl's Crest North. And he is blue-pale. And also, she sees as she

405-

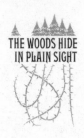

gets closer, he is very pretty. He has what she would now, after this
past fall, refer to as a Byronic profile, with a strong brow and a look
of great gravity set in the bones of his face.

She tries to imagine him down at the Frosty on Friday night, eating soft-serve in the parking lot. Tries to imagine him at the chain
faux Irish pub out on the main drag where the local bank tellers go to
drink Irish coffees and beer. It simply doesn't compute. He is clearly
not of this place, so much so that Em's first thought as she sees him
isn't *Who is he?* but instead *What is he doing here?*

He stops before her and cocks his head curiously. He says, "What
brings a pretty girl out walking on a night with no moon?"

Not the best line she's ever heard, but not the worst either.
"Emiline," she says, "and friends." She sticks her hands in her vest
pockets and shifts her weight back and forth to keep herself warm.
"Old friends I haven't seen in a while." She pushes her glasses up her
nose, suddenly self-conscious of her messy ponytail and "Dungeon
Masters do it behind a screen" T-shirt.

He grins and she sees that under his soft prettiness is a sharpness.
"Well, Emiline, you may call me Ricard. And they are lucky friends
who might earn your company for an evening."

This is all very Gothic and Romantic, but Emiline reminds herself
firmly that by any normal measure he sounds like an insane person. She
wants to play along, but here in the sodium lights in view of the loading dock of her elementary school, she can't, she just can't. "I'm sorry,
look, I'm really not in the mood tonight. Normally I'd love to play lord
and damsel or whatever, but right now I'm just feeling a lot of ambiv-
alence about seeing these old friends and I'm kind of preoccupied."

His grin falls, but in its place is not disappointment or annoyance
but confusion. "In the mood for what?"

"You know, the"—Em gestures up to take in all of Ricard, his clothes, his face, his hair—"the whole dark prince thing. Yes, you're the prettiest thing in the suburbs. Congratulations."

He smiles. "I am pleased that you think me pretty."

"Well, you've worked hard enough at it."

Now that the romance of the woods is gone, she realizes she knows the type well. Overdressed for everything, affects archaic speech patterns, playing a little live-action role-playing dark fantasy game in his head. She is reminded why she became friends with Marcus and Lilith, two of the few people she knew who liked dark fantasy and nerdy stuff, but didn't take it way too seriously, or pour their entire personalities into it. She knew boys like Ricard in high school—smug, patrician, and eager for you to understand how they personally are tortured by existence. Cruel parodies of the Romantic.

Ricard cocks his head as though she has said something deeply intriguing. "Does it seem so?" he says. "It's meant to look natural. Like I woke up like this."

His look is so sincere that she begins laughing, then claps her hand over her mouth. "Most of us don't wake up in eyeliner."

He nods. "I will remember that for next time." His mouth quirks up in a smirk that Em is irritated to find charming. "Anything else about me you would change?"

Em swears loudly. "Stop being so likable! I'm trying to judge you. I don't like fake vampires and all that."

"Well, I am happy to report," says Ricard, "that I am not one of those." He starts into the woods, heading into the dark. "I'll see you again, I think," he calls back.

Emiline watches him slip into shadows until the sound of his boots on the underbrush fades.

Her friends are in the semifinished basement where Emiline has spent probably whole months of her life in aggregate. Em finds herself smiling when she walks by Blackball, Marcus's terrible tiny car, whose many flaws he is constantly trying to hide by endless weird customizations. For the holiday season, Marcus has painted an extremely Gothic stylized crow on the hood in glow-in-the-dark paint, because Marcus does not care about the holiday season.

Marcus himself is lazily shooting pool with no real purpose, and Lilith is sitting up on the back of the couch, her feet on the seat. In addition there is Clyde, who Emiline vaguely knew before, and who is apparently now dating Marcus, and who throws the entire balance of the gathering off. Immediately Emiline feels self-conscious and observed — the prodigal returning. Marcus looks up and grins as she comes down the steps. "There she is," he says. "Come over here and let me beat you at nine-ball."

"You better play with him," says Lilith from her perch. "He's completely insufferable tonight and needs a whuppin'."

Marcus holds up the back of his hand. "I am the night. Behold my nail polish." His nails are very purple. "It's called *Aperotos Eros*," he adds.

"Very Latin," Clyde says.

"Greek," says Em.

"Swinburne," one-ups Lilith. "It's the name of a Swinburne poem. 'Strong as death, and cruel as the grave.'"

"Which perfectly describes my prowess at the pool table," says Marcus.

"You are the gothiest pool hustler ever," says Clyde.

"Throws them off," Marcus says. "They underestimate a dude in eye shadow."

Em pretends to carefully select a cue from the wall; she knows this basement well and knows that they are all equally terrible.

They shoot pool and talk. Em tells them some funny stories from college, feels how odd it is that these people who are so important to her know nothing of these other people who are also so important to her. Says "my friend" and a name in an explanatory tone a lot. They laugh. They tell her stories. They all go to the local college together, and they still hang out together, and they want to tell her about their new friends, too. They think she would really like these new friends. It would be great if Em came down to visit for a weekend. Em nods vaguely. Marcus brings down some of his dad's home brew, and she takes one, though when she last spent time with these friends, she never touched alcohol at all. No one mentions it.

She doesn't mention Ricard, either.

Em's next week is full of Christmas and extended family and answering the same questions over and over. This affords her very few opportunities to flee her parents. She walks the dog. A lot. Well more than the dog needs walking.

Which is when she sees Ricard again. This time he is crossing the street at the entrance to Em's parents' development, walking with purpose, although this is not a place where anybody walks and there is nowhere nearby for him to plausibly be walking from or to. When the dog sees Ricard, she goes berserk, barking and jumping as though in warning. He looks taken aback but then notices Em, and a smile breaks out on his face that Em finds she is very gratified to see. This winter break could be more interesting than she thought. If the dog would ever shut up and stop killing the mood.

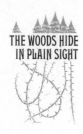

"Sorry about that," she calls over the barks. "Don't take it personally — she does it to kids on bikes too. Uh, hello, also. Ricard, right?"

Ricard is trying to smile at her but is eyeing the dog nervously. "And you are Emiline."

"People just call me Em," she says. The dog has retreated to sitting and growling quietly. "Emiline is a little long and old-fashioned."

"I like old-fashioned," says Ricard. He hesitates. "This is forward of me, but — I should like to see you again. Without the dog perhaps. Dogs are never fond of me."

"It's because you're a vaaaampire," Em says, wiggling her fingers at him in what she hopes will be taken for playful flirtation.

"I get that all the time," Ricard says seriously.

"I can't possibly imagine why," Em says with a little grin.

She begins going for long walks without the dog.

Em has no way of finding Ricard, but he finds her. Perhaps he lives nearby; perhaps, like her, he enjoys the rough cold quiet of walking the neighborhood streets at night. She knows that, realistically, Ricard must wait for her, must pay attention to when she walks and where she goes. Thinking of this, a sinister frisson slides like a cold finger from her neck to the small of her back, which oddly also excites her.

He falls in step with her and they talk. She tells him about how she fled, how she went away to make a project of herself, to transform herself. He tells her that he hopes to stay here, to settle down. This place appeals to him for all the reasons it's meant to appeal: safety, convenience, quiet.

"But it's so antiseptic," Em complains. They are perched together on the handrail preventing kids from falling into the sad little creek behind the public library. Em has a pile of pebbles in her hand, damp with soil, and is pitching them into the creek, one by one. The chill of the steel handrail slices a line across the backs of her thighs. "It doesn't seem like your kind of place at all."

"Nor yours, but here you are," Ricard points out.

"Accident of birth. I didn't choose to be here."

He shrugs. "I have lived all over this country. Right now I live here." He stops, and when she turns to look at him questioningly, he puts his fingertips to the side of her face; it's the first time he has touched her. His hand is cold. He stares at her with his dark eyes, his irises nearly black.

When she goes home, and then the next day when she meets Marcus and Clyde and Lilith for what Marcus describes as their "post-ironic" bowling night, she feels the places on her face where his fingers touched her. She wishes that they had left marks, something that would intrigue her friends, let them know she has a secret.

Ricard never asks for any more contact than their fortuitous meetings and walks, but one night he kisses her, not under a streetlight but in the shadows of a baseball field scoreboard. His lips, his tongue, are cold. He gives her a necklace, a teardrop-shaped, faceted garnet on a thick filigree gold chain. It looks very old. When she puts it on, it shines like a fresh wound on her throat. It has a pleasantly real weight to it, unlike any other jewelry she owns. He asks her to wear it when she sees him, instead of the Celtic cross that she usually wears.

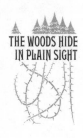

"I have found a forbidden love," Em tells her friends when next she sees them. They are at Lilith's gigantic house for her parents' yearly Epiphany party, and Em notes that she is still able to reliably call Lilith "Lillian" in front of her parents. Some things are programmed into her forever, apparently.

"Oh?" says Clyde politely.

"Yes, but it's a secret," she says. She has had a couple of glasses of wine and is a little flushed. Her ears are too warm, she thinks.

"Do tell," says Marcus, coming up behind Clyde. "Someone we know?"

"I don't know," Em says. "I don't think so. He's older. I never saw him before a couple of weeks ago." She tells them about Ricard, and then when Lilith — Lillian — comes over to see how they're doing, she tells again.

Marcus nods with sagacity at the end of the story. "I can already tell you the punch line."

"This guy is obviously a vampire?" says Em gravely.

"By which you mean a goth kid with too much money," says Lilith.

"Like Lillian," agrees Marcus.

"Shut up."

Marcus puts his hand on Em's shoulder. "No, but seriously, that guy sounds super-weird. There are super-weird people in this town, you know that."

"He doesn't seem weird, really," she says. "He seems . . . old-fashioned. And so serious that he seems a little silly. But sincere. And that makes up for a lot."

"So you're saying that if he was pretending to be a vampire, he'd be a weird creep, but since he's probably actually a vampire, he's okay?"

"Well, I might not have put it that way," Em says defensively.

"I knew it!" Marcus says. "Did you jump through the thornbush today, Em?"

"What?" This from Clyde.

Marcus turns as if just noticing him. "Wow, that last sentence probably sounded completely insane and out of nowhere for you, huh?"

"It did," confirms Clyde.

"Emiline used to make us jump through a thornbush," Lilith says drily. "When we were kids."

Clyde cocks an eyebrow at Em. *Show-off*, she thinks. "I don't know what you're talking about."

"You stand accused, Em," Marcus says. "Of making your poor friends jump through a thornbush just to play with you."

"Explain," says Clyde.

Em sighs. Of course she knows what they're talking about. "When we used to play in the woods, the ones between my neighborhood and the shopping center, I told Marcus and Lillian — we must have been about nine or ten then — that I was going to play in the Real Forest, and if they wanted to come with me, they had to jump through this big thornbush at the entrance."

"You were a little tyrant," says Marcus.

"The Real Forest?" says Clyde politely.

"That's where the faeries are," Lilith says.

"Ah. And you guys actually did it? Jumped?"

Marcus looks a little sheepish. "We told her that she had to do it first, and she just took off and did it. Came down covered in nettles, must have hurt like *crazy*, and this girl stands up smiling. 'See?' she said. 'Are you coming to the Real Forest, or am I going alone?'"

"She was very convincing," says Lilith.

"I'm ready to go to the Real Forest right now," Clyde says. He looks at Marcus. "So you jumped?"

Marcus shrugged. "What were we going to do? *Not* join our friend in the Real Forest? The clearly *superior* Real Forest? And then once we did it once —"

"— you had to do it every time," says Em, smiling. "I haven't made you do that in years."

"Six years, four months, eleven days," Marcus says, and Em pulls a face at him.

"Why the hell did you let her boss you around like that?" says Clyde.

"Well," says Marcus, "it used to drive me crazy, and I'd get mad at Em when I was home and still finding thorns stuck in my socks. But then I would think, 'What if she were actually right? What if she really did see the magic in the world? There's no chance, right? But maybe the tiniest, teeniest little chance.'" He shrugs. "That teeny, tiny chance was worth it. Because how stupid would I be if I had a friend who could see faeries, and when she invited me to join her, I blew her off to avoid some thorns?"

Emiline arranges for all of them to meet at the old wooden playground at the elementary school. It's meant for little kids, but on weekend nights it's invaded by high-school kids who use its wooden castles and forts and tunnels to play tag and smoke and make out. Emiline feels a wave of nostalgia and then realizes that she last spent time here only five months ago.

Ricard appears from between the trees at the edge of the grass. The playground is six or seven miles from where they usually meet on

their walks; she wonders for the first time if he has a car or a bike, and if so, whether he parks it far away so he can make a dramatic entrance on foot. The mystery of it delights her.

Em and her friends are perched atop a picnic table. Tonight, a winter weeknight while kids are still on break from school, they are the only ones there. She introduces everyone around, and then almost immediately an awkward silence descends.

Marcus does his best to break it. "So, do you go to school around here?"

Ricard shakes his head. "I'm done with schooling."

"So what do you, you know, do?" says Lilith. They are not reacting to Ricard in the way Em would have hoped; they are not caught up in the deep mystery of him, just the shallow mystery of fitting him into the patterns they already know. They seem suspicious and troubled.

Ricard smiles in a way that is probably meant to be reassuring but seems oddly predatory. "I'm still working out what it is that I do."

"So you just, like, bum around?" Clyde says. With a start, Emiline realizes why her friends are so dubious. They have fit Ricard neatly into a box she had never even considered for him, that of the guy who graduates from high school and then, unable to leave his well-known world, keeps hanging out with high-school kids, taking advantage of how easily a teenager can be impressed by a grown-up, even a marginal grown-up living with his parents, becoming more pathetic with each passing year. Even as Em thinks of Marcus and Lilith as hopelessly stuck in this charmless town, they at least are in college, are taking the expected next life step, and they are looking at Ricard in the same way that, perhaps, Em sometimes looks at them.

"It's not like that," Em says. "Ricard is new here; he's still trying to figure out his life around here. He's lived all over."

"Can I ask you a personal question?" Marcus says to Ricard, who nods politely. "Don't take this the wrong way, but are you a vampire?"

The direct approach is not what Em had expected, but she has to acknowledge it saves a certain amount of otherwise wasted time.

Ricard looks, for the first time in Em's knowing of him, surprised. And perhaps intrigued. "I am," he says, very slowly. "I am, in fact."

This is not the right answer. "Wait," Em says, trying for a playful tone, "it's not —"

But Marcus is looking right at Ricard. "Prove it."

Ricard now looks even more surprised. "You don't want that."

Lilith catches Em's eye. She looks alarmed; Em feels all of the new sophistication she's tried to show her friends slipping unpleasantly away like a snowball stuffed down the back of her shirt. *You're smarter than this*, Em reads on Lilith's face.

"That's about what I thought," says Marcus, smiling. "You know, I've met a lot of vampires in this town, and none of them have ever been willing to prove it."

Ricard shrugs. Then, with an unexpectedly inhuman speed, he bites Clyde in the neck.

The world is abruptly stilled. The wind stops whistling. They are frozen, the five of them, in a strange tableau. Marcus's smile has dropped, and his eyes have widened; Lilith is gasping, mouth open. Em's gaze is fixed at the point where Ricard's mouth meets Clyde's skin. Ricard's hand is on Em's forearm, bracing himself as he bends over; it is very, very cold.

Clyde's head is thrown back, and in his throat and chest, Em sees his breath rising and falling. She expects fear, hyperventilating, but his breath is sure and slow. He looks surprisingly calm; his only movement is a rapid fluttering under his closed eyelids.

Ricard detaches himself and stands up. Time starts again, and two streams of blood, black in the light, flow unhurriedly from Clyde's neck, over his collarbone, and under the collar of his sweater. Ricard himself has a dark stain of blood on his lips, which he wipes off with two fingers and, watching Em, puts into his mouth to suck.

She should be horrified. She should at the very least be frightened. But instead her head and her body buzz electrically; she realizes her fists are clenched, though she doesn't remember clenching them. The blood on Clyde's neck is *real*, so much more real than anything else here, as though it has been dripped onto a photograph.

After a moment, Marcus finds his voice. "Why —"

"Will that serve as proof?" Ricard says mildly.

Marcus looks at Clyde. "Are you —"

"I'm fine," says Clyde, with more clarity than Em would have expected. He looks at Ricard, back to Marcus, touches his neck. "It was fine. It felt good, actually." He stares at Ricard. "You could have killed me. Could — couldn't you?"

Ricard has drawn a handkerchief from his pocket and hands it to Clyde. "Anyone could kill you," he says. "You could be stabbed with a knife or poisoned or drowned. I am not unique in that ability."

"But —" Marcus begins.

"I *could* have hurt you," Ricard continues, "but I did not. I have no wish to hurt you. I wished only to make a point. And my survival is made much easier *not* hurting anyone. Being a vampire does not mean being a murderer."

"You didn't need to do that," Em says quietly, not looking at him, not looking at anyone.

"But it did serve as proof," he says. "A swift demonstration seemed best."

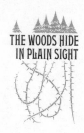

"I'm fine," Clyde says again. "Really," he says to Marcus. He looks back at Ricard. "But don't . . . don't do that again without warning me, okay?"

Ricard nods.

"Do me next," says Lilith.

"No," says Em sharply, to protect Lilith, but also — yes, also out of jealousy. "I think . . . I think we should probably all go. I think we'll . . . I mean, I'll call you guys tomorrow and . . ." She trails off. She only wants to get away, to not allow all of these things to collide any further tonight.

Lilith gets it. "Yeah, I think that's right. Yeah. Come on, guys. Are you coming, Em?"

Em shakes her head. "I need to . . . to figure this out . . ." She cannot yet find words. Her friends look dubious, but they let her stay.

"I thought good vampires only drank blood from animals and stuff," Marcus says as he turns to go.

"There are no good vampires," says Ricard.

"So, yes," he says to Em when her friends are out of sight, "I'm a monster; not a man."

Em feels her blood buzz beneath her veins. Without a word, she slides up her sleeve and holds her wrist out to him.

He drinks from her, only a little. There is no pain. Each pump of her heart drives cold fire through her entire body. He releases her hand, presses his thumb to the wound, draws her closer, and presses his mouth to her neck like a lover. They are in a strange standing embrace; his body is cold, but at every point where it touches hers, a current flows from that point, to her heart, to her throat.

One hand is on her shoulder. With the other he gently lifts her Celtic cross out from under her shirt by its chain, unclasps it, and closes his fist around it. He releases her, takes a step back, and opens his balled fist to show Em. The cross falls to the ground, and in his palm Em can see its shape duplicated in angry red burns, beginning now to blister.

"Doesn't that hurt?" she says.

Ricard nods. "Very much so."

She shakes her head quickly. "I won't wear it. Anymore."

"I would like that."

"I'm sorry about my friends," she says. "They . . . I don't know if they can understand."

"If they are truly your friends, they will come to understand," Ricard says.

Headlights appear in the distance, cresting the hill. Em takes Ricard's burned hand in hers — even the burn is still cold — and, wanting to laugh, wanting to cry out, pulls him into the trees.

She doesn't see her friends and Ricard at the same time after that. It is just too strange. She only has two weeks or so more of break, anyway, and then her parents will drive her back to the mountain village where she reads Chaucer and argues about Plato and looks for faeries under the ferns in the arboretum. She has no idea what she is going to do about Ricard.

In the meantime, their major relationship problem is a lack of privacy. Em can't imagine bringing Ricard home to her parents — he looks young, but not, she admits to herself, young enough to be dating an eighteen-year-old. Ricard is her escape from the

tension of home, and she finds she doesn't want to make him part of that.

It's difficult to find time to be truly hidden together from the world. Neither of them has a car they could park in a dark place for an evening. There are a few dingy local parks, but they are well patrolled, often by parents of Emiline's high-school classmates, suggesting the worst possible discovery scenario. Her parents barely ever go out. And Ricard hasn't told her where he lives and never invites her there, and she never asks.

Finally she smuggles a sleeping bag and a ground pad out of her parents' attic and brings it into her woods. No one, as far as she knows, ever goes there but her, especially in this cold. She feels very self-conscious as she walks down the neighborhood streets with a bed roll under her arm, but no one pays the slightest attention, and once she is in her little strip of woods, she is hidden. She can see out, to the warm amber lights of the kitchens and the cold blue lights of flickering televisions, but no one can see in.

Ricard seems amused by the sleeping bag — he feels neither heat nor cold, he says, but he understands her need. "Even though I can be burned by fire," he says, "I would feel it only as raw pain, without the heat you feel." Em takes off her shoes and socks and her vest and sweater and, after some hesitation, her jeans, under which she is wearing profoundly unsexy waffle-knit long underwear — but at least it will be a much thinner barrier between them.

They get into the sleeping bag and wrap themselves together. Em's T-shirt rucks up, and she feels her bare belly pressed against his. Slowly her warmth begins to seep into him, and it is more like she is embracing another regular person.

"You are leaving soon," he says to her.

This was not what she had in mind when she brought the sleeping bag here. "Yeah," she says. He doesn't say anything, so after a moment she says, "Will you come visit?"

"I want you to stay with me," he says.

"I can't stay here," she says. "I can't live with my parents. I have — you know, I have school and stuff. Look how hard it is just for us to get this much time alone here."

"What if I made you like me?"

"What?" she says, alarmed. She pulls her face away from his. "Like you? Like . . . a vampire?"

He looks in her eyes, says nothing.

"Can you do that?" she says.

Ricard nods. "You must feed from my blood, while being drained of yours. Then you will die and be reborn as one like me."

"I have to die?"

"The path from life to undeath leads through death," Ricard says. "Of this much at least I am sure."

"And then?" she says.

"And then we leave this place," Ricard says. "We travel, we seek a place to settle. We make a life together, you and I." His eyes gleam.

"What about — what about school?" she says. "What about my life?"

"It would be a sacrifice," he says. "A sacrifice of normalcy in exchange for life, for youth, for blood."

"We barely know each other," Em says. But the poetry of it appeals. And "normalcy" is one of the most hateful words she knows. She thinks of herself in four years, done with college, and getting ready to — what? To settle down into some terrible job and worry about her career? To meet someone and move to the suburbs with

them and fight and sulk? Put that way, would she even miss what she sacrificed?

"We would have an eternity for that," he says. He cocks his head at her as if in consideration, in evaluation. "I think that this is a thing that you want, more than you want this 'college.'" He says "college" as if he's never spoken the word before. Em feels the rocks and twigs beneath the sleeping pad, feels deeply, purely embodied. It is immediate and real, far more so than her town, which is almost transparent with falseness, but also more so than the books and intellectual searching of her school. For a semester she has been trying to escape from the mundane world by rising above it, becoming wiser, transcending the everyday, but now she considers what Ricard offers: going not up but down, not rising into air but burrowing into earth. She desperately wants to feel Ricard's slim pale hands move from their chaste place on her shoulder blades. Blood rushes palpably up and down the vessels in her arms and legs, collects in her core. With a single word she can change everything, all at once, no four-year project of painful reconstruction but an instantaneous becoming something new and unnerving and beautiful, like Ricard himself.

So: "Yes," she says.

"You will be damned," he says quietly. "But you will never die."

"We will be damned together," she says. She frees one hand and uses two fingers to pull the collar of her shirt down on one side, to just barely below the top of her bra. "Drink from me," she says, and he bends his head and does. The canopy of trees above is black against the purple-blue sky.

———◆———

"I'm going to become a vampire," she tells her friends the next time she sees them, back at Marcus's house. She expects them to protest, to argue. But they take it as a reasonable career plan. They have no context for the life she made this past fall, the friends she has there, what she plans to sacrifice. Becoming a vampire is as feasible a path, and as strange, as what Em has been doing. They seem not so much troubled as disoriented; they are full of questions, only some of which Em has the answer to (Will we ever see you? *Sure, all the time, just at night.* Will you be immortal, invulnerable? *Mostly, but not to fire or sunlight or holy water.*) It reminds her disconcertingly of the questions they asked when she told them she was going away for school. (Will we ever see you? *Sure, I'll come visit; you can visit me.* Why not just go to school here, where it's cheaper? *Because . . . because.*) None of them ask if they can join her. She gets it. She is the one who goes away; they are the ones who stay.

JOSHUA
LEWIS

The appointed day arrives. Now that Em is meant to become a vampire too, Ricard has invited her to his home; he gives an address that is surprisingly close by, in Fair Lane Manor, an enormous development of exactly identical postwar bungalows. In fact, she remembers, Clyde himself lives in the neighborhood, albeit three miles away at the other end.

She at once understands why he hadn't wanted to show her his house — it is so utterly not Ricard. She had envisioned a lair, some hollowed-out cave under a hill or maybe an abandoned rickety house that everyone knew was haunted. She had not envisioned vinyl siding and fiberglass shutters. *And then we leave this place*, she thinks. *Even the vampires' houses are lame here.*

Using the brass knocker on the front door of this particular house design is an act so familiar to her it is unsettling, something she's done

literally thousands of times before in her life. No one answers, and after a moment she tries the door and finds it unlocked. She steps into the foyer, dim in moonlight that streams through sheer curtains, illuminating dust floating and settling on a completely unremarkable room. "Hello?" she calls, and her voice is lost in the wall-to-wall carpeting; not only does she not get an answer — she doesn't even hear an echo. She begins to look around, and as she does, the house's relentless unremarkability starts to weigh upon her. It's impossible to imagine Ricard picking out sensible table linen and dusting crystal goblets in a china cupboard, Em decides, because it *is* impossible, and now she paces the house with a slightly different eye, running her fingers slightly across the ends of furniture.

The house is opulent in a suburban way, a kind of cheerful beige rococo. Emiline passes through what she labels a "sitting room" and then a "living room" — these names feel right, even though she could not really tell you the exact distinction between the two. In each of these is beautiful furniture, expensive rugs, finery, and as she moves through the house, Em becomes more and more uneasy. Everything is very tasteful and normal, disconcertingly normal, like a hotel lobby or a model home. Has Ricard set this up for *her* benefit? Could he think this would humanize him in her eyes?

She decides no, probably not; this is likely just the camouflage of his house. This is a safe town, a town where kids trick-or-treat door-to-door or collect for charity or come to tell you about their religion, without much worry. And the view of the house they'd get from Ricard's door would not cause worry. Strangely, though, to be surrounded by it here is oppressive. There is a feeling of dread in the back of her throat. Ricard must, after all, do his vampire stuff *somewhere.*

She is wondering if she should be searching for a crawl space or stairs to a basement when she walks into the dining room and finds the women awaiting her.

The dining table is set for thirteen. Its surface shines glossy with moonlight through the windows, and reflected in that surface are the faces of eleven motionless women. They are all dead. Some are long dead.

Em waits for the bottom to drop from her stomach, but it doesn't; her curiosity needs to be satisfied first. Are these other vampires? Ricard's family? They vary in age, though none are younger than perhaps eighteen and none are older than perhaps fifty.

Are they always here? Did Ricard put them here? Will they, unbreathing, nevertheless suddenly turn to look at her, fixing her with the empty gazes of their slack eyes?

She clings to confusion to avoid feeling horror. The women are silent and still. They seem to be mostly clothed in formal dresses, some quite old-fashioned. The uneven quality of the light drapes odd shadows across them.

Em is the only one in the room breathing. The only sounds are her feet scuffing the rug, her breath roaring in her ears, the tick of a grandfather clock in the next room, the hum of a furnace or boiler somewhere below.

You've never even seen a dead body before, she thinks to herself. *Now you've seen a dozen.* She is acutely aware of the rational part of her brain holding back the part of her brain that is screaming and panicking. With a calmness that she thinks might be actual shock — like the medical condition, not just shock in the sense of surprise — she realizes that the women are bolted in place in the chairs, their shoulders and waists pinioned to the chair back with a few long thin steel

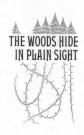

rods pierced through their bodies. That is what is keeping them sitting upright.

The necks of some of the women are horrible. She expects neat wounds, delicate fang holes, and a few of the women seem to have these dainty marks, but a number of the others seem to have had their throats torn out. *Maybe they struggled.*

"Do you want to know their names?" Ricard says from very, very close behind her.

Em gasps and then feels like an idiot for gasping, and then is angry at Ricard for his stupid dramatic entrance, and then is abruptly, coldly aware that Ricard, whatever else may be true of him, undeniably has eleven dead women pinned like butterflies in his dining room. Eleven women almost certainly murdered by him and — even stranger — left here for Emiline to find.

"Why are they here?" she says.

"They're always here," he says. Emiline grimaces, and he quickly adds, "Not here in the dining room, of course. They have their places of rest in the basement, in the cold. I have brought them here as witnesses."

"Of what?" Em is slowly edging her way around the table, putting distance between herself and Ricard. "Are you a serial killer?"

"I'm a vampire," Ricard says. "These are my failures. The ones I tried to turn, to join me in eternal life, but failed."

"You mean you killed them. It was an accident, but you killed them. I thought you didn't kill people. You don't kill people."

"They are my great unsolved mystery," he says. "I keep them cold, below, where rot and contamination can't find them. Someday I will find what I am doing wrong, and I will bring them back, all of them. Where now I am alone, then we will be a whole colony of vampires."

The dark romance of Ricard's vision clashes a bit with the reality of the glowering rictus gazes of the women at the table. Em focuses on their deterioration, the signs of their deaths. Surely they are too far gone to be made into vampires.

But what has happened to the ones who were *not* failures? The ones who he successfully turned, in the past? All gone away?

She steps involuntarily away from the table and finds the wall. She presses her hands against it behind her, feels its cool solidity as she says, "How many times have you succeeded?"

"That is of no matter," says Ricard. "What matters is you and your joining with me. I am sure that I will succeed tonight."

"How many times?" she says, more firmly. She stares at him, and he avoids her eyes.

"It will work with you," he says. "I am sure of it. I have never been so sure."

"It's none," Em says. "You've never succeeded at this, have you?" Anger courses through her. How unexpected. "How hard can it be to turn someone into a vampire?"

Ricard inhales sharply, through his teeth, and as he does he moves fast, not *impossibly* fast as she's seen in vampire movies but faster, certainly, than her. He moves with conviction, in deliberate abrupt flashes, like something stalking prey. And he has his cold hand up against her neck, and he has pushed her head into the wall behind her. Her head rings and pain spreads from the spot. She flinches; she can't help it.

"Do you know what it is like to be alone?" he whispers. His voice is not harsh; he speaks the words as if to a lover. "You are surrounded by family, by friends. Do you want to know"—and his face is so very close to hers—"the great secret of vampires? Do you? The secret is that as far as I know *there are no other vampires.*

"*That* is what it means to be alone — *truly* alone, alone in a way that you cannot imagine."

He lets her go, walks back to the most cadaverous and sunken of the women. He puts a hand on her shoulder companionably.

"Violet. She was twenty years old, and we were in love. I knew her before. I fed from her, purposefully, with her permission, until she was overcome with blood loss and fell dead. I waited for her to arise. She did not."

He moves to the next. "Angela, a widow at thirty-six. I was her younger man, even though I was nearly her age in true years lived. In those days I was romantic. We became engaged. On our wedding night, I fed her my own blood, and then I drained her.

"Clara. By then I was a monster. I terrorized her family, killed and ate their servants. I bled her, ritually, in front of her parents, and fed her both my blood and, when she weakened further, her own mother's blood. She sits still dead before you.

"Laura, the daughter of a wealthy friend. I snuck into her room like a cat and fed her my blood without drinking any of hers myself. Vampire blood turns out, in large-enough quantity, to be fatal to humans.

"Lucy, a lady of low means living alone. I —"

"Stop!" Em yells, and he does.

"Why me?" she says.

"Why anyone?" He shrugs his usual shrug. "You appeal to me, little one. Is it not a great honor to be wanted as my eternal companion?"

"It *is*, but —" *Is it?* "Did you have to *kill* them? Why wouldn't you try things that didn't *kill* them?"

"I did," Ricard said. "And then I tried things that killed them. Death is part of who I am. I am a thing which is, by all normal measures, dead. So *however*"—he slams his hand on the table, and Em jumps a little at the loud *crack*—"one may become a vampire, one will be dead by the time the process is done.

"I cannot turn away from that truth. And if you are to join me, you cannot either."

His gaze is wide and hungry. Under his eyes, the skin sags slightly; to Em, it appears almost gray. In the dimness he could be a black-and-white photograph.

"So what do you have planned? For me?" she says shakily. She tries, very slowly and casually, to shift herself toward the door.

"We shall mingle our blood together," he says, producing a knife from somewhere on his person.

"Uh, so like a 'blood brothers' kind of thing, or . . ." Em is stalling for time. She shifts her weight to her right foot and shuffles her body a little closer to the door.

"No. Not enough mingling of blood with a wound in the hand or even the wrist; I have tried both of those before. My fangs will not draw enough blood flow for that to work." Ricard smiles a surprisingly cheerful smile for someone holding a gigantic knife. "I will draw the blood from your heart and then from my own, and allow them to mingle between us."

"Oh," she says. She glances around the room, hunting for a weapon, a clear path to a doorway, anything. "So you're going to stab me in the heart and then stab yourself. Got it. That's great. So you're a crazy person. I thought that maybe, just *maybe*, under the clean surface of the suburbs lived something dark and vicious and romantic, but instead you're just a serial killer with a vampire thing. I think—" She steps back and her shoulders unexpectedly bump the glass-fronted cabinets of serving ware behind her. They rattle loudly and

unpleasantly. Ricard stays where he is, watching. The knife is down at his side; he doesn't look concerned. "I think that I have thought better of it, Ricard," she says, "and I think that I don't want to become a vampire. And I —" She sidesteps, another loud glass rattling — why is she trying not to break anything in Ricard's house? She is being careful of the possessions of a man who is currently preparing to stab her. "I think, I hate to say it, but I think that . . . I think when I go back to school, this needs to be over."

"I am not crazy," says Ricard. He continues not to move, just to track her with his eyes. "I drink blood. I am harmed, wounded by the light of day. You know these things."

"I know I've only seen you at night," Em says. "I know you drink blood, but again — serial killer! Those guys eat people all the time!"

"I," says Ricard in what is clearly cold rage, "am a vampire, and I must try, until I succeed, to make another of my kind. I cannot know how. I can only guess and try, guess and try, and kill when I am wrong, and mourn my kill. I have been wrong eleven times. Perhaps I will be right the twelfth. If not, I will try again. I have, it seems, all the time in the world." He smiles bleakly and raises the knife again.

Three things happen at once.

Em drops to the floor.

Ricard lashes out with the knife.

And a light as bright as the sun pierces her closed eyes with orange-white fire.

Some feeling has overloaded Em's capacity for thought, which she distantly identified as pain radiating from the knee she has banged hard against the parquet. When, a few seconds later, she opens her eyes, it is bright as day.

Ricard is backed up against the far wall, an arm thrown over his face. Where the light hits him, smoke rises, his skin glows unpleasantly. A terrible smell like burning rubber hangs in the air; several of the women in their chairs have been knocked over and lie staring cockeyed at nothing at all.

The light is coming from a single spot the size of a dinner plate in the doorway. A dark figure steps forward; it is Marcus, holding a huge klieg light at his side like a Gatling gun. He looks grim and waves the light slightly, sending small lines of smoke up and down Ricard.

Em cannot speak. Marcus looks at her with concern. "Are you okay?"

Ricard takes this opportunity to leap for the door and disappears into the back part of the house. Marcus makes to follow him, but he can't move very fast because of the weight of the light. "So much for the element of surprise," he says. "Now we have to get out without him running us down and killing us."

"How — why —" Em shakes her head; it does not clear. She begins to struggle to her feet.

Marcus drops the light, which lands hard on the carpet with a *crack* that sounds like a floorboard breaking. "We thought we should probably keep an eye on you. Lot of creeps in this town."

"Since?" she says.

"Pretty much since he bit Clyde. I mean, he is a *vampire*, Em. Here's what the folklore says. Vampires: sometimes good. Mostly evil, though. Mostly they are monsters and murderers."

"Check and check," Em says wearily.

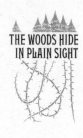

"So we watched you. Followed Ricard home once, found the house, broke in when he was away."

Suddenly he staggers and bends forward, a look of surprise and pain on his face. Ricard appears behind him in the doorway. Marcus coughs and winces, but he doesn't seem to be bleeding, so Em grabs his hand and pulls, and he manages to stagger with her out the other doorway and into the back of the house. *Fair Lane Manor house*, she reminds herself. *I could find my way around blindfolded.* She makes for the open back door and leaps down four cement steps to the back patio. Her knee complains sharply, and she hears Marcus wheeze in pain, but they make it into the underbrush beyond the backyard, and though she feels the bright pricks of brambles and thorns pierce her through her clothes, they quickly pull free and slide down a few feet of scree into a dry creek bed. She can hear Ricard's footfalls, loud against the patio.

"Again with the thorns," Marcus says, pulling one out of his sleeve.

"Where are we going?" says Em.

"Playground," Marcus says. "Blackball."

She orients herself rapidly and takes off. She leaps over huge twisted roots and sharp rocks, stumbles, keeps going. Marcus runs just behind, breathing hard but keeping up.

She can hear Ricard behind them in the creek bed, also running, faster than her. In her mind is the thought of civilization, of human lights and company — but it is late and no one is out on the streets.

The creek bed ends at an overgrown culvert. She scrambles to the top of it and sees they are at a main road. She runs down it, toward the school. When they reach it, she runs down the circular driveway, where the buses stop, and around the side of the building to the

parking lot next to the playground. Blackball is there, the only car in the lot, hunkered down with reassuring solidity, its engine running.

Em risks a look back, and there is Ricard, not nearly far enough behind them. They're out in the open and Ricard is faster and there's no place to hide — could they even get into the car before he caught them? And what then? He'll just find them again later. He knows where Em lives, after all, and now he knows the car.

The door on the far side of the car opens and Clyde emerges. He is holding some large metal sculpture, and she has no idea what it is until he steps forward and a twenty-foot jet of flame emerges from one end of it with an enormous roar, catching Ricard in the face.

Em has no time to consider what this means, because at the same time, the other car door opens and Lilith emerges. She yells, "Catch!" and underhands something to her. Em catches it — a can of pepper spray.

Ricard has stopped running and is trying to figure a way to get close to them, but Clyde is doing a remarkably good job of keeping him at a distance with short bursts of flame.

"Just burn him!" she yells in rage, tremendously loud and echoing in the empty lot.

"I can't!" Clyde calls back. "These things don't hold a lot of fuel! Don't know if it's enough to kill him! And who knows what he can recover from!"

"What the hell are we going to do, then?" she yells back.

Marcus is bent over double, hand braced against the car, still breathing hard. "Trunk," he says.

Clyde's caution seems to be unnecessary; Ricard is getting pretty weakened by the constant gouts of fire and has stumbled and is struggling to regain his footing. Em walks over, and with a feeling of

433-

great satisfaction, she empties the pepper spray into his face. He falls back to the ground and claws at his eyes.

"Stay there," she commands. "Plenty more pepper spray. More fire."

"More theatrical lighting," Marcus calls.

Lilith emerges from rummaging in Blackball's trunk, clutching a huge coil of white nylon rope in triumph.

"You brought rope?" Em says.

"We brought all kinds of stuff," says Lilith. She lifts things out of the trunk to show her. "What do you think? Wooden stake? Garlic rope? Uh . . . repro sword? I think this is supposed to be Durandal."

Em sprays Ricard again and he writhes; confident he isn't about to get up soon, she turns to see Lilith heading toward her with the rope. "Hang on, Lil," she says. "Let me."

Sunrise is at 7:30.

They've decided that's best — keep Ricard here until sunrise, let things take their natural course. Em sits on the back bumper of the car, watching him. She exhales fog into the cold and watches it instead. She and Lilith have lashed him tightly to one of the lampposts, and as they did so, she had a bizarre nostalgic vision of she and Lil nailing together theatrical flats in the high school's shop. It's another odd moment of unexpected congruity: her trust in Lilith's competence, her ability to communicate and get what Em is saying, doing physical tasks together — these are all still there somewhere in her mind. She has never had quite this feeling about anyone before, the way she feels about Marcus and Lilith and even Clyde — utterly familiar and yet still, despite everything, now also utterly strange.

Clyde and Marcus are sitting on the curb of the parking lot, both with cigarettes in their mouths. She gets up and walks over to them.

"You were quitting," she says.

"I think I've earned this one," says Marcus.

She looks at Clyde. "You own a flamethrower?"

"Would you believe they're legal in this state?" Clyde says. "Would you believe there are instructions for building your own that you can just take out of the public library?"

"The answer is yes," Marcus puts in. "Turns out, yes and yes."

"Your boyfriend is a pyromaniac survivalist," she says to him.

Marcus gestures to Ricard, who still smolders as he struggles weakly against his bonds. "You're one to judge."

"Emiline," Ricard calls. His voice is steady despite the way his body shudders with pain. "I loved them. I loved them all. I love you."

"You don't," says Em. "It's just *bait*," she snaps, suddenly furious. "Your love is *bait* for catching girls, for catching . . . warm bags of blood for you to drink. That's all it is."

"I only wanted not to be alone," he says.

He is probably telling the truth. But it doesn't matter.

Marcus drops out first, pleading an early day tomorrow and a short walk to his house from here. Clyde rather sweetly and awkwardly takes his leave shortly thereafter.

"You don't have to stay, Lilith," Em says. "You must be exhausted. I'll watch him."

"I'm staying," says Lilith. "To the bitter end."

Ricard is silent, unmoving, though there's no way he's even

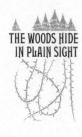

unconscious. He might be trying to endure the pain. Or he might be waiting, recovering his strength.

"It's sad," Em says. "We found out that there really was something magic in the world, and then we have to destroy the only known example of it." Lilith glances at her. "Which we have to do," she adds firmly. "Killing him will save people's lives."

"Ours, for instance," says Lilith.

"But still, it's sad. After this, back to real life. Back to no more magic."

Lilith looks more intently at Em now. "If I left you alone here, you might let him go. You really might."

"No!" says Em. "Well, maybe. Probably not?"

"Not good enough; I'm staying until the bitter end."

"But —"

"The bitter end!" Lilith yells, waving her fist into the sky. A few birds take off from the trees.

"You think I'm ridiculous," Em says. "Don't you?"

"No," says Lilith. "We're friends because you might let him go. I might let him go too. But we both know we can't."

Em snorts. "What are you going to do without me when I go back north for spring semester?"

Lilith punches her on the arm. "When I have to watch a vampire get burned alive, I'll make Marcus come with."

The first rays of the sun begin to pierce through the trees.

Mothers, Lock Up Your Daughters Because They Are Terrifying

ALICE SOLA KIM

At midnight we parked by a Staples and tried some *seriously dark fucking magic*. We had been discussing it for weeks and could have stayed in that *Wouldn't it be funny if* groove forever, zipping between *yes, we should* and *no, we shouldn't* until it became a joke so dumb that we would never. But that night Mini had said, "If we don't do it right now, I'm going to be so mad at you guys, and I'll know from now on that all you chickenheads can do is talk and not do," and the whole way she ranted at us like that, even though we were already doing and not talking, or at least about to. (We always let her do that, get all shirty and sharp with us, because she had the car, but perhaps we should have said something. Perhaps once everyone had cars, Mini would have to figure out how to live in the world as *not* a total bitch, and she would be leagues behind everyone else.)

MOTHERS, LOCK UP
YOUR DAUGHTERS
BECAUSE THEY
ARE TERRIFYING
엄마

The parking lot at night looked like the ocean, the black Atlantic as we imagined it, and in Mini's car we brought up the spell on our phones and Caroline read it first. She always had to be first to do anything, because she had the most to prove, being scared of everything. We couldn't help but tease her about that, even though we knew it wasn't her fault — her parents made her that way, but then again, if someone didn't get told for being a pill just because we could trace said pill-ness back to their parents, then where would it ever end?

We had an X-Acto knife and a lighter and antibacterial ointment and lard and a fat red candle still shrink-wrapped. A chipped saucer from Ronnie's dad's grandmother's wedding set, made of china that glowed even in dim light and sang when you rubbed your thumb along it, which she took because it was chipped and thought they wouldn't miss it, but we thought that was dumb because they would definitely miss the chipped one. The different one. We could have wrapped it all up and sold it as a Satanism starter kit.

Those were the things. What we did with them *we'll never tell*.

For a moment, it seemed like it would work. The moment stayed the same, even though it should have changed. A real staring contest of a moment: Ronnie's face shining in the lunar light of her phone, the slow tick of the blood into the saucer, like a radiator settling. But Mini ruined it. "Do you feel anything?" asked Mini, too soon and too loudly.

We glanced at each other, dismayed. We thought, perhaps if she had just waited a little longer — "I don't think so," said Ronnie.

"I knew this was a dumb idea," said Mini. "Let's clean up this blood before it gets all over my car. So if one of you got murdered, they wouldn't blame me." Caroline handed out the Band-Aids. She put

-438-

hers on and saw the blood well up instantly against the Band-Aid, not red or black or any color in particular, only a dark splotch like a shape under ice.

So much for that, everyone thought, wrong.

ALICE
SOLA KIM

Mini dropped Caroline off first, even though she lived closer to Mini, then Ronnie after. It had been this way always. At first Caroline had been hurt by this, had imagined that we were talking about her in the fifteen extra minutes of alone time that we shared. The truth was both a relief and an even greater insult. There was nothing to say about Caroline, no shit we would talk that wasn't right to her face. We loved Caroline, but her best jokes were unintentional. We loved Caroline, but she didn't know how to pretend to be cool and at home in strange places like we did; she was the one who always seemed like a pie-faced country girleen wearing a straw hat and holding a suitcase, asking obvious questions, like, "Wait, which hand do you want to stamp?" or "Is that illegal?" Not that the answers were always obvious to us, but we knew what not to ask about. We knew how to be cool, so why didn't Caroline?

Usually, we liked to take a moment at the end of the night without Caroline, to discuss the events of the night without someone to remind us how young we were and how little we knew. But tonight we didn't really talk. We didn't talk about how we believed, and how our belief had been shattered. We didn't talk about the next time we would hang out. Ronnie snuck into her house. Her brother, Alex, had left the window open for her. Caroline was already in bed, wearing an ugly quilted headband that kept her bangs off her face so she wouldn't get forehead zits. Mini's mom wasn't home yet, so

she microwaved some egg rolls. She put her feet up on the kitchen table, next to her homework, which had been completed hours ago. The egg rolls exploded tiny scalding droplets of water when she bit into them. She soothed her seared lips on a beer. *This is the life*, Mini thought.

We didn't go to the same school, and we wouldn't be friends if we had. We met at an event for Korean adoptees, a low-ceilinged party at a community center catered with the stinkiest food possible. *Koreans*, amirite?! That's how we/they roll.

Mini and Caroline were having fun. Ronnie was not having fun. Mini's fun was different from Caroline's fun, being a fake-jolly fun in which she was imagining telling her *real* friends about this doofus loser event later, although due to the fact that she was reminding them that she was adopted, they would either squirm with discomfort or stay very still and serious and stare her in the pupils with great intensity, nodding all the while. Caroline was having fun — the pure uncut stuff, nothing ironic about it. She liked talking earnestly with people her age about basic biographical details, because there was a safety in conversational topics that no one cared about all that much. Talking about which high school you go to? Great! Which activities you did at aforementioned school? Raaaad. Talking about the neighborhood where you live? How was it possible that they weren't all dead of fun! Caroline already knew and liked the K-pop soundtracking the evening, the taste of the marinated beef and the clear noodles, dishes that her family re-created on a regular basis.

Ronnie rooted herself by a giant cut-glass bowl full of kimchi, which looked exactly like a big wet pile of fresh guts. She soon realized that (1) the area by the kimchi was very high traffic, and (2) the kimchi emitted a powerful vinegar-poop-death stench. As Ronnie edged away from the food table, Mini and Caroline were walking toward it. Caroline saw a lost and lonely soul and immediately said, "Hi! Is this your first time at a meet-up?"

At this Ronnie experienced split consciousness, feeling annoyed that she was about to be sucked into wearying small talk *in addition to* a nearly sacramental sense of gratitude about being saved from standing alone at a gathering. You could even say that Ronnie was experiencing quadruple consciousness if you counted the fact that she was both judging and admiring Mini and Caroline — Mini for being the kind of girl who tries to look ugly on purpose and thinks it looks so great (*ooh, except it did look kinda great*), her torn sneakers and one thousand silver earrings and chewed-up hair, and Caroline of the sweetly tilted eyes and cashmere sweater dress and ballet flats like she was some pampered cat turned human.

Mini had a stainless-steel water bottle full of ice and vodka cut with the minimal amount of orange juice. She shared it with Ronnie and Caroline. And Caroline drank it. Caroline ate and drank like she was a laughing two-dimensional cutout and everything she consumed just went through her face and evaporated behind her, affecting her not at all.

Ronnie could not stop staring at Caroline, who was a one-woman band of laughing and drinking and ferrying food to her mouth and nodding and asking skin-rippingly boring questions that nevertheless got them talking. Ronnie went from laughing at Caroline to being incredibly jealous of her. People got drunk just to be like Caroline!

Crap, Ronnie thought. Social graces are actually worth something. But Caroline was getting drunk, and since she was already

441-

Caroline, she went too far with the whole being-Caroline thing and asked if she could tell us a joke. Only if we promised not to get offended!

Mini threw her head back, smiled condescendingly at an imaginary person to her left, and said, "Of course." She frowned to hide a burp that was, if not exactly a solid, still alarmingly substantial, and passed the water bottle to Ronnie.

Caroline wound up. This had the potential to be long. "So, you know how — oh wait, no, okay, this is how it starts. Okay, so white people play the violin like this." She made some movements. "Black people play it like this." She made some more movements. "And then *Korean* people play it like th —" and began to bend at the waist but suddenly farted so loudly that it was like the fart had bent her, had then jet-packed her into the air and crumpled her to the ground.

She tried to talk over it, but Ronnie and Mini were ended by their laughter. They fell out of themselves. They were puking laughter, the laughter was a thick brambly painful rope being pulled out of their faces, but they couldn't stop it, and finally Caroline stopped trying to finish the joke and we were all laughing.

Consequences: For days after, we would think that we had exhausted the joke and sanded off all the funniness rubbing it so often with our sweaty fingers, but then we would remember again and, whoa, there we went again, off to the races.

Consequences: Summer arrived. Decoupled from school, we were free to see one another, to feel happy misfitting with one another because we knew we were peas from different pods — we delighted in being such different kinds of girls from one another.

Consequences: For weeks after, we'd end sentences with, "Korean people do it like *ppppbbbbbbbbttth*."

ALICE
SOLA KIM

There are so many ways to miss your mother. Your real mother — the one who looks like you, the one who has to love you because she grew you from her own body, the one who hates you so much that she dumped you in the garbage for white people to pick up and dust off. In Mini's case, it manifested as some weird gothy shit. She had been engaging in a shady flirtation with a clerk at an antiquarian bookshop. We did not approve. We thought this clerk wore thick-rimmed hipster glasses to hide his crow's feet and hoodies to hide his man boobs so that weird high-school chicks would still want to flirt with him. We hoped that Mini mostly only liked him because he was willing to trade clammy glances with her and go no further. Unlike us, Mini was not a fan of going far. When the manager wasn't around, this guy let her go into the room with the padlock on it, where all of the really expensive stuff was. That's where she found the book with the spell. That's were she took a photo of the spell with her phone. That's where she immediately texted it to us without any explanation attached, confident that the symbols were so powerful they would tentacle through our screens and into our hearts, and that we would know it for what it was.

Each of us had had that same moment where we saw ourselves in a photo, caught one of those wonky glances in the mirror that tricks you into thinking that you're seeing someone else, and it's electric. *Kapow boom sizzle*, you got slapped upside the head with the Korean wand, and now you felt weird at family gatherings that veer blond, you felt weird when your friends are replacing their Facebook profile

photos with pictures of the celebrities they look like and all you have is, say, Mulan or Jackie Chan, ha-ha-ha, hahahahaha.

You felt like you could do one thing wrong, one stupid thing, and the sight of you would become a terrible taste in your parents' mouths.

"I'll tell you this," Mini had said. "None of us actually knows what happened to our mothers. None of our parents tell us anything. We don't have the cool parents who'll tell us about our backgrounds and shit like that."

For Mini, this extended to everything else. When her parents decided to get a divorce, Mini felt like she had a hive of bees in her head (her brain was both the bees and the brain that the bees were stinging). She searched online for articles about adoptees with divorced parents. The gist of the articles was that she would be going through an awfully hard time, as in, chick already felt kind of weird and dislocated when it came to family and belonging and now it was just going to be worse. *Internet, you asshole,* thought Mini. *I already knew that.* The articles for the parents told them to reassure their children. Make them feel secure and safe. She waited for the parents to try so she could flame-throw scorn all over them. They did not try. She waited longer.

And she had given up on them long before Mom finally arrived.

We were hanging out in Mini's room, not talking about our unsuccessful attempt at magic. Caroline was painting Ronnie's nails with a color called Balsamic.

"I love this color," said Caroline. "I wish my parents would let me wear it."

"Why wouldn't they?"

"I can't wear dark nail polish until I'm eighteen."

"Wait — they really said that?"

"How many things have they promised you when you turn eighteen?"

"You know they're just going to change the terms of the agreement when you actually turn eighteen, and then you'll be forty and still wearing clear nail polish and taking ballet and not being able to date."

"And not being able to have posters up in your room. Although I guess you won't need posters when you're forty."

"Fuck that! No one's taking away my posters when I get old."

Caroline didn't say anything. She shrugged, keeping her eyes on Ronnie's nails. When we first started hanging out with Caroline, we wondered if we shouldn't shit-talk Caroline's parents, because she never joined in, but we realized that she liked it. It helped her, and it helped her to not have to say anything. "You're all set. Just let it dry."

"I don't know," said Ronnie. "It doesn't go with anything. It just looks random on me."

Mini said, "Well." She squinted and cocked her head back until she had a double chin, taking all of Ronnie in. "You kind of look like you're in prison and you traded a pack of cigarettes for nail polish because you wanted to feel glamorous again."

"Wow, thanks!"

"No, come on. You know what I mean. It's great. You look tough. You look like a normal girl, but you still look tough. Look at me. I'll never look tough." And she so wanted to, we knew. "I'd have to get a face tattoo, like a face tattoo of someone else's face over my face. Maybe I should get your face."

"Makeover montage," said Caroline.

"Koreans do makeovers like *pppppbbbbbbbth*," we said.

Caroline laughed and the nail polish brush veered and swiped Ronnie's knuckle. We saw Ronnie get a little pissed. She didn't like physical insults. Once she wouldn't speak to us for an hour when Mini flicked her in the face with water in a movie theater bathroom. "Sorry," Caroline said. She coughed. Something had gone down wrong. She coughed some more and started to retch, and we were stuck between looking away politely and staring at her with our hands held out in this Jesus-looking way, figuring out how to help. There was a wet burr to her coughing that became a growl, and the growl rose and rose until it became a voice, a fluted voice, like silver flutes, like flutes of bubbly champagne, a beautiful voice full of rich people things.

MY DAUGHTERS

MY GIRLS

MY MY MINE MINE

Mom skipped around. When she spoke, she didn't move our mouths. We only felt the vibration of her voice rumbling through us.

"Did you come to us because we called for you?" asked Mini.

Mom liked to jump into the mouth of the person asking the question. Mini's mouth popped open. Her eyes darted down, to the side, like she was trying to get a glimpse of herself talking.

I HEARD YOU, MY DAUGHTERS

"You speak really good English," Caroline said.

I LEARNED IT WHEN I WAS DEAD

We wanted to talk to one another but it felt rude with Mom in the room. If Mom was still in the room.

LOOK AT YOU SO BEAUTIFUL

THE MOST BEAUTIFUL GIRL IN THE WORLD

Who was beautiful? Which one of us was she talking about? We asked and she did not answer directly. She only said that we were all beautiful, and any mother would be proud to have us. We thought we might work it out later.

OH, I LEFT YOU

AND OH

I'LL NEVER DO IT AGAIN

At first we found Mom highly scary. At first we were scared of her voice and the way she used our faces to speak her words, and we were scared about how she loved us already and found us beautiful without knowing a thing about us. That is what parents are supposed to do, and we found it incredibly stressful and a little bit creepy. *Our parents love us,* thought Caroline and Mini. They do, they do, they do, but every so often we cannot help but feel that we have to earn our places in our homes. Caroline did it by being perfect and PG-rated, though her mind boiled with filthy, outrageous thoughts, though she often got so frustrated at meals with her family during her performances of perfection that she wanted to bite the dining-room table in half. *I'm not the way you think I am, and you're dumb to be so fooled.* Mini did it by never asking for anything. Never complaining. Though she could sulk and stew at the Olympic level. Girl's got to have an outlet.

Mom took turns with us, and in this way we got used to her. A few days after Mom's first appearance, Caroline woke herself up singing softly, a song she had never before heard. It sounded a little like: *baaaaaachudaaaaa / neeeeedeowadaaaa.* Peaceful, droning. She sang it again, and then Mom said:

MOTHERS, LOCK UP
YOUR DAUGHTERS
BECAUSE THEY
ARE TERRIFYING
엄마

THIS IS A SONG MY MOTHER SANG TO ME WHEN I DIDN'T WANT TO WAKE UP FOR SCHOOL. IT CALLS THE VINES DOWN TO LIFT YOU UP AND—

"Mom?" said Caroline.

YES, SWEETIE

"Could you speak more quietly? It gets pretty loud in my head."

Oh, Of Course. Yes. This Song Is What My Mother Sang In The Mornings. And Her Hands Were Vines And She Would Lift Lift Lift Me Up, Mom said.

Caroline's stomach muscles stiffened as she sat up by degrees, like a mummy. Caroline's entire body ached, from her toenails to her temples, but that wasn't Mom's fault. It was her other mom's fault. Summers were almost worse for Caroline than the school year was. There was more ballet, for one thing, including a pointe intensive that made her feet twinge like loose teeth, and this really cheesed her off most of all, because her parents didn't even like ballet. They were bored into micro-sleeps by it, their heads drifting forward, their heads jumping back. What they liked was the idea of a daughter who did ballet, and who would therefore be skinny and not a lesbian. She volunteered at their church and attended youth group, where every-one mostly played foosball. She worked a few shifts at a chocolate shop, where she got to try every kind of chocolate they sold once and then never again. *But what if she forgot how they tasted?* She was tutored in calculus and biology, not because she needed any help with those subjects, but because her parents didn't want to wait to find out whether she was the best or not at them — they wanted best and *they wanted it now*.

Once Ronnie said, "Caroline, your parents are like Asian parents," and Mini said, "Sucks to be you," and Caroline answered, "That's not

-448

what you're going to say in a few years when you're bagging my groceries," which sounded mean, but we knew she really only said it because she was confident that we wouldn't be bagging her groceries. Except for Ronnie, actually. We were worried about Ronnie, who wasn't academically motivated like Caroline or even *C'mon, c'mon, c'mon, what's next* motivated like Mini.

That first day Caroline enjoyed ballet class as she never had before, and she knew it was because Mom was there. She felt her chin tipped upward by Mom, arranging her daughter like a flower, a sleek and sinuous flower that would be admired until it died and even afterward. Mom had learned to speak quietly, and she murmured to Caroline to stand taller and suck in her stomach and become grace itself. The ballet teacher nodded her approval.

Though You Are A Little Bit Too Fat For Ballet, Mom murmured. Caroline cringed. She said, "Yeah, but Mom, I'm not going to be a ballerina." But Mom told her that it was important to try her best at everything and not be motivated by pure careerism only.

Mom told us we were beautiful and special and loved, but that is not to say that she was afraid to criticize the fuck out of us. Once Caroline tried to sing the song about getting up in the morning to please Mom, and Mom just laughed. *Ha-Ha-Ha-Ha-Ha-Ha, Oh Sweetie Ha-Ha-Ha-Ha-Ha-Ha!*

"Mom," said Caroline. "I know the words."

You Don't Speak Korean, Mom told Caroline. *You Will Never Speak Real Korean.*

"You speak real English, though. How come you get both?"

I Told You. I'm Your Mother And I Know A Lot More Than You And I'm Dead.

It was true, though, about Caroline. The words came out of

Caroline's mouth all sideways and awkward, like someone pushing a couch through a hallway. Worst of all, she didn't sound like someone speaking Korean — she sounded like someone making fun of it.

But if we knew Caroline, we knew that this was also what she wanted. Because she wanted to be perfect, so she also wanted to be told about the ways in which she was imperfect.

Mini was the first to actually see Mom. She made herself Jell-O for dinner, which was taking too long because she kept opening the refrigerator door to poke at it. Mini's brain: *C'mon, c'mon, c'mon, c'mon.* She walked around the dining-room table. She tried to read the *New Yorker* that her mother had been neglecting, but it was all tiny-print listings of events that happened anywhere but where she was about five months ago. She came back to the fridge to check on the Jell-O. Its condition seemed improved from the last time she checked, and anyhow she was getting hungrier, and it wasn't like Jell-O soup was the worst thing she'd ever eaten since her mom stopped cooking after the divorce. She looked down at the Jell-O, as any of us would do before breaking that perfect jeweled surface with the spoon, and saw reflected upon it the face of another. The face was on Mini, made up of the Mini material but everything tweaked and adjusted, made longer and thinner and sadder. Mini was awed. "Is that what you look like?" Mini asked. When she spoke she realized how loose her jaw felt. "Ouch," she said. Mom said, *Oh, Honey, I Apologize. I Just Wanted You To See What Mom Looked Like. I'll Stop Now.*

"It's okay," said Mini.

Mom thought that Mini should be eating healthier food, and what do you know, Mini agreed. She told us about the dinner that Mom had Mini make. "I ate vegetables, you guys, and I kind of liked it." She did not tell us that her mother came home near the end of preparations, and Mini told her that she could not have any of it. She did not tell us that she frightened her mother with her cold, slack expression and the way she laughed at nothing in particular as she went up to her room.

Caroline would have said: *I can't believe your mom had the nerve to ask if she could!*

Ronnie would have thought: There's being butt-hurt about your parents' divorce, and then there's being epically, unfairly butt-hurt about your parents' divorce, and you are veering toward the latter, Mini my friend. But what did Ronnie know? She was still scared of Mom. She probably hated her family more than any of us — we knew something was wrong but not what was wrong — but she wouldn't let Mom come too close either.

"Have you been hanging out with Mom?"

"Yeah. We went shopping yesterday."

"I haven't seen her in a long time."

"Caroline, that's not fair! You had her first."

"I just miss her."

"Don't be jealous."

We would wake up with braids in our hair, complicated little tiny braids that we didn't know how to do. We would find ourselves making food that we didn't know how to make, stews and porridges and little sweet hotcakes. Ronnie pulled the braids out. Ronnie did not

eat the food. We knew that Mom didn't like that. We knew Mom would want to have a serious talk with Ronnie soon.

We knew and we allowed ourselves to forget that we already had people in our lives who wanted to parent us, who had already been parenting us for years. But we found it impossible to accept them as our parents, now that our real mother was back. Someone's real mother. Sometimes we were sisters. Sometimes we were competitors.

Our parents didn't know us anymore. They couldn't do anything right, if they ever had in the first place. This is one problem with having another set of parents. *A dotted outline of parents.* For every time your parents forget to pick you up from soccer practice, there is the other set that would have picked you up. They — she — would have been perfect at all of it.

Ronnie was washing the dishes when a terrible pain gripped her head. She shouted and fell to her knees. Water ran over the broken glass in the sink.

Honey, said Mom, *You Won't Let Me Get To Know You. Ronnie, Don't You Love Me? Don't You Like The Food I Make For You? Don't You Miss Your Mother?*

Ronnie shook her head.

Ronnie, I Am Going To Knock First —

Someone was putting hot, tiny little fingers in her head like her head was a glove, up her nose, in her eyes, against the roof of her mouth. And then they squeezed. Ronnie started crying.

— And Then I'm Coming In.

She didn't want this; she didn't want for Mom to know her like Mom had gotten to know Caroline and Mini; she didn't want to

become these weird monosyllabic love-zombies like them, them
with their wonderful families — how dare they complain so much,
how dare they abandon them for this creature? And perhaps Ronnie
was just stronger and more skeptical, but she had another reason for
wanting to keep Mom away. She was ashamed. The truth was that
there was already someone inside her head. It was her brother, Alex.
He was the tumor that rolled and pressed on her brain to shift her
moods between dreamy and horrified.

Ronnie first became infected with the wrong kind of love for
Alex on a school-day morning, when she stood in front of the bathroom mirror brushing her teeth. He had stood there not a minute
before her, shaving. On school-day mornings, they were on the same
schedule, nearly on top of each other. His hot footprints pressed
up into hers. And then he was pressing up against her, and it was
confusing, and she forgot now whose idea all of this was in the first
place, but there was no mistake about the fact that she instigated
everything now. Everything she did and felt, Alex returned, and this
troubled Ronnie, that he never started it anymore, so that she was
definitely the sole foreign element and corrupting influence in this
household of Scandinavian blonds.

("Do you want to do this?") ("Okay. Then I want to do this too.")

Ronnie hated it and liked it when they did stuff in the bathroom.
Having the mirror there was horrible. She didn't need to see all that
to know it was wrong. Having the mirror there helped. It reassured
her to see how different they looked — everything opposed and
chiaroscuro — no laws were being broken and triggering alarms from
deep inside their DNA.

Sometimes Alex told her that they could get married. Or if
not married, they could just leave the state or the country and be

together in some nameless elsewhere. The thought filled Ronnie with a vicious horror. If the Halversons weren't her parents, if Mrs. Halverson wasn't her mother, then *who was to be her mother?* Alex would still have his family. He wasn't the adopted one, after all. Ronnie would be alone in the world, with only fake companions — a blond husband who used to be her brother, and a ghost who would rest its hands on Ronnie's shoulders until the weight was unbearable, a ghost that couldn't even tell different Asian girls apart to recognize its own daughter.

Mom was silent. Ronnie stayed on the floor. She collected her limbs to herself and laced her fingers behind her neck. She felt it: something terrible approached. It was too far away to see or hear or feel, but when it finally arrived, it would shake her hard enough to break her in half. Freeing a hand, Ronnie pulled out her phone and called Mini. She told her to come quickly and to bring Caroline and it was about Mom, and before she could finish, Mom squeezed the phone and slammed Ronnie's hand hard against the kitchen cabinet.

YOU ARE A DIRTY GIRL

NEVER

HAVE I

EVER

SLUT SLUT

FILTHY SLUT

Ronnie's ears rang. Mom was crying now too. *You Do This To These People Who Took You In And Care For You,* Mom sobbed. *I Don't Know You At All. I Don't Know Any Of You.*

YOU'RE NOT NICE GIRLS

NO DAUGHTERS OF MINE

When Mini and Caroline came into the kitchen, Ronnie was sitting on the floor. Her hand was bleeding and swollen, but otherwise she was fine, her face calm, her back straight. She looked up at us. "We have to go reverse the spell. We have to send her back. I made her hate us. I'm sorry. She's going to kill us."

"Oh, no," said Caroline.

Mini's head turned to look at Caroline, then the rest of her body followed. She slapped Caroline neatly across the face. *You I Don't Like So Much Either,* Mom said, using Mini's mouth to speak. *I Know What You Think About At Night, During The Day, All Day. You Can't Fool Me. I Tried And Tried —*

Mini covered her mouth, and then Mom switched to Caroline. *— And Tried To Make You Good. But Ronnie Showed Me It Was All Useless. You Are All Worthless.* Caroline shook her head until Mom left, and we pulled Ronnie up and ran out to the car together, gripping one another's hands the whole way.

We drove, or just Mini drove, but we were rearing forward in our seats, and it was as though we were all driving, strenuously, horse-whippingly, like there was an away to get to, as if what we were trying to escape was behind us and not inside of us. We were screaming and shouting louder and louder until Mini was suddenly seized again. We saw it and we waited. Mini's jaw unhinged, and we only didn't scream because this had happened many times — certainly we didn't like it when it happened to us, but that way at least we didn't have to look at it, the way that it was only skin holding the moving parts of her skull together, skin become liquid like glass in heat, and then

her mouth opened beyond everything we knew to be possible, and the words that come out — oh, the words. Mini began to speak and then we did, we did scream, even though we should have been used to it by now.

DRIVE SAFE

DRIVE SAFE

DO YOU WANT TO DIE BEFORE I TEACH YOU EVERY-THING THERE IS TO KNOW

The car veered, a tree loomed, and we were garlanded in glass, and a branch insinuated itself into Mini's ribs and encircled her heart, and Ronnie sprang forth and broke against the tree, and in the back-seat Caroline was marveling at how her brain became unmoored and seesawed forward into the jagged coastline of the front of her skull and back again, until she was no longer herself, and it was all so mortifying that we could have just died, and we did, we did die, we watched every second of it happen until we realized that we were back on the road, driving, and all of the preceding was just a little movie that Mom had played inside of our heads.

"Stop," said Ronnie. "Stop the car."

"No way," said Mini. "That's what she wants."

Mom's sobs again. *I Killed Myself For Love. I Killed Myself For You,* she said. *I Came Back For Girls Who Wanted Parents But You Already Had Parents.*

"Mini, listen to me," said Ronnie. "I said it because it seemed like a thing to say, and it would have been nice to have, but there is no way to reverse the spell, is there?"

"We can try it. We can go back to the parking lot and do every-thing but backward."

"We can change the words. We have to try," Caroline said.

"Mom," said Ronnie. "If you're still here, I want to tell you that I want you. I'm the one who needs a mother. You saw."

"Ronnie," said Caroline, "what are you talking about?"

From Mini, Mom said, *You Girls Lie To One Another. All The Things You Don't Tell Your Friends.* Ronnie thought she already sounded less angry. Just sad and a little petulant. Maybe showing all of them their deaths by car crash got it out of her system.

"The thing I'm doing," said Ronnie, "that's a thing they would kick me out of the family for doing. I need my real family. I need you." She didn't want to say the rest out loud, so she waited. She felt Mom open up her head, take one cautious step inside with one foot and then the other. Ronnie knew that she didn't want to be this way or do those things anymore. Ronnie knew that she couldn't find a way to stop or escape Alex's gaze from across the room when everyone else is watching TV. *Stop looking at me. If you could stop looking at me for just one second, then I could stop too.*

Mom, while we're speaking honestly, I don't think you're any of our mothers. I don't think you're Korean. I don't even think you come from any country on this planet.

(Don't tell me either way.)

But I don't care. I need your help, Mom. Please, are you still there? I'll be your daughter. I love your strength. I'm not scared anymore. You can sleep inside my bone marrow, and you can eat my thoughts for dinner, and I promise, I promise I'll always listen to you. Just make me good.

They didn't see Ronnie for a few months. Mini did see Alex at a concert pretty soon after everything that happened. He had a black

eye and his arm in a sling. She hid behind a pillar until he passed out of sight. Mini, at least, had sort of figured it out. First she wondered why Ronnie had never told them, but, then, immediately, she wondered how Ronnie could do such a thing. She wondered how Alex could do such a thing. Her thoughts shuttled back and forth between both of those stops and would not rest on one, so she made herself stop thinking about it.

As for Mini and Caroline, their hair grew out or they got haircuts, and everything was different, and Caroline's parents had allowed her to quit ballet and Mini's parents were still leaving her alone too much but she grew to like it. And when they were around, they weren't so bad. These days they could even be in the same room without screaming at each other.

There was another meet-up for Korean adoptees. They decided to go. School had started up again, and Mini and Caroline were on the wane. Mini and Caroline thought, maybe, bringing it all back full circle would help? But they knew it wouldn't be the same without Ronnie.

Mini and Caroline saw us first before we saw them. They saw us emerge from a crowd of people, people that even Caroline hadn't befriended already. They saw our skin and hair, skin and eyes, hair and teeth. The way we seemed to exist in more dimensions than other people did. How something was going on with us — something was shakin' it — on the fourth, fifth, and possibly sixth dimensions. Space and time and space-time and skin and hair and teeth. You can't say "pretty" to describe us. You can't say "beautiful." You can, however, look upon us and know true terror. The Halversons know. All of our friends and admirers know.

Who are we? We are Ronnie and someone standing behind her, with hands on my shoulders, a voice in her ear, and sometimes we are someone standing inside her, with feet in her shoes, moving her around. We are Ronnie and we are her mom and we are every magazine clipping on how to charm and beautify, the tickle of a mascara wand on a tear duct, the burn of a waxed armpit.

We watched Mini and Caroline, observe how shocked they are. Afraid, too. Ronnie could tell that they would not come up to her first. *No?* she said to her mother. *No,* she said. For a moment Ronnie considered rebellion. She rejected the idea. Those girls were from the bad old days. Look at her now. She would never go back. Mom was pushing us away from them. She was telling Ronnie to let them go.

Ronnie watched Mini and Caroline recede. The tables, the tables of food and the chairs on either side of them, rushed toward us as their two skinny figures pinned and blurred. We both felt a moment of regret. She once loved them too, you know. Then her mother turned our head and we walked away.

ABOUT THE
Editors

Kelly Link and **Gavin J. Grant** edited the acclaimed *Steampunk! An Anthology of Fantastically Rich and Strange Stories*. They also started a zine, *Lady Churchill's Rosebud Wristlet*, in 1996, founded an independent publishing house, Small Beer Press, in 2000, and own two letterpresses (in various stages of assembly). They edited the fantasy half of *The Year's Best Fantasy and Horror* for five years, and in 2007 they published *The Best of Lady Churchill's Rosebud Wristlet*.

Kelly Link is a MacArthur Fellow and the author of several acclaimed short story collections, including *Get In Trouble* (a finalist for the 2016 Pulitzer Prize in Fiction), *Stranger Things Happen* (a *Salon* Book of the Year), *Magic for Beginners* (a *Time* Magazine Best Book of the Year), and a collection for young adults, *Pretty Monsters*. Her stories have appeared in the anthologies *The Faery Reel*, *The Restless Dead*, *The Starry Rift*, *The Best American Short Stories*, *Poe's*

Children, *McSweeney's Mammoth Treasury of Thrilling Tales*, and *Fire-birds Rising*, and have won the Hugo, Nebula, Locus, Tiptree, British Science Fiction, and World Fantasy Awards. She worked for three years at a children's bookshop in North Carolina and for five years at Avenue Victor Hugo Bookshop in Boston, and has always loved reading anthologies. Some of her favorites include those edited by Helen Hoke.

Originally from Scotland, Gavin J. Grant moved to the United States in 1991. He worked in bookshops in Los Angeles and Boston, and while in Brooklyn, worked for BookSense.com. He has written for the *Los Angeles Times*, *Bookslut*, and *Time Out New York*, and is still a zine reviewer for *Xerography Debt*. His stories have been published in *Strange Horizons*, *The Journal of Pulse-Pounding Narratives*, *3:AM Magazine*, and *The Third Alternative*, and have been reprinted in *Best New Fantasy* and *Year's Best Fantasy*.

Gavin J. Grant and Kelly Link and their daughter, Ursula, live in (and work on) an old farmhouse in Northampton, Massachusetts.

ABOUT THE
Authors

M. T. Anderson's science-fiction satire *Feed* was a finalist for the National Book Award and a winner of the 2002 *Los Angeles Times* Book Prize. His Gothic historical novel *The Astonishing Life of Octavian Nothing, Traitor to the Nation, Volume One: The Pox Party* won a 2006 National Book Award and a Michael L. Printz Honor, and the second volume, *The Kingdom on the Waves*, also received a Printz Honor. He lives in New England.

Paolo Bacigalupi is the author of the young adult novels *The Water Knife* (a Locus Award finalist), *Ship Breaker* (a Michael L. Printz Award winner, National Book Award Finalist, and Locus Award winner), and *The Drowned Cities* (*Los Angeles Times* Book Prize Finalist and *Kirkus Reviews* Best Book of the Year). His debut adult novel, *The Windup Girl*, was named a *Time* Magazine Top Ten

Fiction Book of 2009 and won the Hugo, Nebula, Locus, Compton Crook, and John W. Campbell Memorial Awards. His short-story collection, *Pump Six and Other Stories*, won a 2008 Locus Award for Best Collection and was also named one of the Best Books of the Year by *Publishers Weekly*. He currently lives in western Colorado with his wife and son.

Nathan Ballingrud is the author of a collection of stories, *North American Lake Monsters*, and a novella, *The Visible Filth*. Several of his stories have been reprinted in year's best anthologies, and "The Monsters of Heaven" won a Shirley Jackson Award. He's worked as a bartender in New Orleans, a cook on oil rigs in the Gulf of Mexico, and a waiter in a fancy restaurant. Currently he lives in Asheville, North Carolina, with his daughter.

Holly Black is the author of best-selling contemporary fantasy books for kids and teens. Some of her work includes *Doll Bones*, a Newbery Honor book and winner of the Mythopoeic Award; the dark fantasy novel *The Coldest Girl in Coldtown*, a *Kirkus Reviews* Best Book of the Year; and *The Wicked King*. She has been a finalist for an Eisner Award and the recipient of the Andre Norton Award. She currently lives in New England with her husband, Theo, in a house with a secret door.

Sarah Rees Brennan is the author of several books for young adults, including the Demon's Lexicon trilogy, the first book of which was an American Library Association Top Ten Best Book for Young Adults; the Lynburn Legacy series; *Tell the Wind and Fire*; and the fantasy novel *In Other Lands*, which she started as a prequel to "Wings in

the Morning." Sarah writes from her homeland of Ireland but likes to travel the world collecting monstrous inspirations.

Cassandra Clare is the author of the Shadowhunter Chronicles, which includes the *New York Times, USA Today, Wall Street Journal,* and *Publishers Weekly* best-selling The Mortal Instruments series. Her books have more than fifty million copies in print worldwide and have been translated into more than thirty-five languages. Cassandra lives in western Massachusetts.

Nalo Hopkinson was born in Jamaica and has lived in Canada for more than thirty-five years. She is the author of the novels *Brown Girl in the Ring, Midnight Robber, The Salt Roads, The New Moon's Arms, The Chaos,* and *Sister Mine,* as well as the short-story collections *Skin Folk* and *Falling in Love with Hominids,* and *Report from Planet Midnight,* a chapbook. She has stories in a number of young adult anthologies, including *Welcome to Bordertown* and *After: Nineteen Stories of Apocalypse and Dystopia,* and has edited and co-edited a number of anthologies. She is a recipient of the John W. Campbell Memorial Award, the World Fantasy Award, and the Andre Norton Award, and a two-time recipient of the Sunburst Award for Excellence in Canadian Literature of the Fantastic. She is currently a professor of science fiction and fantasy in the Creative Writing Department of the University of California, Riverside.

Dylan Horrocks is a writer, artist, and cartoonist who lives in New Zealand. Comics he's written and/or drawn include *Pickle, Atlas, Batgirl, Incomplete Works,* and *Hunter: The Age of Magic.* His graphic novel *Hicksville* has been published in several languages and won an

Eisner Award. His story "Steam Girl" was published in *Steampunk! An Anthology of Fantastically Rich and Strange Stories*. His first published comic strip appeared in a New Zealand children's magazine called *Jabberwocky* in his early teens. He teaches writing and drawing at various universities and art schools around New Zealand, and in 2016 he received a New Zealand Arts Foundation Laureate Award. For some years, he's also been running a steampunk fantasy role-playing game for a group of friends and is slowly writing a novel based on some of the characters and settings.

Nik Houser wrote the first draft of "Son of Abyss" over a five-day period at the 2012 Clarion West Writers' Workshop for George R. R. Martin, aka the "GRRM Reader." He would especially like to thank Kelly, Gavin, Les, Neile, George, and his brilliant classmates for their enthusiasm for this story, and more importantly, for being his compatriots. His short novel *Red Rover* is available as an e-book. In his spare time, Nik enjoys petting stray cats, performing stand-up comedy, and having to write novelettes in five days. He is currently at work expanding "Son of Abyss" into a novel. For free fiction, a list of published works, contact information, and some cartoons, please visit his website.

Kathleen Jennings is an illustrator and writer from Brisbane, Australia. Her comic "Finishing School" was published in *Steampunk! An Anthology of Fantastically Rich and Strange Stories*. Her art has won several Ditmar Awards, been nominated for a World Fantasy Award, and short-listed for the Aurealis Awards, and has appeared in many books. Her short stories have been selected to appear in *The Year's Best Australian Fantasy and Horror*.

Alice Sola Kim is the winner of the 2016 Whiting Award, and her writing has appeared in many publications, including *Strange Horizons*, *Asimov's Science Fiction*, *Lightspeed*, and *The Year's Best Science Fiction and Fantasy*. She has an MFA from Washington University in St. Louis and was awarded a grant from the Elizabeth George Foundation. She currently resides in New York.

Joshua Lewis lives in western Massachusetts with his wife, Cassandra Clare, three cats, and several thousand books. He spends a lot of his time thinking about monsters. As much time as possible, really.

Kelly Link is a MacArthur Fellow and the author of several collections of short stories, including *Get In Trouble*, a finalist for the 2016 Pulitzer Prize in Fiction, *Stranger Things Happen*, *Magic for Beginners*, and *Pretty Monsters*. Her short stories have won three Nebula Awards, a Hugo Award, and a World Fantasy Award. She was born in Miami, Florida, and once won a free trip around the world by answering the question "Why do you want to go around the world?" (Her answer: "Because you can't go through it.") Kelly Link and her family live in Northampton, Massachusetts, where she and her husband, Gavin J. Grant, run Small Beer Press and play Ping-Pong. In 1996 they started the occasional zine *Lady Churchill's Rosebud Wristlet*.

Patrick Ness is the author of the Chaos Walking trilogy, *A Monster Calls*, and *More Than This*. He has won the Booktrust Teenage Prize, the *Guardian* Children's Fiction Prize, the Costa

Children's Book Award, and is a two-time recipient of the Carnegie Medal. He is also the author of two adult novels and a short-story collection. He lives in Los Angeles.

G. Carl Purcell's writing has appeared in *Open City, Fence, Stop Smiling*, and *The Agriculture Reader*; has been anthologized in *A Best of Fence: The First 9 Years* and the *McSweeney's*-edited *Created in Darkness by Troubled Americans*; and is forthcoming in *New Genre*.

ACKNOWLEDGMENTS

Once again we have to thank Kelly's fabulous, patient, and detail-oriented agent, Renée Zuckerbrot, for keeping us on track and (as much as she can) honest. Then, of course, all the authors who sent us such dark, horrible, bleak, excellent monster stories; especially Cassandra Clare and Holly Black, who sparked the idea for this book. Thanks to Holly Black, Cassandra Clare, and Sarah Rees Brennan for substantial and timely help with the pop quiz. Thanks, too, to the Commonwealth of Massachusetts for its wonderful health care.